Books in the *Windfall* universe:
Sixes Wild: Manifest Destiny
Windfall
Sixes Wild: Echoes and other stories

Also by Tempo:
The Book of Monsters, Ironclaw Roleplaying System

TEMPE O'KUN · SLATE
WINDFALL

AN
OTTER-BODY
EXPERIENCE
AND OTHER STORIES

Acknowledgements

Special thanks to Anakuro, Carl Minez, Eljot, Keiron White, Kohaku Nightfang, Megan, Slate, Slip-Wolf, Sophie, T-Kay, and UltraFennec for editing.

Windfall — An Otter-Body Experience and Other Stories

Cover and interior illustrations by Slate

Published by FurPlanet Productions
Dallas, TX
http://www.FurPlanet.com

ISBN 978-1-61450-452-8

First Edition Trade Paperback December 2018

To Sam for getting it done. To Megan for making it fun.

Table of Contents

Wrapping Up

STRANGEVILLE (SAT/4P)

S05E12 "Unusual Fair": A traveling carnival grifts the townsfolk with magical nostalgia. Cassie gets jealous when a bat fortune-teller flirts with Serge, but needs her to fill in the gaps in a vision.

The talk show hosts had been right.

So had the cast, the crew, and a small but passionate Internet fanbase.

Over the final seasons of Strangeville, Kylie had fallen in love with her best friend.

~ ~ ~

Several months prior, Kylie'd been watching movies on the sofa of their Hollywood apartment—pleasant, small, and significantly tidier since a certain husky co-star had moved in. Her mother's voice, muffled through a bedroom door, faded in and out of her attention. Studio talk: as producer and lead writer of a cable TV show, Mom spent a lot of time on the phone, very little of it sounding fun. The younger otter tried not to worry about it; she felt anxious enough already. Worse, she couldn't seem to pin down why.

A knock at the door made her jump. She bounced up from the cushions and onto her tiptoes to peer through the peephole. A scruffy coyote with kind eyes stood in the hallway. The lutrine opened the door. "Jake! It's you... Hi!"

"Hello, Miss Kylie." The coyote doffed a battered fedora. A slim suitcase hung from his other paw. One of her mom's sources, he had a habit of showing up at odd times, with even odder merchandise. His ears perked as he looked over the living room. "Your mother at home?"

"She's on a call from the network." Kylie bobbed out of the way. "C'mon in. I'm sure she'll be off before too long."

He stepped inside and wiped worn-in hiking boots on the doormat. A long tan coat draped from his shoulders, out of place and out of vogue in a Hollywood climate. Those gold eyes surveyed her, then the open door behind him. "You're expecting someone else."

Anxiety wrung her. "Max's due back today. Thought he might've gotten in early."

The canine nodded, muzzle shut on words he held back.

Trying to unwind the tension, Kylie chattered on: "He's back with his family in Montana, since we're between seasons. Guess they really missed him. I know how they feel." A nervous giggle bubbled up, unbidden. "Anyway, what's in the bag?"

His dusty paw hefted the briefcase with an air of theater. "Articles of inspiration."

Jake dealt in knickknacks and curios. Laura had bought a number of them over the years, but kept them in a box in her office, only taking them out when she needed inspiration. Kylie had caught glimpses of them: a strange curl of fossilized bone, a silver shot pourer fingerprints couldn't mar, an asymmetric black orb she couldn't study for long without getting a headache. How Jake and her mother settled on a price also eluded her. Not like her to keep secrets from her daughter, but both seemed to be putting on a show to add to their mystique. Anything to squeeze a little more authenticity out of the actors.

Whiskers perked, the otter nosed in on the case. "Can I see?"

With a coy smile, he drew back and patted the black leather case. "Serious inquiries only."

"You know Mom's good for it." She crossed her arms, standing her ground barefoot on the carpet. "When has she not bought your stuff?"

"I couldn't speak to what she might've bought. I have a terrible memory." A paw rose to his chest. "Occupational hazard."

The roll of her eyes traveled down her body.

Laura appeared at her bedroom door and seemed more frazzled than usual. A breath huffed out of her, tinged with stress. "Strangeville's not getting a sixth season."

Kylie winced. No shocker, but not fun to hear aloud. Last season, when they were slated to be cancelled, Mom and the other writers had crafted the finale to tie up all the loose ends. Everyone loved it, especially the studio who then gave them a half-length fifth season and expected more episodes like the final one.

"How unfortunate." The coyote shifted, briefcase in paw. His ears dipped in sympathy.

The older otter glanced to him, noticing him for the first time, and offered him a shrug. "We all knew this season was our swan song." Sadness seeped through her professionalism. "Though I would've liked to keep singing…"

He nodded, cheery smile now faded to neutrality. "Where will you go now?"

Laura shrugged. "We have some friends and an old family property in New England. It's as good a place as any to regroup while I think of the next big thing."

The coyote's face remained impassive. "That where you came up with the show in the first place?"

Her expression shuttered, cooling her warmth a bit. "Something like that."

Oh, that place. Great. Kylie had been there a few times as a pup, but only to pick up or drop off something. What little she remembered creaked, sprawled, and creeped everyone out. In addition, she remembered it being miles from anywhere, surrounded by overgrown woods on all sides.

The dusky canine straightened.

"They aren't going to stop paying me, Jake." A dark chortle rose from the middle-aged otter, then tilted her head at the office. "We can still talk business."

Together, they left the room, leaving Kylie alone with her thoughts. The end of the show depressed her. It'd been the center of her life for the latter part of her teenage years. She felt the need to get out of the apartment. As soon as Max got back, she'd grab him and drag him out to the movies or something. They had a lot of bumming around to do before the season ended.

Kylie sat up, the little lump of anxiety suddenly swelling to churn at her insides as sudden, terrible realization struck her. Bad enough Max spent shooting breaks at home, but once the show ended he would pack up and go back to living on the farm and she and her mother would fly to the other end of the country and she and her best friend would never ever lay eyes on each other again and what in the world was she going to do?

He arrived an hour later.

Before his bag even hit the floor, she bounced over and wrapped him in a massive hug.

He wagged and held her. "Hey there, rudderbutt." His paw patted her shoulder, off-balance and a little awkward. "Missed me, huh?"

"Yeah." She nuzzled against his chest. It occurred to her that she was holding the hug longer than she was supposed to, but she couldn't bring herself to feel self-conscious. This was Max, the nicest, safest guy in the world. She entertained a fleeting thought that she could stay like this forever, snuggled against warm fluff with strong arms all around her.

It all clicked for her then, like a wayward gear slotting into place. The source of her anxiety, her lack of desire for other companionship, the upswell of relief when he'd come back. Somewhere, without realizing it, Kylie had fallen in old-timey, pining-by-the-window love with her co-star.

Crap.

~ ~ ~

Shooting the rest of the season, the specter of her crush haunted her mind, but the frantic pace of production let her outrun it, if only for a scene at a time. She kept trying to get Max alone, to drop some perfect hint, or make some big, dramatic declaration. But they'd spent years settling into a routine and it proved impenetrable.

If she'd figured it out sooner, she could've come up with some kind of plan. Now, though, she had no idea what to do about it. As she stewed, her thick tail swished the bathtub's steaming water. She scrubbed the air from under her pelt, letting the heat soak her skin.

Of course, she lacked any first-hand knowledge on how to seduce anybody. Or second-hand. Third-hand she had plenty of, but those consisted of the romantic sub-plots to terrible movies. Here in reality, she was on her own.

She stared at the ceiling plaster, her mind tracing patterns in the chaos as she tried to come up with a plan. Her thoughts drifted to earlier that day.

~ ~ ~

Between scenes, the studio break room used to be a hub of activity. Now it stood quiet and empty, only those few people needed for pickups wandering through. Max busied himself at the coffee machine as she tried not to stare at him. For months, she'd been dancing around her growing attraction to him, writing it off as fear of moving away from him. His character had joined the show as a bit part, but now she couldn't imagine the series without him. For over three of the five-season run of the show, she'd worked, joked, eaten, and lived with him almost every day. But how the heck do you tell your best friend that being his best friend isn't enough for you anymore?

The tall, muscular husky set a coffee in front of her, with two creams and a sugar, just the way she liked it. "Just saying, I chewed plenty of tennis balls as a pup. I have a hard time acting like I'm scared of them."

She sipped the steaming beverage. "What, you don't like doing fifteen reaction shots to the same piece of green screen?"

13

He sat across from her and managed to look only a bit comical in the fox-sized chair. "I only have so many ways to look surprised."

"You sure have more than when you started." One elbow propped on the table, she leaned in with a smirk. "You'll be a regular dynamo back in Montana."

He nodded and sighed, his shoulder slumping.

Her whiskers lifted with concern.

He noticed and shrugged, then gestured to the studio. The muscles in his jaw worked over his anxiety. "All this is ending forever."

Kylie fought the urge to slump. The playful banter had been so normal that, for a moment, she'd been able to forget. "Cheer up, Maxie." Her smile weakened, but she was a better actor than he was. "You could stay in Hollywood." She leaned back and crossed her arms, thick tail swishing on the floor. "You're a big-time actor now."

He stirred his black coffee. "I'm not an actor; I just play one on TV."

Her tail tip bumped his shoe. "You'd get gigs."

"Yeah, you're right. But this was all just a special case, you know?" The canine spread his wide, white paws. "My already knowing the lore, you and I getting along, your mom looking out for me: it all sort of came together." One paw brushed back the hair the costume department had him grow out. "It's been fun, but the idea of doing it without you or your mom or the crew…" He sat up a little and straightened his sweatshirt, forcing a brave smirk. "Besides, Serge is basically me. If I got another job, people'd catch on that I can't act."

He'd just looked so brave and sad and hopeful, she'd wanted to kiss him then and there. Or hold his paw. Or even just hug him.

Instead, she'd wimped out and patted his shoulder.

~ ~ ~

Back in the bathtub, Kylie steeped in her thoughts like a mustelid-flavored tea. Hollywood portrayed otters as sensuous and self-confident, so everyone seemed to assume she had seductive powers to spare, not to mention a complete lack of shame. In reality, she'd had enough trouble working up the nerve to buy a sex toy over the Internet. Could she really risk alienating her best friend over a crush?

Deft paws worked a few globs of shampoo into her fur, the lavender scent doing little to allay her anxiety. They had, what, two weeks left of shooting pickup scenes? What could she even do in that time without seeming like a desperate weirdo?

She rinsed the lather and slipped out of the tub. After drying off and brushing her pelt, she eeled into the hallway. Towel wrapped around her, she scampered to her bedroom door just as an idea sprung to her mind. Slinking back into the living room, she rehearsed an excuse to walk past him. Getting a glass of water: that'd work. This wasn't the time for subtlety. Which was good, because she was terrible at subtlety.

Fantasies unfolded about dropping the towel with a sultry look, or him easing it from her wet body with those strong husky paws. From there, matters got steamier than any bath in the world. Ridiculous, of course— even if Max was interested, he was too much of a gentleman for an impromptu romp with his best friend. But maybe, if he saw her in just a towel, she could get the ball rolling. Maybe he'd even make the first move.

The otter paused at the border of lamp light. One paw stroked back a wet lock of hair from her eyes. She steeled her resolve and rounded the corner, swearing to follow wherever the moment led.

The dog lay sprawled on the sofa, muzzle closed in a quiet snore. Those muscled arms hugged a pillow. A t-shirt and shorts draped over his powerful form, hinting at a body she really wanted to get to know better. A book on writing lay beside him on the floor. The ceiling fan whirred, stirring his fluffy coat wherever it lay exposed.

A smile lifted her whiskers. The cold fear in her stomach fading, she padded over and turned off the coffee table lamp. In the faint glow of streetlights stories below, she watched him for a moment. Max living with them had never been the plan; at first, his parents took turns keeping him company at another apartment in the same building. She and the big fluffy canine had gravitated toward each other right away, and before long he ate dinner with them most nights. Whenever his parents had to head back to the farmstead, Kylie's mom had promised to keep him out of trouble. After a season together, they all decided it would be simpler for everyone if they just got a three-bedroom place, which allowed his mom and dad to head back to Montana full-time. In all honesty, Kylie and her mother just liked having someone else around.

He still slept on the lumpy old sofa enough that she didn't bother waking him. His fold-up guest bed couldn't be much comfier anyway. Apartments this close to the studio seemed designed to pack tenants like sardines. Besides, he looked so cute. She resisted a sudden urge to wake him with a kiss, or even a cuddle. He'd be an amazing cuddler, all soft and fluffy and caring.

No. Too late for her to act on her feelings for Max, at least for now. Not like he'd never visit, but the days of him sleeping on their sofa slipped through her paws like water.

The lutrine strode back to her room and climbed into bed. Not a waterbed, the studio had some kind of clause against them, but she'd gotten used to it over the years. Maybe she could get one once they moved back to Windfall? Her recollections of the town, of the massive creaky house there, had faded since her childhood. What would life be like there? What would it be like not living from script to script?

If only she had a script for confessing her attraction to Max. They'd had scenes together on Strangeville for years, working through scripts with an easy chemistry. She almost had more experience interacting with him as Cassie than as herself. Maybe her character could inform her a little. How would Cassie seduce Serge?

Wait.

Why was she thinking about this when she had the Internet to think for her?

In a frantic flop, she rolled over to grab her laptop. A few quick searches later, the fandom's collective speculation on that exact scenario lay before her. Most of them involved Serge ravaging Cassie between scenes. Intriguing, but if she and Max were going to tear off each other's clothes in a fit of un-foreshadowed passion, it would've happened already. Why'd real life have to be more difficult than fanfiction?

The stories with threesomes proved even less helpful, in addition to filling her with irrational jealousy toward several of the CG monsters. Then, of course, came a parade of kinks: she hooks up with a villain; he gets hurt and she has to comfort him with her vagina; she gets hit by a bus so he can console himself by sleeping with the entire cast; him getting her pregnant; her getting him pregnant; him turning into an otter; him as a feral canine on her farm; him as a vampire with the terrible secret of not being a vampire.

After an author-insert story where she was the target of the author's insertion, she sorted the stories by popularity and blocked a few of the creepier keywords. That helped.

The steampunk one cast him as a stoic swordsman and her as an aristocratic airship heiress—creative, though the prose got purple enough to embarrass a plum. Likewise, the forty-chapter crossover fiction appeared impressive, but so packed with references not even she understood half of them. Alien zoologists making them have sex would be nice, but she refused to sit around and wait for UFO abduction; she saved the story on her hard drive and moved on.

The alternative universe with them as regular high school students seemed cute, though it revealed a flaw in her plan: Cassie could see the future, which meant she could foretell Serge calling out her name in a moment of passion. Kylie would have to find her own means of advancing the plot. She corrected little details as she went. His fur smelled of shampoo and safety, not just untamed canine musk. His Russian drawl was fake. In reality, Max's only accent was a touch of cowboy around the edges, though she couldn't blame the average fan for not knowing that.

Another story caught her eye. Set during the camping episode, Serge had gone skinny dipping at a lake to wash the monster of the week off his fur, only to have Cassie catch a glimpse. She watched in secret as water flowed over his sculpted, fluffy body. Before long, he spotted her and cast her a sultry stare as he covered up.

Her imagination dove into the tale, showing Max all naked and muscled and demure, but with a coy smile.

The scene unfolded with her joining him in the lake, finding refuge from the supernatural world in the natural comfort of his embrace. At first nervous, the hot insistence of his erection grew in her paws, melting away any insecurities about his interest in her. Flowery prose followed, blooming into his confessions of passionate love for her.

Her hips rocked against the bed. One paw sank through the sheets and down between her thighs. Still damp from the bath, matters had only gotten juicer. She reached into her nightstand drawer and pulled out an unassuming silk bag. From it, she drew a sleek silicone vibrator; waterproof, of course. Best of all, it made almost no noise, a quality she envied in these matters. It'd proved an excellent investment over the last few months of increasingly frequent use.

Reading on, she teased the toy up and down her slit, then around her tender labia. She clicked it on, savoring the pleasant buzz it translated through her most sensitive regions. Deeper now, with a quiet squelch. In her mind and in the story, he entered her.

The otter imagined him holding her close, sinking deeper and deeper into her. Her every gasp caressed his name. She worked the toy further in; its little rabbit ears vibrated to either side of her clit, sending tingles of delight through her squirming body.

The story described her straddling his hips as he stood in the moonlit water, the night cool around them as passion burned within them. It detailed him pumping into her, worshipping her with every thrust, then clutching her close and howling to the stars as he spurted hot canine seed into her. The hot swell of canine flesh grew within her and filled her every need.

Her body curled around the pleasure surging from her toy. Waves of bliss washed through her body as she suppressed squeaks of pleasure. She wiggled and bounced against the mattress, bucking against the dildo.

Panting, she slumped against the bed and clicked the toy off. She shut the laptop. Her orgasm faded to a sticky memory. Webbed paws swept through the sheets, finding the bed bigger and lonelier than usual. As she rolled up in the covers, she wondered what it'd be like to have that big, probably lonely husky wrap his arms around her instead.

~ ~ ~

A few weeks later, airline passengers hurried past, wrapped up in their own storylines. Inoffensive music echoed down the white-walled corridors, punctuated here and there by the whoosh of a jet. Her mom stood at the counter, helping Max check his luggage, which likely weighed as much as she did. He had somehow crammed three years of his life into it, all his clothes and books and memories in a green canvas duffle.

Kylie bit her lip, trying not to make a fool of herself. Inside, though, she wanted to bounce off the walls, to bar the plane's door, to wrap herself around his calf and insist she was luggage. But cowardice and flight regulations prevented her carrying on or being declared a carry-on.

The husky hefted his laptop bag. "Don't look so down, rudderbutt." He smiled and set a wide paw on her shoulder. "We'll only be a couple hours apart." His other paw lifted, showing an old watch with two time-zones, already set for across the continent. "You know you can call whenever."

She wrung her webbed paws. "I will."

His eyes met hers with a quiet whine, tail still. "You okay?"

Kylie hugged Max like it might keep him from leaving. She pulled back to look him in the eyes. Behind him, the airport metal detector gaped with gray indifference. Her gaze flicked down to his lips. She could kiss him, and the music would swell and he'd wrap his arms around her and he wouldn't go to Montana. All she had to do was kiss him.

She didn't kiss him.

He waved as he headed past the check-in and onto the plane. Final boarding calls. Kylie watched as it taxied down the tarmac and lifted off.

Her mom put an arm over her shoulder. She didn't say anything, but looked on with the sad amusement she always got when new chapters started in life.

~ ~ ~

The three-story monstrosity sprawled from the Bevy family's past to Kylie's foreseeable future. Chipping paint and battered shingles complained of years of neglect in the briny sea air. She did her best to blink away the jet-lag, then sighed. Home sweet home.

Laura grabbed the last box and patted the trailer behind her hatch-back. "Okay kiddo, I'm going to run this beast back to town. You gonna be okay?"

"I'll be fine, Mom." She took the box and rolled her eyes. "It's just a giant creepy house."

"Our giant creepy house. Can't believe it's been twenty years…" The middle-aged otter threw an arm around her daughter. "A good twenty years."

"Has much changed?"

Her mother cast an eye at the woods that fringed the property. "Here's hoping."

The younger otter rolled her eyes, but smiled. As far as moms went, hers was alright, if a little dramatic.

With a final squeeze of her shoulders, her mother bounced into the seat of her hatchback, fired it up, and rumbled down the driveway.

Kylie carried the final box inside and set it down on the cluttered kitchen table. Her mother had labeled and color-coded all their possessions, but the writing on this one had scuffed off. Curious, she sliced through the tape with a claw and peered inside. Old books, diaries, bound in ancient leather covers. She opened one and found yellowed pages flooded with strange, inky scrawls. No name, no date, just an array of strange runes.

Her phone buzzed in her pocket, a familiar custom ringtone. Her heart leapt as she scrambled to fish it out.

Max Saber: {The Internet says our show jumped the shark with the ship-in-a-bottle that turned out to be a voodoo doll ship.}

Her heart raced. Fingers fumbled over the touchscreen as she scrambled to reply.

Kylie Bevy: {Whatever! I liked that one. And we jumped the shark with the printer that murdered people with paper cuts.}

A moment passed. Max Saber: {Actually, that led to creative staff threatening to quit if they weren't given more control. So in the long run, it helped.} Very talkative for one of his texts; while far from stoic, Max tended not to waste words on what people already understood.

Kylie Bevy: {No wonder the fans like you. You're one of them!}

Another minute or so ticked by, leaving her twitching her foot and fidgeting with the phone. Around her, leaves rustled on wind, trees encroaching on the yard from all sides.

Max Saber: {Miss you, rudderbutt.}

Kylie Bevy: {Miss you too!}

Max Saber: {Still up for me coming to visit this summer?}

She smiled, cradling the phone between her paws. She took a moment to savor the idea that he missed her too, then tapped out her reply.

Kylie Bevy: {Count on it. :) }

GROUNDWORK

STRANGEVILLE (WED/9P)

S04E08 "Light Clerical": Sandy is convinced Tammy's new office job is a doomsday cult, but Tammy resists, desperate for a sense of normalcy. Cassie's visions make her an ideal fast food employee.

Standing in the kitchen, Max brewed coffee and stirred crab porridge on the stove. He'd eaten hours ago, as usual. Rice porridge with shredded crab wasn't the weirdest thing otters ate. Actually kind of pleasant, once you got past the pink color. He picked a few more pieces of crab meat from the shells, only a little unsettled at how the carapace yielded like that of an alien he'd been forced to pummel in this very room. He glanced around to the various floor scuffs and wallpaper scratches the creature had left during its attack and exit. He could probably straighten the stair railing a little more.

His gaze crossed the kitchen table to his bedroom. Through the cracked door, Kylie lay sprawled on the bed. His bed. He smiled. He'd really lucked out, having a girlfriend who was also his best pal. Not to mention a girlfriend's mom who didn't get after them for sleeping in the same bed. Well, Kylie was mostly sleeping in the bed: one of her legs and most of her tail hung off in an ooze of spinal contortion. The sunlight shone off the swimsuit-like panties on her upturned rump. A soft, squeaky snore fizzled from the room.

A knock rattled the front door.

Kylie popped upright and whipped her head around for the source of the disturbance, whiskers bedraggled to crazy angles. With a squawk, she flailed into emergency backup PJs—the pastel unicorn seahorse ones that still fit from when she was a kid. She kept them in his room because she'd felt wasteful throwing them away. She fought her way into his shirt and pawed at her red hair, her ability to straighten it limited by the fact that otter paws are very dissimilar from combs.

He trotted to the door, then paused with his paw on the knob. Once his girlfriend appeared halfway decent, he opened it.

It swung open to reveal Shane and Sarah Warren, siblings across species. He saw the cat pretty frequently, since he worked with Kylie. The rabbit was a recent defection from Cindy Madison, the local dog Kylie managed to start a feud with.

"Hey guys." The husky cocked his head. "What're you doing here so early?"

"H-hey." With an anxious wave, Sarah looked up at him. "We have some questions."

Without a word, Max ushered them in. Wouldn't do to have them talk in the doorway. Not that this would be the only conversation about the supernatural in Windfall, even at this hour. He just didn't want to be rude.

The orange feline propped himself beside the doorframe. His grin sharp, he glanced around. "Sheesh, Kylie. I wondered what you looked like in your natural habitat." He nodded at her disheveled hair.

A sputter of outrage rattled up through the otter, gathering strength and threatening to coalesce into words.

Max placed a steaming cup of coffee in her paws, with all her favorite additives.

Sinking her muzzle into the mug, she muttered into the tan liquid.

The cat snickered.

Over her shoulder, the bunny pointed back toward town. "So, Joe's house is now a crater."

Max nodded.

The otter tottered up beside him. Her thumb hooked in his jeans pocket. A slight teapot whistle escaped her muzzle.

"And Shane tells me you showed up at our house in the middle of the night asking where he lived." The bunny leaned around Max to study his girlfriend. "Is there something you guys want to tell me?"

Behind his most stoic face, the husky mulled over how to respond. Was it fair to lie to them about their hometown, even in the hope of protecting them? They were adults, if just barely. And they must have some inkling of the supernatural, if they were here asking about the alien Max and Kylie had tracked down, beaten up, and sent packing. Perhaps it would be best to explain a little at a time, since radical truths could be traumatic.

Clutching her coffee, Kylie vibrated for an instant, then blurted: "Look, the tunnels collapsed, okay?"

The bunny cast her a narrow-eyed glance. "Those tunnels showed no sign of collapsing before you went downtown."

"Caves collapse all the time!" She flung up her webbed hands. "Dirt is treacherous. Trust only the sea!"

Max's gigantic paw settled atop her head. He didn't press down, just resting it there in hope the weight would keep her from bouncing around. She wasn't good with mornings and would probably regret acting like a weirdo in front of the Warrens.

His girlfriend made a low, continuous chitter, which ocellated as he wobbled her gently back and forth. She sipped her coffee with each forward motion, like a drinking bird. Each gulp seemed to perk her whiskers another fraction of a millimeter.

"Please, excuse her." The husky sighed. "She's not usually up this early."

Shane examined his claws. "I don't normally care about this sort of thing—"

"Or anything." His sister glared at him.

He shrugged. "—but if I'm an accessory to something, I should probably know."

"Joe was an alien monster." The words exploded from Kylie's muzzle. Her coffee sloshed.

"Ah okay." Shane ambled across the squeaky floorboards, leveling two index fingers at them. "So if anyone asks, you're a lunatic."

"What Kylie means is…" The dog's brow furrowed in thought. He waited as long as socially possible for an excuse to show up. Nothing. "Yeah, actually, that's pretty much it."

Sarah stood perfectly still, eyes wide. Now and then, her nose twitched in thought. Good thing the windows were shut; a stiff breeze might have knocked her over.

Unreadable as ever, Shane sharpened his claws on the stem of a banana.

Motion snapped back into the bunny, leaving her swaying onto the back of a chair with both hands. "You're serious?"

Max nodded.

Her cotton-puff tail quivered. "Because everybody in this town lies about aliens and ghosts all the time."

Bouncing out from under her boyfriend's paw, the lutrine chattered and lashed her thick tail. "If you thought this was a hoax, would you have come up here?"

"I don't know! There has to be a reasonable explanation." Her fingers swept limp ears back from her face. "I can't just accept somebody I knew wasn't a…person."

"He was a person! Just not an Earthling." Kylie tipped a webbed finger at her. "And also a huge jerk. He threatened to kill us if we didn't give back his outer-space CD-ROMs."

"He threatened to kill you?" Sarah's jaw and ears dropped. "For real?"

"With his alien blade arms." The otter made karate chops at the air, then dramatically punched her palm. "But Max beat him up."

The rabbit's mouth hung open, buck teeth glinting in the morning light. Her ears popped up at Max. "Do you beat up monsters a lot?"

"Only on TV." The musclebound male shrugged. "I'd never been in a real fight before."

The siblings looked the towering husky up and down.

His heavy shoulders shrugged. "People don't really pick fights with me."

The Warrens blinked at the husky for a moment.

The orange tabby turned cool eyes to Max. "So where's Joe now?"

Rubbing his scruff, the husky squirmed. "He's …um…. left this world."

Sarah gave a little hop of alarm. "He's dead?"

Waving a webbed paw, Kylie dismissed the worry. "No, he just hates our planet and isn't coming back."

"He made that abundantly clear." Max rolled his eyes.

Sarah twitched. "If he's dangerous and wanted to leave, why'd you mess with him at all?"

Max contemplated the classic herbivore logic: if all who go into the valley are eaten, don't go into the valley. He'd cautioned Kylie about chasing a dangerous creature into its lair, but ultimately gone along. Had his canine instincts compelled him to take down a threat in his territory. Or maybe that was just his mom's opinion on the matter.

"We had to get involved!" She planted webbed fists on her hips.

Feigning boredom, Shane batted at the pull-cord to the blinds. "If you hadn't gotten involved, would we still be living down the block from a sinkhole?"

"Actually, it would've been way worse if I'd done what I wanted." Kylie's muzzle scrunched up. "This is coming out wrong."

The steps creaked. Laura waddled down the stairs on fuzzy slippers. "Oh wow. You have friends—" She tightened her bathrobe. "—over."

Kylie cast her a dirty look.

The older otter tossed her webbed fingers slowly into the air, hoping to dispel any offense.

Pouring her a cup of black coffee, Max smirked. "Affirmative. Out."

The middle-aged television writer took the mug, rolled her eyes at both of them, and shuffled away. Ascending the staircase, she raised the drink in salute. "Good to see you, guests. I'm off to become presentable."

Sarah watched her go, then turned to Kylie with a whisper. "Does your mom not know?"

The shorter otter scoffed. "She's trying really hard not to know."

"But she wrote the TV show!" Sarah hopped in quiet outrage.

Kylie groaned. "All part of her decades-long not-knowing campaign."

Another agitated twitch of her tail poof, then she spun to face her brother. "Shane, can you believe this?"

"I mean, yeah. Probably." He yawned. "Fits the evidence I've seen."

The rabbit punched her brother in the shoulder. "Why didn't you tell me it was real?"

He rubbed his arm. "I told you a bunch of times it was real."

"You acted like it was no big deal, so I thought you were lying!"

"Like how you don't listen when I tell you not to mess around in the old mines?" The faintest ember of emotion glowed in his voice.

Max's ears perked to attentive triangles. He locked eyes with his girlfriend. Awake and obviously entertained, she cocked an eyebrow to indicate they should wait and see where this was going.

"I know what I'm doing." Sarah crossed her arms. "I'm perfectly safe."

"Except you don't and you're not. Except your entire family has told you your entire life not to go into those mines." A spark of uncharacteristic anger hissed in his voice, like water on hot metal. "They're unstable."

"And apparently full of monsters." She pointed back down the hill toward town.

"Not anymore." The short otter swayed back and forth in thought, then grinned with pride. "Just sayin'."

The bunny rounded on the couple. "So, this is what you guys do?" She flipped her fluffy paws into the air at either side. "Show up in a town and hunt monsters?"

Kylie nodded. "Yes."

Max glanced down at her in disbelief. "No!"

The otter groaned. "Okay, so this is the first in what's likely to be a string of monsters."

Her lover crossed his arms over a resolute chest. "No."

"Oh, come on!" She bounced in place, wiggling with objection as she clung to his arm. "We can't stop now."

The large dog didn't budge, though he looked down at her with concern as she dangled from his elbow.

Sarah cleared her throat and lowered her ears, as if trying to enforce calm on herself. "So, why'd you guys do all this?"

"We wanted to prove my family wasn't crazy." Kylie twirled a webbed finger by her head, then around at the house. "Turns out they were even less crazy that we thought."

The bunny froze for a second, then blinked. "So what happens now?"

Max nodded. "We've kind of been worrying about that."

"Duh!" The otter chattered. "We're going to use our position as TV monster hunters to inform the world about real monsters."

Leaning against the kitchen counter, Shane lashed his long tail. "How are you gonna do that?"

The husky shrugged. "We have a blog. Or will soon."

Tan bunny ears lifted. "A blog?"

"It's basically fan fiction, but I live in the same house as the original creator." His eyes flicked toward the stairs, following Laura's exit route. "And she's going to give everything her stamp of approval before I post it."

"Mom gave him the keys to the kingdom." Kylie elbowed him for his modesty. "Max is now the official lead writer of Strangeville."

"Wow. That's really cool." Sarah nodded, impressed. "I've never known someone connected to a TV show before."

"I'm also the coffee boy." His paw tilted in the direction of the steaming carafe.

"Good luck there." The rabbit fumbled for a gestured and eventually settled on a thumbs-up.

Max nodded with a self-effacing wag. "Thanks."

A phone buzzed. Shane pulled it from his pocket. "Dad wants us to watch the store for a couple hours while he runs errands."

Sarah planted her hands on her hips. "If he wants us, why did he only text you?"

"He's using the royal 'us.'" He regarded his sister, unflappable indifference restored. "It's pronounced 'Shane.'"

She shook her head. "Well, we rode together, so I guess I'm leaving either way."

Shane patted Kylie on the shoulder. "Not every day someone collapse my neighborhood. Congrats. We'll put a tracking collar on Sarah so you don't collapse any cave she's in."

The otter glanced at the lapine in question. "Do you have a Sarah-tracking app?"

"Just let me know if you're going into my tunnels." Her finger poked toward the ground. "Or plan to destroy them."

"Can do!" Kylie offered a paw, which the bunny puzzled on for an instant, then shook.

With a deadpan nod, Shane headed unceremoniously out the door and toward their car.

Sarah moved to follow, but stopped at the doorway and turned around. "Are you guys okay?"

"Yeah, I just need more coffee." The otter hoisted her cup.

"No, I mean really okay." The bunny's paw reached just short of touching her.

Kylie paused in thought, then slowly settled back into motion. "I stand by the coffee thing."

Max bumped her with his elbow.

"I dunno! I've never battled aliens before. And it's cool that my ancestors weren't all crazy, but it's crazy that my ancestors were right about monsters." She throw her webbed paws in the air. "I'm used to being an actor on a silly TV show—"

The dog looked around for Laura with concern.

"—and now I know all this stuff that, if I tell the world, the world's gonna think I'm just another crazy celebrity, lying for attention." The otter wobbled. "So I'm trying to get my bearings."

The bunny looked to Max.

He nodded in agreement.

"Okay, well, keep in touch. Let's talk about this soon. It's not healthy to only talk about monsters; any therapist will tell you that." She ducked into the car. "We'll go to Salad Days."

The car motored away. On the twisting road, it sank below the crest of the hill and filtered into the woods. Soon, only the faint sound of the engine remained.

Kylie flashed him an exasperated look. "Herbivores! Who goes to Salad Days?"

He shrugged. "I hear they have a salad made of turnip shavings."

"That's stupid, but I don't even care because people are coming to us with supernatural problems!" Happiness buoyed her. Her grabby paws gripped his arm to keep her from bouncing away.

He raised a fluffy finger. "They came to us because they thought we collapsed a suburb."

The lutrine sprang from foot to foot, clapping. "Ooooooh, we'll form a mystery club!"

Max stroked his chin. "While I hesitate to bring them into danger, I suppose it's good to have people we can call for backup." He nodded. "Granted, them knowing will make it harder for us to investigate in secret."

"Great!" Still clad in PJs, she twirled around him, tail trailing in a curl after. Her head nuzzled against his chest. "We want to do the opposite of a secret. We only want to keep the investigating secret until we can prove it."

His arm rising to embrace her, the canine stood in silence. A moment of assessment gripped him. He'd started dating his best friend. He'd uncovered extraterrestrial carpentry. Which of those was wilder, he wasn't sure. As he gazed off into the wind-caressed woods, he wondered how the future could top that.

In the face of that, writing a Strangeville blog seemed downright achievable.

~ ~ ~

Max had handed Laura the proposed blog post, still hot from the printer. It was the first one that felt truly finished, so it'd felt good to hand Laura a physical copy. Now, though, as he sat watching her read it, flipping one page every couple minutes, sometimes flipping back, he found this all excessively dramatic. He'd been in writing classes, but the opinion of classmates or a professor didn't hold the same weight as his idol and mentor. That he was writing official fanfiction of her work doubled the pressure.

The cluttered office loomed around him. Awards and memorabilia from dozens of productions stood like sentinels, guarding stacks of manuscripts and hard drives. At the window, multi-colored glass buoys floated in an old net, glowing under ancient dust. Had she put them there? Or had they been hung there by some otter a hundred years ago? So much of her past was tucked into corners of this sprawling house. For all the years he'd worked for her, these gaps made him unsure he'd calibrated the story for the right audience.

At last, she cleared her throat, wiggled upright, and smiled at him. "Great. A couple structural problems, but we can hammer those out together."

The dog's muzzle swung open to emit a sigh of relief. She hadn't hated it. He wasn't hopeless.

"You've been using the series reference guide, though, and your obsession over the show's lore is paying off." She shrugged. "An alternate-reality show like Strangeville lives or dies by its continuity. Fans are going to be demanding for that continuity even more since the property is changing formats."

He wagged. This was going pretty well.

"After all, real life has great continuity."

Max looked up at her. Was she totally oblivious to the fact that she ignored whole slices of reality? The ones related to the supernatural, for instance. Oh well.

She flipped back a couple pages. "Interesting that you have Serge carrying around a small baseball bat all the time."

He nodded, remembering bludgeoning an alien with it. "We found one upstairs."

The otter snickered. "If you're finding your inspiration by cleaning, that's twice as good for me. But you have a good understanding of the characters and setting. You do me proud."

He nodded. This was actually going pretty great.

Leaning across her desk, she tipped the story back to him. "Now do it 49 more times."

His ears popped straight up.

"What? It's not a blog without content. If you can't write a year's worth of content before you start, you don't have a sustainable idea."

The husky squirmed. "I thought I could just post them as I write them."

She shook a webbed finger up into the air. "And what happens when you get a cold?"

He shrugged. "I don't get colds."

"What happens when you get roped into another project? Or when my daughter gets you arrested?"

Max snorted. "Am I likely to get arrested, associating with her?"

"More likely than without." The middle-aged otter waved a blasé paw. "You want a reservoir of content."

He nodded. "How'd you do this on the show?"

"I've been writing Strangeville since I was about your age. Not that I knew what it would become, then. Sometimes, when you start something, you have no idea how it's going to get out of hand. Like Kylie."

A voice from the hallway piped in: "Hey!"

Laura cracked her webbed knuckles one at a time. "If you're going to eavesdrop, I get to make fun of you."

One hand gripping the doorframe, Kylie swung into the room. "What's the point of me learning where all the creaky boards are in this old mansion if I never get to eavesdrop?"

Her mother's battered office chair groaned mechanically as she leaned back to regard her daughter. "Shouldn't you be at work?"

"I was supposed to be at work half an hour ago. I guarantee nobody has noticed." Her fists propped on her hips. "How's life aboard the S.S. Apprenticeship?"

"Hasn't sunk yet." The older otter took a sip of coffee. "He wrote a good first short story."

Kylie's small ears perked up at her boyfriend. "High praise, considering some of the things she'd say to the writing team."

He shrugged. "The special effects budget for prose is pretty generous."

"I still say we could just post as Cassie and Serge." She gave Max a thumbs-up. "We'll buy you a Cyrillic keyboard so you can write his accent."

"While I like the augmented-reality angle, that locks you into events that take place after the show. And thinking of all the stories in order. And in real time." Laura scratched her chin idly. "And into only ever having it from their point of view. And—"

"Yes, I get it, Mom." She rolled her eyes. "You're very smart and creative."

The older lutrine smirked. "It's almost like I've been doing this for a while."

Max sat up extra straight. "Plus, she has some really cool old scripts from the show." He gestured toward a box of hard drives. "I really want to adapt them eventually."

Kylie lifted her hands to either side. "Why don't you just adapt them now?"

"I thought I'd practice on small stuff like this first. TV episodes are pretty long when you write them out." The husky leaned forward in his chair, his bulk making it creak mightily. "Plus, I want to do them justice."

"While I appreciate the thought, you don't need to put me on a pedestal." She waggled a modest wiggle. "They're just half-finished scripts. I don't have any grand designs on them. Take what you can use."

"I will." Ears dipped, the massive canine glanced to his mentor. "Eventually."

His girlfriend slapped him on the back. "Look at you! Being all proud. You do it."

Max swallowed, nervous. "Well, I did it once. And they're only a few thousand words. I guess I can just knuckle down and do it again. And then fifty more times."

~ ~ ~

Kylie popped into her boyfriend's room. "Idea."

Max looked up from his computer. "No."

"TV action show: Covert Otts." She made a gun gesture with both hands, then ducked back into the hallway.

He leaned after her and woofed: "This isn't the 70s! You need more than a species pun as the premise."

Her voice rang from down the hall. "I can't hear you because I'm too covert!"

~ ~ ~

Max wrote another blog post. And another. And the fourth one wasn't as good, but it was done. And then the fifth one he left to percolate. And then he did the same thing to the sixth one. When he was two paragraphs into the seventh one, and was about to abandon it too, he noticed the pattern his life was taking.

He stared at the screen, trying to focus. Half of the outline was there; he just needed to figure out the connective tissues. He'd given up on writing in the living room. And in his bedroom. And in the library. And now he was stuffed into a slightly-too-small chair in a spare bedroom that had mostly been excavated from decades of clutter.

Indistinct otter noises rattled from downstairs.

He lifted his ears and tuned in.

Echoing up the stairs, his girlfriend chattered: "You're stressing out my boyfriend. He's making the noises."

The canine sat up straight. His throat stopped making a high-pitched whine he hadn't known he was making.

"I haven't moved from this table all day." Laura squawked back. "I don't know what you think I've done."

"You gave him an impossible task and now he's going to work on it forever."

"If he's trying to focus, maybe we should leave him alone."

"He's not focused—he's panicking." Kylie got even louder. "I haven't heard him make these noises since he sat on a fire ant hill and didn't want to react because he'd ruin the take."

Max wasn't sure that was entirely true. He'd probably made similar noises when confronting a monstrous alien at the start of the summer. Kylie had been making a lot of noises of her own, so maybe she hadn't noticed. Dog ears picked up a lot that otter ears missed, such as the conversation downstairs. Or two pairs of otter paws climbing the stairs.

The pair of lutrines waddled into the spare bedroom.

Laura pushed up her glasses. "Are you freaking out in here?"

With a long look at the little laptop, he sighed. "I guess."

"Told you." With a wiggle of victory, the younger otter sashayed around to face her mother. "You probably couldn't hear his high-pitched noises because you're old."

She rolled her eyes. "Yes, the upper range of my hearing was mercifully worn away by your childhood."

Kylie squawked her displeasure.

Laura tried in vain to straighten one of her whiskers. "Why are you freaking out?"

He waved a heavy paw at the screen. "I just can't get this stuff written."

A bitter laugh chattered out of her. "That is the primary state we writers exist in."

"When I started off it was all coming together, then..."

"Then you used up all the well-developed ideas and your creative juices dried up?"

The husky looked to her in mild surprise.

"That's the primary thing that happens. Being an artist is just learning how to trick yourself into it happening less."

The large dog squirmed. "I like being relied on."

"And you are reliable." Laura tossed her hands into the air. "That's not the same thing as magically doing everything."

He pondered that. Falling short of expectations wasn't something allowed by his mom, growing up. "It feels weird to not be able to do something you wanted."

His girlfriend snickered. "Yeah, that's because she'd ask you to look like you could beat up a foam-rubber monster." Raising her webbed hands, she clawed at the air playfully. "And then you'd pick up cars and stuff."

"That was a go-cart. Once." He crossed muscular arms over a broad chest. "And that was a lot easier than this stupid blog."

"Max, sweetie, it's online bonus content. We're starting you out small on purpose here." Her webbed paw chopped vaguely at the computer. "You could take years to write these and it wouldn't matter."

Kylie smacked her tail on a battered dresser, causing the attached mirror to wobble. "But we told the Internet!"

With a woof of agreement, Max tilted a paw at his girlfriend.

The elder otter rolled her eyes. "You told that rhino kid's podcast. Which has…" She looked Strange Times up on her phone. "…409 subscribers. There will come a day when you dream of only disappointing 400 people with your writing."

The dog nodded slowly.

"I'm sorry for making you put all this pressure on yourself. I just didn't think about it because you kids both surprise me with what you're capable of." She set a paw on her daughter's shoulder, then turned to Max. "Plus, you're largely self-parenting."

A long sigh escaped him. "I know. I thought I was good at this. I thought I could just sit down and do it."

"If we were talking about how to carve a whistle, sure. Once I taught you, you could do it a thousand times. But you're whittling something new every time you start." The middle-aged otter sat with care on a stack of old cardboard boxes. "It's possible to be creative on demand, but it's not something you can do through brute force. Just like you need a reserve of material for that blog, you need to learn to cultivate a reserve of creativity."

"Don't give him all your secrets at once, Mom." Kylie snorted. "I can't drag him along on wacky adventures if he's an overnight success."

He regarded his mentor. "So what do I once I've made it?"

She shrugged. "Same thing as before. Chop wood, carry water."

His ears rose.

"Yeah! Make him do training like in a kung fu flick." The slimmer otter attacked the air with a flurry of punches and tail-slaps. "Montage!"

Laura lifted an eyebrow at her offspring. "It's an expression. After you become the person you want to be, you still have to do the same work that got you there. People get jealous of talent because they think it means you automatically get to do great things, like you're favored by the gods." Curling her tail, she brushed a spiderweb off the tip. "But the world's full of people with natural talent they don't bother to develop."

The dog nodded, thoughtful.

"There are ways to maximize the odds of getting what you want out of a day of writing. I've been doing this for a while." Laura shrugged. "I can teach you if you want."

The massive canine straightened. "As your...protégé?"

Kylie clasped her hands together under her chin. "Aww, look at him, using words."

"It's good you recruited some outside talent, Kylie..." Her mother chattered a laugh. "...or this never would've made it as a family business."

"He's good to have around." The younger otter ran her paw over his ears.

"To answer you, yes, I'd be your mentor." She extended a paw.

His head tilted at the gesture.

"What?" She shrugged, paw still halfway between them. "You like making things official."

His massive white paw closed around hers and shook it. He wagged, glanced to Kylie, then wagged some more. This was actually going pretty well.

Something Big

STRANGEVILLE (TUE/8P)

S03E14 "Throwback": Everyone but Cassie and Egbert turn into feral monster versions of themselves. They must stop their super-powered friends before they hurt someone.

Max was used to strangers staring. Sometimes they took pictures. Sometimes they whispered and giggled. Mostly they asked if he was "that shirtless guy from that show with the monsters." And he'd say yes, even though he was only shirtless in a few scenes in that one time travel episode, no matter how many times they showed it in the opening credits. Those interactions embarrassed him, sure, but he'd had years to get used to them.

Since coming to Windfall, though, the stares had sharpened and the whispers had lost much of their mirth. Most of them were directed at Kylie: his co-star, his best friend, and now his girlfriend. The whispers always stopped when she got close, which made her tense up.

With a huff of concern, the husky settled into a booth at Pinchy's Diner and worked his tail into the bench's slot. "We may need to throttle back a little."

"On what?" His otter lover crashed into the seat across from him, poking at her phone and muttering. Her round little muzzle never diverted from its screen. She never stopped making tiny, anxious motions and noises as she searched for clues. Never exactly an easygoing little thing, Kylie had been growing more and more tense over the past few days. The two of them had run into one dead end after another while chasing down local legends and weird rumors in an attempt to prove what they already knew: that Windfall's tacky paranormal tourism industry was at least partially based on truth, and that her family's history of chasing monsters wasn't as wacky as it sounded.

He'd have loved to help her unwind, but her focus seemed unshakeable, each disappointment only adding to her resolve. She hadn't wanted to play old video games or take him for a walk. She'd barely slowed down for a smooch or two from him in the last few days, let alone anything more intensive. He'd probably been too subtle in his flirting, but not everybody could be as bold as an otter. Plus, being twice her size, he didn't want to come off as pressuring her for sex. No, better to just let her usual horniness catch up to her. Typically he didn't have to wait this long. "Our more obvious supernatural investigations. The direct approach hasn't really done much for us."

She crossed her arms over her vest. "I can't prove my family wasn't crazy without evidence."

"True." His paw pads traced over the worn corner of a menu.

Her paw swept at the window, finger webs aglow in the sunlight. "Plus, the whole town is full of paranormal crazies. They're just weird about actually handing over the proof."

"Also true. Acting sane would help our case, though." Under the table, he bumped a sneaker against hers. "At least where people can see. You know I'm on board, but it looks bad to climb around inside sinkholes in residential neighborhoods at midnight. Or to buy all the butter in town."

"That wasn't even for anything paranormal!" She chittered in objection and flung her arms in the air. "We had a lot of crabs to cook."

"Right, but it looks like the kind of rich-person crazy that made people think your ancestors were nuts." His eyes scanned the seafood restaurant. The various patrons chatted and ate, mostly done staring. A pair of foxes yapped back to lapping up gossip. Some teenagers stuck napkins on their deer friend's antlers without his knowledge. A twitchy mongoose emerged from the backroom, accepted an envelope from the manager, and waddled over to slip into a booth. Out the windows, autumn sunlight painted a pleasant view of the sea. His stomach growled. In an effort to drag her from her phone, he tapped the table. "Are you going to look at the menu?"

"I'll just have the chowder, like always." She grumbled at the device. "Ugh, why do aliens have to be so hard to find?"

Max glanced around the dining area. His gaze returned to her with a question.

"Don't give me that look. Everyone in this town talks like a crazy person." Her webbed fingers flicked through a series of images for the tenth time. "Most of them are."

The heavily-built husky interlaced his fingers. "You told me to warn you if you were obsessing."

"An alien trashed my living room, Maxie." Those hazel eyes flicked up to him. "An alien who convinced the town my family was crazy."

He steepled his index fingers under his chin. "Yes, I know. I was there. And acting like a weirdo in a public place will clear their name?"

An argument bottled up inside her chest as she tried to come up with a rationale. A second later, it rolled out over the table as a sigh and stirred the napkins. "Fine. You're right."

A lynx waitress padded past and set down a basket of rolls between them. Before she could say anything, though, a splash and a clatter sent her trampling off toward a pack of wolf cubs, their two tired-looking parents, and at least one spilled soda.

The scent of fresh-baked bread drew in Max's nose immediately. With his girlfriend still diving into her phone, he lifted the undyed sailcloth, revealing a half-dozen dinner rolls, shiny with glaze and steaming. The dog swallowed to keep from drooling. He plucked one from the basket and nibbled at it with delicate teeth. The stretchy, wholesome texture dissolved into a burst of heady slow-risen flavor on his tongue. The roll felt exquisite to chew, luscious to taste, and warm to swallow.

Kylie arched an eyebrow at him.

Halfway through his second roll, the canine slowed his chewing.

"Hungry?"

He swallowed. "I guess so."

His girlfriend eyed the rolls, then leaned back to where the lynx server had finished mopping up beverages. "Did you guys change something in the bread?"

"Nah, the good stuff is just usually gone by now." Putting the mop and bucket back behind the counter, she inclined her tufted ears at the far booth. "The delivery came late today. All-natural, stone-ground: good stuff."

A few booths over, the wiry mongoose unlocked a small case hand-cuffed to her wrist, which opened with a pressurized hiss. She unshackled the cuffs and cooed at a lump of dough within. "Are you hungry, my pet? I bet you are…" She uncorked a glass flask and anointed the blob. "A little water first? You must be parched. Wouldn't want you to dry up, would we?" With great care, she opened another vessel and shook pale powder onto the object of her affection. "A new version of the Mother Flour, yes. No more coarse grounds wreaking havoc with your gluten." Snap! Snap! Two rubber gloves stretched over her quick paws. Her digits caressed the dough first, then kneaded the layer of fresh material into it. "Oo-hoo-hoo! You like it already; I can tell."

Transfixed, the otter stared. "Weird…" She snapped a picture with her phone. "And she's like this whenever she drops off bread?"

"I guess." The waitress shrugged fluffy shoulders. "Doesn't always massage the starter dough on-site, but whatever. She's a bit eccentric, but you can't argue with the results." She took out a small notepad and pencil, sharpening the lead of the latter on her paw pad. "What can I get ya?"

Kylie didn't even look at the menu, still studying the mongoose. "Fried clams."

Max dug through the menu and found the tiny sandwich section in the back. "Cheeseburger. Could I get it on one of these buns?"

"So long as the cooks haven't eaten them all since I was back there, sure." The lynx tossed them a toothy smile and slunk back to the kitchen.

The otter's tiny ears perked toward her boyfriend, even as she kept spying on the baker. "Maxie, do not tell me you're still eating it."

With a shrug, the husky obeyed and continued eating the rolls. "Thought you were getting the chowder."

"Soup doesn't travel well." Her whiskers hung with nonchalance, though her keen hazel eyes peered with interest at the baker.

With a jolt, the mongoose finished massaging her sourdough starter. Max turned his muzzle to the window, wondering if their staring had caught her attention. But then she jolted to digging in her purse and smacking on some lip balm. Apparently, she always moved like she was being slightly electrocuted.

Meanwhile, the husky had reached the bottom of the basket of rolls.

The mongoose trotted past. Her suitcase said "Yeast India Company – All-Natural Breads" on the top in an ornate script. She zipped out the door, scooted to a moped with a massive bread box on the back, and locked the briefcase inside.

Kylie vibrated in her chair, beaming.

With a sigh, Max waved to get their server's attention. "Could we get those to-go?"

~ ~ ~

On a deserted stretch of backroad, Max crouched in a ditch, fighting back the urge to slink back to the car for his cheeseburger. Under an overcast sky, the husky watched a lone figure totter and curse her way down a rocky path to the ocean. She scampered along the shore using a small strainer pail to fill a larger bucket, maybe fifty meters downhill.

Beside him, Kylie rolled over in the grass, her cream-colored middle exposed as her t-shirt rode up. "Ugh! Is she still messing around?"

A low woof of confirmation escaped his muzzle.

Her webbed hands stuck up toward the color-washed sky. Her sneaker heels scuffed dry autumn grass. "We should get some camouflage clothes." She brushed some of the dust from her pastel purple Sugar Gliders band t-shirt, which she'd had since middle school. What little growth she'd gone through since then made it tighter in interesting ways. "You know, for our spying."

"Few things are as conspicuous as camouflage." He flattened his ears to his skull as the mongoose peered around, oblivious to them. "It makes people ask questions."

The lutrine fished the takeout container from its plastic bag, opened it on her stomach, and began eating fried clams. "Questions more awkward than 'why were you two laying in that ditch?'"

"I can think of a good lie." He looked her up and down. "Or at least a good eyebrow waggle."

She stuffed another fried clam in her muzzle. "You can't just wag your way out of every situation."

"It's worked on you so far."

The otter chittered at him, then popped yet another fried clam into her mouth. She wiggled in contentment, scooting closer to him against the evening chill. Her body lay along his, a warmth he couldn't ignore.

He felt the familiar pumping of primal hormones through his veins. It didn't help that she'd waded back into the deep end of paranormal research, meaning he'd been running around with a sexy otter for the last few days with little or no time to lend his libido a paw. Jumbled fantasies filled his head: play-wrestling with her, tossing her on the bed, tearing her clothes off...but she was such a tiny little thing. Acting on those canine impulses could hurt or scare her, so he always let her take the lead.

For the moment, she seemed to have no intention of leading him to the bedroom. She'd rolled to her stomach and watched as the mongoose hauled the sloshing bucket of seawater back up the path to her moped. The scrawny female slapped a lid on the container and chucked it into the storage box on the back of the vehicle, then hopped on and puttered off.

"She's making a break for it!" Kylie popped up and raced back toward her own car, juggling fried clams. "C'mon!"

Max followed her around the bend of the road and wedged himself into the passenger seat of the otter-sized car. He carefully avoided sitting on the still-wrapped cheeseburger. He took her container of fried clams so they wouldn't spill.

With a chatter of pursuit, the otter cranked the ignition. The tiny aquatic car sputtered to life and trundled off after the vanishing moped. They bounced down the uneven road as gray clouds rolled up the coastline toward them. She whipped down a turnoff, the box on the back of her moped at a wild tilt.

Undeterred, the otter tailed her at an inconspicuous distance. The Amphicar bounced along the uneven gravel. The harpoon gun tumbled from the back seat to rattle around with a pawful of ancient pull-tabs and oyster-shell shards. He'd never met her great-uncle who'd owned this car, but the guy could've at least vacuumed under the seats before vanishing from the face of the Earth.

Another bump in the road smacked the canine's head on the rods of the ragtop roof. His ears lowered as he slunk down, only to have his knees whack against the dashboard. A quiet whine trailed from his muzzle. "Could we slow down?"

"Gotta keep her in sight." Kylie double-checked that the propeller weren't engaged as the underpowered little car struggled with a modest hill. The center console consisted of chrome levers and knobs shaped for webbed paws. Her fingers danced over them with obvious relish. Otters liked gripping things, and his girlfriend was no exception. Pleasant memories about what she liked gripping distracted him for a lovely instant.

Then his shin whacked the glove compartment. Old maps and scrawled notes spilled onto the floor. He growled. The ocean sparkled to their left as he strained to pick up the various dry pens and yellowed documents. The maintenance log stated the car was thirty years past due for having its propeller sharpened.

With another reckless turn, the mongoose motored around a bend. Kylie revved the Amphicar as much as she dared, but arrived at a four-way stop with no sign of the baker. The woods around them lay silent. The roads snaked around hills, obscuring any view they might have had of their quarry.

The cheeseburger sat, faintly warm, in his lap.

"Stubborn, spikey crab carapace!" The otter whipped her head around looking for any track or trace of the moped. "Where'd she go?"

Quietly, the husky unwrapped his cheeseburger. Best to take advantage of the stopped car before she picked up the scent again.

She flashed him a look of frustrated desperation. "What're we supposed to do now?"

Stopping a millimeter away from his first bite, he cocked an ear at her. "I just wanted lunch. You're the one who wanted to follow the bread lady." He handed her back the box of fried clams.

"She's seriously suspicious." She popped open the box, placed it between her thighs, and munched on the breaded mollusks. Her sleek paws fished the little binoculars from her fishing vest pocket as she surveyed the woods. "What'd ya think? Alternate wheat dimension? Secret grain cult? Ghost flour?"

He sniffed at the cheeseburger bun. It smelled tasty. Weren't ghosts supposed to not have a smell? Or be just a smell? He didn't remember, probably because he was too hungry. He bit into the cheeseburger. It was as delicious as expected: succulent beef, balanced condiments, fresh lettuce and tomato, and of course a nice springy roll.

"And now she vanishes?" The binoculars never left her eyes, even as she neared the bottom of the oyster pail of clams. "Pretty weird, right?"

"Yesf." The husky took another bite of his burger. It really was very good, even if it was going cold. Juices and sauce had soaked into the bun. Wasn't soggy yet, just mingling flavors. He wagged. He might be in a cramped car on some back road outside a supernatural tourist trap, but at least he was with an otter who loved him—and eating a really good hamburger. "Mmm."

"We need more info." She poked around on her phone, finding few damnations of the Yeast India Company beyond its limited production. "Internet's not turning up much. Even in Windfall, 'uses supernatural ingredients' isn't something you put on your website."

"Well…" He chomped another bit of the vanishing burger. He really had been hungry. "Unless you can think of a better idea in the next five seconds, I say we call Karl."

She took a breath to object, halted halfway through it, and rolled her eyes. "Fine…"

He wagged and wolfed down the last of the hamburger.

~ ~ ~

Max knocked on the heavy steel door, where a coat of cheery paint obscured years of dents. Beside him, Kylie groaned, arms crossed.

Footfalls vibrated through the concrete stoop. The door opened to reveal a burly rhino in a well-worn fleece shirt blocking all light from the interior. His beady black eyes sized Kylie up, which didn't take long, then locked with Max's gaze. A stoic moment ground away. "Ain't you those kids from the TV?"

Max nodded, in the unusual position of having to look up at someone.

He shorted an unreadable huff, then jabbed his horn toward the living room. "Better come in then."

A matronly rhinoceros with tiny horn-rimmed glasses stomped in from the kitchen. "Oh! Hello! Can I help you?"

"We're just here to see Karl."

"He's downstairs." She offered a thick, gray hand. "I'm June, his mother. Are you two staying for dinner?"

"No-o-o-o-o." The little otter vibrated as her paw was vigorously shaken. Once released, it opened and closed a few times. "We just had a couple quick questions."

Karl's dad snorted. "You kids these days and your questions. Don't know when to leave well enough alone. I was friends with Joe for twenty years and he never asked me a damn thing."

Karl's mom tipped her head back, knocking a little plaster from the ceiling. "Maybe if you'd had more actual conversations, he'd have told you where he was going. You've talked more about that beaver since he disappeared than you did in the two decades before that."

Her husband only repeated his snort.

She turned her head to shout to the basement. "Karly, honey! Your friends from television are here!" Propping her mighty fists on stalwart hips, she gestured for them to head down. "You'll recognize his room. You're on the door!" Her laugh shook the walls a little.

The husky smiled and nodded. Placing a paw at Kylie's back, he guided her downstairs. They tromped down into the dim basement and knocked on the partly-open door. The Strangeville poster taped there had been signed by the whole cast, so he must've actually touched it at some point in the past. Life as a minor cable TV star was weird like that. When a moment passed with no sign of their fan, he knocked again—louder.

A series of crashes and stumbles progressed toward the door. Electronic music started playing the middle of a song. The door swung open to reveal a tall, plump rhino. Headphones swung wildly from his horn, cord dangling. His tiny eyes went wide. His breath sped, spiking his tone higher and higher. "Uh, hey guys! Didn't hear you come in." A frantic hand straightened his disheveled hair. He finally noticed the headphones hanging off his horn and gave an embarrassed grin as he disentangled from them. "What's up?"

"We're on a case." The otter flipped the phone into her paw like a police notebook, then showed him a photo of the mongoose. "What can you tell us about this lady?"

He blinked. "Isn't that the lady who sells bread to Pinchy's? It's good stuff."

Kylie looked up at a considerable angle, very serious. "We need whatever you can tell us."

"You might want to grab a seat." His horn bobbled in the affirmative. "I'll see what I can dig up."

They walked into the messy, but large bedroom. Karl took a moment to frantically closed some browser tabs. Max pretended not to notice. Kylie appeared genuinely oblivious. The husky sat on the sofa, which was surrounded by podcast recording equipment. Instead of squeezing in next to him, Kylie sat on his lap.

The husky buried his nose in her hair for an instant, before remembering where they were. Trying to look casual, he eyed stacks of Mana Clash cards on the desk. Looked like the rhino was building a new deck.

Kylie wiggled in his lap. Her thick tail brushed against some interesting places, which she seemed oblivious of. "So she sells them bread?"

"Oh yeah." The rhino grabbed a seat on the office chair before his computer. His hands settled over a massive keyboard. The gray and white brick of plastic pinged under his thick fingers. It had to weigh at least two kilos. He pulled up a file of notes on his computer. "She makes all their bread bowls too."

The otter gasped, paws to her muzzle. "I've already been contaminated!"

Max patted her shoulder. "Anything in your files about her?"

"Heh, well, I don't have big dramatic filing cabinets like on the show, but…" He paused for a blink. "Wait, you're asking me for help on a story for your new Strangeville blog?"

"Well, yeah." Max nodded. "You're our expert on mysterious local happenings."

His pointy ears popped up. "I'm the Egbert? Wow. Aw…" The perk of his ears faded with slight disappointment. "I always saw myself as more of the Damon, ya know?"

The husky suppressed a snicker at the notion of Karl squeezed into the porcupine badass's signature leather jacket. "I guess you've got the natural armor angle."

Kylie chattered with impatience. "Boys, can we focus?"

Karl tapped his massive fingers together. "I mean Max is still the Serge, and you're still the Cassie, so…"

Trying to let the fanboy down easy, Max twirled his paw between them. "I don't know if you're really the motorcycle type."

The rhino perked up. "They make motorcycles for rhinos!" He started to search the web for pictures. "They start with a forklift—"

"Karl! Karl." She waved webbed paws. "What can you tell us about the bread lady?"

Max smirked. A part of him wanted to hear where that was going.

"Right." The rhino clicked back to the text document and searched for bread.

A series of deep thuds announced Karl's parents walking around upstairs. It occurred to Max that he was standing directly under at least two full-grown rhinos. He cast a suspicious eye at a nearby support beam.

Their fan didn't even look up. "Don't worry; basically the whole house is made of steel."

Max shared a concerned look with his girlfriend.

"Hmm. Not finding very much. Looks like she runs her company out of her home—the addresses are the same." The rhino pulled up a map. "She's south of town, in the hills."

"Any reports of death from eating her baked goods? Or possession?" She looked at her husky boyfriend. "Or brainwashing?"

"Well, that Yeast India Company has really positive reviews." His thick fingers scrolled through a string of social media comments. "So maybe brainwashing?"

Kylie bounced on the husky's lap. "Wait, you have an address?"

Max cleared his throat, trying to pretend he didn't have a sexy lutrine grinding on him. "I thought you said you didn't have that much information on her."

"Yeah, it's on her business card. Or, at least, it used to be. The new ones just have a FoodieFoto link and a bunch of weird symbols." He tilted his horn at the screen. "She must take orders through there, since I still see her catering events."

The otter wiggled with excitement. "You never went there to investigate?"

He shrugged his heavy shoulders. "I didn't think 'makes tasty bread' was a good reason to break into her house."

"Yeah, that'd be crazy." She waggled her phone at him. "Could you send me that address, please?"

"Sure!" He copied it into an email for her. "Do you guys have any questions about other residents?"

"Nope!" The otter popped up from her boyfriend's lap like a fishing bobber. Her tail curved for balance as she angled for the door.

Max stood, glad that his hoodie was long enough to help hide his erection as he stood to follow. "Not today, but I'm sure we'll have more soon."

Ears drooping a little at their sudden exit, the rhino hooked a thumb at his computer. "Because most of my files are way more thorough."

The husky snapped a finger at him. "That's why you're the Egbert."

Karl grinned, ears waggling sheepishly.

The husky trotted after his lover up the stairs. On their way out the door, they swept past Karl's mom, who had somehow produced a large glazed squash in the time they'd been there.

~ ~ ~

Armed with the address, they poked along the back lanes surrounding Windfall until they came across a nondescript strip of land. It had a little house, a modest barn, and plenty of tree cover. Most importantly, it had a familiar little moped parked in front of it.

Letting the car putter to a stop, Kylie whipped a pair of small binoculars from her fishing vest. Her paw on his chest pushed him back into the seat for a better view.

Max rubbed the top of his head and the front of his shins. His tail felt oddly comfortable, however, in the seat's generous tail slot. Maybe if he started wearing skateboard pads whenever Kylie drove, he could learn to tolerate the Amphicar.

She watched as the mongoose emerged from the house toting a massive grain sack. "There she is! I bet she has alien mind-control spores in there."

The dog sniffed absently. Smelled like rain. "You mean like in Season One?"

"Hm?" Her paw rested on his thigh as she leaned forward. The binoculars tapped the windshield.

The canine tried not to think about how good her touch felt, or the gradual swell of his arousal. "Strangeville. Before I joined the show." Max watched both her and the house warily, unsure when she'd dash out of the car and drag him along. "One of the first episodes in the Tribunal arc."

"Ah." A smirk quirked the corner of her muzzle. "Sometimes I forget I'm dating the show's biggest fan."

His massive paw covered hers. "Or at least yours."

The otter lowered her binoculars to flash him a quick smile, then looked back at the property. "Ugh!" The otter wiggled with displeasure. "How is she still not doing anything?"

A few dozen meters into the property, the baker tottered across the driveway. Her middle did a belly dance under the heavy sack. With a yowl of strength, she let it thud to the earth and flung open the door to the shed. Inside sat a huge granite millstone.

Max lowered his ears and sunk lower in his seat, hoping she wouldn't turn around and notice them.

With a chatter of excitement, Kylie shoved the binoculars into his paws.

He took them and peered at the strange baker. She hauled the grain sack up to the massive stones and began to pour it onto the stone surface. The instant the sack was empty, she streaked under the mill's heavy crank and slammed the barn door. A sharp chatter carried through the mossy trees. Seconds later, a massive grinding sound followed. The husky found himself reminded of the canned sound effect of stone doors sliding open.

The otter held up her phone, recording. "What's she doing?"

He shrugged. "I don't know. Wheat magic?"

She cocked an eyebrow at him. "You can't have magic and aliens."

His eyebrow rose without permission. "I'm not sure that's an actual rule."

A sputtering light, weak at first, flashed from the gap around the barn door. Brighter and brighter it became, until it flared like a welding torch.

Max lowered the field glasses and rubbed at his eyes. A whimper trailed from his muzzle.

Kylie kept recording. "Whoa!"

He blinked away the afterimage. A purple blob obscured the center of his vision, forcing him to look at the building sidelong. "What was that?"

"That was totally some kind of magic!" Her webbed finger jabbed toward the windshield. "Her all-natural bread is all-supernatural!"

Still blinking, Max watched as the runes and spirals sparked as the millstones ground on. "I don't know if we can conclude that yet."

She gripped at his shoulder, tugging on sleeve fabric. "We have to tell the world."

"Assuming you're right…" He thought back to the juicy cheeseburger of hours before. "If we expose her, won't she stop making the bread?"

They sat silent for a long moment. The slim mongoose kicked open the door, toting a massive bucket of flour. A faint cloud followed her to the house. Back on the grindstone, only a faint spark here and there on the great stone wheels spoke of the energies that had crackled there seconds before.

"Okay. Fine. Maybe." Her eyebrows sunk like river stones. "But we're putting this in the blog."

His tail thumped against the otter-shaped seat. "Warm people up to the idea. Preheat them for the coming proof."

"But we still have to figure out exactly what she's doing." The lutrine wiggled in her seat and flailed at the events that had just unfolded. "For all we know, she's using nightmares to power her magic."

"So it's magic?" He cocked an ear.

She stuck her tongue out of her cute little muzzle. "Shut up."

The big canine clicked the covers back on the lenses of the binoculars. "So much for that."

Phone still in her paws, Kylie popped open the car door and hopped out. With a whisper of footsteps, she slunk toward the barn.

His triangular ears dropped with a groan. "Or not."

He followed her across the cluttered and brambly woods. Moss dangled from ancient trees. The distant crack of thunder rolled in from the sea. Together, they dashed across the driveway and around the back of the barn.

Under Kylie's paw, the old wooden door squeaked open. She eeled into the dim space, over boxes and around dusty machinery.

By the time Max stubbed his toes down the same path, she stood rubbing her paws together over the massive granite millstones. Upon inspection, the great stones appeared to have been retrofitted for this purpose from some kind of forgotten shrine, with some faces of the rock freshly cut and others still covered with ancient lichen. Its massive wheels lay etched with strange symbols, jagged things arranged in no pattern Max could discern. As Max examined them, they almost seemed to shift and rearrange when he wasn't looking. He found he could never find a particular symbol again after he'd looked away from it. As he opened his mouth to give voice to his growing unease, Kylie took a step toward it, eyes glittering. Her fingers stretched out for the surface…

He grabbed her by the back of the vest and yanked her out of reach of the rune-etched stones.

"Hey!" Her voice came as a choked squawk. "What's the big idea?"

"Sorry." The big dog shrugged. "It looked like you were going to touch it."

Her eyes carried the special kind of pity reserved for beloved but daft dogs. "I was gonna touch it."

"Then I'm not sorry." His grip tightened on her garment. "We did five years of TV show on this. Touching random artifacts is how you summon demons."

Her fists propped on her hips. "Oh, there're demons now."

"Magic alien demons." He nodded and let her go. "Don't touch it."

With a displeased chitter, she settled for just taking video of the apparatus. "But we're getting a sample." She pulled small plastic bag from her fishing vest pocket.

"Deal." He took the bag and stooped to collect a bit of flour from the ground.

She looked a little disgusted. "Ew, from the floor?"

"We're not going to eat it. We're going to study it." Whispering, he scooped a pile of the white powder into the bag, then zipped it sealed. "I know that's going to be tough for someone who forgot not to eat the giant dumpling squid."

She sputtered, leering at him from around a stone possibly repurposed from some occult altar. "That's not the same and you know it!" She poked the crank. Nothing happened. She gave it a quick turn. The millstone rolled, but no weird lights appeared. She braced to turn it one more time...

Thunder boomed. Close.

The walls shook, rattling loose dust in thin plumes and helixes.

The husky found himself stepping immediately to her side. A glance revealed his otter girlfriend standing very straight and looking around with concern.

A serious look passed between them. He pocketed the evidence. "Quit while we're ahead?"

She only hesitated for a second, then reached for his arm. "Sure."

Footsteps.

Faint snaps of profanity neared, sounding quite a bit like the mongoose straining under another heavy weight.

Max ducked. The otter did likewise. As one, they started shuffling back toward the side door. He strained to listen, even as he tried to keep his ears down and out of sight.

The mongoose staggered into view, face obscured by another burlap sack of wheat. Dumping it on the wheel, she seized upon that massive handle and cranked it up and down, ripples of effort translating down her long spine. One granite wheel rolled atop the other, grinding the grain to powder. The old female began to mutter, low and continuous. The words were too low to hear, but the cadence was bizarre, and many of the sounds seemed to be produced at the back of the throat. Green light sparkled along the etchings, gathering at the point of contact between the stones. Here and there, little licks of lightning flicked out, curling around the wheels or arching to nearby pillars. By the growing light, Max saw her eyes had gone glazed, unfocused.

The pair of intruders stood at the side door, a fair ways from the action. Max glanced to his girlfriend, assuming she'd be about ready to leave. Instead, he found her recording the proceedings with keen interest. With his quietest groan, he picked her up around the middle and backpedaled out the open door. Sometimes, it paid to be big.

The outside air hung heavy with moisture, drizzle spraying down in fits. Sweeps of wind stirred the trees. The birds had gone quiet.

The otter finally turned off her phone. "Fine, fine."

Clouds darkened the sky, deepening the shadows of the forest below. After ducking into the trees, they beat a swift retreat. Max found himself actually pleased to be crammed back into the Amphicar, at least for the moment, as his girlfriend fired it up.

He shot her a testy look. "What happened to quitting while we were ahead?"

Those webbed paws waggled on the steering wheel. "Um, she came back and started grinding alien flour in front of us? And there was a big crazy light show?"

"Yes, and we know a ton of special effects professionals." He crossed his arms over his damp hoodie. "I thought we were letting this one go."

"We are!" She pulled back onto the main road. "I did!"

"And you stuck around recording her because…?"

She grinned, still riding the endorphin rush. "I was just getting 'special effects' footage for the blog."

"That really upped our odds of being caught. She could've called the cops."

A second or two passed while rain pattered on the windshield. "Okay, so maybe we need to back off."

"A little." He wiggled the water from his whiskers.

She drove on a little way, then her bright laugh splashed against the gray din of rain.

"What?" He couldn't help a small smile.

"Nothing." Her hazel eyes shone his way. "It just occurred to me that nobody's going to believe us about a magic bread lady."

~ ~ ~

The looming rainstorm met them in the driveway. Max unfolded himself from the confines of her aquatic car and squished up the gravel to the front porch. His fur soaked up the rainwater as he tried to shield a takeout bag of rolls.

Kylie padded along as raindrops bounced off her sleek pelt. Once inside, she kicked off her shoes and spun on tiptoe to face him, scarfing down the remains of a roll. "These are actually really good."

A quick shake cleared some of the water from his fur. "Hand-milled, you know. You could almost say they're out of this world." He waggled his eyebrows as he stashed the remaining rolls in the fridge. As he passed the stairs, his ears popped up. "Judging by the classic rock coming from your mom's room, she's deep into some project."

"You don't think she got talked into working on that 'kid lawyers' show?" She snagged her laptop from the kitchen table.

"I don't think even she could salvage that." He eyed her computer, hoping she wouldn't dive back into research instantly. Padding across the dining room, he followed her to his room. She smelled really good. She always did. "What are we going to do now?"

With a leap and a chitter, she bounced onto his bed. "Keep researching Bread Lady, obviously. She could lead us to something people might actually believe." She wiggled forward to her laptop.

His paw settled atop hers on the trackpad. "Or we could watch a movie."

The otter looked up at him with automatic defiance.

He met her eyes and cocked an ear. Without a trace of shame, he drooped his muzzle, dropped his ears, and opened his eyes extra wide.

Her expression softened in a moment. A sigh of surrender left her a little slumped. "Okay, that might be a good idea. Bread Lady isn't an obvious threat."

The husky wagged. It was nice that she listened to him once in a while. "What do you want to watch? Vow of Violence? Kevlar King Charles?"

They settled on a low-budget action flick from south of the border. Rain pattered down the window panes. Wind whipped tree branches outside, the forest a dark rollick. Imperfect subtitles sprung up like dandelions along the bottom of the screen.

He sighed with contentment. Watching bad movies together on the bed, just like the old days: the only difference now being how close he got to cuddle her.

Max sniffed in disbelief. "I get that she's really good with spatulas, but you'd think the Federales would make her carry a gun."

The otter rolled her eyes, then rolled a shrug down her body. "Then she wouldn't be La Espátula."

He squinted at the screen. "We've also had no explanation for why these spatulas are so sharp." Onscreen, the lead actress hurled one such implement through the bulletproof windshield of a getaway limo and into the chest of its driver.

The movie exploded onward until the credits rolled.

Kylie gave the scrolling names and theme music a sidelong look. "So the intrepid Mexican cafeteria worker single-handedly destroys the drug cartel...with spatulas." She tilted her head at the screen. "Is this sexist? I honestly can't tell."

Beside her, the husky nodded. "The jury's still out, but justice...has been served."

She punched him in the shoulder. "Dork."

His arms closed around hers, a hug to impede any further strikes. He took a deep breath of her scent; it always calmed him, reminded him of old times.

As the movie file ended, she reached for the keyboard. Closing the media player and switching to her web browser, she clicked over to a site Max recognized as one of Windfall's local supernatural forums.

With a woof of offense, he pushed the laptop to the headboard. "Oh no, you're taking the night off."

"Hey!" She squirmed to reach it, but his arm around her middle kept her in place. "Lemme go, fluff brain!"

He chuckled and made no move to release her. "No way."

"It's my computer!" Her deft fingers poked at his ribs, unleashing a burst of tickles. "I can investigate on it if I want!"

With a yowl of laugher, he snatched up her paws in one of his. It just made sense to get on top of her, since she was being such a scallywag. It was important to restrain her paws if he wanted to win: after years of rooming together, she knew all his ticklish spots.

For a short little otter, Kylie was actually pretty strong. Her whole body rippled in a wave atop the bed, the combined force of her legs, tail, and back flinging him back. The mattress springs creaked under the strain, not for the first time, of their bodies moving against each other.

Heartbeat picking up, he pinned her back to the bed and unleashed a playful growl in her ear.

With a giggle, she nibbled at his neck fur. "Nah-om-om-om!" Her hips bucked up into his, bucking him just far enough back to break her hands free. She gripped around his back, wrestling him into a roll, trying to get the upper paw.

Unfortunately, they ran out of bed.

For an instant, they teetered in limbo at the edge of the mattress, then slid into an inextricable flop to the floor. Max winced as he took the brunt of the impact on his elbows, cradling Kylie to his chest to keep her from hitting the carpeted floor. His eyes opened a half second later. "You okay?"

"Yeah. No harm done." She sounded winded and wry as she squirmed in his grip. "You can let me up now, Maxie."

He pondered her, still panting from the exertion on the bed. She was warm against him, her scent stirred up by their roughhousing. Her butt pressed against his belly, her long tail between his legs. The position made his sheath twitch, and for the first time in days, he didn't feel the need to stifle the urge. He slipped his paw from its protective position against her sternum, slipping it up instead to encircle her smaller paw, pinning it in place as he gave a playful growl in her ear. "What if I don't want to?"

The shiver that passed through her was intensely gratifying. Curling her fingers against his, she twisted to look up at him with those big, pretty hazel eyes. "Okay, then. What do you want to do?"

Still keeping her gently pinned, he nuzzled her throat, drawing a long lick along her jawline. "I want you, rudderbutt. Just like this." As he slipped his paw under the hem of her shirt, he rocked his hips forward, pressing the growing heat of his crotch against her upturned ass.

She gave a strained little moan, arching to press against his caress as he traced her ribs. "Oh, wow. That's so much better than my idea." Her rump waggled against his crotch.

He ground his hips forward. The steady return of his erection did not pass under her radar as it pressed under her tail.

"Ooh, bad doggy." A more insistent grind followed. "You'll do anything to distract me."

"Mmmhmm." His deep growl breezed through her silky auburn hair. His paws migrated between her thighs, teasing along the underside of her rudder, pressing its ample curve against his crotch.

Those bright white top teeth pressed her bottom lip for an instant of anticipation. "Or do you just like humping my tail?"

He gave it an extra grope. "You do have a cute tail…"

With a scoundrel's snicker, she writhed free, her spine arching like liquid sex. Her glance simmered up at him. "I think I like this plan, Maxie. We've never done it doggy style…"

He got up to his knees for a better look. His erection prodded a tent in his pants. Idly, his paw traced atop it as he watched her.

She rolled to all fours. Legs spread, the otter arched her back to present herself to him. With a mischievous snicker, she waggled her jeans-clad backside his way and snaked her tail under his t-shirt. "Better get these clothes out of the way."

Led by the nose, he tripped over her scent while getting to his feet. He shimmied out of pants and boxers, then danced out of his socks. With a final moment's thought before her scent overtook him, he double-checked his bedroom door was closed and locked. Trotting back to her, the red tip of his erection gleamed against the snowy white of his belly. He took her by the paw and helped her back to her feet.

As soon as his crotch was within reach, webbed paws teased and toyed with his emerging cock. Her touch flowed over his length, tugging his sheath back and smoothing the fur of his balls. She stretched up and nuzzled teasingly close with a kiss-me look. He obliged her.

Embracing her, Max fell through a haze of arousal into her kisses. He drove his tongue into her mouth, mind spinning as he struggled to divide his attention between kissing the otter and removing her clothes. Fumbling to undo the tail clasp of her pants, he slid them and her underwear down enough to let them fall to the floor, then returned to squeeze her ass and draw a squeak of pleasure from her. They were forced to separate as she hauled his shirt up over his head, and he took advantage of the interruption to peel her out of her vest and shirt, pulling her back to him and resuming the kiss and hooking his arms around her to tackle the clasp of her bra. He was getting pretty good at it; only a few seconds of fumbling and the light, practical garment fell away, exposing her small, pert breasts to his eager paws.

Kylie moaned as his paw pads played over her nipples. Then, with a mewl of regret, she pulled back and out of his arms, dancing away to lean against the footboard of his bed, and Max had to pause to admire the sight of her. She was panting slightly, her chest heaving, those perfect little breasts swaying. He followed the smooth lines of her body over her rounded hips, past her flare of auburn pubic fur to her plump, ready sex.

He swallowed, his fervor buried for the moment as he felt the need to speak, to tell her how amazing she was. There needed to be a new word for Kylie, something that encompassed "fun" and "gorgeous" and "adorable."

Especially "adorable," as she bit her lower lip and gave him the same hungry look right back.

But, as he opened his mouth to fumble for something halfway romantic, she beat him to it. Gripping the footboard as though to steady herself, she blurted: "You're really, really good looking, Maxie. Like, crazy sexy. I love watching you get turned on." Then she was turning away, vaulting up onto the bed, tail swaying for balance and seduction. She crawled until she was near the pillows, turning back to look over her shoulder at him with fluid grace. "This is the way you wanted me, right?"

Max could freely admit the sight of his best friend and lover with her rump in the air, tail raised in eager invitation, was one of the best things he'd ever seen. He joined her on the bed, drinking in the curves of her body, the scent of her arousal filling the air. Seeing how eager she'd become, he couldn't resist tormenting her just a bit, caressing the backs of her thigh up toward her rump, stopping just short of her slick, gleaming sex.

"I can't believe we've never done it this way before." Kylie murmured into smooth fabric, rubbing her face against the blankets, chasing his scent. She gave her upturned rump a wiggle with a chitter of giddy anticipation.

He was still enjoying teasing her, running his hands along her sides, brushing his fingertips along the curve of her ribs. He leaned in to plant a kiss to the small of her back. "Why's that?"

She caressed her tail against his naked chest, eyes drifting shut in pleasure at the petting. More of his weight settled on her hips as he slipped forward, and she turned her head a bit so he could nuzzle against her jawline. His cock brushed the fur of her inner thighs on its unhurried path to its destination, a wonderful inevitability, and she shivered in obvious anticipation. "Well, you know..."

A pause, as he struggled to finish her thought through the haze of his lust. Then he heaved a sound somewhere between a sigh and a groan into the fall of her hair. "Because I'm a dog?"

She had to twist to grin at him, and despite her best efforts she didn't look very apologetic.

With a deadpan glare, he sighed. "I don't know why we're the ones who got saddled with the name. It's not like every other species does missionary."

"Maybe you have some crazy inborn talent for it." She bit her lower lip, bouncing her hips up against him emphatically. "We should find out."

That got a smile from him. He leaned up to lick her ear, rocking her forward slightly to get her rear end higher. One paw took hold of her tail base, thumb caressing the sensitive underside. "You're lucky you're cute."

She gave the tiniest of happy squeaks as the slick tip of him brushed her entrance. "It does come in handy."

A playful growl rumbled down his throat. He pressed his hips forward, sinking into her a millimeter at a time. Her folds parted with slick welcoming heat.

The otter spread her legs further. A chirr from her round little muzzle begged wordlessly for more. Those cute webbed paws clutched his pillow to muffle her louder noises, even as her tail waved across his chest like a winding river.

His sheath slid back as he sank further into her. Once he'd hilted, he paused a moment to soak up the sensations. Hot breath filtered through her hair, each pant an affirmation of how much he loved her. The urge to thrust overwhelmed him, though, and soon he was riding her with an increasing rhythm and enthusiasm.

His lover, his co-star and best friend for years, squawked into the pillow —a sort of high-pitched keen of pleasure— as he penetrated her again. Her toes curled against his thighs, tugging at the fur there. Back and forth her hips waggled, working his shaft against every surface of her passage.

He thrusted harder, damp fuzzy balls slapping against her mons. The room filled with the sounds of the lovemaking, the slick slurp of him pulling back audible over the rain. His paws gripped her hips, shoving them back against his. He grunted with effort as he claimed the sexy little otter under him.

Her every squeak urged him on. The bed rocked under them, her laptop tapping against the headboard.

He rocked atop her, driving his canine length into her lovely depths. Those paws, massive compared to her own, stirred her pelt with care, even while gripping her for carnal leverage. His hips slapped against hers with urgent force, flattening her breasts on the mattress. Wet slicks echoed through the room, counterpointed by the deep grunts of pleasure.

A squeak of joy escaped her throat: high-pitched and super cute. Her ears flicked back in a blush. She shoved her face into his pillow.

Max growled into her round little ears; the raw vibration rocked her to the core. Pressing himself flush as he could against her, he relished the soft flesh of her labia against his sheath. "How're you holding up, squeaker?"

"M'good." She groaned, spreading her legs a little wider to give him easier access. "You feel really deep like this, Maxie. And don't call me that."

Her obvious enjoyment only upped his determination. One paw gripped her hips, while the other slipped under her midriff to massage her clit. As he work it in steady circles, her body bucked hard against his.

For a moment, all she could do was squeak back at him, face still buried in the pillow. Then she cleared her throat and attempted a sultry purr. It came out more like a balloon squeak.

The husky froze, then woofed a massive laugh.

"Shut up!" She squirmed to escape his gaze, but not his dick. "I can't help that I only make stupid peeps. We can't all sound like sexy diesel engines."

"I like it when you peep." Leaning up to nuzzle her hair, he shifted inside her. "Tells me I'm doing a good job. You're the best squeaky toy ever."

"That's not helping!" She hid her face in a pillow again to bury a giggle.

"Kylie…" His paw pads caressed her silken cheek. "I think you can feel just how much I like our soundtrack." He let a rumble of his lust creep into his voice as his hips rocked forward to press a growing knot into her.

The otter shuddered as he spread her legs wide. A slight vibration to her hips told him one of her paws had slipped between her legs.

His balls swung with every thrust, slowed only by the fluff on them. He unleashed a growl of passion past her ear: "So you like how I sound, rudderbutt?"

Face-deep in the pillow, she squeaked in agreement.

"And you like the feel of a big hard husky cock inside you?" He teased her with his knot, never quite going inside.

"Maxie!" Her tail bumped back against his chest as she tried to capture that canine bulge.

After a second, he relented. He pressed his whole length inside her, knot a tight fit past her slick entrance. His hips worked faster into her than ever, dragging it in and out of her. As her passage clenched down around him, a sudden wave of ecstasy swept him away. The tight tension of her around his knot squeezed a gasp from him. His world crashed into a single sensation: that of climax within his mate. Every shudder of his straining body spurted hot passion into her. Satiny slickness spread his seed along every surface within her passage. Surge after surge of pleasure lifted his balls and raced down his length to flood her waiting wetness, leaving her all the wetter.

Not that the otter ever complained about being too wet. She panted. That telltale wiggle returned, swishing her ample tail through his stomach fur.

He shuddered as his orgasm faded to afterglow. Pushing her tail a little further to one side as he leaned in, he mouthed a deep growl to her ear: "You gonna come for me? I want you to come on my cock when I tie you."

A sharp squeak answered him. "Since when can you talk dirty?"

His shrug translated across her back. "It's easy when I've been having dirty thoughts about you all week." He slipped back into a deep, seductive tone, still panting. "I want you to, you know." His paws found her breasts and toyed with her stiff nipples. "I love seeing you cum." He rocked his hips to tug at the knot within her. "I love feeling it around my knot."

She tensed under him and muffled a mighty squeak into the pillow. Her toes gripped the sheets. That tight passage pulsed up his length, squishing his hot cum around. Her eyes closed as she shoved her hips back into him.

Max straightened, still tied. Not wanting to kink her tail, he carefully lifted it and resettled it on his other hip. This motion, of course, caused all manner of pleasant sensations to press around his knot.

The otter appreciated them too, from the low chitters that rippled through her voice. The sound sharpened as her tail base rubbed along his stomach. Endorphins making him adventurous, he slid a hand between them to explore the spot's sensitivity, letting her hand guide his. His gambit paid off, eliciting a dreamy coo from Kylie. Her body relaxed against and around him. Her tail uncurled and drooped atop his thigh. Her whiskers drooped to the pillow.

His lutrine lover turned to gaze up at him through messy auburn hair.

He leaned for a nuzzle, which melted into a kiss on the side of her muzzle. One disadvantage of this position was that he couldn't make out with her. It had other benefits, though. Her body felt lovely up against his. Every little move her body made brushed it against his.

A tender moment passed in calming silence. Rain traced down the window as their heartbeats slowed and the familiar spell of sleepy satisfaction

crept over Max. He rested his chin on her shoulder and sighed a happy sigh.

She patted his arm. "Wow. You were pretty pent up."

He blushed and buried his muzzle in her hair. "Yeah."

"Why didn't you say something?"

"You were sniffing out clues. You seemed really set on it." He shrugged. "And I didn't want to be pushy."

Her little ears went up. "Pushy?"

He rolled his shoulders, feeling a tinge of embarrassment. "Yeah. I mean, I'm like twice your size. I can't just throw you into bed and have my way with you."

"Not sure I'd complain about that." Her hazel eyes watched him in the reflection of the slightly-fogged window. "You're my boyfriend, after all. You're allowed to have needs."

The term made him smile. He rubbed a paw down her flank. "You're small, though, and sometimes I worry I could hurt you. Or make things awkward."

"We did all our own stunts, remember? I can handle a big fluffball like you." She toyed with the fur of his wrist. "In case you didn't notice, I like how big you are."

That made him smirk. "Oh?"

"Not just like that." She placed a gentle kiss on the inside of his wrist. "You make me feel so safe, Maxie. Sometimes I feel like I could just bury myself in your fur and be safe from everything. All this crazy paranormal stuff feels so much less insane if I have you watching my back. Besides, I like that I can trust you."

"Oh?"

"Yeah." She nuzzled into his palm. "To be good to me. And I know how much work you put into being careful." He was close enough to her ear to watch the pink inside darken with her blush. "And if you want to toss me into bed or pin me to a wall and have your way with me, I don't think I'd object."

He nodded, nose between her round lutrine ears. "Mmm. This was pretty good."

"And your bigness has all sorts of benefits." She squeezed down on his buried cock, eliciting a woof of pleasure from the dog. Her paws spread across the head of the bed. "I don't know if I'd even have the courage to track down monsters without you."

Still tingling, he rested his muzzle atop her head. "Pretty sure you still would, but that you'd just die."

"Hey!" Her elbow prodded his ribs. "I'm tough!" She squirmed with outrage, tugging at his knot, unable to turn and face him. "I totally bit an alien handyman that one time."

Chuckling, he patted her shoulder. "I'm kidding; I'm kidding. You're tough."

The otter sniffed, placated. "I had no idea you were holding back."

His ears lifted.

"I mean, I kinda noticed I was always the one to initiate sex. I thought that just meant I was the horny one."

He smirked. "I get horny too."

She squirmed. "Yeah, but when we're in friend mode, you totally pick me up and toss me over your shoulder when I'm being a brat."

His ears flicked up. "So you admit you can be a brat?"

"Not the point here, mister."

The husky rolled his eyes. "Pinning you to the couch because you've deluded yourself into thinking you can win a wrestling match with me is one thing." He swished his whiskers with an anxious whimper. "Pinning you to the couch because I'm horny and your tight jeans are driving me crazy…makes me feel like I'm controlling you."

Still tied, she scoffed. "Yeah, good luck with that."

He laughed a little. "Tell me about it…"

For a moment, she pursed her lips. "Remember the episode where everyone but me and Egbert were turning into feral monster versions of themselves?"

The husky kissed his lover's neck, rumbling as he caressed her belly. He could tell she had at least one more climax in her, and to his mild surprise he found he did as well, his knotted cock pulsing once more in the incredible tightness of her passage. Automatically, he recited: "'Throwback.' Season Three, Episode Fourteen. Something like six and a half stars on IMDB."

The tilt and bob of her head told him she'd rolled her eyes. "Right, that one. Well, remember the part where you changed right in front of me and chased me around the house?" She reached for her computer, which had been forgotten against the headboard. She woke it up with a flick across the touchpad and opened a site from her favorites.

With an absent kiss to her shoulder, he peeked curiously at the laptop as the screen lit up. "Yeah, I think so. Mostly I remember tripping over the coffee table because reflective yellow contact lenses make it hard to see, and then I remember the makeup people yelling at me for ripping out my fur extensions.

The otter chuckled. She clicked a link and the screen transitioned to a column of text. "Well, it was worth it to inspire this fic. One of my favorites. Basically, what if I hadn't locked you in the basement and escaped up the coal chute?"

He raised an eyebrow. "I seem to recall my motivation being that I was out for blood."

"Yeah, well, turns out you had other bodily fluids in mind." She gave a little shiver that made his cock surge. "Mmm, it's all feral and passionate, but still with a tender core, ya know?"

"Sounds fun." Slipping his paw down to caress a brazen finger along the joining of their bodies, he let his teeth graze the shell of her ear as he whispered: "You should read it for me."

Her nervous chuckle lasted just long enough for her to brush hair from her face. "Okay, um, let's see. Cassie peered over Serge's shoulder, watching him pore over the recipe to the counterspell. Part of her wanted to insist that she take the risk, since she had more experience with magic stuff, but another part of her was glad he had offered, happy that he wanted to protect her."

This scene felt familiar, and a little ways off from where it needed to be. "Skip ahead." He moaned, giving a little thrust that jostled his reawakening cock inside her and grinning as she squirmed.

Scrolling rapidly through the paragraphs, his otter murmured. "Mmmph, oh gosh, okay. Let's see, you start to change before you finish, can't make it in time, big scary transformation scene, chase me out into the living room… Okay, here we go: Cassie moaned into the carpet, the tatters of her shirt and panties swaying as Serge bucked into her. Monstrous hands held her wrists, pinning her down, but she wouldn't have gone anywhere if she could. He —mm!— claimed her and she loved it, arching her hips to meet every thrust of his huge, hard cock inside her. She felt hot breath on her nape and shivered, picturing him bent over her, covering her, pressing as much of his body against hers as he could. When Serge's tongue slipped along the arch of her neck, she turned to meet it, completely trusting. This was Serge, after all, her Serge. She knew in her bones he would never hurt her." She twisted to look at him, her mouth open just enough for a gasp. "See, Maxie? Even in crazy primal sex stories you're a big softie."

Max grunted, willing his eyes to focus as he kept up the steady roll of his hips. He couldn't get much motion going —she was super tight— but whenever he could coax a shudder out of her she would clench wonderfully around his knot. So he teased and caressed her, his free hand traveling up and down her body, fluttering over her nipples and navel and clit as he pretended to be patient so she'd continue.

"S-She felt a sudden extra resistance to his thrusts, a growing swelling at the base of his cock as it sheathed itself in her. With a jolt, she realized it must be his knot, and that the sex-crazed creature that had once been her best friend wanted to stuff it inside her and—umf, Max!" She whimpered into the sheets. "Faster. Ah! Please— Ah, yeah. J-just like that."

The husky abandoned mere teasing as the story approached its climax, sinking his paw between her legs for a merciless assault on her core. He caressed the straining bud of her clit, grinding his knot against her inner walls in an inexorable rhythm. "You're almost there, rudderbutt. Just a little more."

She shook her head, squirming against his chest, fists buried in his bedsheets as her body convulsed in pleasure. "It's too much, Maxie. I can't keep re-reading—"

"You can." His voice rumbled against her shoulder as he arched over her, feeling her body rippling around him, wanting more than anything to see her hit one more peak. "I know you're close, Kylie. You can do it. Just keep reading."

Kylie strained for the laptop, struggling to get the screen back into view. "Sh-she didn't have time to wonder if it could fit before it was inside her, stretching her out wide, filling her with his hot flesh! Serge only managed a few more thrusts before it was too big to come out of her, locking them t-together. With a howl of triumph, Serge gripped her tight as wave after wave of white-hot cum filled her tender womb, claiming her innermost places with his essence." She shuddered as the husky's cock throbbed at the description, but persevered, too stubborn to back down now. "Then she felt him twist, bearing down on her until his jaws closed on her scruff. She felt a pinch and sting of teeth as he gripped her, marking her outside as well as in, making her entirely his!"

This was just the sort of opening Max'd been waiting for. With a slowness that hid his growing desperation, he threaded his muzzle through the short, silky fall of her hair, nuzzling along the line of her spine. At the appropriate instant in the story, in just the right pause in her reading, he opened his jaws and gave the back of her neck a sharp, playful nip.

The otter squeaked in shocked delight. Her whole body stiffened. That cute little muzzle rolled against the mattress as she wiggled, still tethered by his buried cock. Those round ears tipped back through her dark red hair as her form undulated against him, body-surfing on a wave of climax.

His knotted length throbbed within her, somewhat sore but not yet ready to come unstuck from her. He found himself teetering on the edge of another orgasm, the side effect of being teased all day. Frantic need compelled him as he curled fingers around his sheath and under his balls, rubbing as much as the space between their bodies allowed. Arousal spiked fast within him, overwhelming him in seconds. A deep growl rattled his throat as he emptied his balls into his writhing lover, her passage welcoming every drop with gripping passion.

Max's second climax turned his muscles to overheated gelatin, and his vision swam with the buzz of pleasure. Rather than put his faith in his trembling arms and risk squishing Kylie, he slipped an arm around her middle and guided them both down onto their sides. The otter didn't protest, merely snuggling back against his chest and pulling his arms around her.

They lay like that for some time, the husky caressing her belly as he listened to her heartbeat slow. He considered trying to get one of his blankets over them, but that would have taken too much effort. With a kiss to the back of his lover's neck, he murmured: "Does that fanfic have any more chapters?"

She made a sleepy sound, drawing his other arm tighter around her chest. "Eh." Her webbed paw waved a vague gesture in the direction of the still-humming laptop. "It does, but it gets weird. Long story short: half-monster husky-otter babies and hardly any more sex scenes."

He huffed a laugh into the warm scent of her hair. "Alas."

Her tail teased his shins. "So, you liked the fic?"

"Mmmmm, pretty good, but I like the real thing better." His fading knot slipped slowly free. Muzzle over her shoulder, he watched as thick fluids beaded down her waterproof pubic hair to drip on the sheets, like rain down the window glass.

"And did you catch the part where, even though Serge was big and strong and being a little rough, Cassie was right there with him because she trusted him? Think there might be some kind of message there?"

He chuckled. "Yeah."

Her trembled gasp concluded with a sigh. Free now to move about, she turned to snuggle closer against him. Her smooth pelt mingled with his fluff, her muzzle slipping perfectly into the hollow of his shoulder. "You have my permission to throw me over furniture anytime."

His arms curled around her. "I'll remember that next time you're obsessing."

She giggled against his arm. "Not much of a deterrent."

"I've known you long enough to know you can't be deterred..." He kissed her hair. "...only distracted."

HARD SLEEPER

STRANGEVILLE (SAT/4P)

S05E07 "I, Dogbot": Sandy steals a robot from the Tribunal, which is super-strong and obeys every command. She programs it to protect Cassie, giving Serge an identity crisis.

Seated on the sofa, Kylie looked up from the Strangeville fan fiction she was idly reading. "Is waking a guy up by going down on him a real thing?"

Across the room, under a laptop, Max sat up. A quiet woof escaped him at her immodesty. "How would I know?"

"I dunno!" A bit late, she remembered to check if her mother was in earshot, then continued. "Guys talk."

"Guys also lie." The husky scoffed and refinished typing up something on his computer. "If half the stuff my high school friends swore was true actually happened, my hometown would be twice its size."

"It seems like a real thing." She tapped a claw on the phone screen. "The writer wrote it very convincingly."

He shrugged. "Every crazy sex thing has probably been a real thing at some point." Straightening, he made a faint effort to see her phone. "Are you reading porn of our characters again?"

"I'm trying to." Her lithe body wiggled in place. "Don't worry. It's all canon now."

His thick arms crossed. "That's still a little weird."

"I prefer to think of it as crowdsourcing." The otter twirled a paw in the direction of the internet. "Besides, it's completely unrealistic."

The husky winced. "Would my ego survive you explaining that?"

"No, not like that." She rolled her eyes. "They just don't know you like I do."

A deep bark of laughter rose from the dog. "I should hope not."

"If they knew how hard of a sleeper you were, they'd never bother writing this kind of story." Snickering, she shook the phone at him. "I could try to wake you up all sexy with a blowjob, but you'd just sleep through it."

"What are you talking about?" He smirked at her over the laptop screen. "That would be the best reason to wake up ever."

She stuck her tongue out at him. "Yeah, except you're like that Serge knockoff robot from the final season."

A nostalgic look crossed his muzzle. "It was weird how the costume department gave it a cast of my face." He glanced sidelong at her. "Does the robot come up in these stories?"

"Oh, yes!" A chitter of glee echoed through the old house. "But he's more of a sex toy than a character."

"I guess that's better." His head tilted to one side, then the other. "But where were you going with that?"

"You switch off for exactly eight hours a night." She squawked at him. "And nothing can interrupt your recharge cycle."

"I am pretty sure a blowjob would wake me up, rudderbutt." Chuckling, he shook his muzzle. "But you're welcome to try."

The first inkling of a scheme arose in her mind. She grinned. "I'm just saying: I know you better than some fan fiction author."

"And I'm glad you do." He gave her an earnest smile, then returned to typing. A moment later, he paused with academic appreciation. "Man, that was one of the stronger episodes of Season Five."

"Uh, yeah! We'd finally graduated from being sidekicks." Under the innocent guise of looking up more pornography, Kylie swiped over to her alarm app and set the time to an obscene hour. This was totally going to be worth it.

~ ~ ~

The warbling synth of a phone alarm hauled Kylie from her dreams. Webbed paws flailed at the device, but only succeeded in knocking it to the floor. She flopped out of bed to chase it, slinking halfway to the carpet before she could locate it and switch it off. Whatever she had been planning for this early, it totally wasn't worth it. Clawing her way back into bed, she tried to ooze deeper into her pillows, curl up atop the mattress, and bury her whiskers under the blanket, but to no avail. Sunrise bleared through the woods and glowed across her window. As she lay surrendering to wakefulness, she wondered what had possessed her to set an alarm. Thoughts had to swim upstream through molasses. Did she work today? The shop never opened before 10am. Flying out to record DVD commentary? No, that wasn't for months. Maybe she could just ask Max.

Max—that was it!

The otter bounced out of bed and eeled around the room. Stuffing the phone in the elastic of her shorts, she stretched. Her tail almost reached the floor as her fists reached nowhere near the ceiling. Her sleek form flowed out the door into the hallway. Padding across the old wood floor, she knew by instinct which boards squeaked after months of sneaking around the sprawling, ancient house.

Max had always been an early riser, with the power to fall asleep on command and sleep like a log. Kylie, meanwhile, usually flipped and flopped for ages beforehand and woke up at the slightest noise. Worst of all, he always downplayed the difference. Today, she'd get some payback. And prove to that daft dog that she knew him better than he knew himself.

She took the north staircase because the south one shared a wall with her mom's bedroom. Not that she had anything to hide, just yet. The slim otter crept through the living room, with an anxious titter. Her paw paused on his doorknob. With incredible slowness, she turned it and peeked through the cracked door. There her boyfriend lay, sprawled out on the guest bed. The sheets only partly covered him, as if kicked off in the night. Husky fur had great insulating properties, which she'd discovered during their cuddle sessions.

Slinking into the room, she made sure to close the door. With her luck, this'd be the morning Mom made good on her promise to surprise everyone with breakfast and see into the room from the kitchen. With a steadying breath, Kylie eased a knee onto the mattress and lifted the sheet.

Max wore loose charcoal-blue boxer shorts. She'd seen them a few times, though usually just long enough to get her paws on them and throw them across the room. They brought out the colors of his pelt pretty well. Just like Maxie to dress well only when nobody would see. Her fingers traced the fly of his boxers. With care, she unbuttoned and spread the fabric, then squeaked with joy. She always adored looking at his package and having him asleep brought the advantage of him not getting shy. The soft white fur of his stomach changed to a patch of black at his pubic region, leading down to his very full white sheath and the silk-furred orbs beneath. His sheath already looked plump; she wondered if he'd been dreaming of her.

She traced a hand over his hips, then down between his muscular thighs. One throb at a time, her boyfriend's pink canine cocktip emerged from its hiding place.

Max sniffed and rolled his head to one side, nose twitching.

Kylie smirked. She ran a paw up and down his growing length, eliciting a moan from her sleeping husky. It pulsed under her palm, its naked heat growing as it stiffened. She took hold of his sheath and worked it up and down over the smooth flesh. Her other paw meandered to those delicate, white-furred orbs and rolled them around. Deft fingers lifted his balls through the opening in the shorts.

The canine's head lay against the pillow, eyes closed. As the seconds passed, his breathing deepened, though his girth still throbbed in her paw.

She stroked the hot surface of his shaft. Otters loved grabbing things, holding them, exploring them, yet nothing had ever felt as right in her paw as his smooth, hot dick. Her fingertips caressed his opening, spreading a drop of clear, sticky fluid. With nervous care, she rubbed it along his full length, then marveled at how that slight lubrication changed the feel of his cock under her paw pads and webbing.

The canine whimpered in pleasure, panting. His legs stirred against the tousled sheets.

She'd always loved how sensitive Max was, given he was built like such a tough guy. The otter bit her lower lip and watched with her hand around him, wondering if he'd wake up.

A tremor of tension ran through his hips, but the husky's tongue lolled out of his muzzle in dreamy wonder. He'd never look that undignified awake—at least, not before orgasm.

Rubbing her thighs together at the thought of Max's climax, the otter decided she'd teased him enough. She stared down the length of his erection with a grin, then licked her lips. Her paw closed around the base to hold it steady. She rubbed her silky nose against its contours, then gave the side a gentle, tasting lick. Starting with a light kiss to the tip, her mouth spread wide around the thick canine cock, muzzle wrapped around it, feeling its weight and heat on her tongue. A soft hum of pleasure rumbled deep inside her chest as she tasted her boyfriend's precum-slicked member. She took inch after slick inch of red husky dick into her muzzle, pausing every inch or so to suckle, coaxing out a little more of his juices.

Max groaned in his sleep and twitched a paw at his hip, but gave no other signs of waking.

The lutrine bobbed her head, sucking as hard as she dared. Really, him waking up wouldn't be terrible, but it would ruin her plan. Her tongue swirled around the head of his cock, then down to push his sheath, just like she knew he liked. This exposed the swelling bulge of his knot, which she squeezed with her pinkie finger as she returned to sucking his tip. He dribbled hot, plentiful precum into her muzzle, but she'd never minded a little extra moisture. With a swallow, she dove back down and let him fill her whole muzzle with his thick canine shaft.

Whimpering with desire, the husky's hand drifted onto his lap, then curled under his knot. His other hand slipped around the back of her head, fingers interleaved with her hair as he sleepily tugged her muzzle down his length.

Giggling around his dick, the otter's paw replaced his at rubbing behind that ample bulge. She eased just a little further down his dick, until her lips kissed at the knot. One more strong suckle and—

Max gasped, one powerful arm lifting his back off the mattress while the other held her close with frantic need. His hips gave a short, sharp buck into her warm, slick muzzle.

She coughed at the unexpected movement, but redoubled her efforts. Her lips closed around his shaft, tongue dancing along his length to flick at his knot. Proud of her efforts, she watched his sleepy expression shift from distraction to ecstasy.

The dog groaned and tension fluttered through his fluffy bulk. His cock twitched in her paw and over her tongue. The next instant, a volley of creamy heat spurted against the roof of her mouth. She pulled off and stroked the dribbles of white over his crimson shaft. It rolled in beads over the slick fur of her hand and pattered over the cotton boxers. With a nice coating of his own cream, the texture of his shaft slid under her fingers.

Hips jerking as he came, the husky's whimpers of pleasure faded to a panted afterglow. Still his heartbeat throbbed in her grasp, along with the occasional twitch. The husky sat up a little, blinked at her once, and flashed a dreamy smile.

She froze. She'd have to come up with an excuse. Not that he'd need much of one considering—

He slumped back to the pillow and passed out, leg twitching.

"Seriously?" Stifling her whisper, Kylie rolled her eyes at her canine boyfriend. A final string of heat dribbled down her palm, drawing her attention to his slick and shrinking shaft. The otter smiled with pride and reached to wipe her boyfriend's juices from her whiskers, then stopped herself. Instead, she reached for her phone.

~ ~ ~

Max awoke nose-deep in soft otter fur. Stirring, he found his best friend had curled up in his arms. Her supple body conformed to his so well, he hadn't even noticed.

She twirled in his embrace to face him. Those soft hazel eyes greeted him with the delicate joy of fresh wakefulness "Hey."

"Morning, rudderbutt." His paws traced her from nape to tail, smoothing her well-worn t-shirt. "Get lonely last night?"

"Mmmhmm…" She nuzzled into his neck fur. "I'll have to sneak in more often."

Mixed feelings stirred within Max at that: Laura thought the two of them dating was cute, but the husky suspected discretion was the better part of not offending your girlfriend's mom. He'd been the one to insist they at least keep up the pretense of sleeping in separate rooms.

She poked him in the ribs. "You don't even remember me climbing into bed, do you?"

He shook his head and tried to put into words how natural she felt against him: a best friend's touch layered with a lover's caress. His tail swept under the covers, and he held her closer.

A chitter of amusement emanated from her with a shrug. "Of course not."

He woofed a quiet laugh. "What's that supposed to mean?"

"Nothing, Maxie." She patted his paw and wiggled for the edge of the bed. "I think you need some breakfast."

He lifted an arm to let her out. "What about you?"

With an amused titter, she shrugged. "I've already had a snack."

The husky's ears tilted as glanced around the room for tuna melt crumbs. "Okay? What, leftovers?"

"Freshly made." Sleek hips swayed her out of his room, dragging his gaze all the way to the door.

As the fabric of his boxers shifted, sticky fur tugged his balls and sheath. Heat flushed his ears. She couldn't have. He must have gotten riled up by her scent and come in his sleep. Against her. The covers and Kylie had hidden its scent, but, with her gone, he smelled like sex.

Sneaking up and shutting the door, he stripped out of his boxers and tossed them in the hamper. Never had he been so glad the guest room had its own shower. He couldn't remember the last time he'd had a wet dream; not since his mid teens, at least. As the hot water raced over his body, he lathered a little extra shampoo into his pelt. If Kylie smelled spunk on him, he'd have to fess up about coming against her and that road lead to no end of teasing. Of course, she may well have woken up to his nocturnal humping, in which case his fate was sealed hours ago.

After a thorough shower, he shook the water from his fur and stepped out to towel off. He could hear banging about in the kitchen; a rarity since neither of the Bevys were early birds. He hurried into some clothes and trotted out into the entryway.

Kylie sat at the table behind a phone and cup of coffee. She looked up, then crossed her legs. "Hey, handsome."

With a shy wag, he padded across the tile and planted a kiss on her cheek. He nodded at the phone. "What're you up to?"

"The usual. Checking the networks, responding to fans." Her eyes flicked between him and the phone. "I promise social media's not as scary as you think."

He shrugged. "I'm still liking Howl."

"Howl was founded by cats who didn't want to hear about tennis balls every ten seconds." She rolled her eyes. "I'm talkin' about non-anonymous social media used by non-canines. Being a minor TV star's pretty cool; you have enough fans that they're excited to talk with you, but the crazies don't think you're worth locking in their basements."

He pondered the notion. "I guess I have time, now that I'm unemployed."

"Good." She squirmed, pleased. "I'll get you the passwords."

His ears popped up. "What?"

She opened new pages on her phone and handed it to him.

He flicked through the sites, one for each of his various social network profiles. "Why'd you make these?"

"So no one else could." Pride wiggled down her frame. "You're famous, remember?"

He swiped through the accounts. "These are all verified."

"I talked to your agent." She leaned back in her chair.

"My agent is your mom!" He jabbed a finger at her second-story office.

The otter crossed her arms and nodded. "That made it very easy to get a meeting."

"No wonder she gave up on getting me to sign up." He scrolled down through the entries. "You've been posting as me?"

She shrugged and took a sip of coffee. "Everyone we talked to agreed I was the most qualified."

"That explains all those high-angle shots you take of me." He blinked at the parade of Maxes on the screen. "My gallery is full of hero-poses of myself."

The smirking lutrine dipped the mug in his direction. "I play the angle that you've still got some acting ambitions."

"Apparently only for shirtless roles." He thumbed through a few shots cropped to leave the existence of his pants to the imagination. "No wonder that Ukrainian kibble company thought I'd do a commercial in my underwear."

In the comments section, he found a backlog of notes people from in his hometown.

"Don't worry—I've been replying." She patted his knee as he sat. "You're super polite and super stoic, so it's easy to make them feel like you care in a dozen syllables or so. Or maybe a serious emoji." Her face donned a too-serious expression.

He chuckled at her, then snorted at the phone. "None of these people knew I existed in high school."

"Yeah, but then you got famous." Her supple body oozed back into the chair.

"This explains a lot of awkward conversations I had when I was home." He glanced to her. "When do you even have time to post all this?"

"Once in a while I wake up and can't get back to sleep right away." Her tail swayed to nudge his calf. "You wouldn't know what that's like."

"What's that supposed to mean?"

"You sleep like the dead and aren't a zombie in the morning." She set down her coffee cup.

"That's an exaggeration."

"I thought you might say that." Kylie snatched back her phone with a grin, tapped through a few menus, then handed it back.

The rectangular screen held a well-composed self-shot photo. The image showed an otter's smile, smeared with semen. Over a sea of monochrome fur, a webbed paw gripped the knot of a very familiar-looking dick. His.

Max's ears shot up in shock as he fumbled to hide the screen and scoured the kitchen for evidence her mother had teleported in to see. "Kylie!"

"Now do you believe me that you're a heavy sleeper?"

"If this gets on the internet, it'll outlast cockroaches!"

"I made sure it didn't identify us and I'm not posting it. Besides..." Her round muzzle brushed against his chest as her blue eyes beamed up at him. "...that could be any otter sucking off any husky. Internet's full of the stuff—believe me, I've checked."

Max's paw cupped her face. "I'm sure you have." His thumb stroked her cheek ruff as he leaned forward for a tender kiss on her smiling lips. His tail stirred the air behind his chair. He ran a hand down her flank. "Speaking of which, it seems I owe you an orgasm."

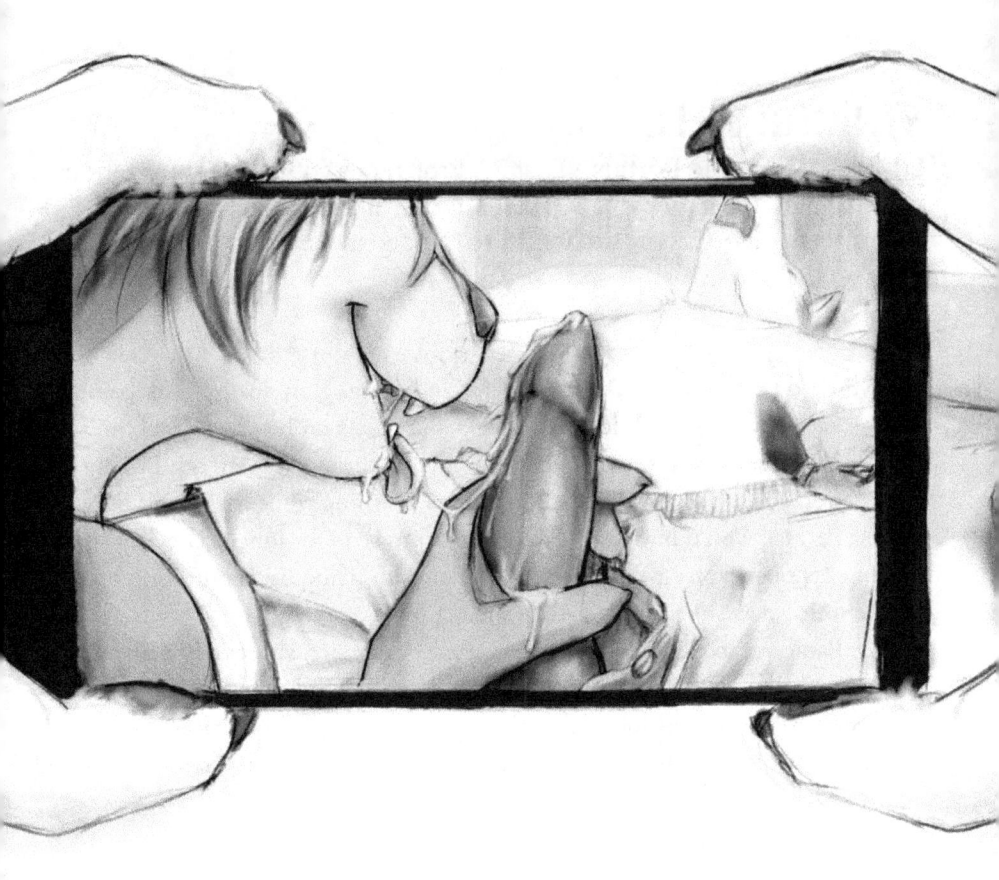

Forget-Me-Nots and Told-You-Sos

STRANGEVILLE (TUE/8P)

S02E04 "The Nine Portals - Part 2": Prof. Egbert uncovers a mysterious text that could seal the Nine Portals, but only if the team can translate it in time. Meanwhile, Cassie and Serge are trapped in a barn by a massive toad.

Kylie had been in the makeup chair for an hour as glow-in-the-dark paint was carefully applied to look like veins and runes on her finger webbing. The script said they showed she'd be filled with mystical energy, but the practical effect was that she couldn't touch anything while they dried.

As luck would have it, she had a husky to send for lunch. They'd been out of chopsticks, so he just kept popping sashimi into her mouth by hand. He smirked as she munched each bite happily.

Paula, a raccoon makeup artist, knelt beside her, alternately using an impossibly-tiny brush to apply paint and a beaver-grade blowdryer to blast it dry. Her dark eyes focused with singular intensity on her work. She'd already airbrushed the same paint into the fur of Kylie's arms. This was the more detailed work, though.

The teenage otter, however, wiggled with contentment. She felt queenly, being waited on as she sat in a battered, vinyl throne. Maybe she could have Max bring a palm frond to fan her. The prop department probably had a plastic one stashed somewhere.

Lance, the lead lighting guy, prowled in to test that the paint would glow properly under UV light. He was an ocelot, about as tall as Max's chest: the perfect size for scrambling up and down rigging.

Max smiled and headed back to the set.

The golden feline glanced over and watched Max leave. His tan eyes turned to shine on Kylie, brow stripes shifting with amusement. "I know what you tell the fans and reporters, but come on: are you guys dating?"

The lutrine sat up. "What? No!"

His sleek paw waved idly. "Just saying: you guys are pretty fond of each other." That supple tail swished through the air as he pranced around the makeup chair. "Always hanging off each other, always touching each other."

"Ugh!" Kylie rolled her eyes. "We're friends."

"A friend who moved in with you." He tossed the black light between his hands.

She gripped the chair and earned a dirty look from the makeup artist. "And my mom."

"And who just fed you two rolls of sushi by hand." His chest puffed up under a slinky black shirt.

Through the hole in the back of the chair, she lashed her rudder at him. "Shut up, Lance."

Paula didn't look up, still painting. "Hey, give the girl a break."

"I'm just looking out for her." The ocelot lifted his palms, shaking his hips side to side. His gilded muzzle flashed the captive actor a shameless look. "Or maybe for Max."

Expression unchanged, Paula turned the blow-dryer on his face, blasting his whiskers.

Lance yowled and scampered back. "Fine, fine." With a snicker, he padded out of the room. "I was just curious."

As if she'd never been disturbed, the raccoon got back to painting. "Ignore him. You don't have to tell him anything."

A huff of breath steadied Kylie. At least she had one ally. "Thanks, Paula."

The makeup artist nodded. Her dark eyes flicked up to Kylie for an instant. "You can totally tell me, though."

~ ~ ~

Kylie shuffled out of the makeup department. Paula had commanded her to hold her hands out like a surgeon going into an operating room, which only made her feel more self-conscious. Not that anyone paid particular attention to a painted otter on the set of Strangeville, but every adult who passed by seemed likely to ask her about Max next.

At least she knew exactly where to find the dog. She waddled through a half-assembled demonic gateway to the catering table.

Max stood, unobtrusive, in a corner. He looked up, muzzle-deep in a steak sandwich. That fluffy tail wagged as he spotted her.

"All done." She lifted her hands, fingers starting to feel sore from being spread so long. "Full of arcane power."

Swallowing, he nodded with approval. Already taller than everybody except the giraffe boom mic operator, his teenage body seemed intent on converting all red meat into muscle mass.

She resisted the urge to plant her hands on her hips, fearing another hour in the makeup chair. Instead, she settled for flapping her hands at him. "You were allowed to come back, you know."

"I was planning to after another couple sandwiches." Blue eyes shy, he brushed a lock of dark hair behind his ear. "I don't like to get in Paula's way."

The otter groaned. "Wish you would've…"

He raised an eyebrow.

Her eyes rolled. "She and Lance think we're dating."

He chuckled. "Them and most of the fandom." Then he assembled a few more sandwiches and stacked them on a paper plate. Stocked up, he followed her back toward the set.

Traipsing over power cords and dodging around crew, Kylie led him onward. "What's up with that?"

He shrugged, wolfing down another sandwich.

They stood at the edge of the set, watching crew try to install fake fireplaces upside-down in a mirrored corridor. Once they were done, she could get up there and shoot this stupid magic scene. And then she could stop spreading her increasingly-strained fingers. This was turning into a long day.

The crew fed the glitter fans and watered the fog machines.

Kylie half-crossed her arms, then grumbled at herself and returned them to their doctoral position. "They must be taking this episode seriously: they busted out the green screen."

Nodding, her canine companion finished his final sandwich.

Without even thinking, she snagged a wet napkin from the pocket of her vest and scrubbed a smear of mustard from his pristine muzzle fur. She took care not to screw up all that stupid hand paint.

Max, recently used to her fussing over him, leaned down without a word to give her easier access.

And that exact moment is when a spotlight clicked on over them, aimed by a snickering ocelot. Instantly, this illumination drew the eyes and awws of all crew present.

The heat she felt on her cheeks had nothing to do with the spotlight's glow.

~ ~ ~

Years later and a continent away, Kylie opened her front door to a delivery of a massive pastel bouquet. She signed for it with idle curiosity.

The delivery greyhound tipped her hat and departed, loping back toward a white van emblazoned with "Floral Authority, Inc." and "Your most flowerful ally!" in leafy-green lettering.

Turning, the lutrine shut the door with a bump of her tail. A nice enough bouquet, really. Pale blue flowers, with some whites and pinks, all with buttery yellow centers. The prodigious bundle of blooms burgeoned from its plastic wrap.

Max knelt on the floor, tapping tiny nails into loose skirting boards. He'd pried the boards off to run networking cable, uncovering ancient wallpaper in the process. He looked up at her and tilted his head.

"Hey, I have no idea." She bumped into a chair, unable to see past the expansive bouquet.

Her husky boyfriend stood and took the flowers. In his giant paws, the bundle looked almost reasonable.

She used a webbed paw to block her voice from going upstairs. "You think it's one of mom's old flames?"

"They usually sent roses." His wide nose sniffed the blooms delicately. "And wine. Or just wine and additional wine."

The otter nodded. She'd seen her mom both drink and auction off expensive gift-wine, depending on the value and how much she liked the sender. "Okay, so maybe a crazy fan?"

Max shrugged. "Karl does know where we live." He located a small white envelope in the foliage and handed it to her. "But you'd think he'd take the excuse to see us in person."

Her claws neatly sliced the top of the envelope. "Better not be from some creep."

The card had an ornate heart on one side. She flipped it over to find text in immaculate calligraphy: "We told you so."

"Those creeps!" Her indignant chatter filled the entryway. "It's from the crew!"

In the kitchen, Max looked up from filling a vase in the sink.

"Don't put them in water!" She punched her fists down at her sides. "Then we have to keep them!"

He looked around for the kitchen shears, eventually settling for a sushi knife. "They're just flowers, rudderbutt."

"That is a bouquet of mockeries!" Kylie jabbed an accusing finger at the pastel blooms.

A single, effortless slice took off the bottoms of the flower stems at a smooth angle. "We should be happy that people are happy that we are happy."

"That is the most canine thing you could possibly say." She waggled a finger at his muzzle.

Eyes closing softly, he nodded with serenity. "We dogs are a wise people."

"I could have been dating you for years!" She threw her paws in the air. "Additional bonus years!"

"But we were hanging out all that time anyway." He shrugged his broad shoulders. "The only difference is that we would've been having sex sooner." With a grin, he set the vase on the table. "And we've been making up for lost time."

She crossed her arms, feeling sullen and not entirely sure why. "But dating you is so much cooler than just being friends…"

His thick fingers made little rearrangements to the flower configuration. "For all we know, if we dated before this, we would've broken up because we weren't ready." He slipped an arm around her shoulders. "We just took our time. And it seems to be going okay."

"It makes me feel like I suck at knowing who I am. Casual acquaintances wander by and do a better job." She buried her muzzle against his chest. "If I didn't know that I was in love with you, how much else do I not know about myself?"

"I think that might just be…life?" The husky patted her back. "Nothing is for sure. Until you die."

She chittered up at him: "And that's the most Siberian thing you could say."

"Hmm." His chin lifted in thought, then shook in the negative. "No, it would have to include something about straying away from your pack and getting eaten by ice monsters."

A sigh rocked her lithe form. "I just don't like people lording over me that they were right and I was wrong."

He leaned in and rubbed his muzzle atop her head. "Who cares about being right compared to being happy?"

"Great." She mumbled into his shirt. "More dog wisdom."

He put on his best enlightened tone of voice. "Sometimes dog wisdom is everybody wisdom."

Grumbling and grudging, Kylie admitted to herself that he might have a point. At least she had a big, fluffy husky to hug. If that meant she had to receive mocking flowers occasionally, perhaps life wasn't all bad.

Tied at the Dock

STRANGEVILLE (TUE/8P)

S02E17 "A Test of Gill": Cassie suspects new swimwear is turning the team into sea monsters. She and Serge must uncover the truth in the face of faculty trying to keep it quiet as the state finals approach.

Max sat with his otter girlfriend, drinking slushies and watching the commotion out the window. He rested against the wall, hoping to appear casual and unobtrusive. As unobtrusive as a two-meter husky can be, anyway. Beads of moisture rolled down his extra-large slushie onto his white-furred paw, the plastic refreshingly cool amid the summer heat.

On the street, Cindy Madison, the cocker spaniel from the tourist trap next door over slunk toward a shiny sedan, tail between her legs. She yanked on the handle, snarling when the door didn't budge. She leaned back against the car with a well-practiced pout, arms and ankles crossed.

Kylie watched with amusement from where she sat on the countertop. Halfway through a fish burrito, she looked up and wiped her mouth with a webbed paw. "So, we need to capture a monster."

"Not Cindy, I hope?" Hot sunlight streamed through the shop's glass door to warm his lap. "She's been trying to catch me all summer and I don't want any part of that."

Cindy's father followed with a beach umbrella and cooler, clad only in a speedo. As he set them down, the car popped unlocked due to the proximity of his keychain. A passerby shouted "Lookin' good there, Mr. Madison!" In response, the older dog turned to point duel fingers with a smirked click of his tongue. Paws on the four-door, Cindy tilted her head with an unheard groan of despair.

"I'm serious." She took a drag of her blue-raspberry beverage. "A real one. For proof."

The big husky rolled his eyes and indulged a sip of his own slushie. The supercooled cola splashed onto his tongue, the ice crystals melting against his gums. His thick coat meant it was easier to cool him from the inside out.

Outside, Mr. Madison had fallen into an extended conversation with the passerby. His daughter glared at him from the passenger side, attempting to psychically compel him to unlock the car. Every meter or so he'd stop and then drive again; her outraged barks rattled the store window.

A metallic crinkle rustled next to him. After a brief fight with the foil, the otter emitted a chatter of victory. She nibbled a flake of white fish from the burrito wrapper. "Or at least get some video. Good video, not the blurry junk we get of the skitters."

Eyes fixed on the otter, he took another icy gulp and gave her a chill look. She looked cute up there on the countertop, legs swinging, ample tail twitching beside the cash register. She looked much better in this store than, say, being attacked by a murderous extra-dimensional alien.

"C'mon!" A groan of exasperation wiggled her supple body. Against the dark hues of the nostalgia shop, her brown pelt almost disappeared. Her teal Sturgeon Emergency band t-shirt stood out, however, clinging pleasantly to her streamlined curves. "We totally survived the last one. It can't be that dangerous."

He sighed, cool breath teasing his nose in the summer heat. "Can't you be happy nothing's trying to kill us?"

She propped a fist to her hip and jabbed her seafood-stuffed tortilla at the window. "The whole town still thinks my family was crazy the last hundred years."

"You know better." The dog glanced outside. His eyes narrowed to half-lidded as he monitored the Madisons' departure.

Now well past the shop, Cindy's dad concluded his game of very gradually driving away and unlocked the door. She climbed in with a visible huff and began barking at his grinning face. They drove off, the yaps of pique audible over the rumble of the engine.

Leaning forward in the antique chair, Max kept his ears and tone relaxed. "Why do you care what other people think?" His paw pads rested against the cool of the icy cup.

"I'm a minor TV star." She chomped a massive bite out of the burrito, chewing with frantic little teeth before a greedy swallow. "Caring what other people think has basically been my entire life up to this point."

He took another long slurp. The level of the cola slush sank to scant clumps. Sucking air through the slush with disapproval, he met her gaze. His ears rose with the patient determination not to validate her dangerous notion. That'd been his role in their friendship for years, though the monster focus was more recent. Prior, he'd mostly worried about keeping her from driving into bad neighborhoods or driving at all.

"Besides, you're a gigantic sled dog! You cracked that alien sucker like a lobster." Her hands smacked invisible bludgeons onto an invisible foe.

He did not remember it being that easy. He mostly remembered it being scary. "There are many powers in this world, for good or for evil." He tilted the last of his ice slush at her. "Some are greater than I am—and against some I have not yet been tested."

She scoffed and munched the last of her burrito. "I've been going over local sources and I've found one that seems consistent." Pulling the phone from her pocket, her webbed finger flicked through some screens. "There's got to be something buried in all this hype and delusion."

The husky nodded, finished his beverage, and cleaned up the scattered food wrappers. With any luck, this impulse would simmer for a while, then maybe lead to a stakeout in a nice restaurant. A steak restaurant, if he dared to hope. He nuzzled in to kiss his girlfriend goodbye, then padded out the door and back toward her house.

~ ~ ~

Sunlight streaming in his bedroom window, the husky lay reading in bed. Around him, the ancient house creaked and settled. The sheets smelled like his girlfriend, putting an extra wag in his tail. In a moment of rare indulgence, he buried his nose in the pillow and breathed deep. The aggregate of a thousand memories surged through him, leaving him quietly radiant.

The otter herself flailed into the room, breathless and wild-eyed. "Maxie! You're not gonna believe what I found."

Shaken from his revelry, he sat up. His ears perked at her. "You're probably right."

"Remember my Uncle Thomas?" She padded and paced around the floor. Webbed toes gripped at the carpet in anxiety to swim in pursuit of a lead. "From the crab feast?"

Max recalled the crab festival with a moan of satisfaction. Never had a country dog eaten so much shellfish in one sitting. "The one who brews seaweed beer?" He shuddered at the salty, umami memory.

Her sleek form slipped in and out of the pool of summer sunlight at the center of his room. "He told me about this lake monster that's supposed to be on the property."

"Is that worth investigating?" A shrug rolled his heavy shoulders. "We live in a town where every gas station claims to have full-service ghosts."

She sputtered like an underwater bottle rocket and bounced toward him. "I was looking for references to it in the journals and I found this!" Her webbed paw proffered a yellowing instant photo. The sides had come unglued, but the image held what looked like an aquatic reptile peeking up from the lake like a periscope. Kylie beamed with pride over picture.

"Not to dash your hopes, rudderbutt, but this could be action figure floating in a fish tank." Squinting at the photo, he stroked his whiskers. "Not sure people will accept that as proof of supernatural life."

With a huff, she propped fists on curvy lutrine hips. "Would you have believed me about an ageless alien living in the silver mines two months ago?"

"Okay, so the evidence we have is your seaweed-farming uncle's story and a possibly-staged photograph?"

"And we'll have more once we investigate the lake." A little bob of excitement bounced her. Her cuteness reached dangerous levels. It threatened to drag him along on another crazy misadventure.

Sitting up, he closed his book to look up at her with suspicion. "Define investigate."

Her paw attempted to fan away his worries. "No no no. We're just gonna take a look around. Nothing serious..."

~ ~ ~

Max trudged through two feet of muck, his calves aching from the unusual exertion. Steady panting and occasional shade did little to cool him against the summer sun. After hours of slogging, the only evidence he'd found along the perimeter of the lake had been his own. He looked up to find he'd circled around to where they'd started.

A few meters toward the center of the lake, Kylie bobbed to the surface with a contemplative look. The mid-summer sunshine gleamed like gold off her pelt. Water rolled off her in easy drops, leaving her face almost dry. Those delicate whiskers alone trapped beads of gilded light.

Dripping and silent, the husky watched her eel toward him. It'd been a long afternoon and evening, but at least it was over. With the lake searched, Kylie could look for evidence in a less exhausting way.

She glided through the water with infinite ease, then popped out at the shore. Mud and water fell from her sleek pelt and streamlined underwear, leaving her cleaner than she dove in. With a thoughtful mutter, she shook the water from her hair. "So much for the shallows."

He slogged out of the murk and mire, small plants clinging to his muddy jeans. He tried to brush them off, in vain. Ears popping upright, he looked up at her. "You're kidding."

"Well, we have to check the bottom." Her arms flew up at how obvious the statement was. "It could be hibernating there like a frog."

His ears lifted. Without a towel, it would take him the better part the day to dry, and when they got back to the house he'd have to shower again to get the lake scum out. He suppressed a growl of complaint.

"And yes, I know you lack my amazing water-repellant properties. Here." She dug into her pack and threw him a big, fluffy towel to dry his big, fluffy pelt. Her round little muzzle flashed him a winning smile. "It won't be a big deal. Really."

~ ~ ~

Clad in a wetsuit, snorkel, goggles, and flippers the husky clomped to the edge of the dock. The lake shone like flawed mirror glass, a shimmering imitation of the sky. Max stood with his paws on his hips. His gaze cast over the lake, then back to his girlfriend with suspicion. "You're not planning to eat the lake monster, are you?"

"No!" The otter wiggled in indignation. "…Unless it's a giant crab. Or an eel. Eels are pretty delicious."

He double-checked his clothes and phone wouldn't fall off the dock. "Because we spent like a week diving for that giant dumpling squid in the bay, which turned out to be earthly in origin."

"That was rumored to be supernaturally delicious." She flowed around him like a whirlpool of chittering assurance. "This is strictly to prove my ancestors weren't crazy."

"From now on, I'm picking the monster…" The husky heaved a heavy sigh. "Do we even know what this 'sandbar stalker' is supposed to look like?"

"Reports vary." Kylie padded up behind him. "Gills, claws, teeth, glowing eyes."

"Great." He glanced back at her. "Aren't you getting changed?"

"Nope." She shoved him into the water.

Flailing, Max scrambled at air for an instant, then plummeted into the drink. With a gurgled yelp, he splashed in, hung for a moment in the distorted light, then bobbed back up in a mass of tiny bubbles. Like the wetsuits they'd used on set, the air in his fluffy coat would keep him afloat until water seeped in, like a sub's ballast tanks. Shaking the droplets from his goggles and coughing, he doggy-padded around to see the platform. "Hey!"

His girlfriend stood, paw on one hip, and watched. "It's just water, Maxie." Her tail swayed in amusement.

His ears flicked back over the band of the snorkel. "You coming in?"

"One sec…" She shrugged out of her vest and, with a lithe bow, set it on the dock. With her phone safe, she smirked at him, hopped, and slithered past the water's surface. Only a slight ripple radiated from her dive, the otter herself vanishing from his sight.

Max peered around the depths, wondering where she could've gone.

She tapped his shoulder. "We gonna look for that monster or what?"

~ ~ ~

Hours later, a very soggy husky slogged to the shore. Water dripped from his ears, his whiskers, his tail.

"Hmmm. Well, I have some weighted nets in the carriage house. Let's grab those and dredge the lakebed."

The waterlogged dog gave her a narrow look and squished with each step on the grass.

Kylie followed, taking almost none of the lake with her. "C'mon, Maxie, you can't be that tired."

"Afraid I'd disagree." He pulled his snorkel off and panted. "I'm not a torpedo like you. You're welcome to keep looking."

"I'm not monster hunting alone!" She wrung her webbed paws, and slunk close. "Can't you just play my underwater body guard a little while longer?"

"Not today, Ky." He sat on the dock with a wet splat. "Let's get some fish sticks or whatever."

She rolled her eyes. "What are we? Toddlers?"

The dog shrugged, trying to fence in his weariness. "I like fish sticks."

Her paw patted his chest. Tiny droplets of scum scattered from the impact. She shook her paw and the slime actually shook off. "You'd make a terrible otter."

He squished at least a cup of water from his tail fluff. "Yeah. Tell me about it."

~ ~ ~

An hour later, they arrived at the sprawling ghost-gray hulk of Bourn Manor. Kylie headed for the kitchen, but her boyfriend took her paw and led her upstairs.

Her eyes met his. "What?"

He offered her a soft smile. "Just come with me."

With only a minor mutter of confusion, the otter followed.

Max was a patient guy, but enough was enough. On the kitchen table, Kylie's laptop displayed a webpage selling scuba tanks and rebreathers. If he didn't want to spend the rest of the summer soggy, something would have to be done.

They crossed the hallway and opened a creaky door. Motes swirled on shafts of light, twenty years of dust aglow atop whatever possessions Laura had deemed not worth selling.

Max crossed his arms with a slight wag. "Where are we, Kylie?"

The otter crossed her arms to match his, a defiant gleam in her eyes. "You know where we are."

His muzzle tilted down at her. "Humor me."

She heaved a sigh and puffed her bangs out of her eyes. "This is my great uncle Leister's old room."

Nodding, the husky patted her shoulder with one thick paw. "And what happened to him?"

She glowered at him for a moment, then slumped. "He went crazy hunting monsters and it ruined his life." She arched an eyebrow at him. "You're not exactly a creature of subtlety. You know that, right?"

Starting to wag again, he smiled. "It's a dog thing. A proud lack of guile going back thousands of years."

Her chuckle sounded forced as she hugged herself, looking around the dusty, neglected room. "You must think I'm pretty silly, getting so worked up over some stupid urban myth."

He pulled her into a hug, gently nuzzling the top of her head. "I think you're passionate and determined, rudderbutt. They're two things I love about you." He lifted her chin. "The proof is out there, Kylie. We'll find it eventually. But in the meantime, the world hasn't ended yet because of these things, and if we don't come up for air now and then we might get so caught up in this stuff we forget about the real world."

She smirked at him. "You rehearsed that."

He chuckled. "A little."

She laid her head on his chest. "I like your use of 'we.' Very diplomatic. As though you ever obsessed over anything."

The husky's arms tightened around her. "Well, there is one thing."

Kylie let out a soft sigh, pressing herself into the embrace. Finally she pulled away and punched him in the arm. "Come on, you big sap. Let's go order pizza or something."

"Attagirl." The canine followed her out of the room, closing the door behind them.

~ ~ ~

"Maxie? You awake?"

Merciless poking assailed the husky through the heavy curtain of dreams. The canine opened bleary eyes to find an otter-shaped silhouette leaning over his bed. Kylie stood, almost bouncing with excitement: she'd somehow gotten even nuttier since they started dating. Nonetheless, his tail thumped once under the blankets. "Hey."

Her lithe form twirled and plopped down on his bed. "Put some clothes on."

"Well, that's the opposite of what I expected to hear." He groped for his watch on the nightstand, but only knocked it to the floor. Sleep clung to his mind and impeded his every attempt at wakeful interaction. He rubbed his eyes. "What time is it?"

"Middle of the night." A bounce bobbed her atop the bed. "C'mon! I wanna go down to the lake."

"Aw, really?"

"Just trust me." Whiskers mingling with a giggle, she kissed him lightly on the nose. "And keep quiet; pretty sure Mom's asleep."

The dog groaned and rolled out of bed, having decided long ago to trust at least some of Kylie's crazy impulses. He pulled on some clothes and slung a heavy flashlight into his jeans pocket. His phone and knife followed onto his belt. It'd been a while since they'd been stalked by any extra-dimensional monsters, but wandering the wooded and eerie ground of Bourn Manor at night had a history of attracting them.

Old floorboards creaked under his paws as he followed the lutrine around the corner and out the front door. They padded across the field that passed for a lawn. Max cast a look back at the sprawling and slouching house they'd emerged from. Otters were a cute bunch, Kylie in particular, so he continued to be mystified that her ancestors could have commissioned a structure so creepy.

A warm, cloudless night, the soft heavy breeze suggested Autumn wasn't far away. On a winding game trail, they trudged through the forest. Her swaying walk caught his gaze and wouldn't let go, even in the patchy moonlight that streamed between the gaps in the canopy. He knew better than to ask where they were headed: a grin of mischief had spread across her face. Max just kept at her heel, even as branches swatted and roots sprung up underfoot.

Just as he started to wonder if they were lost, Kylie perked and wound through a tangle of undergrowth. Max broke through it to find the glassy surface of the lake before them. It glistened in the moonlight, shimmering a near-monochrome image of the woods and sky. From this angle, he recognized the old wooden dock stretching toward the lake's center, a few colorful water toys tethered to the supports. Far across the surface, faint window lights shone: summer cabins.

"So lake again?" Tail swaying, he touched her arm.

She nodded and leaned closer. "Mmmhmm."

"And it's somehow different now?"

"Yep!" Her hands wrung as she bounced from foot to foot.

The dog peered into the night. "What now?"

Max blinked at the rippling water. In his half-sleep, he had thrown on the clothes he'd been wearing that afternoon. "I'm not sure what you're planning to find here, Ky, but I didn't think to bring my swim trunks."

She turned to give him a slow blink over one shoulder. "Who said I was planning on finding anything?" With a chitter of mischief, the otter flowed out of her garments. Before Max could process what was happening she stood nude, sleek fur aglow under the full moon. "And you won't need your swim trunks, Maxie."

He could only blink dumbly as she swept up to him, small breasts bouncing with her movements. Still, he didn't resist as her paws helped him out of his clothes. With that familiar blend of affection and anticipation in her eyes, the otter stole a quick kiss and dragged him toward the shimmering surface of the lake.

Ears drooped and warm, he glanced around the woods. Running around naked, even at night and with Kylie, wasn't something he'd made a habit of. He trotted into the lake after Kylie. The water's chill crept further up his legs with every step. He whimpered as it reached his crotch, somehow feeling colder than before.

All the while, she led him on, her streamlined body slicing the water as she backpedaled. Her smile never faded as it sank under the surface.

The dog stood on the squishy lakebed and watched as she swam. A passable swimmer, Kylie outclassed him.

The dark form of his girlfriend flitted around. Her body undulated under the water, head to tail waves of motion propelling her, blending with the soft waves she stirred. She darted and dove, like a ripple of moonlight. Her body brushed his thighs, sweeping water through his fur.

The husky shivered, and not just from the chilled water. The canine lumbered through the chest-high water after her, now and then getting close enough to have her tail slip through his grasp. He stumbled forward, then bumped into her crotch-first. His ears blazed hotter as he felt her whiskers traced through the fur of his sac.

With a playful grip of his rump, the lutrine nuzzled against his balls and sheath before slipping out of reach. She surfaced just long enough for a flirty laugh, then vanished with a star-lit splash. The longer she teased him, the more obvious it became what'd happen when he caught her.

He lost track of her, then turned as pressure touched his tail. He woofed in surprise as she swam between his legs.

Webbed paws groped him. The otter bobbed up in front of him with a smirk.

He held her close, whispering in her ear. "So, what're you thinking?"

Kylie's fingers traced his soaked fur. "Maybe I'm planning to teach you the ins and outs of underwater sex."

He quirked an eyebrow. "And you're an expert?"

"I'm an otter!" Chin-deep, she gave an indignant wiggle. "And I have the Internet!"

Tantalized by the texture of her fur against his peeking tip, he nodded. "So, you're well-versed in theory."

"It can't be that hard." She squeezed his sheath.

"Mmmm." He closed his eyes, savoring the feel of her paws on his crotch. "Unlike you, I find breathing a hard habit to break."

"Who says you're the one underwater?" Eyes catching the moon, she sank and vanished into night-dark water.

The canine searched the lake, but found not so much as ripple of his girlfriend.

Then her muzzle found his cock tip.

Her lips pushed back his sheath, exposing more bare shaft to the cold water, then to the warmth of her mouth. That velvet tongue traced all around the underside of his dick. Without breaking the surface, her webbed feet paddled to stop her floating. Bobbing under the surface and along his length, she gripped his hips and took him deep.

Max panted, eyes half-lidded in pleasure. He never thought having Kylie suck him underwater would leave him the breathless one. Hot passion soared, even as he stood in the chilly water. His fingers traced her hair, which drifted in slow motion as he resisted the urge to play with his sheath. He wanted to let this situation happen. He'd gotten off in the shower a few times as a teenager, but that paled in comparison to every little lick dragging him closer to spraying thick canine cream into her wet and waiting muzzle…

Then she stopped and swam around him, giggling.

"Hey!" Before she could escape again, he grabbed her by the waist and dragged her to the surface. "Get back here, rudderbutt."

With a squawk, she wriggled and splashed at him. Water rushed off her body to course over his hands. Her tail swept between his knees, stirring currents through his fur. "Oh? What could you want from an innocent little otter like me?" Her thick tail brushed under his balls.

Even as his last dry fur got soaked by her pelt, he tightened his grip around the slippery otter, holding her close to keep her from squirming away to tease him even more. Her body felt so right against his as they stood naked as the stars in the boundless expanse overhead. Even in water up to his chest, he could feel her warmth. "I just want you to finished what you started."

She pressed her breasts against his questing paws, angling her head to the side so he could bury his nose in the crook of her neck. Her whisper stirred the fur of his ear. "Are you gonna fuck me, Maxie?"

He shivered and his cock lurched, pressing between the cleft of her rump and tail base. He slipped a hand down over her belly, into the water, and cupped her mound, grinding his fingers against her hidden slit. "Yeah…"

The otter leaned back against his chest, spreading her legs for him as he parted her tender lips to bury a finger in her molten passage. She let out

a squeak as he massaged her inner walls, already eager and very slick. She tightened on his fingers and wrung water from his fur. "Awesome."

"But first…" Max slid another finger into her passage, curling one then the other against the spots that made her squirm most. His fingers worked in and out. He jostled his thumb over her clit.

The lutrine squirmed, stirring the water at their waists, rubbing her thick tail base over his stiffening cock. One leg hooked around his to give him easier access. With the night sky shimmering off the surface of the water and the moonlight on her sleek pelt, she rocked her hips against his paw.

His tail wagged under the water. He stroked faster, faster than he could sustain for long, but she felt close. His muzzle met her ear, cheek pressed to her water-repelling hair. Her breasts fit his paw just right, a perky pawful each as he tweaked one nipple then the other. Twisting his arm a little, he rubbed his palm over her clit and wiggled his fingers as deep as they could reach.

Her breath caught—her body tensed—her hips bucked. Her head rolled back so hard it pressed the water from his chest fur. "Oh! Oh! Ooohhhhh…." A few more joyful squeaks, then she shuddered, moaned, and melted into his arms.

Holding her as she recovered, he decided he couldn't ignore his erection much longer. Not with her rubbing her tail back against it in a giggly haze. He considered turning her around and wrapping her legs around his waist, but decided they'd probably tip over. Looking around for options, he spotted an inflatable raft tethered to the dock. He picked her up with ease, carried her wiggling form to the shallows, and bent her over the raft. In the thigh-deep water, he stood, smiling at her exposed rump.

Legs dangling into the water, she lay across the raft. Her raised tail swayed, drops of lake water falling from its curve like the strings of a harp. She smiled over her shoulder, inviting him to come play. Her voice took on a sultry note. "Like the view?"

He set a paw on her back, testing the buoyancy of the raft as he caressed her sleek pelt. His free paw closed around his sheath and angled himself between her thighs. Half-hard from the teasing, half-soft from the cold water, he stroked himself against her slit.

"I want you, Maxie." The lutrine's hips rocked back on him. Her dark body stood out against the cheery yellow raft like a cloud against the moon. The heat of her juices clung to the tip of his cock. "I want you inside me…"

Fully on board with this idea, Max stepped closer, which only bumped the raft away. Even when he managed to grab her slippery hip and pull her against him, figuring out how to sink in from this new angle proved tricky. As his length glanced off her slit and against the edge of the rubber raft, he grunted at the unexpected texture and fumbled at trying to line back up.

"Let me." She reached back, wrapped a webbed paw around his girth, and guided him to her welcoming entrance. "There, push in…"

Easing forward, he sank into her. In the few dozen times they'd had sex, she'd never felt so wet. He'd acclimated to the chill of the water, but it just made her feel that much hotter around him. A shudder of pleasure chased down his shaft, sending a dribble of his juices to mingle with hers. She felt incredible, like warmth and exquisite tightness. She smelled incredible, like years of friendship and nights of passion. He pinned the raft against the dock and pounded harder into her. The raft bobbed, sloshing as he shot another pulse of precum into her depths.

She reached between her legs, playing with her clit, pressing it against his shaft as it pumped deep inside her. "Are you gonna knot me?"

He shuddered at her words, teeth set at the pleasure radiating from the warm slide of friction where their naked flesh met. "Want me to?"

"Mmhm!" With a nod, she bit her lip. Her legs paddled in the water, then wrapped back around his to pull him even deeper. "I really wanna feel it."

With a growl of arousal, he bucked harder against her. His knot slipped inside her, sending a rush of bliss through his tense body. Instinct howled at him to do it again, and he obeyed with glee. Each thrust pressed back his sheath and popped his growing knot inside her. She felt tighter and tighter around him, his bulge barely able to fit. A whine of tension escaped through bared teeth. Any moment now, he wouldn't be able to pull back out of her and he knew it. He craved it, craved it with every facet of his being. He thrust harder.

"Ah yes, Maxie!" Her cheek rocked against her forearms. Squeaks rose from both the otter herself and her paws against the rubber surface as she scrambled for purchase to slam her hips back against his.

With a paw on either flank, the husky plunged into her, sinking his bulge between her stretched folds for the final time. Whimpering with wonder, he buried his full length in the otter he loved. He wanted to give her everything: his heart, his knot, his now, his forever. His first shot spurted against her walls, followed by another and another, each adding to the luxurious slickness around his cock. Even tied, he thrusted; cool water splashed against his thighs, tightening his balls. Hilted deep in her, his knot throbbed larger, filling her.

Kylie's fingers sped against the front of her passage, then shivered as orgasm overtook her. A chittering gasp spilled across the water before she buried her face in the rubber raft with a deep moan. Her passage squeezed his knot tight, wringing into her more pulses of rich canine seed.

Max's body trembled as wave upon wave of bliss washed through him. Paws gripping her waist, he ground against her, lips in a silent howl of wonder. His orgasm ebbed, draining his will to stand upright. Kissing the curve of her tail, he slumped atop her, floating in the heady silence of after-glow atop the cheap rubber raft.

His girlfriend drowsed under him, afloat on satisfied sighs and fading waves. He breathed her scent, mixed with those of the water and the woods. Her body felt as warm under him as it did around his cock, bent over and around the curves of the raft. He wagged. Droplets scattered from his tail to patter the rubber surface.

In the distance, through his daze, a flicker of moonlight caught his attention. He could've sworn he saw the gleam of moonlight on a reptilian head staring back at him. But then he blinked and it was gone, just a ripple spreading over the water. His gaze cast again and again over the surface of the water, but found nothing. The notion of investigating occurred to him, perhaps even in the raft, but, for better and worse, he found himself buried knot-deep in Kylie.

Whatever haunted the lake, it would have to wait for another day. After all, the fantastic creature buried on his penis was far more important than any that might be swimming under the water. He blinked at the empty shoreline behind him, then leaned to her ear and whispered: "You remembered to bring towels, right?"

Pack Lunch

STRANGEVILLE (SAT/4P)

S05E08 "Insincerely Yours": While studying curses, Sandy inadvertently enchants herself with a sarcasm hex. Mistakenly following her directions, Serge and Cassie drive off to fight a pineapple demon.

The sun in his fluff, Max strode down quiet streets, distributing polite nods to townsfolk. The older the people, the more likely they'd comment on "what a nice young dog" he was. Not that the husky minded; it just embarrassed him, like when Strangeville fans spotted him. A quick stop at the diner and he emerged with two polystyrene takeout boxes.

The quiet of small town streets was interrupted only by the occasional hoot of tourists parading inflatable UFOs between hoax museums and hanging healing crystals from their minivan rear-view mirrors. Across the street, a store selling flat globes and emphatic screeds in support thereof shared floorspace with a "craft your own alien artifact" shop.

After sniffing around downtown, he passed the gift shop, he also passed a cocker spaniel baking conditioner into her fur in the midday sun. Pretending to doze behind sunglasses, she shifted to spread her legs a little, which just so happened to brush a foot along his calf. He hurried by, pretending to be fooled by her pretend slumber.

Undeterred, she lowered her sunglasses to smarm at him. "Look at you, walking alone in this part of town. Finally ditch the fishmonger?"

"On my way to see her right now, actually." He tilted his head toward the store next door.

"Too bad." She rolled to her stomach, her ample breasts arching her back in a curve that ended with a long tail over her bikini bottoms. "I could really use a pair of big strong paws to spread fur conditioner on my back."

He hefted the takeout containers. "I'm actually in a bit of a hurry."

"Two coats please…" Without looking, she waggled a slim aerosol can at him. "And it only works really well if you rub it in."

He examined the back of his own paw. "Good to know, but I really ought to be going."

"Don't be shy, Max." A flirty whine rose in her throat. "I'm sure a Hollywood pooch like you could teach me a trick or two."

"They actually apply fur conditioner the same way there." He resolved to take the back door out of the shop. "I'll see you later, Cindy."

"So you're cool with not having a pack?" Her legs crossed as she rubbed in a little more fur conditioner. "Thought huskies were all about that sort of thing."

He froze. "I have a pack."

"She doesn't count, though, right? She's an otter. Anybody but a canine will ditch you eventually." A sharp tang if bitterness leeched into her tone, hidden with a sweet smile as she glanced at him over tipped sunglasses. "I mean, we all play around outside our species. But she can keep up with you for, what? Half a kilometer?" She waved the bottle along the length of the street. "I've seen you out running, and she's never with you."

He blinked. Kylie could out-maneuver him, sure. But otters weren't built to run in straight lines. He found her waddle cute. It showed off her butt. He decided not to get into a discussion of butts at the moment. His girlfriend's booty, however, left little room in his mind to build a rebuttal.

"And when was the last time you were in a good howl?" The cocker spaniel gave a playful woo to woo him. "You know: canine culture."

His most recent howl had been with some high school friends back in Montana. To give him a proper send-off, they'd had a big bonfire by a lake. They'd exchanged howls: coyote, wolf, dog. Even their one fox friend, often too cool to yowl, joined in. It'd been a blast. Sure, they'd had to double-check some more obscure ones by streaming them on their phones, but it had been a very satisfying in a primal way. Some of those howls were thousands of years old. Maybe older. A couple non-canids at the party made some noble attempts, but they weren't built for it. Weird to think Kylie couldn't join in an activity he found so easy and natural.

Cindy smirked at his silence, then nuzzled the side of the conditioner bottle. Her silky tail swished in the sunshine. "I bet I could make you howl."

His eyes rolled. He hefted his takeout boxes. "Gotta go share the results of my hunt. Canine culture, you know."

"Don't go too far." She called after him, with a too-sweet simper.

At last, he slunk past her to the small, time-beaten book and record shop. In the window, a placard with faded psychedelic lettering asked "Remember the 60s?" which he didn't; however the price sticker indicated it'd become a valuable relic in its own right. A hint of otter-scent drifted through the screen door, warming the husky's heart. The canine poked his nose in the door. The scent of old paper sharpened the air. Varnished wood leant an amber glow. Dust spiraled in sunbeams. A pretty otter sat reading at the counter. His otter.

Kylie glanced up from a worn paperback. "Hey Maxie."

He smiled. His tail thumped the doorframe. "Hi."

A wave of amusement translated down her supple frame. Her body amazed him. Always had, even on set; she flowed like water while he thumped along behind her like a cinderblock in cargo pants.

Padding over, his paws ended up on her hips. Cramped filming quarters and years on the road between locations had squeezed out any distance between them. He wasn't sure when it'd gotten so easy for them to touch each other, but he was pretty sure she started it. The touching had just gotten a little closer once they'd started dating.

Without standing, she tilted her head to meet his gaze. "How're you?"

His tail swirled more dust as he smiled at her.

"That good, huh?" She scratched under his chin, doing it just right.

A shrug jostled his shoulders as he relaxed into her affections. "Mmmm…"

The otter glanced down to the plastic bag. "What's in there?"

"Oh." He took out the takeout boxes and set them on the counter. "Lunch."

Eyebrow raised, she sniffed at him, then scowled. "Did Cindy ambush you again? You smell like bubblegum and bitch."

He rolled his eyes. "Didn't let her distract from my objective." He opened one box on the counter. "Tuna salad panini."

She licked her lips, then kissed his.

Wagging, he unpacked his own sandwich. Not fish. He did occasionally get tired of sea food. He took every opportunity to vary his diet when they ate out. "So: weird to not have a caterer on-site, huh?"

"Who says I don't?" Without asking, she stole the pickle from his takeout box.

Smiling around roast beef, he looked around the shop, then at his girlfriend. "This place is always a wreck. You like working in a permanent garage sale?"

Hopping to sit on the counter, she smiled down at him and relished the viewpoint almost as much as the fish. Not often she got to be taller than him. "It's a good place to look for clues."

"Clues for what?" He cocked an ear.

"Supernatural junk. I've been here for months and I hear new rumors on a daily basis—mostly from the tourists, but some locals too."

His muzzle bobbed a nod. "Consignment store recon?"

She looked up, muzzle-deep in the fish sandwich. "You can learn a lot from people's old junk."

Max glanced to a wall of vintage food posters, several of which advertised ingredients he was pretty sure were had become illegal in the intervening years.

Her gaze followed his. "For example, I learned whoever had those was super old and saw no reason not to eat gelatin at every meal of the day."

He nodded, then pointed to the endless shelves of vinyl records. "That half of the store could fit on a cheap phone." His eyes flicked to the stacks of novels around them. "So could this half, come to think of it."

"People don't buy content here." The otter spread her webbed paws. "They buy physical chunks of nostalgia."

Max chewed in consideration. "You've been talking to a certain blasé-faire cat again."

Her arms crossed under pert breasts. "He's my only coworker."

He cast a glance around the shop. "He's not in today?"

"Nah, helping his parents with something." She licked the last of the fish from her claws. Bobbing closer, she brushed crumbs off his whiskers. "Won't be back until close."

"Good." The husky leaned up to deliver a smooch to her muzzle.

Kissing back, she giggled and straddled his lap. Her paws sunk through his fluff to the base of his tail. "You know, this is one of my favorite things." Her other paw traced his tail base.

Shy heat flushed under his fur. "Oh?"

"Being close with you, just hanging out and talking. I missed it, after the show ended." She gripped the wagging appendage, stroking his soft fur. "It might even be my second favorite thing."

"Second?" He wagged harder.

Her webbed paw cupped his crotch and squeezed him through the fabric.

Ears tilting askew, he sputtered. "Uhmmm…"

Still scratching his ears, she groped his plumping sheath. "Like that?"

"Uh-huh…" The dog wiggled in pleasure.

The otter giggled, then glanced around the empty shop. "I need your help with something in the back." She slipped off the stool and flowed past him with a teasing look.

"Okay." He followed her swaying tail to the stockroom. Only one entrance. A dusty window streamed sunlight across boxes of books. Motes floated, lit aglow. The dog saw books, boxes and boxes of them, and no obvious work. "So, what'd you need?"

Her thick tail shut the door. "This." Prancing with excitement, she pushed him to a corner. Those brown eyes shone with mischief. Slender paws rested over his racing heart. That wide nose rose to his, rubbing with silent affection as their lips met.

Max could have sworn he could hear his heartbeat, but then felt his tail drumming on the wall again. He could feel himself grinning like an idiot.

The otter pressed against him eased back from the kiss, eyes closed as she whispered up to him. "Silly doggy."

He stood, frozen with glee for a moment. His arms rose to embrace her.

They kissed again. Her body felt so right against his, melding along him with supple intimacy. So familiar and yet so different from how she'd always felt. A few months ago, he never would've imagined doing this with his best friend. Any attraction he'd had, he'd dismissed as random horniness. Spending a summer with her had changed all that. Amazing how tracking down an extra-dimensional monster could bring two people together.

Her soft muzzle met his now, rather than just pressing into his shoulder. Those eager paws didn't just rest on his back; they caressed his fluff through the thin fabric of his shirt. Years together had made their touching normal, even reassuring; those touches came more intimate now, though every bit as safe.

One more kiss, then her hands trailed down his body as she knelt at the dog's feet. A rascal's grin shone up at him.

"Kylie..." He stood, stiff and trusting. "What're you doing?"

With a giggle, she knelt to nuzzle the crotch of his pants. "Just checking inventory." A deft claw hooked his zipper, flicking it up and down over his straining budge. Her muzzle pressed along his thigh, she looked up at him with lutrine longing. "Take your pants off for me?"

The husky gritted his teeth, ears sinking in surrender as he glanced to the door of the stockroom. His thumbs toyed with the button of his jeans. "What if someone comes?"

Her nose rubbed up and down his crotch. Every word vibrated temptation through his length: "That's sort of the idea, Maxie."

With a whine of desire and a blush of shyness, he unzipped his pants and pushed them down to his ankles.

She rested her chin on his stomach and toyed with the hem of his shirt. "This too?"

Max swallowed, then pulled off his t-shirt. He folded it over the rungs of a upturned chair and wrung his paws, feeling exposed.

Chittering with glee, his girlfriend ran webbed paws down his chest, then fondled his sheath and balls through his boxers. "And these?"

Pulling down the dark fabric, he felt it slide down his legs and tail to join his jeans. He stepped out of the garments and leaned against an antique desk, well aware how she could make him lose his balance.

Gentle otter jaws nibbled at his sac. Nosing up, she caressed the peeking tip of his member as it poked from the sheath.

He gave a nervous chuckle and rested a shaky paw on her hair. "Happy now?"

"Mmmhmm..." Warm hands closed around his length. Paw webs stroked pleasure up and down naked flesh. That wide otter nose bumped his balls. Breath on his cock warmed the pink inside his ears. She pulled back a few inches, grinning, and paused to make sure he was looking her in the eyes before she extended her tongue for a delicate lick of his member. She paused, pretending not to notice his shivering as she rolled the taste around on her tongue. "Mmm..."

Max whimpered and slid to sit on the floor. His toes curled in his shoes as he felt himself extend against her forehead. A thin string of fluid brushed onto her fur, leaving a shiny dark streak. A nervous chuckle formed in his muzzle. "Sorry."

"I don't mind getting wet." The otter glanced up at him, stroking back a stray lock of red hair, then, with only a moment's hesitation, kissed his dribbling tip. She smiled at his taste. "Especially with you."

An unsteady smile crept across his muzzle.

Stroking with both paws, she nuzzled white fur and red flesh. That wide otter nose traced up and down his tender flesh. The sunlit room sat silent, except for the wet sounds of her kissing along his length. Those big brown eyes glinted mischief as her muzzle enveloped his dick.

Max gasped. His cock grew along the hot confines of her mouth, while his knees grew weak. Her eyes held a look of delighted determination, though, so he straightened, gripping an old desk for support.

Looking up, she giggled around his dick. A delicate paw tugged his sheath back and forth, bunching it against suckling otter lips. Velvet fur and a satin tongue explored him in playful worship as she knelt between his knees.

His wide paws trembled onto her head, cupping her face. A bulge in one cheek, then the other bumped his palms—a bulge he recognized as his own cock. A whine of wonder and he squirted precum against the back of her mouth.

The otter coughed off him, clearing her throat.

Concern lifted his ears. "Kylie?"

"S'okay." One paw wiped her lips, the other gripping his thick shaft. She gave his tip a giddy kiss. "It's just hard not to get greedy." Her lips closed around him again, not diving so deep this time.

"You really like...?" He gripped the sides of the desk and grappled for composure. "I mean..."

"I love your dick." Kylie gripped the stiffening canine length and waggled it back and forth, grinning. Her webbed paw stroked the sheath along his rampant arousal.

"Yeah?" Max, seated on the desk, bit his lip in pleasure and stroked her hair. His other paw groped at the faded paper calendar. On the tip, afternoon light caught in a crystalline sheen of saliva and precum.

"Mmmhmm." The otter hummed as she licked his sheath down, eyes closed, breaths deep. When she spoke, her lips stayed pressed to his dick. "Feels nice on my tongue." One paw gripped gripped his impending knot as her muzzle slipped down his shaft. Suckling bared flesh, she curled her tongue around his girth in leisurely licks. A faint heat dribbled against her soft palate, then down to her busy tongue. She smacked her lips with blatant enjoyment, meeting his eyes. "Tasty too."

116

His tail wagged against her breasts, even as those pointy ears dipped under the weight of a blush. He watched, transfixed, as she lapped up the sides of his shaft.

Giggling, she bopped the tip against her waiting tongue, causing the large canine to twitch in pleasure. One dainty paw toyed with his balls while the other waggled his erection against her lips. "You like this too, Maxie?"

"Ah..." The dog took a breath to compose himself, then managed to stammer: "Y-yeah..." He stroked her auburn hair as she suckled his bright red length. His thighs tried to close on her, but he fought to hold still, afraid she might stop. The tight confines of his sheath, stretched by arousal, hugged the growing base of his cock.

A paw supported his sac, thumb caressing thin fur with delicate care. Feeling his knot, she worked his sheath behind it, just like he'd shown her that night in bed. A brief worry that she might not remember what he liked got washed away by her supple tongue. Clear fluid dribbled down the side of his cock. Pulling off, her lips chased it, catching up just behind his canine bulge.

Ecstasy.

Max growled with passion, the first shot of orgasm racing up his shaft. No sooner had it splattered on her shoulder, than another surge of tingling tension rushed up from his balls, squirting thick cum to drip on her muzzle.

Kylie gasped, wringing him in surprise.

He bit back a howl as a small fountain of his rich canine cream coursed down his length, collecting on graceful otter paws. Blast after blast of his heavy white spunk rolled down over her fingers. She sealed her lips around his tip and sucked, tasting his salty musk, exploring the throbbing tip with all her tongue's surfaces.

His ears, already pinned back with pleasure, sank further as he realized the mess he'd made. A deep blush glowed under his fur. "Oh! I— My— I'm, uh, sorry?"

"Settle down, silly doggy." She examined the strings of sticky fluid on her pelt. And clothes. "Pretty sure it'll wash out. Did I...do a good job?"

The dog slid to the floor, still dripping, tongue lolling out as he sat.

"Good." The cum-splattered mustelid wiggled with pride. "Let me grab some paper towels." She skipped out the door, smiling all the while.

Swathed in afterglow, the husky sat, panting. His drooping erection hung over white balls, connected to the floor by a thin strand of semen in the dusk light. In a dreamy haze, he watched as his knot faded, then shivered as his sheath slipped back over it.

Kylie eeled through the door with a roll of paper towels, dabbing at the wet mark on her shirt. She plopped down in front of him with liquid grace, tail curled around her crossed legs.

With a shy little look, he pulled on his clothes, then leaned in close to her. As he helped wipe clean her whiskers, he whispered into the silence: "So quick question about that door... Does it lock?"

She tossed a wad of paper towel into the waste bin and turned to lock the door.

With her distracted, Max rolled to his knees and grabbed her around the midriff. He nuzzled under her shirt and into smooth stomach fur.

The otter squeaked, wriggling in his grasp against the antique desk. Her sneakers traced little lines across the tile, tail in a shy curl. "What're you doing?"

He unzipped and spread the fly of her pants with a wolfish grin. "Returning the favor."

The garment slipped down with a rustle of fabric over fur. Relieved of her pants, the lutrine lifted her legs and rested her ankles on his shoulders.

Max nuzzled her crotch through the thin cotton of her panties, then nosed it aside. His tongue traced her folds. Her flavor teased his tongue. Eager otter juices slicked her thin fur, coating his muzzle to the whiskers. Gentle paws tugged her panties down to give him more room to lick.

She gripped his ears and rocked on her tail. "Mmmmm, higher..." Her cute little butt scooted onto the desk, legs spread to give him better access. "Yeah, right there..."

He stroked her tail base, blunt canine claws scratching fur so often hidden under her shorts. Deeper he licked, tongue sinking into silken folds. His lips massaged the hood of her clit, making her whole body wriggle.

"Ooooohhh…" Webbed toes gripped his shoulders, tugging his pelt through sock fabric. Her tail swished atop the desk, powerful enough to jostle her whole body. The heavy desk knocked against the wall in time with her wiggles of pleasure. Her breath caught on a moan, slender paws slipping under her bra to play with her nipples.

Max licked on. Saliva slicked over sleek fur, past the curve of her rump to her muscular tail. He lapped faster and faster, as deep in her as he could reach. His nose ground to her nub. A grin spread on his muzzle as he drove her wild.

Her streamlined form shuddered atop the desk, one paw to her mouth as she squeaked in delight. Ankles hooked behind his head pulled him tight to her passion. The lutrine bucked against her lover's mouth, tossed on waves of ecstasy. Rapture enwrapped her, even pinning those cute little ears down against her auburn hair. After a moment of exquisite tension, she relaxed, her gasps the loudest sound in the stockroom. Tiny aftershocks traced through her limbs and left her twitching at his every breath.

As her legs released him, the dog licked his chops, looking up from his girlfriend's crotch with a head tilt. He laid his muzzle on her stomach and reveled in the intimacy, affection, and tasty flavors of lutrine cunnilingus. Breathing together in a sticky cuddle, he decided he should bring her lunch more often.

"Mmmmm. That was lovely, Maxie." She glanced at the evening glow spreading through the window shade. "I should probably get back to work, though. I've gotta close up shop soon."

He stroked her bare knee. "I'll help."

The otter giggled and stroked his relaxed ears. "Aren't you sweet."

Still reeling from his orgasm and her scent, he rose to give her ear a brazen lick. "I'll be even sweeter when I get you home."

Her wiggle of scandal and delight made his heart soar as his thoughts raced back to the house and between the sheets of her bed. It was going to be a fun night.

As he helped her tidy up, his thoughts wandered back to what Cindy had said about her. Kylie might not be a canine. She might be wiggly and manic, but she cared about him and tried to make him happy. Thinking back on the best packs he'd seen, the most stable and effective ones, they'd always looked out for each other like that. He'd just have to keep making her happy in return. A pretty cool deal, now that he thought about it. No wonder canines made such a big deal about packs.

In the Dark

STRANGEVILLE (SAT/4P)

S05E10 "Egbert Over Easy": Egbert starts attending meditation classes and calms down. A local museum curator schemes to take over the city with with resurrected dinosaurs.

Kylie's webbed fingers rolled over the steering wheel. "I just don't like the idea of haunted houses anymore." She tapped the breaks as a family of foxes bobbed across the street, dressed as a string of papier-mâché traffic cones.

As the orange sunset cast the autumn night in ember hues, aliens, undead, and monsters of all ages filled the streets of Windfall. Idling through the middle of it, an otter sat in her mom's hatchback.

Her big canine boyfriend sat folded up in the passenger seat, paws on his lap, dressed as a green dinosaur. Sunset light cast an orange halo through his fluff. The husky turned from looking at a platypus dressed as an aircraft carrier and cocked an eyebrow at her. His sky blue eyes studied her over that blocky white muzzle. "Okay."

She pulled back her little red riding hood for a better view of the road. The trouble with dating the dog who'd been your best friend for years is you can't pretend not to know his body language. "I mean, we found an alien running around my actual house who was totally willing to kill us." Two enterprising young giraffes had dressed as a pair of telephone poles. She slowed again to let them cross the road. "I just don't like being scared. What if I freak out next time something crazy happens?"

"You won't." He patted her thigh, looking infuriatingly earnest.

Her sigh left her chest feeling empty, though under less pressure. "Easy for you to say."

The husky nodded, thought, then spread a thick paw in the air between them. "It is. But I know you're a tough little thing." He adjusted the fabric hood of his dino costume, its serious eyebrows judging the automotive upholstery. "Anyway, Shane and Sarah are our friends. It's good to do things with friends."

A string of muttered squawks trailed from her round muzzle. He had a point, which made her feel unreasonable and grouchy.

He set a heavy paw on the shoulder of her bright red bodice. "Look, if you need to bail, tell me and I'll kick down the nearest wall or something."

She flashed him a little smile of trust. "You're a good dog, Maxie."

His tail thumped the seat, the sound dampened by the spiked, fabric tail-sleeve. Out the passenger window, in a rather meta move, a ferret had dressed up as a candy bar for trick-or-treating.

She steered her mother's hatchback into a residential neighborhood. Max didn't like Kylie's car, even though it was the best car ever. It could drive on water, after all. Sure, it was a little small, but he looked cute with his knees crammed up against his chest.

"I didn't think we were doing costumes this year." He wiggled his fingers at her, clad in overlarge dino-claw gloves. "Usually, you try to coordinate a matching one with me." He woofed a chuckle. "Those matching costumes were always a hit. Remember when we went as Saturn and Soyuz rockets?"

"Oh, I remember." She rolled her eyes, then returned them to the road. "Even with you and your appetite around, we were eating oatmeal for months to get that many cardboard cylinders." Her tongue poked out at the memory. "Anyway, I wanted this one to be a surprise."

Muzzle aimed at the windshield, his gaze flicked to her ruffled white bodice and crimson knee-length skirt with matching cape. "It certainly was..."

"Besides, you're already coordinated with it." Her paw reached over to caress his thigh. "You're my Big Bad Wolf."

"Okay, so you're sexy Red Riding Hood on purpose." He patted her paw warmly. "I wasn't going to say anything. I wasn't sure you knew."

She squawked in mild offense. "What's that supposed to mean?"

The husky shrugged. "The skirt's a little bit short for grandmother's house, but I didn't know if that was for my benefit or for easier swimming."

Straightening her skirt, she leaned in close and whispered. "You like my skirt, Maxie?"

His gaze traced over her supple form. "Uh huh."

"Wanna hear a secret?" She wiggled from hips to shoulders. "I'm not wearing any panties under here."

His ears popped up. Those bright blue eyes flicked to her hemline. "Seriously?"

"Nah." She punched his shoulder. "But now I've got you thinking about it." Pulling up outside the Warren residence, she beeped the horn once.

Sarah bounced out the front door and down the sidewalk. A clear plastic dome sat over her head like a soap bubble, curling her ears forward. Her moon boots glittered in the street light. A plush alien carrot peeked from the pocket of her puffy silver jumpsuit. Matching gloves and a jet pack with ribbon streamers completed the costume.

Her brother, a bored orange cat, padded after her in a t-shirt and jeans and got in the car. Not even adopted, though Kylie'd been fooled for months. Thanks to the magic of in vitro fertilization, they were, as Sarah put it, "uterus buddies."

As she dropped the car into gear, the otter peered at him around the driver's seat. "Shane, you seem to have forgotten your costume."

"Nah." He gestured to his white t-shirt, which had "Error 404: Costume not found." written on it in black marker.

Sarah's groan of disgust echoed in her homemade space helmet.

"We should get moving." The feline pointed from between the front seats. "The haunted house closes at midnight."

Jack-o-lanterns flickered on every doorstep. They passed a pair of armadillo twins, dressed as a matched set of pill bugs. Along the side of the street, a store called Wibbly Warbles advertised "the largest selection of theremins on the East Coast."

Kylie watched the proprietors demonstrate their wares to a couple of platypus clients. She tilted a webbed thumb in its direction. "Does that theremin shop only open for Halloween?"

Shane rolled his slitted eyes. "It should. I don't know how they stay in business the rest of the year."

His sister fought to keep the seat belt from pulling off her space helmet. "You know, just like the rest of Windfall."

The otter snorted.

The slim tabby poked a claw between the front seats. "Turn here."

She pulled into the parking lot. The Windfall Chamber of Commerce event center displayed a canvas that read "of Horrors" over half its sign. Kylie navigated the hatchback into the parking lot. The entire building glowed with strings of flickering electric candles.

The otter's eyebrows lifted, whiskers spread. "I was expecting somebody's house."

Sarah leaned up from the back seat, bumping her helmet into the dome light. Her excited breath fogged the front of the sphere. "Windfall takes Halloween seriously."

They exited the car and crossed the parking lot. Kids of all ages ping-ponged between the parked cars, fueled by candy. The great glass doors stood half-lit, cloaked in cobweb fabric. In a line around the second story, demonic skulls blasted fire from their eyes with a distinct odor of propane. Streaks of fake blood traced down from the roof and onto the off-white walls.

Kylie gaped up at the transformed civil building, feeling small. She fought the urge to cling to Max's arm. "I, uh, thought these haunted houses were supposed to be all plastic skeletons and jack-o'-lanterns."

Shane thumped her shoulder. "Yeah, that's not how the folks in Windfall roll. My dad spent a couple years helping with this thing. He said they feel like failures without at least one ambulance visit per year."

"I guess it was two or three competing houses at some point, and they got really competitive." Sarah orbited around them in her homemade spacesuit. "Lucky for us, they decided to combine their efforts before anyone resorted to property damage."

They padded in through the front door. Kylie stifled a groan when she saw who was taking the tickets.

Cindy. The cocker spaniel who worked next door to her and had decided Max was too hot to date outside the species. She stood in the lobby, taking the occasional ticket and looking bored. The busty canine was dressed as a witch, to the extent as she was dressed at all. The broad-brimmed hat contained most of the costume's fabric. The cape had the acreage of an unfolded napkin. The skirt appeared to be underwear. The bat-shaped bra struggled to stay aloft under the weight of her bust. Luckily, her boots made up for the lack of modesty, easily reaching mid-thigh. Spider-themed lingerie-grade mesh covered her arms, in what could only be considered sleeves in a technical sense.

"You're here?" The spaniel crossed her arms over her cleavage. "Don't you have your own spooky house to haunt?"

The otter chattered with displeasure and shoved all four tickets into the spaniel's paws. "Don't you get cold, riding a broom in that?"

Her eyes distributed glances like nasty little trick-or-treats. A dagger-sharp glare at the otter. A nasty glance sent Sarah scampering ahead. A look of mild recognition for Shane. A jealous leer for Max, which turned to a head-tilt when she saw his rudimentary costume.

Max raised his dinosaur-claw gloves with a shrug. He offered a helpful: "Rawr?"

"Wow, Max, you look…" Tilting her head back and her muzzle away, Cindy stepped back, unsure what to make of the larger dog. "Is that supposed to be a dinosaur?"

He shrugged, sharing a smirk with Kylie. "It's the only thing I could find that fit."

The smaller canine crossed her arms with a predatory smirk. She looked him up and down. Mostly down. "I can think of something else you'd fit into."

His eyebrows closed ranks. "I already have a costume, though."

She stepped forward, one hip at a time. "Then maybe I could interest you in my goodies."

Max didn't react, except to look around, feigning confusion. "I don't see a candy bowl."

As usual, Cindy refused to get the message. She put a paw on her hip, her long silken tail stirring the short skirt. "Not yet, you don't."

"Aaaaaand we're leaving." Kylie turned to go.

The husky clamped a paw on her shoulder and towed her toward the lobby. "Bye, Cindy."

Snickering, the cat caught up to them. His sister's ears blushed against the inside of the space helmet.

The otter grumbled. "I knew I should have had an axe with this costume…"

"Just ignore her." Sarah moon-bounced up with a shrug. "She's at a weird place right now."

Kylie cast her an incredulous glance. Cindy had been a jerk long before Max visited for the summer and ended up staying. She suspected the rabbit just didn't want to believe she'd been friends with a total bitch, but said nothing.

They continued into the lobby, which had been infested with zombie lawn gnomes and electronic portraits that morphed in sinister ways. Beyond lay a darkened hallway, constructed out of painted chipboard.

Cindy's dad popped out from just inside the tunnel, clad in a black and crimson cape. "Ah! Fresh blood! Welcome to Windfall's oldest and spookiest house of horrors." The spaniel cackled, showing a set of plastic fang extenders. "Stay together. Stay on the track. Stay alive. For legal reasons, we must ask that you not touch the actors. Bwahahahaha!"

Kylie rolled her eyes and pushed the group onward. Whatever lay ahead, it couldn't be worse than sticking around near the lobby where Cindy could come back and perv on her boyfriend. They passed through a curtain of heavy, tattered, black felt.

When rubber snakes dropped down from the ceiling, Kylie jumped, but managed to laugh. When a creature with a mishmash of predator traits prowled past, she grit her teeth until her jaw hurt. When a cycloptic elephant skull peeked around the corner, a chill welled in the pit of her stomach. When what she'd assumed was a mannequin jumped up —clad in filthy pajamas and bloody eye bandages— to paw at her, she screamed at a pitch that only dolphin sopranos normally reach and clung to her boyfriend.

Without even flinching, the dog's thick paw closed around hers. He smirked down at her and wagged his cloth dinosaur tail.

"Shut up." She didn't loosen her grip.

The group pressed on, past fog machines and sickly-green strobes. Small air cannons blasted tiny plastic spiders at them. The hallway twisted and turned, with hidden hatches opening at random. Usually, masked faces hid behind them, but at least one reached out with a sticky tendril and caressed their ankles.

They passed into a nautical section of the haunted house. A pirate skeleton draped over a ship's wheel, while two others lay on the floor with cutlasses jabbed through each other's ribcages. Piles of rigging and rotted sail lay atop mounds of seaweed.

Kylie scampered up, eager to get to something more familiar. The floor had been warped to give the impression of moving over waves, but any otter worth her salt was never a step or two away from sea legs. It took more than piles of flotsam to spook a lutrine.

A massive heap of seaweed in the corner rose to leap at her. Its cold tendrils whipped out at her. "Blllaaaaarrrr!"

The otteress shrieked and wrapped herself around her large canine boyfriend, almost tripping him. Her paws gripped at his shirt and costume as she clung to him for dear life.

Sarah likewise sprung about a foot in the air, then landed with a giggle.

A very familiar horn stuck out of the top of the swamp creature as it retreated to its hiding place.

"Wait—was that Karl?" She realized she was hiding behind Max and popped upright with embarrassment.

Shane's tail lashed in silent amusement. His green eyes flicked around the room, catching the strange light in unnatural flashes.

"Oh sorry!" The monster lifted some of the fake vegetation to reveal a small, dark, excitable eye. "I thought you were a little kid!"

A sputter of outrage issued from her round little muzzle. "I'm older than you!"

"I've gotta get back." The rhinoceros called above the spooky soundtrack and thumped back into position for the next group. "Have fun!"

Kylie drew in on herself, feeling foolish. Only a few rhinos lived in town, and if she'd taken half a second to think she could have realized that none of them were exactly threatening. She needed to calm down and stop acting like a pup.

A green dragon roared down from the rafters, spreading leathery wings. Flames wooshed down from its maw. For an instant, the passage gleamed with the flare of firelight.

The otter leapt, flailed at the air, and almost tripped backward over her own tail. A thrill of cold disquiet ran through her body, calmed only a little by the familiar husky paw that steadied her from behind.

Bouncing back from the commotion, Sarah squeaked with surprise, then laughed. Shane, as usual, trailed behind and gloated at their every scared reaction.

The bat in the dragon mask wiggled wing fingers at them and pocketed the lighter she'd used for the fire-breathing. "You can start the maze at any of these doors, but choose wisely. You never can tell what lies ahead."

Smarting from the Karl incident, she waved Max off. The otter stomped to the farthest door, yanked it open, socked the dangling paper skeleton, and slammed the door after her.

Through the door, she heard him gave a whine that hurt her heart as much as the scares had hurt her pride, but soon his claws clicked along the floor to another door.

Endless twists and turns awaited her. At one point, she had to eel through a hallway filled by giant bladders of air. As soon as she escaped from that, a fog machine blasted her with a rain forest's worth of humidity. Otters can see through water and air just fine, but the mixture sent her stumbling. She punched her way through a heavy curtain, bounced off some walls, then tripped into complete darkness. Using the uneven wall as a guide, she pressed on, swearing as she bumped into pillars and struts. "Ugh!"

Kylie fumbled for her stupid, useless keychain flashlight, turning the feeble LED on the walls and confirming her suspicions: She'd somehow gotten so turned around she'd wandered into the catacombs of the civic center, a narrow brick hallway stretching off into the blackness, devoid of either life or Halloween decorations.

She huffed, mostly to put some sound into the eerie silence. Wonderful. Now she had to fumble around in total freaking darkness, hoping to find her way out of the accidentally-creepy portion of the building and back into the part that was deliberately creepy. And then she'd have to explain where she'd been, and Shane and Sarah would think she was an idiot, and Max would get all worried because he'd assume she'd been scared, and just because that was true didn't mean—

"Excuse me, are you lost?"

"Yauagh!" Kylie articulated, shooting three feet straight up in the air as her heart and stomach abruptly switched places. She landed awkwardly, falling against the wall as she turned her light on her assailant.

An otter stood before her, but not a river one like her. She stood several inches taller and her white-tinged muzzle had bristly whiskers. She wore a black windbreaker with frightfully neon highlights.

"Whoa, chill." The matronly sea otter held up webbed paws. "You wander off the track?"

"Yeah! Sorry…" The river otter made herself start breathing again, her entire pelt on end. "I got turned around in the dark."

"Well, you don't look like a teenaged thrill-seeker, so I believe you." The taller female wiggled her bushy whiskers. Her costume consisted of 80s clothes grabbed from the back of a closet, but her mom had tried to pass that off as a costume before, so it didn't seem too weird. "I keep telling the scarers they need to make sure they shut the doors."

Kylie grinned. Most adults assumed she was in her mid teens, which gets old after half a decade. Must be because she's a fellow lutrine.

"Edith." She offered a paw. "I work here."

The younger otter shook it. "Kylie. I'm lost here."

"That's a rad little costume." The sea otter glanced at her get-up. "Red Riding Hood?"

"Yeah. I got separated from my Big Bad Wolf. He's dressed as a dinosaur. Probably with a space bunny and a cat."

The older otter arched an eyebrow. "Gotcha. What's the cat going as?"

"Wet blanket, like always."

"Ah, normal clothes." She clicked on a flashlight and pointed it down the corridor. "Let's see if we can find them through the scare-holes."

"Scare-holes?" Kylie followed her through the struts and electrical cords of the access passage.

"It's what we've always called the little doors that open on the main track." She popped open a porthole and poked her whiskery nose through. "Back in my day, we only would've had one track to check, but now they've got this maze. I've been pushing for a water fixture."

Kylie tailed the larger otter as she spied through various peepholes on the track. Muted music echoed from the other side of the walls, less scary now that she in a less creepy context. Her paws still wrung each other, feeling cold.

"You don't seem to be that excited to get back." The taller lutrine peered through another panel, letting in a curl of fog. "Haunted houses not your scene?"

"I thought they were!" A shrug rippled down Kylie's flexible spine. "And then I got here and..." She paused for an instant, then figured it couldn't possibly matter to vent to a friendly stranger. Plus, the jumble of feelings in her guts felt like they had to be said out loud to get untangled. "I used to like getting scared. Then some actually scary stuff happened and now I'm all weird about it."

The other otter nodded. The concern in her eyes could be spotted even in the dim light.

"Nothing bad actually happened, really. I didn't get hurt or anything." Her hands squeezed into fists for a moment as she gripped at the thought. "But, it turns out there's a lot I don't understand about how the world works. And now the fun kind of scary is just...gone. Ya know?"

The older girl nodded and fostered a slight smile. "Well, it's probably not gone forever. We wouldn't stay in business long if it worked that way." Ignoring the screams and scampers within, she slunk under a rise in the tunnel to access another part of the maze. Here, she peered through a heavy black curtain, but to no avail. "The more you get scared in a fun way, the easier it gets to enjoy it. The whole town is based on the idea of being drawn to scary stuff."

"Easier said than done..." The river otter snapped her muzzle shut. This random lady didn't want to hear her whine.

The sea otter didn't seem phased. "For me, Halloween's about laughing at your own fear, finding a way of looking at it that takes back its power over you. Get the blood up and those feel-good brain chemicals going." She considered. "Also, candy."

Though a little worried her guide was about to burst into a children's cartoon song, the younger mustelid pondered that notion. What would it take for her to feel safe again?

Edith checked another passage, then wiggled her whiskers in dismay. "Starting to think this is a lost cause." She waved her flashlight at a distant orange exit sign. "Let's just get you outside. You can catch your friends when they come out."

The pair of mustelids padded out one of the event center's many back doors.

The taller otter let the door slam behind her, clicking locked. "Okay, just cruise around the building and you'll see the main exit." She pointed a webbed digit. "If you see the lobby entrance, you've gone too far."

Kylie nodded at the closed steel door. "Aren't you stuck out here too?"

"Nah. This is my personal entrance." She gave the locked door handle a practiced jiggle and popped it open. "Hang loose—and think about what I said."

After her rescuer vanished into the dark, the younger otter stood for a moment. The door closed. Then a distant and familiar whimper caught her attention. Around the corner of the building, she glimpsed the Maxosaurus milling around the crowd, clearly looking for someone.

The otter cleared her throat. "Hey Maxie!"

His ears popped up. Those blue eyes brightened on her.

She slipped through the loose crowd toward him. "You got through fast."

"I hurried." He trotted up to her. His fingers traced her arm. His muzzle chewed a question or two he was trying not to ask.

She squirmed, remembering how she stormed off. "I didn't mean to make you worry."

He bent down to bump his nose to hers. "It wouldn't have been as much fun without you anyway."

Her muzzle angled up to give him a little kiss. She started to think of how to explain how she wandered off the track without sounding stupid, but then a space bunny and a sourpuss exited the building. The pair waved them over.

Sarah moon-bounced over. "What'd ya think?"

With a quick glance up at her boyfriend, the otter shrugged. "It was actually pretty cool."

"I know, right?" She beamed from inside her clear helmet, then shoved her brother toward the car. "Come on. The high school always hosts a super great Halloween party."

~ ~ ~

A couple hours later, Kylie sat to one side of the Windfall High School cafeteria. Shane and Sarah had led them there, only to vanish into the crowd to talk to old friends. Meanwhile, the otter pretended to text on her phone while a DJ showed unnatural enthusiasm for a loop of royalty-free Halloween songs on stage in the gymnasium. The door between the two large rooms opened and closed with each passing student, muting and unmuting the music.

The otter sat in a corner near the entrance, nursing watery punch and deep thoughts. That Edith lady had made an interesting point. How could she take control of her fear? An idle paw in her pocket clicked her keychain flashlight.

The massive husky could be seen weaving around clusters of teenagers and young adults. Max sat down beside her, two tiny cups of punch in one massive hand, his third plate of snacks in the other. Nearing, he smiled down at her, juxtaposed by the serious eyebrows of his dinosaur costume. "May I kick down a wall yet?"

"Could you? Maybe it's just because I don't know anybody here, but I'm feeling a little too old for this party." She took the offered cup and glanced to the cafeteria door. "These high school kids keep making jokes about extracting your DNA. Mostly the girls."

"Yeah." He munched on some sections of submarine sandwich. "I heard one tell her friend to go Isla my Nublar." A couple gulps drained the small cup of punch. "I suspect she failed Spanish."

With a subdued chuckle, the lutrine pocketed her phone. A teenage fox padded past with a samurai sword and at least eight extra tails. The otter leaned against her husky boyfriend's reassuring bulk.

He patted her shoulder. "You doing okay?"

"Yeah." She clicked the flashlight a few more times. A soft crinkle in her pocket reminded her what else lay there. A wild plan started clicking together in her mind.

At her pause, he took her by the paw and led her through the crowd to the front door. They angled through the thinning crowd and out into the chill night air. A short jaunt saw them across the parking lot and back into her mother's hatchback wagon.

As they crossed town, she passed by the event center again, its haunted house trappings dark. The parking lot stood empty. The whole place looked deserted. Kylie got an idea.

On an impulse, she veered into the lot.

"What are we doing?" The husky cocked his ears at her sudden course correction.

She pulled up around the back of the building. "I wanna take a look around." She hopped out of the car. "C'mon."

The dog made a series of growly grumbles, but followed.

She reached Edith's personal door and, after much shaking, jostling, and rattling, didn't get it to so much as budge. She chattered with frustration and tried again. Same result.

He raised an eyebrow. "So, by look around, you meant you wanted to throttle a door handle?"

"I swear this is the door she let me—" Click. The faulty door clicked open. She swung it open the rest of the way with a squeak of pride. "Told ya."

Max padded after her, giving the space a wary sniff. "Okay, so we're trespassing."

"Exploring." She popped her head out to make sure no one had seen them enter, but the parking lot was as dead as ever. She shut the door and clicked on her feeble flashlight.

"Uh-huh." The husky clicked on his much better flashlight, sweeping the beam through the dark and cramped passage. "Exploring what exactly?"

"Fear. Love. Sex." She gestured dramatically around the access corridor, flashing the light across her face. Taking him by the hand, she led him deeper into the building. Anxiety and anticipation bubbled up inside her. Could she really go through with this? Sure, the place was deserted, but someone could have forgotten something and come back. Even the nice sea otter lady from before wouldn't approve of her shagging her boyfriend next to a pile of exotic gourds.

"Okay, if the writers had tried to make you say something that cliché on the show, you would've thrown a fit." He growled a nervous laugh as he ducked under a strut. Those pointy ears scanned the dark corridor. "Sounds like nobody's home."

"See? You should trust me." Passing through another door, they emerged onto the scare track. Instead of eerie music, silence awaited. Here and there, dim lights cast intricate shadows through the dangling rubber snakes and fake tree branches. Her heart racing, she still took a moment to appreciate the serenity of delicate color. Dragging him to the start of the maze, she flashed him a big grin. "I'm good at getting in just the right amount of trouble."

Several shades of light painted Max's monochrome fur in complex overlays. "Now there's something Red Riding Hood might actually say."

Spinning to face him, the otter sauntered closer. She wiggled and puffed out her chest, making sure her breasts stood out in her red bodice. Her round muzzle nuzzled up under his blockier one. A webbed paw cupped the front of his jeans. "My, what a big cock you have."

He cast a nervous glance around the darkness. "I don't know about this, rudderbutt…"

"Come on." She rubbed her supple body against his. "The whole point of this was to overcome my fears. I never feel safer than when I'm with you."

A whine escaped his throat. "But you said we were just taking a look around."

Her webbed paw closed over the bulge at the front of his pants. She arched up to nuzzle his neck fluff, under the green dinosaur hood. "Are you complaining?"

"Not exactly…" His feet shuffled on the floor, taking a stance that allowed her to rub against him without tipping him over. "…but I don't know if it's worth the risk. Someone might hear."

She knelt in front of him. "Bet I can change your mind." Her webbed fingers deftly pulled his boxers down. Though only the red tip of his cock shone in the dim light, his sheath felt firm and plump. She kissed the slit, savoring the faint salinity of his precum. Gingerly strokes worked the sheath down, then up, again and again over that smooth shaft. His balls rocked against the elastic waistband.

The dog himself leaned against the wall. His blue boxer briefs slid down to his knees. His hips shuddered as he didn't resist her efforts. "Kylie..."

"Shh..." She brushed the head of his cock under the soft fuzz of her chin. "Someone might hear."

He gave a muffled woof at the stimulation. A faint wet heat collected where his tip touched her chin. Upon pulling back, she saw a thin sheen of precum, shimmering in the surreal lighting, tempting her to lap it up.

The otter dove forward, engulfing his length with an eager little muzzle. Her smile bobbed up and down on her boyfriend's hardening dick. "Mmmmm." She drew out the sound of her moan to make sure it vibrated through his flesh. Her tongue swirled and twirled, tasting his arousal as it leaked even more from the tip.

A growled moan echoed down the empty corridor as he leaned back against a wall strung with fake cobwebs. A dinosaur-gloved paw settled behind her head, not pushing, just encouraging, letting her know it felt good. His other paw gripped a mossy stone pillar for support. His expression got hazy, mouth open as he panted.

After a minute or so of loving suction, the otter pulled back for breath. She caressed her boyfriend's fluffy balls as he trembled before her. She reached into her side pocket, past her keys to a plastic-wrapped object. Her paws left Max's cock to open the crinkly and stubborn wrapper.

"Are you unwrapping candy?" Those sharp ears popped up again. He didn't even sound offended. Dogs.

"No!" With a strategic nibble, she managed to open the plastic package. The glow-in-the-dark ring of rubber radiated light into the dark room. "But it is supposed to be a treat." She spat out the chunk of wrapper. "I dipped into our supply." She'd ordered a box of canine novelty condoms online. Thus far, they had been a lot of fun, if not strictly necessary for an interspecies couple.

His face lit up in the dim room. That green dinosaur tail wagged a little against the wall. "Wow, that's actually glowing really well."

"I've been charging it up in my pocket with my keychain flashlight all night." Careful not to puncture the thin material with her claws, she eventually ascertained which side was the inside. "I wasn't sure where we might end up having sex, so I thought I'd better bring a way to find your dick in the dark."

"You've never had trouble with that before— Mmmf!" He bit back a woof as she unrolled the condom onto his jutting erection. His length throbbed as she settled the band of the condom at the opening of his sheath.

She nuzzled in against his glowing member, then took it in her mouth. The condom's faint chemical taste distracted her only a little from the pleasing heft and girth of his cock. She made sure to get a little extra spit on him before pulling off. "Mmmm, now there's a nice treat."

With a light growl, he pulled her close and pressed her to a wall with a hungry kiss. The glow of his dick pressed between them, its light catching in his white fur. His eyeshine glinted as he rubbed his muzzle along hers with a growl of lust. "Horny little otter."

Her chitter of amusement melted into a sultry laugh. "Big sexy doggy." By the light of Max's dick, the lutrine scurried up her lover and wrapped her legs around his waist. After a brief but chittery squabble with her skirt and panties, she managed to reach a paw down to guide his cock in. Heat and moisture met her already-eager slit. A waggle of her thick tail rocked her hips, sinking onto him an inch at a time. The texture of the condom was a little grippier than his naked cock. This might have been a problem had she not been fairly wet already.

His strong arms held her easily off the floor. Delicate whiskers mingled with her own. Those green fabric dinosaur claws gripped her rump, rocking her hard onto his harder dick. Heavy balls dragged across her tail base. "Uhh! Mmm! Yeah!"

"Keep going!" She gasped as that thick canine cock buried in her slip-pery little otter passage. Every time he hilted in her, the surge of fullness drove a squeak from her throat. The grippy texture of the condom dragged in and out of her tender folds. Her paw dove between them to rub at her clit. The sensitive webbing rolled over her even-more-sensitive nub. Her passage clenched around him. "Nghh! Take me, Maxie. Oh!"

With a roar any dinosaur would've been proud of, he gripped her hips and buried his phosphorescent length in her. Even through the con-dom, she felt the swell of his knot, getting bigger with every heartbeat. He growled into her shoulder. "Hhhhrrrrrrrrh!!"

With a heavy moan, the otter gasped. Her tail bucked, swinging her hips hard onto his spurting dick. Head thrown back, her red riding hood fell back from her flattened ears. Pleasure coursed through her body. Instinct caused her to clutch at her lover. Her hips wiggled against his, riding as far as his knot allowed, wringing every possible pleasure from her stuffed-full climax. "Mmm..."

For long, loving minutes, they leaned together against the wall. His breaths slowed against her ear. Tension evaporated, even as her body tingled with energy. She couldn't believe what they'd just done, what they were still doing, but it felt incredible. Of all the emotions she was feeling, fear was still there, but it was far down the list. Her webbed paws stroked along his broad back, feeling him pant. Just as she started to wonder if his legs would give out, she felt his knot slip free. A final gasp passed between them as she struggled to ease down without tripping them both.

The faint light returned as he pulled free, then pulled the rubber off his length and tied it to prevent spilling. "At least there's no mess to clean up."

Her panties slid helpfully back over the sticky fur of her mound in a sweep of unexpected sensation. Giddy, Kylie giggled. "We're not gonna use it to light our way home?" She straightened her panties, lips wet, but far from the usual dripping. Normally, his thick canine seed would be running down her tail at this point.

"I don't feel the need for my jizz to guide us." Once Max got his junk sorted away, he gave her a quick kiss and leaned to her ear. "We'd better go." He placed a palm on the crash bar and popped the door open. "I don't want to explain why this whole place smells like sex now."

As they stepped outside, the otter bobbed around him with a bubbly giggle. "Want to catch up with Shane and Sarah?"

"Nah, let's text them and head home." He pulled her close, ducking his muzzle into her hood to nibble at her ear. "I still really, really want to see you take that costume off."

Kylie chittered in anticipation. As the door closed, she caught a glimpse of dull metal in the moonlight, a flash of a familiar face. She stopped the door, leaning back inside to look more closely. On the wall hung an old bronze plaque with an embossed portrait of a sea otter with bushy whiskers and a cheery smile.

In memory of Edith Jetsam

1942-1986

Died installing an unauthorized aquatic component to the annual haunted house. We honor your dedication, if not your methods.

Kylie let the door shut, hiding the plaque. She stood on the narrow concrete step, mind buzzing, something cold twisting in her chest.

"Hey, something wrong?" Max looked down at her with concern on his muzzle, phosphorescent condom dangling in his grasp.

"No..." She shook her head. "It's nothing." She took his paw and walked from the alleyway.

Home for the Holidays

STRANGEVILLE (TUE/8p)

S02E12 "One Big Happy Calamity": The Order of the Hidden Claw makes its final preparations for the summoning of the Unending Ones. While their house is being fumigated, Sandy and Cassie stay with Serge's family.

Airports were loading screens, Max decided, rather than real places. You could land in the airports of a thousand cities and leave without any local dust in your fur. You had to step outside for that. They even smelled like nowhere: cheap coffee, cleaning agents, and hasty departure. The crowd he pressed through as politely as possible, a feat made easier by most species tendency to get out of a two-meter canine's path. They all scrambled along to their connections, their own plot lines. His girlfriend buzzed rapid-fire messages at the phone in his paw.

He felt sore. Airline seats were not designed for him, though no cubs had been seated behind him to dab jam on his tail, which was nice. Hefting bags stuffed with collectible card games, he walked out the main doors. A crisp breeze traced his nose, nothing compared to the winds of Montana. People complained about the wet chill here, though the husky's thick fur protected him from that pretty well. He'd brought waterproof winter clothing as a concession to his mother, in a bid to distract from her demands that he come back for every holiday and eventually just stay on the farm. It didn't work. He hadn't found a good time to mention the supernatural reality he confronted with his former castmate.

A silver-blue hatchback puttered up somewhat faster than necessary, braking to emit a smiling otter. "Maxie!" She rounded the car and crashed into his chest with a hug. "Hey!"

"Hey rudderbutt." With a wag, he lifted the chittering otter in his arms. Her delicate scent swept his mind through a thousand tender moments in her company. She felt fluffier than he remembered, maybe even silkier, but he had been gone a couple weeks.

"Check it out!" She twirled against him and fluffed her chest toward him. "My winter coat grew in!"

Max glanced around at the passing passengers. Most of them were jet lagged enough not to notice if he touched his girlfriend's chest fluff.

Before he could quite make contact, the car behind hers honked, sending the otter into the air. She scrambled for purchase, then shook a webbed fist at the impatient airport patron. "I'm having a reunion here!"

Through the windscreen, the driver, a panther in a flowery blouse, raised thick paws in a gesture of not understanding. Beside her, two cubs clawed and bit at each other, their murderous efforts hampered by booster seats.

"Ugh! Fine!" Kylie scrambled back into the car.

Max placed his luggage in the back and sat in the passenger's seat. The car sank a centimeter or two. Clods of wet snow smacked on the windscreen as they navigated the maze of parking lots. The car only got stuck once, and it only took a steady push to dislodge it. The highway, better-plowed, passed under them uneventfully.

She very pointedly didn't look at him. "Been enjoying the pictures?"

He felt a flush under his fur. "Nightly."

"I hope you're not threatened." Her hazel eyes flicked to him, then back onto the road. A smile rose on her muzzle like the tide.

His paw came to rest on her thigh. "Happy for the help on team ottergasm."

"Oooh. That's good to hear." She wiggled in the driver's seat. "You inspired the purchase, ya know. I needed something to get me through three weeks without you."

The husky nodded with pride. "I suspected as much."

"Remember that night you were stuck in your uncle's vacation power-point and we were texting the whole time?"

He straightened in his seat. "You were using it then?"

"Mmm, the whole time." Her giggle lifted his ears. "In your bed."

"That's…interesting." Max nodded, feeling quite lively in spite of the long flight. He adjusted himself in the seat and tried to rein in his imagination. "Couldn't tell by the glow of the glow-in-the-dark dildo."

"I left it in your dresser, in case the hallway nightlight goes out." She changed lanes and cast him a sparkle of a look. "Not that I'll be needing it now that I've got the real thing back."

The husky rolled his eyes, then rubbed his paw back and forth on her thigh. He'd missed her in so many ways.

"Not that I'm opposed to sharing." She bit a mischievous smile as she snuck him another glance.

"That's…not something I'd ever given any thought to." Picturing the dildo, he did some geometry in his head.

She snickered. "I have."

"Of course you have." He shook his head. "Maybe, if I can get a little familiar with it first."

"Well!" Her eyebrows rose, then she flicked on the turn signal and ease over to the off-ramp. "Go team ottergasm."

Exiting the highway, they cruised through the streets of Windfall. A cascade of lights and decorations swept past in a blur. The town square boasted an array of pop-up businesses, including a roasted nut pavilion staffed by a tussle of squirrels. At the entrance to Bourn Holt, a small aquatic automobile perched alongside the road, with evidence of several attempts to motor up the hill. With several centimeters of snow on its roof, the Amphicar keeled halfway into a ditch.

His eyebrows drifted up. "Speaking of things wedged into places they aren't designed for…"

"It's designed for water, not snow. Couldn't get up the hill." She winked at him. "Got down it really well."

"I bet." He resolved to haul her little car back to the house as soon as weather allowed. "So, what's it going to be like?"

"The usual Yuletide celebrations, plus Max, equals great." She squeezed his paw.

He wagged in the confines of the seat's tail slot. His family might have tried to guilt him into staying, but now that he was half a continent away, he could relax with his girlfriend and learn more about her ottery ways. "Sounds relaxing."

"Any previous year, yes." Kylie gave a quiet sigh. "Mom's got this crazy scheme in mind where all the relations come over."

The husky calculated how many otters could fit in Bourn Manor and quickly found it came to more than he could imagine. "We do have the space."

"Yeah, but I barely know them." A glum look fell on her rounded muzzle. "Mom remembers everybody from back when she grew up here."

He nodded. "Well, everybody older than us."

"I just..." Her webbed fingers gripped the steering wheel. "Bourn Manor's only starting to feel like home. I feel weird about having a whole extended family sail in there to remind me how I don't know anything about it." She stared out into the fading day, almost the shortest of the year. "The things I've found out about it haven't all been great thus far."

"Except the family tradition of monster hunting. That's kinda rad."

She smirked at the winding road leading into the property. "There is that."

"The trouble with families is they're composed of people." He patted her knee. "People are complicated."

She smirked at his wisdom. "Well, if she does summon a horde of otters down on us, I'm sure she'll find some use for a big strong dog."

"Finally, something she and my mother agree on." He stretched his still-sore muscles within the confines of the car. "And what about you?"

She pulled into the driveway. Bourn Manor hunched under its many-sloped roof, the overhangs of snow giving it a resentful air. His girlfriend parked the car and popped up to smooch his cheek with a cheery chitter. "I'm sure I can think of a use for you too."

~ ~ ~

Snow tumbling serenely around her, Kylie watched as her boyfriend chopped firewood. As a husky, the winter chill had little visible effect on him. She, on the other paw, wore several layers of insulation and only felt remotely warm because her hunky boyfriend had just taken off his shirt. Her booted feet stamped to keep the blood moving.

Heavily muscled and slowly panting, Max brought the axe down with tireless ease. Must be nice to be gigantic. He was twice her weight and mostly muscle, even under all that fluff. The halves of the log spiraled off the stump. His heavy paws lifted another log out of the snow and set it atop the low, ancient stump. Another swing split the piece cleanly.

"You're pretty good at that for a city kid." Webbed fingers wiggling in her mittens, she wrapped her arms around herself.

"Har har. I'm still a farm dog, thank you." With a crack that echoed through the woods, he split another log. "Being on your mom's TV show didn't erase all my outdoor knowledge." Those sky-blue eyes flicked to her. He paused and leaned on the axe. "Rudderbutt, you don't have to be out here if you're cold."

"Are you kidding?" Her ears popped up inside her stocking cap. "First winter coat, remember? What's the point if I don't use it?"

His gentle gaze swept over her. "You are looking fluffier."

"We can't all be immune to the cold by default." She wiggled her head a little, remarking at the novel sensation of added insulation. "Besides, watching you exert yourself shirtless is my favorite hobby."

The dog rolled his eyes and got back to work.

After another ten minutes or so, he finished chopping a large pile of logs. She picked up an armful of firewood. Throwing his shirt over his shoulder, he picked up three times as much. Here and there, clumps of snow tumbled from branches in silence. They tromped back through the woods to her sprawling ancestral home. Across its various roof slants, the structure bore the weight of the snow with stern indifference. Colorful lights blinked on the deck railing, diffused by a layer of fresh powder, providing an island of multicolored cheer against the gloomy bulk of the mostly-empty building.

Paused on the front steps, the otter studied the unusual glow. She'd have thought of it as alien, but the only alien she'd met favored sickly yellow light. "Neat. I've never seen lights under snow before."

"The magic of LEDs." Crunching up the walk behind her, he stopped too. "My parents still have giant incandescent lights. They just melt their way free."

The pair entered Bourn Manor. Stamping their boots clean, they crossed the living room and set the firewood by the hearth. Festive knick-knacks glimmered atop dark wood shelves. A pine tree had been crammed into the living room, the top bough bent against the ceiling. They'd only reclaimed a fraction of the maze-like old mansion, the part her mom called "the old house," since it had been the mother mushroom from which the rest of the dwelling had sprouted.

Mutters and clatters rattled from the kitchen. Her mother unpacking additional Yuletide cheer, no doubt. Maybe some more of those glass buoy lights.

His big paws brushed bits of bark off his arms and into the hearth. A smile found his muzzle as he looked to his girlfriend. "What do you guys do for the big dinner?"

"A giant salmon." Her mouth watered at the idea of the flakey pink delight. The saliva felt cold, another unexpected side-effect of a real winter. "We always have one. We'll have to get an extra-giant one since you're here." A wiggle of excitement shimmied up her body.

He suppressed a snicker.

"What?" She eeled right up into his face. "You dare laugh at my people's traditions!"

"Wouldn't dream of it." He bumped his nose to hers, his breath warm. "That's just very ottery."

She bounced up to kiss him, then settled easily into his arms. "You're okay? Your family's not going to come drag you away?"

"They'd never find us in this maze of a house." He patted the base of her tail. "Don't worry your rudderbutt, rudderbutt."

"Yeah, yeah…" Kylie rolled her eyes. She had a slight tendency to obsess and knew it. Being from a long line of monster hunters and a short line of TV producers, she at least came by it honestly.

With another kiss, the canine trotted backward toward the door. "I'm going to bring in the last of the firewood." His furry bulk slipped out the front door, trying to minimize the roll of winter air entering the house.

Slithering past the dining room, the younger otter swung into the kitchen, hanging off the doorframe with one paw, feeling painted-over scratches under her webs.

The middle-aged river otter chattered grumpily as she fired off a few quick texts, then stuffed the phone back in her pocket.

"Hey Mom?" She kept her voice casual. "What would you say to a turkey?"

"Hmm." Laura stood from rifling through old boxes of exotic pots and pans. "Probably: 'I have no idea how to cook you.'" Setting aside a large roasting pan, she crossed her arms under her breasts. "But I'm happy to try for the sake of our resident husky."

Happiness wiggled down her supple form. "Thanks Mom."

"You won't miss the braised salmon?" The elder otter leaned forward and tapped a claw on the pan lid.

"Well yeah, but we'll just have it next week or something." She tried to play it casual. No sense in handing her mom more to tease her about. "You haven't bought it yet, right."

"I haven't." She flipped the flaps of a box closed with her toe. "And I suppose someone somewhere on the Internet has posted turkey-baking advice…" She pulled a phone from her pocket and started searching.

Kylie nodded. That was easy. Maybe she'd do a couple other little things to help him feel at home.

~ ~ ~

Weeks passed and a festive air permeated the house on the tailwinds of an evergreen pine. Seated on his bed, browsing the Internet, Max swore off social media after a sustained barrage of his family's holiday photos: bonfires, tobogganing, feasting all the relations. Had they posted this many pictures previous years? He'd been tagged in all of them and appeared in none. It had to be a psychological operation by his mother. Ears perking at a burst of otter profanity, the dog looked up from his laptop. A blend of spicy scents had been seeping under the door for the past hour, keeping him from finishing any of Laura's writing assignments. He rose, opened his bedroom door, and padded across the entryway to the jingles and clamor in the kitchen.

Cloying steam filled the room. Howled carols blasted from a water-proof phone on the counter, surrounded by open containers of spices. At the stove, his otter girlfriend stood on a step-stool to swirl a long-handled ladle into a massive pot with great enthusiasm. Small splashes pattered on the surface of the stove, which appeared to be supporting the weight for now.

A quick tap of his knuckles on the doorframe and he leaned against it. He'd been a big guy since his early teens and had learned to actively not sneak up on people. He didn't bother to hide his amusement, however.

"Oh hi, Maxie." She straightened an ancient oyster-print apron. "Wondered how long this holiday magic would take to summon you."

He stepped up behind her and rested paws on her curvy hips. "Stealing a page from my mom's cookbook, eh?"

The otter stirred with pride, sloshing more. "Aww, you knew because of the smell?"

"That and it's the only cider recipe I've seen that could be sailed across." He craned his muzzle over her shoulder to look at the almost-full lobster pot. "This is way too much for us, even with your relations."

"My entire family's coming over!" Her deft brown paws propped atop his big clumsy white ones.

149

Resting his chin atop her head, he chuckled. "Yeah, but they're all small."

Mock defiance chattered from her muzzle as she brandished the ladle at him. "We're not that small. You're just twice normal size."

"And yet you don't complain about how big I am…" A couple centimeters was all it took to bring her rump to his crotch. Thanks to the step stool, her tail fit very pleasantly against the bulge in his pants.

A pleased chitter rattled from her muzzle as it angled to brush under his jaw. "No, I suppose you have your uses." She kissed his extra-thick fluff.

He'd brushed extra well, so she didn't even get shed fur on her lips. He wagged. After a few pleasant seconds, he noticed a bowl of tiny green and red dog biscuits, too uniform to be homemade. He picked up one of each and sniffed: turkey and cranberry, respectively. "Why'd your mom have me carry in a turkey?"

Kylie glance to the barely-closed refrigerator. "She didn't want to throw her back out."

He nuzzled her unusually-fluffy cheek ruffs. "I thought fish was the dish."

"It was. But I thought it might be nice to bring in a little of what you're used to." She shrugged. "So I stalked your family online, then stole their recipes and music playlist."

The musical woos and woofs soared to a very familiar chorus. Max gave a pleased sigh, tightening his arms around her. "I appreciate the thought, but you don't need to do anything special for me."

"You're missing out on your family." A squirm of guilt caused her to slither in his arms.

"You guys are my family too. You especially." He squeezed her middle. "Being part of your life is the plan, rudderbutt."

With a small squeak of relief, she nuzzled into his chest.

~ ~ ~

In the living room, Kylie lay on the floor, scrolling through the Internet one phone screen at a time. Outside, wet snow fell. The world outside her door had become a slush drink flavored with inconvenience.

Across the dining room, floorboards intended for the weight of otters creaked under a much greater burden. Max trod into the room looking gloomy, phone in paw.

She studied his face, not bothering to get up, but bothering to soften her tone. "How's your mom?"

"Demanding." He sighed, closed his eyes, and relaxed his posture.

She arched an eyebrow. "I thought you were going to talk before you left."

"I did." His triangular ears tuned in on her. "She had a conversation saved up about how I should ditch you guys for two holidays in a row." He glanced at, then pocketed his phone. "This was just her resurrecting the ghost of conversations past. And informing me I'm coming back for New Year's Eve."

Kylie squirmed through a long moment. "But you're not going back... right?"

"No, I'm not going." His ears rose with his tone, though in confusion and frustration rather than anger. "She needs to learn I'm an adult and she can't stop me."

"Yeah." She inclined her muzzle at the window. "Especially on ice."

Looking down two meters, the dog crossed his arms. "These talks are usually indoors."

"It's a husky household." She swished her tail into his ankle. "You probably have ice floors."

"We have carpet floors." With one foot and no apparent effort, he rotated her ninety degrees.

"The point stands. She's not that much bigger than me, and you toss me around like a throw pillow." Her arms flopped to the sides. "Just keep walking."

His muzzle unfurled a sad smile. "That's what I'm doing."

~ ~ ~

Sprawled over the sofa, Kylie let the holiday happen around her. Snow tumbled past the window outside, dusted with color by the setting sun. The dining room table groaned under the weight of a slew of side-dishes. Her mom clattered around in the kitchen, muttering into her phone. The stress of uncertain plans radiated through the house. The younger otter watched her boyfriend's butt as he poked around inside the fireplace, which proved therapeutic. His fluffy tail swished over jeans pulled tight over his rump.

Across the room, those heavy white paws assembled an intricate structure from sticks and logs. He'd tried to explain to her the complex theories behind how to build a fire, but she told him to save time by just showing her.

With an impatient chitter, the otter rolled belly-up, head dangling toward the carpet. "Wouldn't it just be faster to spray the logs with lighter fluid?"

"Much faster." He tore apart some old cardboard boxes for tinder. "Maybe even fast enough to burn down the house."

"Otter houses can't burn down. They have too many pools." She could think of four, not counting large bathtubs. She reached into a mixing bowl of caramel-drizzled popcorn and dropped the tidbits one at a time into her open mouth. They had a pleasant crunch. "True fact."

The dog emitted an agreeable grunt. A mixture of rude lutrine sea shanties and howled canine carols drifted from her mom's battered stereo. After another five minutes of building the most flammable log cabin possible, Max struck a match and lit the cardboard. The ancient material ignited with stuttering eagerness, giving off a faint musty smell from its decades in the attic. New boxes were saved for repacking.

The fireplace crackled brighter, casting hues to match the sunset. The massive pine filled a quarter of the room. A sparse scattering of ornaments hung on its boughs like carolers lost in a vast forest.

She pondered the tree. "We shoulda bought more decorations."

Sitting down on the sofa, he shrugged. "We can add more over time."

She snuggled up to him. "So, you'll be around to help add them?"

"Yep." He threw his arm around her shoulders. "Besides, you can't just buy decorations. You have to be given them over time. And quietly throw out the ones you don't like."

Alone for the moment, the younger otter elbowed her boyfriend. "So, how's this compare, Maxie? To what your family does?"

Scanning the room with his ears, he gathered a response for a moment. "Quieter."

Kylie snorted. "In spite of Mom's best efforts."

He soaked up the ambience for another second, then turned those bright blue eyes to her. "Saner."

She tilted her head side to side. "Not a word usually associated with my family, but I'll take it."

A glance at the dining room table, then he growled a chuckle. "Lacking a yule-log meatloaf."

"A what?" She peered at him to clues. He had to be making that up.

"A very large meatloaf…" He spread his paw almost a meter apart. "…festively decorated."

"You could have asked for one." She bopped him in the shoulder.

He shook his blocky muzzle, then hooked a thumb toward the dining room. "A turkey that size brooks no rivals." As his stomach growled, the scent took him by the nose until he was facing the origin of the savory scent. "I really want to get started on that thing."

"Still worth it?" Her gaze floated up to his like a brave balloon. "Being here instead, I mean."

His strong arms closed around her. "Mmmhmm."

Having finally convinced herself to trust him to know when he's happy, Kylie cuddled up to his warmth with a merry chirr, disrupted only by muffled chatters from across the dining room. "I can't believe Mom is still on the phone." She tumbled to the tree and snagged a small present. "Here." She tossed the box to him. "Open your family's gift."

He caught and considered the box. "Can we start without Laura?"

Carrying a small gift for herself, she flopped down on the sofa beside him. "We always do one the day before." She paused, then groaned when he didn't move: "I give you permission, Maxie."

A cardboard cube, slapped with postage, almost vanished in his giant white paw. His knife flickered from his pocket and whispered through the tape sealing it. Inside, nested in crumpled bakery parchment, lay a coffee mug. He turned it so she could see the text: "The mountains are calling and I must go. - John Muir" soaring through a blue sky.

Kylie glanced from cup to boyfriend. "From your mom?"

He nodded with resignation.

"Subtle." She wiggled a little straighter on the sofa to see the paper and foil sticking out of the mug. "What's all the stuff in it?"

He pulled three little mylar packets free. "Mana Clash booster packs, from my sisters." A small envelope rattled around the ceramic enclosure, which he plucked out and read. "And something for you, from my dad." He offered it to her.

She opened it to find a delicate bundle of tiny gray-blue feathers and yellow spots. "A hat pin?"

From the vantage point of his height, Max peered with approval down at the object. "He ties flies."

She examined the hat pin for traces of insects, which only made him chuckle at her.

"Fishing flies. It's a Gray Ghost Streamer." He unfurled a paw toward it. "It's supposed to look like a smelt."

She plucked it from the packaging to examine in the firelight. "Huh, it kinda does. I guess I could wear a smelt on a hat."

The husky nodded. "Or you could fish with it and not be a weirdo."

"Wait, I'm an otter, so I know how to fly fish?" She noodled in place, then poked him in the ribs. "That's a little presumptuous."

He captured her poking paw. "You've worn a fishing vest every time he's seen you, in person and on TV."

"I guess that's fair." With her still-free paw, she examined the business end of the fishhook. "Did I tell you I found the spare spears for the harpoon gun? They were in with the lawn darts."

"Oh good." The dog rolled his eyes. "I was really worried about that."

"Well, if you're opening your gift from your parents, I'll open mine from Greg." Looking down at the present in her lap, she rubbed her paws together greedily. "Come on, Pinchy's gift certificate…" She shook the parcel. "Okay, maybe taped to canned oysters?"

Laura appeared in the living room doorway. "Well, Max, you can start on that turkey leg you've been eyeing for the past hour. No sense letting the food go to waste."

The canine's ears shot up, instantly departing the conversation. He quietly rose, patted his girlfriend's mother on the shoulder, and practically dashed to the dining room.

For a moment, the middle-aged otter stood and looked around the massive, mostly empty house. A heavy sigh sank her shoulders. "Nobody's coming."

Max's face craned back into the doorway behind her, ears up, plate already full.

Kylie watched her mother stalk into the room. "Nobody?"

The older otter collapsed into an easy chair. "The relations are worried about the roads, so they're having dinner at Thomas's place like usual."

"Can you blame them?" The dog woofed from the next room. "Even I'd hesitate to drive through the mashed potato you guys call snow." He hooked a clawed thumb toward the window. "Low visibility too."

"I guess I shouldn't be mad, but Thomas didn't exactly fight to get them out the door." With an agitated wiggle, she shoved her phone in her pocket. "That old grog-monger…"

Her daughter tossed both hands in the air. Her uncle Thomas ran a brewery just shy of the Canadian border, a few hours' drive away. "I thought he was on your side."

She shrugged. "More like willing to go along with me."

Kylie's small ears flicked down with a grumble. "So it's just the three of us, stuck in this giant house, with Turkeyzilla."

"And an industrial drum of cider." Already at the dining room table, the husky ladled himself another mug.

"You watch your tone about Turkeyzilla." She waggled a finger at her child. "Cooking it was a three-day ordeal. We've bonded."

Max reappeared in the doorway, juggling a steaming mug and a massive turkey leg. "At least you have a year to prepare now."

"True." The plumper lutrine allowed herself a sigh. "I may have been in producer mode, thinking I could call the shots and everyone would fall in line. We were gone for twenty years, and there's been significant tradition drift."

"We are up one husky, though." Kylie leaned over the arm of the sofa to make sure he'd hear. "He's big enough to count for several otters."

"He'd better, with all the food we have." The elder otter took off her glasses and rubbed the bridge of her nose.

Returning, Max nodded, muzzle buried halfway through a massive turkey leg.

Kylie waved her still-unopened present. "We're opening gifts from estranged parents."

"Well!" She huffed into a half-smile. "I suppose I should open mine from my estranged ex."

Ever helpful, the dog fetched said gift from under the tree, carrying it gingerly in the paw not full of turkey. He handed it to the spectacled otter.

"Thank you, Max." With the patience that comes from being old, Laura drummed her paw pads on the object. "Go ahead and open yours, sweetie."

Kylie shredded the paper in a burst of glittery scraps. Inside the flat box, she found a filigree cheese wedge with a built-in opera glass. "A sextant? Is this an add-on for the Amphicar?" After finding a brochure for a floating camper trailer in the car's service manual, she'd believe just about anything.

Laura sat back, smiling fondly at the little brass gizmo. "That's an old Bevy heirloom."

She rocked the tarnished metal back and forth in her paw. "What? Did Greg pinch it when he left?"

"Very funny." She turned the large package over in her paws, causing it to glug softly. "I gave that to your father a long time ago. When he was looking for some direction in life." She picked at the wrapping on her present, looking for the edge of the tape. "As it happened, his direction was a little different than mine, that's all."

"Ah." Kylie peered through the scope at the twinkling lights, then set it on the coffee table in an aesthetically-pleasing manner. "I'm sure it'll tie the shots of my biopic together someday. I'd better save it."

Pushing up her glasses, Laura's voice took on a directorial tone. "See that you do. You're living in a very authentic props department." With that, she abandoned decorum and her claws tore through the wrapping. The paper fell away to reveal a bottle. The dark amber liquid sloshed in glass designed to look like a bundle of sugar canes with one taller in the center. The cork bore a tuft of dried and slightly-crumpled leaves. Her face lit up. "Oooooh, the good stuff."

The younger river otter's eyebrows rose. "Since when do you get more than a gift card from Dad?"

"It's not like we don't talk, kiddo. And we did just move back to his home state." She gripped the bottle in both webbed paws, then used her tail to launch herself off the sofa. "I have just the place for this…" Without explanation, she vanished into the kitchen.

Dabbing his muzzle with a napkin, Max lifted pert ears to his girlfriend.

Kylie let out a soft sigh as glass clinked in the next room. With all the prep work her mother had done over the past couple weeks, who knew what secret fruitcake she might ignite and wheel in, next to the giant pine tree and the roaring bonfire. Where had that fire extinguisher gotten to?

A couple minutes later, the middle-aged otter sailed back in with a tray of creamy drinks.

Her daughter's ears popped up through her hair. "What's that?"

"Eggnog." She handed her daughter a glass. "Served in the best crystal that I didn't sell—and fortified by rum."

He sniffed the drink. "Um, Laura, you put rum in ours too."

The former TV producer gave him a weary look. "Drink the damn eggnog, Max."

He drank the eggnog. His triangular ears cycled through a few different settings as he sipped. His expression struggled to remain the same, though his electric blue eyes widened.

Cradling the geometric glass in both paws, Kylie stuck her tongue in the liquid. Beneath the nutmeg, the burn of rum was quickly quenched by sweet cream. Not bad.

"Well, Max, if we're only going to only have one extra person in the house…" Kylie's mom raised her glass to him. "…I'm glad it's you."

The hulking canine smiled shyly and tinked his glass to hers. "Thanks for making me feel at home, even before Turkeyzilla."

"We've been trying to make the old place feel homey." Laura took another sip, then wiped the nog from her whiskers.

Kylie tapped her beverage to the other two. "And we are, one dusty room at a time."

Over the lipstick-blurred rim of her glass, she looked at the younger lutrine. "High praise from my surly child."

"Must be the spiked nog." The slimmer otter poured another gulp into her mouth. "Shameful, all this underage drinking."

Snow piled up outside. Steam radiators gurgled and gargled. The fireplace crackled and flickered. The drinks vanished, leaving a warm glow of camaraderie. Their appetites made a small dent in the feast on the table.

"What were the old dinners like?" Kylie nibbled asparagus one stalk at a time, happy the informal setting allowed her to just pick them up with her fingers. For a plant, they were oddly fish-like in crunch, if cooked right. "Before you left to make it big?"

"Magnificent." Her mother raised her fork in salute to absent company. "The whole place was packed with laughter and stories. Some of them were even true." A spark of nostalgia entered her voice as she watched the ghosts of holidays past. "Every otter with even the faintest connection to the Bevy line could show up and most of them did."

Max contemplated the nutmeg floating on his second eggnog. His brow furrowed in a way that Kylie had learned spoke of a thought percolating. "Laura, you sold some stuff inside Bourn Manor..." He shifted his gaze to her mom, using his extra-polite voice. "...but the real money was always in the house and land."

"Mmhm." Laura swirled hers around, as if pondering how much more rum she could fit.

"You never considered selling it?" The dog cleared his throat. "Not that I don't appreciate it."

"Never when I had work, and never earlier than one in the morning." The plump otter looked out the window with a wry grin, watching the snowfall and lack of headlights in the driveway.

"Why?" The question hung in the tinseled air for an uncomfortable length of time.

Sitting back in the easy chair, she shook her head. "It was always my emergency fallback. A few times, I was a month's rent away from slinking back here. I never had to, but having that option made me confident."

Nodding, the husky's voice remained soft, though it gained a hint of the playful banter they used when he and Laura brainstormed. "You could've rented it out."

Peering down through her glasses, she chased a stray clump of sweet potato around her plate with a fork. "It never felt right, someone else living here. We TV producers are well known for our mawkish sentimentality."

He coughed a laugh through his drink.

The older otter looked up with amusement. "It's true, though. I have good memories of this house. I want more of those." She smiled at her daughter. "I want to fix the place. Make new memories."

"Mom, you old sap." She flashed a smirk to her mother.

Laura stretched and oozed off the sofa. "Ugh! All this revelry has tired me out. And this eggnog has clearly written me into a holiday special." She waddled over and hugged both of them. "I'm going to bed."

Kylie watched her mother head up the stairs, then listened as her footsteps receded into the master bedroom. The dog beside her watched the

fire crackle and the snow fall in patient peace. Curled up with Max, minutes passed a breath at a time, as the creak of the floorboards moved to the
bathroom and eventually back to the bed.

Time to set her scheme into motion. She wriggled to her feet.

Max's ears rose with her, lifting a question into the air with the softest
whine.

"Stay there, Maxie." She flowed out of the room with barely a backward glance. "I'm just getting another present for you."

His tail thumped on the cushions as she scampered back to her room.

~ ~ ~

Max took in the picturesque scene before him: snowfall, a low fire, and
more pine tree than the room was designed to accommodate. The room
was dark, lit only by firelight and little white LEDs. It looked like a post-
card. Sure, it wasn't his family home, but it was rapidly becoming a home
to him. He found himself smiling at the idea.

An excited chirr drew his attention toward the stairs. His otter girlfriend crossed the landing and stretched a paw up the doorframe, clad in a
bathrobe. And only a bathrobe, if her bare thighs were to be believed. She
watched him with a sensual chirr. "Hello, Maxie."

He blinked, brain trying to catch up to her appearing "Hi."

She padded into the living room, got some wrapping paper stuck to
her foot, kicked it free with an offended chitter, and crawled into his lap.
Her arms slipped over his shoulders to play with his scruff. "I'm really glad
you're here."

His eyes darted down to her cleavage. "Yeah, me too."

She leaned in and kissed him. Then, biting her lower lip, she lifted his
paws to the ends of the robe belt.

Playing along, he double-checked that Laura hadn't suddenly appeared
downstairs, then pulled loose the bow. He'd assumed Kylie would be naked
under the robe, but it fell away to reveal silky undergarments: diaphanous
white with threads that sparkled like new-fallen snow. The garment hung

like a curtain of mist, secured to her breasts by a single ribbon bow. A matched pair of panties glimmered from under it, again secured only by a shimmering ribbon atop her tail. His ears sprung up in surprise. The blush under his fur felt hotter, somehow, than if she'd just been nude.

Giggling scandalously, the otter bounced off his lap and did a little twirl in the firelight. She wiggled and babbled: "I thought the shiny satin was a bit much, but in the firelight it looks pretty good. The great thing about lingerie is it'll last forever, since you only wear it for a few minutes before it comes off. Unless, ya know, it works so well your husky boyfriend uses his teeth. But don't use your teeth, even though that would be kinda hot. Anyway, what'd ya think, Max?"

Standing, he took her by the paw and drew her into a slow kiss. He pulled her against him as they made out. His tongue slipped into her muzzle to trace those pointy lutrine teeth and her supple lips. Even as he leaned down over her, she edged him back to the sofa until he sat down with a muffled bounce of springs.

She squirmed with joy along his body. Her curvy form flowed between his knees as she ran her paw down his chest. "Now lemme unwrap my present…" Her grabby brown otter paws quickly shucked him of his shirt. Delicate claws scratched under his chin as her other palm pressed atop his crotch.

"Out in the living room?" His ears flattened shyly. "Won't your mom hear?"

"She was snoring in bed by the time I came outta my room." Kneeling between his legs, she nuzzled the crotch of his pants. "Some people can't hold their egg nog."

Even more pink reached his ears. "Kylie…"

"Shush…" Her eager fingers seized on his fly. "You unwrapped your present; now it's my turn." Her paws undid his fly and tugged his boxers out of the way. With an eager chitter, she leaned down and kissed deeply into his sheath. As he hardened on her tongue, she played with his balls, then pulled back to admire her work.

The canine panted, his dick in his girlfriend's paws. With a grunt, a fresh bead of precum rolled down from his tip.

She lapped it up. With a hot breath, her round muzzle eased down his length. A full second of her looking up at him with satisfaction coaxed an unexpected pulse of precum onto her tongue. She sucked and slurped. Slowly, she explored every delightful sensation she could evoke in him. Through the pleasure, he noticed her hips bounce on her other paw. After several lovely minutes, reluctantly, she pulled off, working her tired jaw.

Smiling, he cupped her cheek ruff and admired how sexy she looked beside his wet erection.

She nuzzled into his touch, then pressed him to the soft fur of her other cheek. "I do really like your dick, Maxie."

He whimpered at her words. "Yeah?"

"Mmmhmm." Pumping with her paws, she stroked her finger webbing over his canine bulge. "Might be a size too big."

A pulse of arousal hardened him further. Leaning in, he pressed his muzzle to her ear and growled: "Let's make sure it fits."

With a giggle, the otter oozed straight to the floor. One webbed paw pulled her panties aside, while the other spread her entrance. The naughty gleam in her eye shone brighter than anything else in the room.

The canine prowled down atop her and between her waiting thighs. Her soft outfit, almost as lovely under his paws as her newly-grown pelt, slipped under his touch. Already fully hard, he found her wet and eager. Her hips twisted and humped up his length.

That powerful tail propelled her up against him. Her toes caught on his waistband to pull his pants and boxers down fully. Knuckles to her mouth, she snickered at his gasp.

He shuffled the rest of the way out of his garments, then stalked atop her. His paws gripped her dainty shoulders as he worked his girth into her. He did everything possible to increase the frequency of those happy squeaks. The growl in his throat gave him pause with how predatory it sounded. A few strokes later, though, he was back up to full speed.

With no mattress to absorb the impact, his every thrust squeezed a squeak from her. Half-lit by colorful lights and the fireplace, her head rocked back and forth in pleasure.

The dog whined, banging his hips down onto hers. An exotic flourish of sensation, the silken panties brushed against one side of his length as he worked it in and out of her. With a sudden urgency, he bounced his knot against her sopping folds. A squelch, and he was inside. Breath caught in his throat. A twitch started in his balls and squirted up his length with a rush of ecstasy.

His lover squirmed with pleasure, her tail curling between their legs. Webbed paws traced his body, urging him on with eager grips at his fur. As his passion emptied into her with a spreading warmth, she chirred with unabashed delight.

Atop her, he slowly regained his breath. He slipped free the bow at the front of her lingerie, exposing her cleavage. He lapped at her nipples in turn, cupping her modest breasts.

She squirmed on his knot. "Mmmmmmm. Maxie, that feels nice…"

Still breathing hard, he reached down and massaged her clit against the swell of his buried cock. The faint squish of his cum seeped around his length, making her slick passage all the slicker. His fingertips worked in gentle circles, faster and faster, until she was a whimpering wiggle of happiness under him.

"Mmf! Yeah!" Her hips bounced up to his as much as the tie allowed. "Like that! Mmmmmf!" With a trembled surge of strength, she clutched to him, her passage gripping his sensitive cock.

Having been focused on his labors, Max yipped softly in surprise as his dick slipped free. A glance between them showed his pink length swaying, half sheathed and dripping. He sat up to see his climax seeping out of her, white as the snow falling outside the window. After a moment's appreciation, he gathered their clothes and lifted her in his arms.

"Mmmmm." She snuggled against his chest. "Where're we goin', Maxie?"

"I'm carrying you to bed, rudderbutt." His cock cooling in the scandalous air, the husky made his best efforts to reach his bedroom before he dripped on the carpet. He did take the time to press his lips to her hair and whisper: "To tie you again before you pass out."

His lover squeaked, wiggled, and ruffled her muzzle into the fluff of his throat. Wet passion trailed down the waterproof fur at the base of her tail. It seeped into the fur at the crook of his arm, igniting a blush under his cheek fluff.

Slipping through the door, he padded across the darkened room to lay her on the bed. He lay beside her. As his paws drifted over her, he noticed a bow, just like the one over her cleavage, atop the tail of the garment. Tucked warm in bed, visions of unwrapping more presents tomorrow danced through the husky's head. Eager paws untied it, leaving him to remark how easily her panties pulled free. He really wanted to see her come again. Even though he'd just come, another option occurred to him. Fumbling at the nightstand, he obtained a silicone sex toy from the top drawer. The slightly-squishy phallus emitted a faint glow, just enough to light his paw. Its respectable knot gleamed along its shapely length. Maybe someday, he'd let her use a toy on him. Maybe. But for the moment, he spread her legs and teased the tip of the toy along her sopping slit.

The otter chittered agreeably. The bed creaked under her. Her bared chest rose and fell. Her round little muzzle beckoned for a kiss and he decided it wouldn't be in the holiday spirit to be stingy. Her lips pressed warm and soft against his.

Pressing in softly, he marveled at how easily she could accommodate the dildo. Even the knot only hesitated a moment before gliding inside, lubricated by their passion. Then again, she'd had another knot in her just moments ago. He blushed under his pelt at the thought. His dick poked valiantly from its sheath.

All four lutrine paws gripped the sheets as he worked the toy in and out of her. Lewd sounds filled the air, a far older and more primal tune for chasing off the midwinter blues. Her tail swished along the smooth fabric. In and out the dildo pressed, leaving the otter wiggling for more. Eventually, she grabbed his hands and pressed it urgently to her entrance. Her body stiffened, forcing a gasp from her. Max wiggled toy's knot deep inside her, just like she'd mentioned in all those naughty texts. The little extra effort made her head rock in redoubled pleasure. "Mmmmmm!"

He nuzzled in against the side of her neck and listened as her breathing caught up in the quiet darkness. For a minute or so, he left the knot in her. She'd told him how much she enjoyed the fullness. Only when he felt the increasing need to cuddle her half-naked form did he draw it free and return it to the nightstand, quite sticky. Curling up with his lover on the cold December night, he felt his retreating erection slide against the satin-smooth nightie.

"Mmmm, but Maxie…" She whimpered against his neck fluff, half asleep. "I wanna do it again."

A chuckle rumbled in his chest. "Later, rudderbutt." He wrapped careful arms around her, not wanting to give her a crick in the neck. "I'm not going anywhere."

Mollified, she muttered contentment and settled into slumber against him.

Fading fast, he held her against him and enjoyed the afterglow. His breathing steadied as sleep settled over him. Good food, good cheer, good sex: a really excellent day, truth be told. And if he happened to wake up with an otter and an erection, the festivities might just continue. His chin settled atop the otter's head. Her scent teased his nose, soft and welcoming. He sighed. It might not be the homestead, but curling up with Kylie always felt like home.

Movie Night

STRANGEVILLE (WED/9P)

S04E07 "Occult Classic": Prof. Egbert accidentally uploads a ghost onto his computer from a haunted videocassette. It must be appeased to safeguard his notes on magic.

Outside Bourn Manor, clouds rolled by and leaves danced on their branches. Inside, a takeout box from Pinchy's filled the kitchen with a delicious fried shrimp smell. Beside it, an otter refrained from eating them with great selflessness as she attempted to assemble a vegetable platter.

Kylie, having never paid particular attention to how a veggie tray was structured, dumped a whole bag of baby carrots onto a plate. "Is it too late to tell everybody not to come over?"

Her boyfriend sliced celery with calm, careful strokes. "They're probably already on the way."

"We could shut off all the lights." Briefly fighting to unseal a bottle of ranch dressing, she resorted to gnawing it open, then spitting out a stray piece of paper label. "And lock the door. And—"

The dog buried each length of celery under the edge of her carrot hill. "It's just a movie night, Kylie."

She upended the ranch bottle and blasted it into a bowl. "I'm fine with movie nights that aren't in my weird, creepy house."

Rolling his eyes, Max plucked one radish at a time from the farmers' market bundle, breaking off any unappetizing leaves and setting them on the plate. "Most people would say that's a bonus for movie night."

"Most people aren't still a little sensitive about being seen as crazy based upon their crazy house." She seized a bell pepper and raised a cleaver over her head to strike.

Giving a weary sigh, he plucked the knife and then the pepper from her grasp. "We've known them for a year. We have to let them come over to our cool house. We told them they could come over." The husky pointed toward town. "If we tease Karl with it any more, he's going to bounce in through the window."

She watched as he cut up the pepper with care but no expertise. "Still."

"They don't think you're crazy." He arranged the pepper slices around the perimeter of the tray, casting her a smirk. "Any more than you actually are."

"But they've never really been in my giant creepy house." She gestured at the sprawling manor house. "It's an urban legend!"

"We're not even urban." He shrugged. "We're a suburban legend, at most. That's much less spooky."

She jabbed a webbed finger at the end of the driveway. "That 'ghost tours' bus still stops by the edge of the driveway."

"Yeah, but now your mom goes out in her bathrobe whenever she sees them. That seems to be the answer."

"Bathrobes?" She picked up the ranch bottle again and tried to shake out the stubborn remainder.

He shook his thick muzzle. "No, showing everybody we live here and that it's just a house."

A knock rattled the door.

Kylie, clutching the empty ranch bottle in both hands, realized that was a weird thing to do when friends arrived. She chucked it at the trash bin, only to have bounce off the wall with a white splatter. She then realized having a gobs of goo running down the wall was also something abnormal and dove for a dishtowel.

Max, unperturbed, trotted over and opened the front door.

Shane and Sarah, siblings exhibiting completely different degrees of giving a fig, stood on the porch. A drizzle of rain pattered on the old wood planks. Gray clouds clogged the sky.

The orange tabby nodded at his husky host. "Hey." With fluid ease, he slinked into the dining room and cleaned his glasses.

"Hi Max." Sarah offered an antsy smile, long ears drooped. Tip-toeing inside, she hopped out of her shoes and set them politely out of the way by the door. Ears up, she peeked into the kitchen and spotted Kylie scrubbing ranch dressing off the wall like a totally normal person and offered her a small wave.

Surrendering to the the idea that she had been caught wrangling salad dressing, she cast the offending dish rag into the sink and bore the veggie tray out toward the guests in triumph. "Snacks! Also, hi!"

Sarah smiled. "Thanks for inviting us over. It's good to see you."

Shane nodded at the otter, then leaned against the wall and started cleaning one finger claw with another.

His sister elbowed him in the ribs. "Say hello."

He rubbed his side. "We work together. We've worn out 'hello.'"

The rabbit shrugged an apology.

Kylie snickered.

Max, meanwhile, had taken the appearance of the veggie tray to begin conveying other snacks from the kitchen to the living room. The husky hustled back and forth, towering and domestic.

A series of excited thuds clattered on the porch. Muted voices radiated through the door. A heavy hip bumped the wall. An eager chirp rattled the window glass.

Kylie set the plate of vegetables on the dining table and reopened the front door.

There stood a rhinoceros and a bat. Karl had a mini camcorder strapped to his horn. He was dressed in his nicest Strangeville fan t-shirt, the one with cartoon versions of the cast surrounding the obvious lack of an alien ghost dragon.

Meanwhile, Rune held a boom mic in one wing and was fiddling with the device with the other. A green shirt, which lacking sleeves looked like a well-tailored pillowcase. On it's front, ye olde font spelled out "It's gonna be dicey!" over a cup spilling polyhedral dice. Over it, she wore a vest with what Kylie considered a very useful number of pockets.

An electronic beep arose. The bat nodded. "Horn-cam is active."

The rhino's tiny eyes alighted on the otter and he straightened with a grin. "Hi, Kylie!" A tiny dance in place creaked the boards of her porch. "Can you close the door so we can get a shot of it opening?"

"Oh, okay." Kylie shut the door, then swung it open again. "Wait, why?"

Karl blinked. A tiny red LED on the device on his horn also blinked.

Already holding the boom mic over Kylie's head, Rune looked up from double-checking the recorder on her vest. "For Strange Times."

The rhino waved a thick hand at the ancient house. "You said we could come to Bourn Manor."

She propped her fists on her hips. "I said you could come to my house."

"Which is Bourn Manor." Shane tipped a finger at her. His tail swished with sass.

She stuck her tongue out at the cat, then turned back to the newest guests. "I meant that we should hang out. Like normal friends."

"We're friends?" Karl's tiny ears popped upright.

"We're normal?" Rune scratched her stomach with one foot.

Carrying a heaping bowl of popcorn shrimp, Max paused parallel to the doorway. "Pretty sure we count as friends."

The rhino grinned and gave him a thumbs-up.

Juggling the bowl to be cradled against his broad chest, the husky managed to return the gesture.

Kylie emitted a noise that made everyone look at the rusty door hinges. "Just come in. We've got movies to watch."

Karl nodded with excitement, then gingerly took hold of doorknob and closed it. On the other side, he began a very excited introduction about opening the door.

"Are you kids just opening and closing doors?" Laura padded down the stairs. "Is that the new fad?"

The younger otter groaned. "My mother the comedian, ladies and gentlemen."

Sarah gave her a wave almost identical the one she'd given Kylie.

Shane shrugged. "The evening is way more about doors than I expected."

The door opened yet again and and this time Karl got past the threshold. "Whoa, cool." His horned head swung around, camera on his horn capturing it all.

Rune followed him back inside, carrying the boom mic ahead of her like a lantern. The brown-eyed bat gave her a shrug.

Then he noticed who was standing on the stairs. "Oh! Hi, Ms. Bevy! It's Laura Bevy, creator of Strangeville!"

"Hello...you." Laura pushed up her glasses. "Quiz time: remind me how we met."

"We met at Kawaii Con!" The rhino beamed, as if reciting a key moment of his life. "I came up to the table and you signed a bunch of stuff while you were drinking coffee."

Glancing to her daughter, the older otter lifted her palms. "Story checks out."

"Mom, this is Karl and Rune and Shane and Sarah." She pointed to each of them in turn.

"Ah, excellent." Interlacing her fingers as much as webbing allowed, she leaned over the stair railing. "Always nice to meet people who will put up with my daughter."

He bounced in place, clattering every framed photo and knickknack in the surrounding rooms. "Oh wow. I can't believe we're in Laura Bevy's house."

Laura looked the rhino up and down. Mostly up. "You did realize you were coming to Kylie Bevy's house, right?"

"Yes! But still—it's just unbelievable." He squeezed.

She nodded gently. "I'm impressed you're impressed."

Max caught Kylie's eye from the living room. Amusement perked his ears. At least everybody else was having fun with her embarrassing mother.

Laura looked the group over. "Say, you're a group of eighteen to twenty-five year olds. How would you like to be a focus group?"

"I think we're supposed to watch a movie." The spotted brown rabbit glanced at Kylie.

"We'd probably skew your results." Rune lowered the mic half a meter so she could talk near it. "Karl already spends most of his disposable income on things you make."

The middle-aged lutrine laughed.

"Mother, don't conscript the guests." Kylie hoisted the heaping veggie tray and paraded it to the living room. "They're normal people here to have a normal evening."

"Then I will leave you to your normalcy. Try not to make too much noise after ten. If I'm still awake then, I want it to be the coffee's fault." She retreated upstairs.

The guests followed Kylie into the living room. After bonking her boom mic on the ceiling, the brown bat telescoped it back down to a reasonable length and strapped it to her back. The recorder its cord ran to, however, still blinked "recording" over and over on its screen.

"So!" Kylie brandished the remote. "Do you guy want to watch Wraith Street or Unwelcome Geists? Oh! Or Killer App?"

Shane raised a half-hearted paw. "Why would we watch haunted house movies when we're inside the spookiest haunted house ever?"

Why did everything in this town have to revolve around what was spooky? She waggled the remote at him. "That is not one of the options, Mr. Warren."

Karl raised a polite finger. "I'm okay with seeing more of the house."

Bowl cradled in one wing, Rune munched merrily on popcorn shrimp. "I'm also okay with seeing more of the house."

The otter crossed her arms. "You've barely even seen this part of the house."

"From the outside, it looks like it's all jumbled." Sarah wrung her fuzzy hands. "Sort of like a cave system."

"Only one way to find out." Shane ambled past her, just so happening to pass her and re-enter the dining room.

The other three guests glanced between each other, daring each other. Then, one by one, they all trailed along after Shane. Sarah padded. Karl brushed against the wall to avoid bumping Kylie. Rune brought the bowl with her.

"Hey!" The lutrine chattered with objection. "Where are you going?"

Turning to his winged friend, the rhino touched thick fingers to his smiling lips. "We're exploring Bourn Manor."

"You can't just explore it!" She flung her arms to either side. "I live here!"

Shane cast her a dry look. "Then you explore it and we'll go with you."

Wordless, Max stood by the sofa as all four guests drifted past him. He held a cheese and cracker plate. With a shrug, he set some cheese on a cracker and started eating.

Kylie shook a finger at her boyfriend. "I have enough trouble without you joining in."

He leaned in, his breath smelling like cheddar. "Rudderbutt, I don't see why this is a big deal. We can let them see the house, if they're so curious."

She followed the rest of them out of the civilized area of the house and into the realm old boxes and dusty knickknacks. Just one hallway brought them into the wilderness of her family's past. "What if they find something weird?"

Still popping shrimp into her mouth, Rune chirped back at her. "I found something weird already." With one foot, she reached under a small table and tugged free a green paper packet. She held it up to the group for inspection.

Karl zoom in. Literally, by zooming his head, and its horn-cam, toward the find. "An artifact!"

As Kylie got closer, she saw it was a pack of gum. Tiny pine trees adorned the wrapper. Decades had faded the ink. The whole thing bent at a sharp angle, as if the few forgotten sticks of gum had gone brittle and snapped at a clean angle.

"Is this gum…" Ears up, Sarah tilted her head. "…tree flavor?"

"Pine." Shane swished his tail. "It's a beaver thing. We had a poster for it at the store once."

With a disappointed sigh, Rune pirouetted and placed the packet deftly on the table it, between an old lamp and a cigar box with knitted mittens reaching out of it. The table itself now wobbled.

They came to the ballroom. After getting a resigned nod from Kylie, her boyfriend creaked open the heavy doors that sealed it. Kylie flipped on the light. Everybody else made little impressed noises. Rune clicked her tongue, like a camera shutter capturing the moment.

Ornate tin sheets girded the room from the floor to about knee height, allowing it to be flooded with water. It depicted seahorses pulling shell chariots, each crewed by a revel of merrymakers of various species. A dinghy, overflowing with silk flowers and splashed with garish colors, lay pitched in a corner. Classical columns stretched up into the room and connected to nothing. Shorter columns held vases, most with dried flowers still visible. A heap of bunting in the corner had become a nest for something, or several generations of something. And above it all, three massive sea-glass chandeliers loomed, their piece's irregular colors and shapes worked into glowing tapestries of ocean, beach, and riverside scenes.

And it was crammed, wall to wall, with dusty bric-a-brac.

The rhino tiptoed into the ballroom's sea of junk, recording it all for posterity and the Internet. Attempting to peek into an umbrella stand, he clinked his horn against bundle of colorful glass buoys hanging from one wall. "Oops." He checked them for cracks, but found none. "Sorry. I shouldn't interfere with the site."

"It's not a site." Kylie muttered and waddled after them. "It's just my house."

Rune regarded a suit of armor that had been waterproofed with ornate enamel. All the while, her wing fingers continued popping fried shrimp into her muzzle. "You really do have a cool house. Even when I peeked in the windows as a kid, I never imagined it would have this much stuff in it."

A spike of discomfort sputtered through Kylie, though she couldn't find a reason to object to looking into a house nobody lived in. Even if she now lived in it.

"Is it okay to look in the boxes?" Sarah tapped on a cardboard box with one polite claw.

"I'm looking in the boxes." Shane looked in the boxes.

"No!" The otter balled up her webbed fists. Could she really expect nobody to look in all the boxes laying around? She'd been peeking into them for months and never found anything that exotic. "I mean, maybe? Since when are boxes better than movies? And I can't be held accountable for anything you find."

Wagging beside her, Max watched the group's antics. "I can stop them, if you really want."

"With brawn?" She debated the merits of having her boyfriend toss everyone back into the living room.

"With shame." The dog continued to eat cheese and crackers.

A heavy sigh slumped her supple frame. "No... That would only make them want to look more. They'd probably just leave for a glass of water and get trapped under a stack of old fishing magazines. At least this way we can keep an eye on all of them."

The husky nodded, then dislodged an oyster-shucking knife from the wall. He placed it discretely into the nearest vase.

Kylie got the distinct impression this was not the wildest party that had been thrown here.

The feline picked his way through the bric-a-brac to the bar in the far corner. Once there, he recovered several bottles of questionable liquor, which raised the guests spirits.

Her webbed paws pressed to her face. "Seriously, Shane?"

"I didn't put this here." He shrugged, a dusty bottle of gin in either hand. "I only found it."

"It's bad enough to wander around my house on a walking snack tour." She waved for him to put the booze back. "We're not also getting drunk."

Rolling green eyes, the tabby set both bottles back on the counter and continued invading the privacy of her long-dead relations. He reappeared behind the bar and donned an old apron.

Max leaned into frame of the horn-cam. "The cast of Strangeville does not endorse drinking unknown alcohol you find lying around."

Karl giggled. "This has been a public service announcement."

"Isn't gin made from juniper berries?" Sarah looked up from peeking inside a tin of stained doilies. "Who bought all these tree-flavored things?"

Leaning on the bar, tail flicking with mild amusement, Shane smirked. "Are you sure you're not a beaver, Kylie?"

The lutrine scoffed. "How about I bit you and you tell me if they feel like beaver teeth, wise guy?"

The cat shook his head, though his nose was already drifting over an opened bottle of dark bitters.

Rune tottered back over to Kylie and offered access to the somewhat-depleted bowl of popcorn shrimp.

Unwilling to let her pride turn away fresh popcorn shrimp, Kylie snagged a handful of them and began consoling herself with their crispy goodness.

"You get these at Pinchy's?" The bat smiled as she straightened one of the elastic bands holding on her glasses.

She nodded, happy to talk to someone her own height for once. Being short was a pain in the neck. "Yeah."

The bat continued to snack. "Good stuff."

She'd bought them mostly for herself, but she was pleased at least some part of having guests over had gone more smoothly than expected. "Are shrimp a bat thing?"

Rune shrugged her wings. "Insectivore."

"I guess that makes sense." Kylie nodded. "Bugs are just land shrimp."

The bat nodded.

As they watched, the trio discovered old bedsheets, half of a boombox, and an unopened novelty cast-your-own-anchor kit. Warmth clung to the room. With the doors usually shut, the air conditioning hadn't reached in here.

Kylie found herself not super upset that movie night wasn't featuring any movies. A little upset, still, but nobody had found evidence of a murder. Or a monster skull. Actually, a monster skull might be okay, in the long term.

Shifting under the boom mic strapped to her back, the bat turned to her. "I don't think we've ever actually been introduced. I'm Rune." She extended a wing.

The otter shook it, unsure which of them had brought the crumbs to the handshake. "I'm Kylie."

"Yeah, I know." The slender mammal gave her a gleaming-white, dorky grin. "I do a podcast on you."

A chitter of amusement rattled from the lutrine's muzzle. "Right."

"Thanks again for letting us see the place, even if it wasn't what you planned. Karl's been talking about it for days. It's a local landmark."

"Everybody keeps saying that." Kylie watched as her friends and boyfriend waded out into the ballroom until they were waist-deep in boxes. "Surprised nobody snuck in."

Shaking her head, Rune hooked a wing thumb at the evening light seeping in at the far end of the ballroom. "The windows were all locked."

"You walked around checking my windows?" Kylie took another handful of breaded shrimp.

Her wing fingers wiggled. "Flew."

The otter crossed her arms. "Still."

"I was eleven. It was a dare." Her voice went sing-song around a bite of shrimp. "It was that or let my friends fall off the third story trying to get in."

"Fair point." With a nod, the lutrine smirked at a realization. "I suppose it's my fault you couldn't get in until now."

The bat's ears rose. The mauve-striped elastic bands around them stretched, tilting her glasses back a few degrees. "Oh?"

"After raising me, Mom got pretty good about locking things." She jerked a webbed thumb toward the same large windows at the ballroom's far end. Rain pattered against the panes.

Rune brushed some crumbs of shrimp breading from her rusty throat fluff. "You spent a lot of time climbing in windows?"

"No, but baby-me tried to fall out of a few." Shrugging, Kylie tossed another shrimp into her muzzle.

The brown bat blinked, as if that was a really normal statement for someone to make and she expected more. Then she nodded. "I'm happy you didn't. The show has been super good for Karl."

"Good how?"

"Lots of ways, I guess. He leveled up!" She squeaked a snicker. "Made some new friends. Learned tech stuff for the podcast. Had people listen to him for the first time."

"You didn't listen to him before?"

"Well, yeah. But bats listen to everybody." Her ears wiggled. Those glasses moved again.

Kylie decided the bat was pretty cool. Even if she had to share the shrimp with her. She'd have to get twice as much shrimp next time she had a bunch of lunatics over to rummage through her house.

"Can we find someplace to wash up? I've got grease on my wings now and I don't want to touch all your family heirlooms like this."

"You could just not touch them at all."

"Wouldn't be much of an investigation."

Kylie directed her to the bathroom in the guest suite. Upon returning, she found the group had unearthed a dozen busts of various species—cartoon proportions with unsettling realistic details. She smiled as Max, Sarah, and Shane parade them in front of her.

"Who would buy these?" The rabbit studied a three-quarter scale ceramic bust of hers species, the finish only somewhat chipped.

"How should I know?" Kylie cursed whatever weirdo relation had bought these creepy clay heads and also whoever hadn't smashed them the first chance they got. "They're probably older than all of us added up."

"But what are they for?" Sarah offered her the rabbit one, which she did not accept.

"I don't think they're for anything." Shane attempted to imitate the snarl on a cougar bust. "I think they just are."

Max arranged the remainder of them in a neat line on the bar, then considered them for a moment and turned them all to face each other.

The otter reminded herself that this could be a lot weirder. Old junk like this could be found at a garage sale. Maybe a two on the crazy scale. A little part of her wanted them to find proof of the supernatural, naturally. That would be the opposite of showing her family was a bunch of crackpots. With a little luck, this would be the weirdest thing they found.

Rune wandered back into the room. "Why are the windows in your bathroom crazy thick?"

"What?" Kylie eeled around to face her.

"The windows." The bespectacled bat clicked her tongue and pointed back at the guest suite. "The glass sounds like it's about a meter deep."

"That can't be right." She looked back toward the other guests.

Rune rubbed a damp wing on her shirt. "It could be some kind of acoustic trick, but it's super weird. Probably worth investigating."

Kylie winced. Enough investigating was already going on. The rain was still coming down outside, though, so maybe nobody would notice.

But, across the ballroom, Sarah's ears were already up.

Karl turned to her, horn-cam still blinking. "What'd she say?"

The bunny lifted a paw. "Something about a super weird bathroom."

A nervous chuckle bubbled up from the otter. She tried to think of something to distract everybody with, but figured pretending to faint would make her seem more insane, not less.

The siblings and Karl picked their way back through the sea of boxes toward Rune, who led them straight to the suspicious bathroom.

Max drifted to her side like a two-meter cloud of fluff and reassurance. Instead of using his gigantic strength to pick up all their guests and carry them to the living room to watch a movie, he offered her a resigned shrug.

With a low and bitter chitter, Kylie waddled after the crowd. Movie night was spiraling out of control.

The expedition trooped through the hallway and into the guest suite. By the time she caught up to them, everybody had crowded into the bathroom. It was not a super weird bathroom. It had nice shell motif on the white tiles. The windows looked like very normal privacy windows, all rippled glass like a disturbed pond. Sunlight shone in, with the faint shapes of water droplets running down them.

Rune sat on the sink. Sarah looked around, hands folded. Karl was grinning at himself in the mirror on horn-cam. Shane had wandered into the spacious linen closet.

Kylie lifted a webbed paw at the far end of the room. "Those windows?"

"Yeah." Rune shrugged, then clicked her tongue at the windows. "All three of them sound super deep. Like a meter."

All three windows looked like three quite ordinary, if large, glass panes. The wavy texture prevented anyone from seeing in, since they were on ground level. It wasn't frosted glass, just the plain kind, so abstract shapes presented the full colors of the woods outside. Basically, they looked like the glass blocks hip people used to separate their kitchens from their dining rooms, just bigger. Everybody watched raindrops trace down them, like some kind of out-of-focus noir film.

Eyes half-lidded with vague incredulity, Shane lashed his tail. "How can the windows be that thick? They only go outside."

Prancing delicately over the seashell-lidded toilet, she balanced on the edge of the tub and tapped a wing finger on the glass, which made a deep ring. "Because the wall is a meter thick?"

Sarah's ears lifted at Kylie. "Does this bathroom stay really warm in the winter?"

The otter blinked, unsure. "Not that I noticed? But I only come here when people are using the other bathrooms." With only three people in the house, that almost never happened. But it sounded less crazy than her explained how she'd made sure to use all the bathrooms at least once while moving in, as a sort of challenge to herself.

Karl peered over them, horn-cam capturing the scene. "Could it be a window into another dimension? Existing outside conventional space-time?"

The otter felt the crazy-meter rising and blurted out the first reasonable solutions she could think of. "It's probably just pipes."

Everybody turned to look at her.

Reverting to classroom protocol, Sarah raised a paw. "Pipes?"

"Yeah! Water pipes." Her brain shuffled through a very small stack of architectural knowledge. "Pressed against the glass, so they sound huge to echolocation."

Ears wiggling in thought, Rune casually cartwheeled to hang from the shower rod by her feet. "Pretty sure that's not what's going on."

With a series of polite grunts, Max squeezed to the far end of the bathroom and stood in the tub. He pressed a triangular ear to the wall. "I don't hear any pipes."

Kylie forced herself to smile, then saw in the mirror how manic she looked. Her acting skills were getting rusty. "Well, that was a dead end. Back to movie night?"

Spinning by from one foot's grip to another, Rune examined the window sill. "Unless we can find a way into the wall."

Karl bounced, shaking dust from the light fixtures. "My dad has a sledgehammer."

Shane shrugged. "The garden shed probably has something we can break through a wall with."

"No!" The otter slapped her tail on the sink cabinet. "You are not demolishing my house."

Sarah raised her paw again.

Everybody looked at her, the pressure of which caused her to hesitate. Her ears dropped. Her hand stayed up.

Likewise falling into classroom etiquette, Max pointed to her.

The rabbit puffed up, then made complex gestures. "When I run into problems like this in caves, I sometimes can solve them with math. Measuring."

"So you need a tape measure?" Her brother leaned against a wall, vaguely disappointed.

One paw smoothed the fur of her long ears. "I usually just use a rope."

Max squeezed past everyone again, then returned with a coil of extension cord so ancient it had cloth insulation.

The rhino studied the diamond-patterned fabric with beady eyes. "Aren't those a fire hazard?"

"Only if you plug them in." He handed one end to Karl.

After comparing the inside of the bathroom to the hallway outside it, Sarah compared the two lengths. She shrugged at the group, holding uneven lengths of cord. "About a meter off."

"This place was added to a bunch of times. I'm sure it's just the outside that's jagged in or something."

The rhino walked around the corner and reappeared on the small porch facing the bathroom windows from the outside. Her mom had called it the smoking porch. The red LED of his horn-cam glowed in the rain. He reappeared a second later. "That wall is completely flat." He jerked a heavy thumb toward the row of windows in the hallway parallel to the mystery wall. "The windows look the same as these, except they're that wavy glass."

Sara bundled the extension cord into a neat coil. "What's that mean?"

Shane shrugged. "Optical illusion?"

Karl tapped his fingertips together. "An extra-dimensional space?"

Rune scratched her chin and dangled herself from a light fixture. "Or it's built to fool people."

Kylie groaned. Much as she hoped it was proof of the supernatural, she also hoped it wasn't stuffed with bodies or something.

Max sniffed the wall.

Conflict squeaked inside the lutrine. She refrained from asking why he was encouraging this, since she was in the habit of prodding him into investigating the unknown. "What are you smelling?"

"A draft is coming out of this seam in the wall." The husky flicked out a pocket knife, snapped it open with a flick of his clawed thumb, and gingerly slipped the blade into a gap in the wood paneling.

The flustered otter flung her arms in the air. "Don't stab the house!"

The guests, meanwhile, looked at each other with obvious delight, except for Shane who only smirked.

"It's just open space…" He ran the blade up along the seam, then heard a clatter. "Found a latch, I think." Prying the crack just a little wider, he stuck a claw in it. In a silvery glint, the knife clacked shut and vanished into his pocket. As he slipped the rest of his claws in position, his cool blue eyes flicked back to everybody else. "I'm going to open it."

The rhino giggled with glee and checked that his horn-cam was still recording. "Okay, ready!"

His powerful shoulders rippled under his t-shirt as he pulled the panel back. With the crunch of forgotten dust, a door-sized section of the wall came cleanly away. A thin wooden dowel bounced out and rolled into the hallway. He pulled the paneling free, revealing a dark space inside. Dust shook off every surface, rattled free by the opened door. It cascaded down like a thousand tiny waterfalls and hit the old floorboards to form a hazy wave that pushed inextricably out into the hallway.

As the others crept past him to peer inside, Max leaned the chunk of wall against another wall.

Kylie's heart raced. The world closed in. She melted back as everybody pressed forward. This whole night had been a current sweeping here to this moment when everybody realized what a bunch of nutcases her entire family line had been.

Big fuzzy hands settled on her shoulders.

She looked up at him. Then she chanced looking ahead.

The space within hunched under the weight of an insane past. Shelves bowed under jars of briny liquid, strange shapes suspended within. Scribbled maps, drawings of skittering creatures, and blurry photos hung tacked to the walls, strung together with pale string and a heavy mist of spiderwebs.

"Whoa." Sarah blinked, ears up.

"Cool!" Karl balled up his fists in joy.

"Huh." Shane stretched to see over the brown bat.

"Told you." Rune unfolded a wing into the dusty space, scything through countless cobwebs to tink a tiny claw on the glass. "Thickest windows ever."

~ ~ ~

On the porch, Kylie and Max waved their guests off. Wind hissed through unseen leaves. Bugs chirped in the woods. The red glow of taillights flickered between the tree trunks, vanishing in the direction of town.

The husky rolled back and forth on his feet, making the deck boards creak. Just as she started to wonder if he was trying to wear out the porch, he sighed. "So."

She raised an eyebrow at him. "So?"

"So..." His muscled arms extended in front of him in a restless stretch. "Remember how you were the social one in this relationship?"

She propped her hands on her hips. "What's that supposed to mean?"

He leaned on the railing and looked out over the moonlit forest. "Back in Hollywood, you were always charming people, chatting them up, even though we were just the kids on the cast."

Watching him, the otter nodded. "Okay."

"But here..." He waved a thick paw between the manor and the town. "...you're suspicious of everybody."

A sharp laugh escaped her throat. "Because I was cool and a little bit famous there! Here, I'm a feature in the roadside freak show." She leaned beside him on the railing and put on her best carnival barker voice. "Come pay a nickel and see the craziest family of otters on the Eastern Seaboard, just north of the demonic barbecue smoker and the cafe built at a 20 degree angle."

He sniffed, amused. "Well, yeah. People are going to whisper stupid rumors if you never let anybody in."

Riding a swell of pettiness, she stuck out her tongue. "I don't like weirdos poking through my weird family's weird junk."

He smiled at her, then tilted his head back at the house. "Rudderbutt, I have cleared out and sorted so much weird junk in this house."

"You don't count." She wiggled a little closer and rubbed her tail on the back of his thigh. "I trust you."

Wagging, he leaned in and kissed the side of her head. Then, arms resting once more on the railing, he spread his hands toward the night sky. "You can trust other people too."

"But they're showing up for the weird junk!" She jabbed a webbed finger at the road their friends had departed on.

The dog's eyes narrowed with patient amusement. "I'm talking about letting people into your life, not just your big spooky house."

"I know…" A drawn-out groan trailed out of, leaving her slumped atop the "But if I let them in, they'll see all the junk I haven't sorted out. What if it's scary or makes them see me differently?"

He nodded. "That can happen. But everybody has junk they're dealing with."

"I guess." She flicked away a moth that landed on her arm.

"What do you think they thought of you and all your weird junk?"

"Rune was cool about it. Sarah was nice, but she's always nice. Shane was a pain in the tail, but we already knew that. Karl's, well, Karl."

"Yeah. It's good press for the blog at least. Gives the fans something to chew on."

"You sound like Mom."

"Your mom knows what she's talking about." He rubbed his paw pads together, the faint moisture from the rain reflecting the deck light. "Though she could stand more social contact too."

"Definitely. She's going a little stir-crazy, and not just from ignoring that aliens exist." She rolled her eyes, then drifted into quiet thought for a couple seconds. "Guess it's easier to see when other people aren't sorting out their weird junk."

The dog nodded.

She hugged his arm and nuzzled his shirt sleeve. "You're pretty smart for a big oaf, Maxie."

He rested his chin atop her head, whiskers brushing along her ears. "Trying not to get typecast."

Squeezing her boyfriend close, Kylie peered out into the dark landscape of Bourn Holt. The outbuildings stood as wild frontiers of unsorted junk. Behind her, the house loomed like the past. But, with a fluffy boyfriend to hold, a cool mom somewhere upstairs, and friends just as weird as herself down in town, it felt a little more like home.

An Otter-Body Experience

STRANGEVILLE (TUE/8ᴘ)

S03E15 "Serge in Value": A coin collector turns any who wrong him into rare coins from their birth year. Cassie accidentally spends Serge and has to track him down.

I

Alone with her in the laundry room, Max was blowing his girlfriend's mind.

"Maxie, you're magical!" She chittered, wiggling in place at his impressive performance. "How are you even doing that? I didn't even think that was possible."

Her mother poked her head in the door of the laundry room, where it branched off from the kitchen, a piece of toast in hand. "What are you two doing in here?"

"He's folding a fitted sheet." The younger otter flailed gestures at him, her pretty sundress dancing in waves like a breezy meadow. "We have to keep him."

Laura rolled her eyes and headed out into the living room.

Seated on the floor, he placed another folded bedsheet into the laundry basket.

The laundry room was T-shaped, branching off the kitchen. A washer, dryer, and sink lined its far wall. A small counter and some shelves filled the rest of the small space. Nestled at the center of what they'd reclaimed of Bourn Manor, it didn't have any windows and so electric lights hummed faintly, just loud enough to register with canine ears.

With large, careful paws, he continued folding linens. "I'm home all day, you know. I'd put in your laundry." He checked that his girlfriend's mom wasn't stopping by at that moment. His voice dropped to a whisper: "I help make it dirty."

Her front half inside the dryer, the otter snickered as she gathered the last clothes from inside it. "Nah, that'd be weird."

The husky tilted his head. "Why is it weird?" He sat cross-legged, his knee against the metal of the washing machine. The sleek modern appliances shone in brushed steel contrast to the outdated decor of the dim laundry room, lit by a single clear lightbulb, it's ancient filament glowing. Between it and the dryer, the room felt noticeably warm under his thick husky fur.

"Let me have my secrets, Maxie." Kylie stood. Her lutrine body, clad in that thin green-and-yellow sundress, contorted into a sultry double-curve, hand on one hip. Her other hand dumped clothes into the basket to be folded.

The ionized smell of static electricity crackled in the air, backed by the rich scents of laundry soap and hot fabric. The dog's nose sifted through them, finding the more subtle scent of his girlfriend too. "You have much better secrets than 'my clothes get dirty when I wear them.'" He continued matching socks, which was made both easier and harder by her wild variety of sock. "You're my girlfriend. It's not like I've never seen your dirty clothes."

"I don't know... I guess I want to stay mysterious and seductive to you." She sighed as she bent to pluck a stray pair of panties off the floor. Her sundress twirled. "Not all gross and boring."

He patted her shoulder. "Except I love you. That's not gross and boring."

"You big sap." Her clawed fingertips traced his hand. "Love you too."

His tail swished on the tile floor. "So you're okay with me doing your laundry then?"

Making a noise like a creaky door, she delicately punched clothes into an overfull hamper until they stopped spilling out, then stopped in thought. "Ask me in a couple years."

A woof of laughter left his throat. "Oh, so we'll still be dating?"

"I'm not letting you go." She started chucking wet clothes from the washer into the dryer. "You know how to fold fitted sheets."

Phone in her paw, Laura waddled into the room. "That's the spirit, kiddo."

The dog shrugged. "We have a very laundry-centered relationship."

"All the best long-term relationships are based on linens." Somewhere, through a tinny speaker, a crowd laughed. "Or so I'm told." The same unseen crowd hooted and catcalled.

Kylie jabbed an accusing finger at her mother's mobile phone. "You promised to delete that sitcom soundboard app!"

"I know. It's just so much easier than actually writing for television." Laura pressed another button and her phone made a crowd's worth of sad, sympathetic clucks and murmurs.

"Mom!" The younger otter swiped halfheartedly at the device. "I will revoke your phone privileges."

Laura lifted the device out of her daughter's reach. "I revoke your privilege-revocation privileges."

Max glanced at the phone, just above eye-level. He could intervene, but didn't want to be pushy. That was a bad look for a guy bigger than everybody else. Besides, he was thinking. He wasn't the quickest on the uptake with personal issues, but Laura usually just snarked at her daughter; these shenanigans were atypical. Probably a side-effect of being cooped up in the house. She used to go out with friends, or even on dates, but both had stopped when she moved across the continent. Maybe she needed social contact beyond the two of them. He tried to think of a way to mention that, again without seeming pushy. One didn't spring to mind.

As a means of truce, Laura stuffed the phone in her pocket. Then she looked around the room. "Kylie dear, you seem to be doing an awful lot of laundry. Is something the matter?"

"Yeah, Mom. I've been having these weird responsible feelings." Kylie reached for another fabric softener sheet, but found only an empty box. She hopped for a top shelf, but couldn't reach the new box.

Much as he liked watching her bounce, he lifted her up. Her curvy body provided just the right kind of handholds to grip her by the waist.

With an elegant arch of her entire body, she plucked the box off the shelf. Once she was back on the floor, she popped up on her tip-toes and kissed him on the cheek. "Thank you, Maxie."

He wagged.

Laura hit another sound-effect button. Mawkish swooning filled the room.

Kylie groaned. "Mother."

"I'm going. I'm going." Laura waved a webbed paw. "I'm off to the gardening store."

Max's ears flicked. Laura's preferred flower store was a big nursery in the next town, and travel time alone would keep her out of the house for more than an hour. He turned his attention back to Kylie, plans beginning to form as he watched her sway like seagrass in her simple sundress.

"They have a sale on water plants. Need something for the reflecting pool." She waddled off and cut through the dining room. Her keys jingled. "Don't burn down the house while I'm gone. I'm still looking for a good insurance policy."

Her daughter grumbled. "It'd just go out when it hit all the pools in the east wing."

"See that it does." The front door opened and shut. A few seconds later, her car started up and puttered away.

Kylie shook her head. "She's so weird."

"Of course she is." The dog chuckled and folded a pair of jeans. "She's basically an older version of you."

"Hey! I'm no Mom-clone, mister." She squawked and shook a wet sock at him. "Are you just a smaller version of your mom?"

Max looked back and forth between his broad shoulders. "If anything, my mom is a smaller version of me."

She propped her fists on her hips. "How'd that happen, anyway?"

"My paternal grandmother is a timber wolf." He held up a paw at grandmother height, far above Kylie's head.

"That's what every husky in Hollywood says so they can get wolf roles." Her thick tail bopped his knee while she reached to pull clothes from ever-deeper in the washing machine. "You're probably just a mutant."

"Then you're dating a mutant." He placed the last of her dry clothes in the basket in a neat stack, then stood.

"Well, thanks for using your mutant powers to help me." Her clawed hands made lightning-shooting gestures at the folded laundry.

The dog shrugged. "I like being useful. It's why I let you climb on me to reach things."

"You're not just a mobile step-ladder." She folded his arms around her, then nuzzled his chest. "You're my boyfriend."

He nodded and squeezed her supple otter body. Her breasts pressed to him, as streamlined as the rest of her.

She wiggled up him to tuck her sleek head under his chin. "I'd want you as my boyfriend even if you couldn't fold fitted sheets."

He wagged. He still felt gigantic and intimidating sometimes, but not around her. She sure seemed to like that he was powerful. She trusted him. He smiled.

Kylie smiled back at him, bounced up to kiss him, and then spied something at the bottom of the washer and eeled from his arms to grab it. In a single, fluid motion, she oozed over the lip of the washing machine and into it. Her rump waggled, feet off the floor, as the otter struggled to reach some garment at the back of the device. That powerful tail swayed and lashed, sticking straight backward in the air while she sought her prey.

With a playful wag, the husky placed a paw about halfway up her tail. "Well, hello there."

"Hey!" She struggled in the tight space. "What do you think you're doing?"

"Just enjoying your rudder-butt, rudderbutt." He caressed the ample curve of her bottom through the think cotton of the sundress.

Her legs kicked at air. "Oh, so Mom leaves the house and you just start groping me?"

He woofed a laugh. "You grope me all the time!"

"Well, yeah." She echoed from inside the washer drum. One webbed foot pressed off his leg as she tried to navigate inside the machine. "Otter paws are naturally grabby."

He rolled his eyes, then noticed the hem of the dress as her inclining tail lifted it higher. "Are you not wearing panties?"

Her tail dropped, and a paw lashed up to gesture at him. "I'm outta clean ones!"

Gripping her by the tail, he raised it, exposing her naked crotch. The faint pink of her flesh, the creamy white of her underbelly fur, the green and yellow of her dress: it all painted a pretty picture. His free hand traced down her tail, her rump, her inner thigh…

"You scoundrel!" Her powerful tail wiggled, not quite breaking his grasp, just enough to object to the teasing.

His fingertips traced up and down her slit. Teasing claws traced along the thin fur of her pubic mound. Tender paw pads worked to spread her lips.

Her toes splayed. Her tail trembled in his grasp. Squeaky whimpers echoed into the room. "N-no fair, Maxie! Let me outta the washing machine if we're gonna get dirty."

The husky chuckled and had mercy on his lover. Gently, he angled her down and free of the washer. He took extra care not to squish her boobs against the side or bump her head on the central pillar. As her feet reached the floor, he watched as the sundress fell to a modest position. "Better?"

She twirled to face him and poked him in the chest with one webbed finger. "You great hulking horndog! Teasing an innocent little otter while she's trying to do responsible adult things!"

"I'll give you an adult situation." He pulled her close, cradling her slender curves as he deepened the kiss. The cotton of her sundress ran soft under the pads of his fingers as he slid a paw up her belly to cup her breast, squeezing it through the flimsy barrier. She arched into his touch with the sweetest little mewl, and he rumbled in satisfaction to find she wasn't wearing a bra, either.

"Max…" She breathed against his muzzle, only to hiss in pleasure and cling tighter to him as he brushed his thumb across her hidden nipple. "Maxie, we're supposed to be getting the clothes clean, not making them all wrinkly."

He blinked, hesitated, hand lifting just a little off her chest.

"I didn't say stop, silly dog." She guided his hand up, across her throat, to where her sundress tied behind her neck. "Help me with this?"

His large paws carefully unfastened the back of her dress. He lifted it over her head, figuring the girliness of a garment was inversely proportionate to its durability. With care, he placed the garment atop the washer.

Arms raised like an Olympic diver about to take a plunge, she wiggled proudly in her nudity. What little modesty otters started with had vanished when they'd started dating. Smiling, she draped webbed paws on his chest. "And it's just as well because I need to get changed for work and —oh look— all my clean clothes are right here." She swept a paw at the hamper of clothes he'd folded, then smiled sweetly up at him. "Lucky me."

Reaching forward, he let that smirk draw him in. Even as friends, they hadn't been very shy about touching each other. She'd started it, of course. Otters were pretty handsy with people they liked. But he'd picked it up. Gripping her flanks, he picked her up too, without even bending down.

Surprise chattered from her round muzzle. Her lithe form wriggled, relying on his strength to keep hold of her, even as her feet left the floor.

With little effort, he placed her on the dryer. His whole life, he'd tried not to call attention to his size, his strength. It spooked people. But, with a small and trusting girlfriend, he could show off a bit. It made her wiggle with glee in a way he found very enticing. He knelt before her and nuzzled her knees apart. Following the scent of her arousal, he traced along her sleek thigh fur. His nose bumped the warmth and moisture of her tender slit and he set to licking. The laundry room, warm before, now felt positively hot.

She watched him work with avid interest. Chitters of pleasure rattled through the laundry room. Her hips rocked, testing out positions. Her sleek legs traced over his shoulders and down his back. That powerful tail swept back and forth along his chest.

His tongue danced over her clit in spirals and sweeps. Moisture collected on his chin as it grew all the harder under his attentions. He reached up and pressed the start button. The dryer shook. Either the machine was especially powerful or she hadn't properly balanced the load again. As he contemplated which was more likely, he redoubled his efforts at lapping inside her.

The vibration shook right through the otter and into her moans. "Uh-h-h-h-h-h-h-h…" Her silky folds trembled against his mouth.

Max kept licking. That seemed to be the trick with Kylie. Lucky for both of them, dog tongue lapped the competition. He slipped his tongue as deep as he could into her, trailing along her sensitive walls. Her scent, once obscured by laundry, intoxicated him.

The otter unleashed a squeak like the world's loudest door hinge. Her thighs squeezed on the sides of his head, then bounced up and down. Her feet pressed on his shoulders. That supple body strained against the dryer's control panel, tilting the whole machine back with the force of her orgasm.

Licking along at the same speed, even as his head jostled around by her orgasm, the husky stayed focused. His paws gripped her rump. Best not to let her wiggle off the machine.

Kylie trembled back down onto the shaking dryer. Her arms, legs, and tail fell limp. Her muzzle hung open, breasts rising and falling. After a minute of panting, her eyes opened. She reached down and stroked his ears.

His eyes met hers. His tail wagged. He nuzzled her inner thigh.

Bundled up in the forgotten dress, her phone rattled against the sheet metal lid of the washer.

The canine stood and offered her a paw.

She took it and let him pull her forward. With a lazy grumble, she oozed off the shaking machine and onto her feet. Groping at her balled-up dress, she reached into the limited pocket real estate and drew out her phone. "Huh. Shane wants me to cover for him."

He cocked an ear.

The small lutrine pushed his shoulder. "We have to keep up appearances that it's a functional store." She shoved the phone back into her pocket. "He has some meeting later."

Straightening, the canine gave a deferential nod.

"Aww, hey. Are you sure?" She groped the front of his jeans, now quite tented. "Washing machine's still going." One webbed paw patted the appliance. "I bet you could bend me over it…" Her teeth traced over her lower lip as she wiggled in front of him. "…I bet you could finish before it does."

A blush flared up under his snowy fur. It was really tempting, but he didn't want to keep her from work. "We can do something tonight, rudderbutt." He traced a paw along her jawline. "I don't want you to be late."

"Normally, I wouldn't care very much, but Shane needs me to cover the last few hours of his shift. Has some kind of meeting he has to go to. And then he and Sarah are getting conscripted for some kind of family chore bonanza. They're replacing all the grippy traction stickers on the cave walkways this afternoon."

He nodded. Since defecting from her position as Cindy's minion, Sarah had found Kylie a superior friend. Which made sense: Kylie was pretty great. "I'll walk you down."

Smiling up sweetly, perhaps still a bit euphoric from orgasm, she took his much larger paw in hers. She bounced up to nuzzle his cheek. "Aww, you just wanna be with me?"

He wiped her juices from his whiskers. "That and I owe Karl a duel in Mana Clash."

"I see." She made dramatic, little card-dealing gestures. "Being a wizard is your real priority."

He threw an arm around her slim shoulders. "You weren't complaining about my magic a minute ago."

~ ~ ~

A spring evening rolled in on a light mist, spreading through the streets of Windfall. In the town's only game shop, a small spaced crammed with comic books, Max stood, playing a card game with the excitable rhino. Board games and role-play books lined the walls, along with the occasional promotional sword. Mylar-bagged snacks perched on shelves overhead, like balloons strewn with exotic lettering. Glitter dice sparkled in a gumball machine. Before the husky spread a wizard duel's worth of Mana Clash cards on the countertop.

Behind the counter, a plump and cheery rhino watched him with a mixture of trembling glee and nervous anticipation. The card stock rectangles nearly vanished in his armored hands. His dark eyes flicked between his options and the table situation, mapping out options.

A brown bat in a purple "This Side Up" tank top dangled from an exposed pipe on the ceiling. She alternated between pushing down her large glasses and quietly munching sour gummy worms. "I seriously never see cards this old."

Max glanced down at the cards; his looked faded, not due to abuse, but older printing technology. "I've been out of the loop for a few years." He studied his hand. He should've added more Mana-Bird Eggs to the deck. "And I mostly got cards when I was little."

Her shirt stirred by the nearby ceiling fan, Rune looked him down and up. "Hard to imagine you ever being little."

"Yeah, it gets harder for me to imagine every year." He played another realm card, then summoned a grey-muzzled constable. Then he tapped a giant cowering acid-hound to sniff out more realm cards. The dog's thick knuckles knocked on the glass countertop. "Done."

Blinking, Karl paused to study the card, like a museum curator studying some long-misplaced exhibit. Half the cards Max played were printed before the rhino entered kindergarten, bought with the dog's grade-school allowance. The rhino squinted at the tiny text. "These textured backgrounds make it hard to read."

"Back when the game only had 300 cards, you didn't need to read as much." In the canine's pocket, his phone buzzed. He grabbed it, thinking it might be another Howl notification about an excess of BBQ ribs. But, alas, the screen showed a text from his mom. Another text about how nice it would be if he moved back to Montana. He sympathized: she didn't like having him so far away. Family was important. Kylie and Laura were family to him too, though, and they needed him more. Plus, they didn't push him around about it. He stuffed the phone back into his jeans pocket and tried to get his thoughts back on the game. His opponent didn't seem to have noticed, still reading the walls of tiny text on his cards.

Dangling by one foot, the bat finessed a lemon-shaped coin purse from a cargo pocket. The cuffs of her pants clung in place, elasticized, as she plucked out a fiver and fluttered it on the counter like a falling leaf.

The rhino popped the cash register drawer and glanced to her. "What'll it be, Rune?"

"More worms, please." She swung back and forth happily. "And could you get—?"

"—whatever one feels like it has the most sour powder." He dropped the packet of candies in her wing fingers. "Already had it set aside."

With a peep of excitement, she bit the bag open before he finished counting her change.

Max smiled. He tried not to come during crowded times, but Karl's friends seemed pleasant enough. "Your name's Rune? That's pretty cool."

Her ears flicked up, bashful. "It's Prunella, actually. But, yeah, everybody calls me Rune."

The rhino snorted, grinning. "Except her family."

Max raised an eyebrow. The three sat in silence for a couple seconds, accompanied only by the whir of an air conditioner.

Surrendering hope the topic might be bypassed, she rolled her eyes and fidgeted with the packet of gummy worms. "They still call me Prunie."

After a moment's consideration, he decided a commiserative nod was the right reaction. "That's rough."

She offered an upside-down shrug. "You are who you are, ya know? Your family has seen your whole version history, so it's hard to become someone else to them."

The canine nodded. "I'm in the middle of that too."

Rune smiled and tossed a sour gummy worm into her muzzle, then caught it with smooth skill. Traces of sugar lingered on her fuzzy nose.

With a quiet cackle, Karl slapped down another card: a giant serpent. "Okay, I cast Sand Spewer and I blow up that realm." He poked a heavy digit at one of Max's cards.

Surveying his options for a moment, the canine then picked up a card. "I sacrifice a gadget to Mirror-Polisher. That redirects the destruction effect to your only desert-type realm. Since your Sand Spewer has desert-home, it dies."

The pudgy rhino straightened, one of the few town residents tall enough to look Max in the eye. Not that he usually did: he still seemed dazzled by his TV heroes emergence into real life. "Desert-home?" His heavy fingers poked at his phone as he searched for the term.

The canine's blunt claw hovered over the card text. "It's what the game called that ability, ten years ago. It comes up in some of the tie-in novels."

"You're in trouble now, Karl." The bat giggled. "Somebody finally has more arcane knowledge of the rules than you."

After a blink of amazement, the shop attendant put away his phone. "I still have Gorgak, the Nameless One." His thick grey finger poked the card, though not enough to bend it. "His ability is you can't name him for the purposes of your spells."

"He has a name, though." Max peered down at the card. "It's Gorgak."

"A-a-ah!" The rhino waggled a thick finger with obvious pride. "You're naming him." He started turning cards sideways. "I attack with him and all my mold-demons…"

"Why are you running sand serpents and mold-demons?" Max turned a paw palm-up at the cards. "They hate each other in the lore."

"They do?" Karl stared at them around his horn.

"Well, yeah. Think about it." He tapped a paw pad beside on of the monsters. "Mold-demons serve Quag, Queen of the Mindsuckers. She wants to flood their deserts…" He shrugged, figuring the other gamers knew the rest.

"Huh." The rhino scratched his chin. "See, I just put them together because their abilities work with one another."

Rune nibbled another gummy worm. "This is fascinating."

Fun facts aside, Karl's Gorgak monster wasn't a big problem, but it was one he had no answer for. It couldn't be intercepted or targeted, so he now had a countdown until he lost the game. Max's main trick was a good defense until he could bring out powerful monsters later. The old cards he relied on just weren't made for this situation. He used his Beguiling Bard to distract the mold-demons, but had to take the rest of the damage, hoping he'd get a lucky draw soon.

Up the street, a familiar putter rattled. An amphibious car rolled into view through the front windows. With a jingle and a bang, Kylie exploded from the vehicle and burst into the game shop with the tinkle of a tiny bell. "Maxie! We've got a lead!"

The husky's ears popped up. He glanced to Karl, trying to think of a polite way to excuse himself from the game.

His opponent broke out into a giant grin and mouthed the word "a lead." Cards in one hand, he flipped him a thumbs-up with the other.

With a deep breath, the canine turned back to his girlfriend.

Eeling around a display of potion-themed energy drinks, Kylie popped up beside him. "C'mon!" She took him by the paw and, feet scrabbling on the tile floor, towed him from the store.

"I guess I'll see you later, Karl." The two-meter-tall dog amiably allowed himself to be dragged along. He tipped a finger at the game. "Watch my cards, would you?"

Blinking, Karl gave a confused wave. "Umm, sure!" He began delicately scooping up the cards. "Later!"

Glancing to her friend, the bat dangled in surprise and whispered. "Does that happen a lot?"

As Max and Kylie hurried out the door, the rhino shrugged. "I guess that's how being famous works."

A scattering of clouds did little to hide the sun. Light winds traipsed in from the sea, unfurling the alien-faced banners strapped to the sides of a kiosk selling novelty balloons at inflated prices. On the street, a cluster of tourists with dowsing rods followed unseen forces and the advice of their paid instructor, who did her best to steer them out of traffic. Even in Windfall, motorists had limited patience for unseen forces.

With a sudden stop, the lutrine twirled to face him. "Wait a sec. Are you sure you wanna skip out on your game? I kinda dragged you away." She peered back through the game store window. "I can scout it out first, then text you."

Max shook his head. "No, no. I should go and make sure you don't jump down a mineshaft."

Chittering with pique, she wiggled in front of him. "Why would I jump down a mineshaft?"

He shrugged. "I'm not saying you won't have a reason. I'm just saying you might jump." Leaning in, the dog murmured beneath the drone of street hubbub. "Mind telling me where we're going?"

"Okay, so!" She rubbed her paws together. "Shane's boss called and had him attend the Chamber of Commerce meeting. That's why he needed me to cover for him."

His triangular ears flicked up. "Isn't Shane's boss also your boss?"

"Shane's my boss. This guy can't be my boss if I've never met him. Anyway, while Shane's there eating all their snacks, he hears about this weird little chunk of land they're dealing with." The short lutrine shoved a phone in his muzzle. It displayed a map. "Up in the hills. Guess who owned it?"

The dog blinked. "…I know, like, six people in this town."

She swatted his arm. "Joe! Alien handyman and property speculator." She chittered with pride at her discovery and yanked on his wrist. "What'd ya wanna bet it's where he crashed his spaceship?"

Allowing himself to be hauled along, the dog nodded. "If he had a spaceship, wouldn't he have left in it?"

Wiggles of impatience undulated up the otter before him. "Not once he totaled it."

"Ah yes." He nodded. "Why fix it? Much easier to punch a hole in the fabric of reality."

An elderly mink tottered by, trailed by the scent of musk and medicated cream. Hefting her bag of groceries, she paid absolutely no mind to their conversation about extraterrestrials. She tottered into a small apartment building. Vinyl howls from the Newfoundland Dogs Choir roared from within. Reality seemed fine, at least by Windfall standards.

Rounding on her Amphicar, the otter vibrated with excitement. "You comin' or not?"

Rolling his eyes, he found himself smiling. "With you, always."

"Great!" She crammed him into her tiny car.

Max squeezed into the seat, with a complaint from the suspension. An extra seatbelt component shook loose from under the headrest, clattering to his lap. "Why is the car growing additional shoulder straps?" He examined the thick canvas ribbon and tried to clip it into place, but it barely got halfway across his chest. "Are these aftermarket otter seatbelts?"

Kylie shrugged as she slid behind the wheel, clicking the additional belts into place with the careless ease of practice. "Yeah, we're basically torpedoes, so we need extra straps to keep us in. Mom remembered this car was built in the 70s and ordered them online." With a turn of the key, the petite four-cylinder engine sputtered triumphantly to life.

"And what is our target today?" Not for the first time, the husky tried in vain to adjust the seat further back.

"The truth." She threw the boat-car into gear, which obediently scooted into traffic. She squawked the horn at wandering diviners in the roadway, then glanced back to her boyfriend. "Duh."

~ ~ ~

Evening fell slowly on the hills around Windfall. A fine mist lingered in the shade and hollows. Songbirds chirped and flittered, bobbing through the shadowed branches and diving to nab unwary bugs.

Kylie parked on some forgotten gravel road the GPS insisted was nearest to their objective. After prying her boyfriend out of the car, she dragged him into the dense wilderness surrounding the property. In spite of short little otter legs, she noodled her way through the forest. Her streamlined frame offered little for branches to catch on. When she hit a rocky outcropping, she wriggled up it with fluid flexibility.

Her husky boyfriend tromped after her, mulching the undergrowth with every stride. "Rudderbutt, should we really rifle through the possessions of the guy who almost killed us?"

The otter rounded on her boyfriend and counted on her fingers. "He's in another dimension. He's not going to find out. He made it pretty clear he's not coming back." Then she threw her paws in the air. "Who better than us? We have some idea what's in there."

Max nodded. "Ah yes: as the people who ruined his life, we are the most qualified to steal his stuff."

"We didn't ruin his life." She wiggled past a low tree branch, then fished a single-serving of jerky from her fishing vest, ripped it open with her teeth, and tossed it to him. "He hated it here."

The canine snapped up the treat in mid-air, with a grateful wag. "We can't be the first people to notice alien handymen." His powerful muzzle contorted to speak politely as he munched on the leathery beef. "Don't you think we should check in with some kind of authority?"

Kylie stuck the wrapper back in her pocket. "What authorities? Sooner or later, tourists are going to find this." She jerked her thumb toward town. "You wanna just leave it to some wandering lunatic?"

"You're right." Swallowing the last of the jerky, he rolled his eyes. "Better left to us local lunatics."

Her stride swayed more than usual. "Maxie, put yourself in my shoes…"

Amused, he sniffed. "Seems like a good way to ruin your shoes."

"Gotta prove the supernatural, Maxie!" She answered in a show tune sing-song voice, traipsing around a tree trunk. "Restore my family honor and blame everything on Joe!"

"Shouldn't be too hard, since he's in another dimension and can't defend himself." The husky nodded. "I just have this other goal where we don't get poisoned by some alien snack."

Sputtering, she straightened her posture. "I don't put random things in my mouth!"

"No comment, but you could get poisoned by touching it." Those pretty blue eyes narrowed at the distance. "Or irradiated."

She shrugged pointedly at him. "Why would he eat radioactive food?"

"I have no idea. That's my point." He lifted a wide white paw toward her. "We know very little about Joe's biology, except that he had no particular resistance to pepper spray."

Without missing a stride, she swung a fantom bludgeon. "Or blunt-force trauma." Flowing atop a half-buried boulder, she spun to face him at eye level. "I'm still proud of you every time I walk by that bent stairway rail."

"Thanks." He smiled and kissed her, then lifted her by the armpits and into a hug. "I tried my best to straighten it. You think your mom noticed?"

The river otter groaned as she was set down. "She's trying very hard to not notice any of this."

The pair continued, trudging through forest and gossamer fog. A setting sun glowed like embers on the dew of the trees. Breaking through one more patch of trees, they arrived at a small Quonset hut, slightly buried in the side of a hill. Its interlocking steel plates shone dull with age, forming a half-tube structure. Patches here and there had been expertly touched up with silver rust-stop paint. Moss draped it. A large tree, as big around as Max, grew against one side, carefully manicured over half a century to not damage the front wall. Here and there, the concrete pad it sat on had been expertly patched. A steel door, painted drab gray, stood bolted and locked, also without a speck of rust.

The lutrine stood, pondering the structure for a moment. "You know, for an amoral alien killing machine, Joe was a pretty good handyman."

Max nodded. "Yeah, your mom's roof came out really nice."

She nodded back. "Guess he had time to learn."

"Next question…" The husky leveled a narrow look at his girlfriend as he drew a pair of bolt cutters from his backpack. "You sure this isn't illegal?"

Kylie grunted and shrugged.

With a roll of his eyes, he set them in place and snapped the cheap padlock free with a single flex of his arms.

The door whispered open. Inside, a dark space lay filled with orderly rows of crates and boxes. Here and there, tools hung from racks or propped against walls.

Kylie eeled into the room and started picking up everything she could get her paws on. "Otters have been salvaging lost loot for centuries." She popped open a dusty glass jar and found it full of roofing nails. She set it down and scampered around the Quonset hut, looking for more interesting treasures. "It's the law of the sea."

Max lifted the flap of an ancient cardboard box with a careful claw, then glanced at her. "We're on land."

"Earth's mostly sea, though. I'd say it applies." Her paws settled on a lever, which she pulled a few times before realizing it connected to a jack and not some kind of secret chamber. "I'm related to lawyers, ya know."

He clicked on his flashlight and scanned the top shelves. "Disbarred, I presume, if their legal advice is anything like yours."

"Don't be an old biddy, Maxie." She snatched a drill from a box and cranked it a few times, considering its possible applications in oyster-shucking, then abandoned it. "Being in the same dimension is nine-tenths of the law."

"Fine, but I reserve the right to cancel this expedition if we find anything really dangerous." He shone his flashlight around the gloomy space, glinting through some jars with murky contents. "Or that makes our teeth hurt, like those alien whatsits in his subterranean lab."

"That's how we'll know we're on the right track." With a wiggle of whiskers and hips, she straightened into a heroic pose. "We otters are also expert navigators."

"You're a river otter." He crossed his thick arms. "Don't pretend you're some oceangoing hipster who's never set paw on terra firma."

"Fine, I'll use my extensive land knowledge." She chattered sass at him over the neat stacks of boxes. "Oh look, what do we have over here?" She unfurled a paw at a spider in one corner of the ceiling. "A land crab in its web."

He unleashed a heavy canine sigh, which stirred dust from an upright tool chest. He opened it to find perfect rows of tools, complete down to the smallest ratchet. A tiny, possibly involuntary, nod revealed his approval.

The otter rolled her eyes and misaligned a stack of shingles with her sneaker. It took considerably more effort than she'd expected. For a fleeting moment, she hoped that meant the shingles were magic, but closer examination revealed that shingles are just heavy.

Max turned to look at her, then glanced down at a row of shrink-wrapped wood panels. "Have to admit, I was expecting something spookier. This mostly seems like a normal shed." He scuffed across the concrete floor. "Oh hey. Those new cabinet doors your mom ordered for the kitchen."

"Huh." She crouched down and examined them. Under a thin layer of dust, finished red wood shone. "They came out pretty nice."

The dog rolled his eyes, jerking a thumb toward the front side of a one such door. "What's with otters putting nautili on everything?"

"The nautilus is a noble beast!" Her flashlight shone on him accusingly. "The real question is why you landlubbers put artichokes and pine cones on bedposts instead."

"Ferns, pineapples…" Max sniffed around the dark and cluttered shed. "Victorians went nuts for anything with a Fibonacci sequence."

"Still, good that we found them." Her claw flicked at the clear plastic wrapping on one door. "I think Mom paid a lot for them."

"Oh yeah." He chuckled, examining some lengths of either bone or driftwood. "She's been complaining they never turned up. She thinks Joe is in hiding somewhere, living it up on her sweet, sweet cabinet money."

Kylie's gaze caught on two abstract-patterned strips of fabric, splashed with 90s hues, muted by a thin layer of dust. She picked them up to find they contained a metal core. A chitter of excitement leapt from her muzzle. "Hey! I remember these!"

"What are those?" Max tilted his head to examine them. "Unmarked rulers?"

With a groan, she rolled her eyes and stepped over a stack of new shingles. She swished the straightened bracelets back and forth before him. They felt like the sturdy kind, not the cheap ones that broke after a few tosses across the room to see if they'd latch onto your friends. Idle paws drummed the colorful lengths on his chest. "Were you never a tween, Max?"

"Not physically." He shrugged broad shoulders. "Straight from puppy to adult when I hit middle school."

"They're snap bracelets." She slapped on her wrist, then grinned as it curled snugly into place with a clatter. "They're fun. So fun they got banned from my school."

He watched her peel the bracelet free and whack it back on again. His eyebrow rose. "Because you constantly snapping them was a distraction?"

"That and you can slap them on the unsuspecting." She smacked the band down on his wrist.

The husky studied the band of rainbow cloth wrapped fully around his wrist. "I don't wear a lot of jewelry, aside from my watch." He studied both his hands, watch and bracelet contrasting sharply in their degree of whimsy. "I guess at least it's symmetrical."

"See?" She waggled her matched bracelet under his nose, then spun to spread her paws at the collected junk. "Breaking into an alien's storage shed is already paying off."

His triangular ears perked up. "What's that sound?"

The lutrine bounced up like a buoy. "What sound?"

"High-pitched whine." He swung his heavy muzzle around, seeking the source. "Booby trap?"

Her little ears twitched. All she heard was his breathing, her breathing, and the leaves rustling outside. "What kind of trap would Joe set?"

"Don't know, but he had hundreds of years to think of one." He grabbed her by the shoulder and marched her out of the Quonset hut.

"Hey!" She dropped a can of varnish from the 70s. It clattered to the concrete floor, sloshing, still liquid inside. Her sneakered feet scuffed along after the overreacting dog.

Those pointy ears swiveled. "I still hear it out here." His head whipped from side to side, mouth a thin line. "I think it's coming from us." He lifted the wristband to his ear. His gaze flicked to her. "Is yours—?"

A brilliant flash seared their every nerve.

Max's howl vanished in her own squawk of panic.

Vertigo churned in her stomach as she found herself an alarming distance from the ground. Through blurry vision, she saw the horizon at a wild tilt. Her limbs felt distant. Her tail felt light, her chest heavy, and her whole body plummeted.

A heavy thump later, Kylie found herself sprawled on the ground. Her head throbbed. Her ears rang. Her limbs numbed. "Okay, maybe he did set a booby trap…" The leaves and branches of the forest rattled with a painful clamor. She opened her eyes to an intolerable brilliance, struck through by a tangle of red lines. "Augh!" She threw paws over her face. "Something's wrong with my eyes. It's like kelp's growing in them."

"I see it too." Behind her, she heard him sit up and croak through his words. "I think we're seeing blood vessels."

Her paws gripped the doorframe to help her stand—she looked around, mystified. The door had shrunk. It stood just above eye level now. She squinted at her surroundings, but her nose kept getting in the way of seeing it. She gripped her nose, then noticed her paws. Blocky and white, with blunt claws. "…Max?"

He grumbled through an usually high-pitched growl. "Yes?"

She looked back at a fluffy, monochrome tail. "I don't wanna freak you out, but I may be a dog." Her gaze, still obscured by veins, found a small, hazy figure beside her.

"That's reassuring." Max nodded, studying his webbed paws. "I'm pretty sure I'm an otter. You, specifically."

"Okay." She took a deep breath. "Not going to freak out." Her ears popped up as she realized a quick way to verify if she wasn't in Max's body.

She grabbed her crotch. Pain spiked up from her testicles through her entire body. "Oww!?"

Watching her, he sighed. "Please refrain from punching yourself in my nuts."

"Shut up! I haven't totally figured out what I'm doing yet." She staggered and almost fell over. "And why's everything blue?!"

He shrugged his tiny shoulders. "Because I have blue eyes?"

Pressing massive paws to her eyes, she groaned. "Seriously?"

Max tried to cross his arms, but was impeded by his breasts. "Do I look like an ophthalmologist?"

She grumbled, which came out rather growly. "I'll tell you once I can see."

Wind blew through the leaves. Birds sang in the woods. Crickets chirped in the rustling grass. They sat, breathing and not freaking out, as their vision slowly returned.

"Okay…" He took a deep breath. His webbed paw grasped her fallen flashlight, which still threw a cone of light across the forest floor. "Let's not panic."

"Actually, let's." She barked in his general direction. "This seems like a panic situation." One of her giant paws rose to her chest. "Wait, this is how you sound to yourself? Your entire chest vibrates when you talk."

"It does. That's normal." Propped against the wall of the steel shack, Max sat up, then inhaled and exhaled deeply. "Theory."

"Yes?" Her gigantic fingers ran down her arms, bumping into the abstract-patterned bracelet.

He held up his wrist, clad in identical neon fabric. "The snap bracelets have betrayed us."

She barked a laugh that was only slightly hysterical. "I never thought I'd see the day." Even through blue-tinted vision, she could see he still wore his. "Maybe we should take them off?"

"Hmf." He tugged at it with obvious unfamiliarity toward both hand and bracelet. "Are they always so hard to take off?"

She woofed, then flinched at the unfamiliar sensation of the sound in her vocal cords. "No, you dork. They just pull right off." She pulled at the bracelet on her heavy canine wrist. It wouldn't come free. It felt like the spring steel and turned into cast iron. Her thick, blunt claws scrabbled across it, but found no seam, only a continuous abstract retro pattern. "What the…?"

"Forget about the bracelets for now. Maybe we just suck at motor skills now." Unsteady, he managed to stand with the help of the doorframe. "Maybe something in the shed set them off?"

With a heavy breath, she struggled to her overlarge feet. "How about you figure it out while I stay out here and scream for a bit?"

He paused, then nodded. "Okay." He waddled inside.

Yelling as Max felt pleasingly loud—it made birds scatter from treetops. Walking took more getting used to, but she figured it out. Once she was done pacing in front of the entrance, screaming at the wilderness, she realized the spots had cleared from her vision, though the world remained stubbornly blue. This revealed her own now-colossal hands clearly. After a smidgen more screaming, she got ahold of herself and returned to the shed.

There, she found Max picking up and setting back down a jar of tacks.

She gripped the doorway, finding it had surprising give under her claws. "Any clues?"

"No." He turned to face her and his tail knocked over a bin of paint stir sticks, which he ignored with eyes closed. "Feeling better?"

"Yes." Her hands balled into fists so hard they hurt. She hadn't thought that was possible. "You seem to be taking this pretty well."

Walking toward her, he shrugged, though the motion got out of control and sashayed down his body. "I'm in shock."

Kylie nodded. She was starting to feel better. Probably from the screaming. Always nice to know you can still scream. "Do you need to lie down?" She looked at her enormous dog paws again. "It helps to close your eyes, when the weirdness builds up too much." She took her own advice for a moment, then looked back to him.

"I'm okay." He shook his head so hard his whiskers swished. "Though I'm having trouble with the…" He gestured toward his chest.

"Boob jiggle?" She snickered. It came out like a pant.

"I was going to say 'different weight distribution,' but that is distracting too." He shook his head, ears dipping shyly. "Were these bracelets with anything else? Something that might be controlling them?"

Kylie glanced down at the wristband, then back to the shelf. Only a faint outline in the dust revealed they'd ever been there. "No."

"Hmm." He tried to stroke his chin, but finger webs outsmarted him so he gave up. Again, his eyes slid down to the bracelet on his dainty wrist. He strained to pull it free. It didn't budge.

"Let me try!" Kylie seized on the wristband and yanked, grunting with effort. No effect.

"Stop. Stop." Max waved his tiny paws at her. "If you break them, who-knows-what will happen."

Letting go, she shook the tension from her hand. She panted a little. "Aside from how distracting it is that your breath shoots out the side of your nostrils…" She stretched and touched the ceiling. "I think I'm getting used to being you."

"Then you're a couple decades faster than I was." He peeked into boxes, one after another, then finally wheezed a weird half-chitter, half-groan. "I don't know. Maybe, if we get away from this Quonset hut, we'll go back to normal?"

She finished poking at every centimeter of the bracelet, finding no hidden buttons. Her next impulse was to gnaw the fabric layer off, but stopped herself. Probably a bad idea to chew on the supernatural, especially with somebody else's teeth. "Worth a shot." She nodded, still distracted by the muzzle obscuring the bottom half of her vision. "Before we go, we should grab anything else that's obviously supernatural."

"Good idea." He surveyed the shed. "Well, nothing is glowing yellow and made of bone, so I'm not sure how we'd know."

"Okay, so maybe anything of value?" She propped her fists on her hips.

"You do your mother proud, but I don't see anything to burgle. Aside from her long-lost cabinet doors." He gripped the edge of an old shop table, lowered his muzzle and closed his eyes. "I might need to lie down."

Her tail felt super light, just flying around like a rogue feather duster. No wonder Max was such a slow swimmer. "I guess all this stuff won't go anywhere."

Nodding, Max staggered for the door. His top half wobbled like an unstable jelly. "I don't know if we should try to carry anything in this state."

Kylie nodded, her head jolting about unsteadily. "Ugh!" She lumbered after him. "I feel like I'm made of stale licorice."

"That's what we non-otters call 'having bones.'" He grabbed a length of heavy-gauge wire on his way out and jammed it through the latch, then tried to bend it. It sprung back into place. He tried again, but only managed to get it to bend a few degrees, in spite of a mighty squeak. He sighed. With a look of defeat, he stepped out of the way. "Kylie…"

She stepped up to the door. "What do you want me to do?"

"Just bend it so the door won't blow open." He grabbed her giant paws and wrapped them around the ends of the wire. "We don't need rain or wild animals getting in."

She twisted the steel wire like taffy. Tough paw pads even kept it from hurting. After a few more twists just for fun, she stood back to admire her work. "Huh! It's pretty cool to be strong."

Max rolled his eyes. Bracing himself against the occasional tree, he picked his way back down the hillside.

She snatched a woody pine cone from the forest floor and pulverized it in one paw. "Ouch! Wow, I totally just crushed that. I'm bleeding a little."

He gave her a sidelong look.

Dusting herself off, Kylie realized her gigantic form had considerable strength and durability at its disposal. After a few experimental bounces, she figured out how to keep her balance with a much lighter tail. She closed a fist around a pine cone and pulverized it. As the dust trailed from her hand, a smile lit her face. She stomped merrily downhill, hefting rocks, breaking branches, smashing underbrush. "This is great!"

Max traipsed with care. His newfound booty seemed to throw him off balance with every step. "Slow down."

"I'm a monster truck on legs! I'll never have to slow down again!" Turning back to look at him, her heavy paws fumbled and flung her face-down into the dirt. She tilted her muzzle up from the ground, shook the leaves off, and grinned. "This is amazing. I'm barely even hurt."

"Be careful with that body." He offered her a hand to stand up. "I need it back."

She took it and yanked him off balance. "Sorry."

He staggered and swept long hair out of his face. "Just take it easy. This won't get any easier if we're also dealing with a broken leg."

Getting borrowed feet under her, she proceeded through the woods at what she considered a normal pace. Sure, this situation was really weird, but soon noticed her boyfriend wasn't keeping up.

He tromped along, tripping over his own tail. Almost falling again, he growled. Then he giggled.

She slowed. "What's so funny?"

He bounced along the game trail, ears low. "Nothing." He simpered again.

"Tell me!" The bark came out much louder than she expected.

His tiny balled-up fists popped out to either side. "Walking as you really tickles, okay?"

"Tickles?" She snorted. "How can walking tickle?"

He squirmed in place, hips waggling as he tried to put it into words. "It just does."

"What are you even talking about? This could be a clue." She threw her arms in the air, almost flinging herself off balance. "Why does it tickle?"

"Because I'm not used to having a vagina, Kylie!" He sputtered, irritated and manic. "I don't know how you just scamper all over with all the feedback coming from this thing."

A howl of laughter echoed through the trees, a blast of sound she could never had made as an otter. Those wide, white paws zipped to her mouth, too late to stop the sound. "Sorry, Maxie. I don't mean to laugh. I'm just here, bouncing along."

Adjusting his jeans, he trotted along, bow-legged and self-conscious. "Let's just keep going."

Plowing through another patch of shrubs without slowing, Kylie barked with glee. "Man, I can just run forever." She jogged backward to face him. "See you back at the car."

"No! Wait! Carry me!" Several meters back, he flailed through the underbrush after her. "I always carry you!"

"Ugh, fine." She trotted over and picked him up. The effort flung him into the air like a pillow, if a very squeaky one. When he landed back in her arms, it hardly took any strength to keep hold. "Ha! You're super light like this. No wonder you're always picking me up."

He grumbled as she threw him over her shoulder, then twisted around to see where they were going. His tiny paw splashed the beam of the flashlight around the dim woods.

At long last, the ground leveled out, and they reached the edge of a twisted gravel road, on which perched a tiny aquatic automobile. Night had seeped out from the shadows of trees and onto the paths between them.

Kylie set down her boyfriend. "Okay. I think we can say getting away from the shed didn't help." She looked back up the slope. "Let's just go home and regroup. I don't wanna climb the mountain again."

His dark pelt almost invisible in the dusk, Max brushed himself off, having particular trouble getting dirt off his fishing vest.

Free from the worry of tripping and flinging him down the mountainside, Kylie bounded along through the grass. Her body demanded more oxygen, so she decided to practice panting. She bit her tongue instantly with the next step. "Ow!" She stuck it out to check if she was bleeding. She was not.

"That's my tongue." Waddling up, he squinted in the fading light. "And I'll thank you to be careful with it."

"It just goes all over the place." She waggled it out of her muzzle to demonstrate.

Arms crossed, he stumped across the unmowed ditch. His tiny ears sank flat against his red hair, which was still largely contained in a ponytail. He looked cute like that, all serious and tiny. She then realized that's how she'd looked all her life and huffed with pique.

An electronic chirp rattled through the seaside air. Searching through the countless pockets of her fishing vest, he pulled out a phone and failed to unlock it. The screen glowed against the dark, a sharp rectangle of civilization in the wilderness.

She stuffed a paw in her jeans pocket, pulled out his phone, and handed it to him. "Phone trade?"

He nodded. "Phone trade." The device looked gigantic in his borrowed paws, almost a tablet.

"It's just mom wondering what we want for dinner." She scowled at the sleek device, which almost vanished in her big white paws. "Ugh, this phone is tiny and impossible now."

His hazel gaze flicked up to her. "Then you'll understand how I feel."

"About my phone?" She propped wide white paws on her hips. "Or about me?"

Max said nothing, only casting her a look as he waddled toward the car.

Hands on her hips, she stuck that large canine tongue out at him. "You can't be having that much trouble if you're sassing me already."

Finding the car locked, he searched through a few pockets before securing the keys, mostly because of the attached plastic oyster with googly eyes. He unlocked the door before tossing them to her and slipping into the passenger's seat.

Max watched as she contorted herself into various configurations to fit behind the steering wheel. He said nothing. A faint amusement touched his otherwise distant expression. The smirk grew over time, until he stood grinning.

After her fourth try, she climbed out and shook a heavy finger at him. "Shut up, you!"

He rolled his eyes. Seated in a now too-far-back seat, he clicked it forward several centimeters, then several more, until his tail wasn't pressed to the back seat.

Her efforts to enter the car resumed, rocking the vehicle back and forth.

In the face of such disturbance, her boyfriend began locating the various parts of the seatbelt. "You're going to tip the car over."

"So I'll just use your body to roll it back on its wheels." She looked fully over the car, which itself was an interesting perspective. "It's not that deep of a ditch."

"Not something I've tried…" He peered with concern out his side window. "…though it's unlikely to improve the car."

Arms flailing, she heaved the most gigantic sigh of her life. "Look, do you wanna drive?"

"Not especially, but if it gets us home alive…" With a sigh, he unbuckled himself and exited, then rounded the car and slithered into the driver's seat.

She dropped the keys into his webbed paw, stomped to the passenger's side, and folded herself into the confines.

"Don't shut your tail in the door." He clipped himself into the four-point harness, feeling a bit like a race-car driver. After checking that Kylie had compressed his entire body into the car, he fired up the engine. "You'll want to adjust the seat." He watched her fiddle with the levers for a moment before continuing. "Then you'll want to adjust it more, but you can't. It doesn't go back any further."

The seat clicked back a few centimeters. Then it stopped. His girlfriend cast accusing looks at everything around the seat. "Are you sure?" Knees braced against the dashboard, she rocked back and forth in the seat.

"Oh, I've checked." In his voice lingered a deep weariness.

Scowling as she banged her knuckles on every possible surface, she mouthed the words back to him.

Coaxing the transmission into first, he puttered off down the road.

At every bump, she hit her head on a rod in the convertible roof. "Okay. I think I see why you resent the ottermobile…"

The boat-car drove admirably until it reached the slightest gravel incline, at which point it handled like a greased surfboard down a staircase. He trampled the brake with both feet, but only made it fishtail. Teeth clenched, he didn't dare look to her. "It's even worse behind the wheel." Trying to turn on the headlights, he activated the propellers. "Why can't anything in this car be normal?"

She watched the trees crawl past. "You're going like ten. It's gonna take us forever to get home."

He downshifted to first. "At least we'll make it there."

As they turned a corner, the sparkle of the Atlantic broke through the trees. "Sheesh, Maxie: just drive it into the sea." She swept a paw toward the ocean, whacking her fingers on the window pane. "Maybe you're better at steering boats."

Hunched down over the wheel, he grumbled a convincing otter mutter and trundled on. "Plan."

"Yes?"

"First, we go home to regroup." He threaded the car down rutted back roads, wincing whenever the undercarriage bottomed out. "Then, until we figure out how to switch back, we lay low and act like each other."

"Why?" In her mind, the path to validating her family's past opened up before her. "I was thinking more of a 'tell the whole world' plan."

"Because people are going to think we're liars or nuts. We're not even the most convincing act in town." He used the turn signal, even though no other cars were visible. "And people being wary of us won't help with finding a cure."

"You'll have to go to work as me." She fought to buckle the seatbelt over her barrel chest. "Shane might have more info."

He chanced a glance at her. "I'm not sure I can act like you."

"You know me really well. Just don't swim into shark territory. You'll be fine! You've known me forever!" Kylie bounced and smacked her head on the ceiling's steel support rods again. Wondering if she had a bruise, she rubbed a paw between her ears. "How hard can it be?"

They drove through town, surrounded on all sides by the faintly surreal. In one yard, an extended family of foxes chatted casually around a giant metal horned skeleton sculpture. Fruity smoke rose from its blackened helm. A vixen in an apron opened a panel on its armor to remove a rack of exquisitely-smoked ribs. The fox kits cheered and scampered around the offering in a swirl of wagging orange-and-white tails.

As they neared the house, the faint voice of her mother muffled through the windows. In the porch light, Max stopped his girlfriend and brushed off her bulky frame. "White fur shows any dirt you get on it."

Glancing down at the twigs and dirt she'd accumulated, Kylie tried to help, but soon became distracted. "Whoa." She rubbed up and down her forearms. "I am so fuzzy."

"Quit it." Max hissed, reaching for the door. "Your mom's going to think we're on drugs."

"Are you sure we're not on drugs?" Her paw raised with the question. "I don't think we've ruled that out. Might be more likely than body-switching."

Hand on knob of the screen door, he paused in thought for a moment, then turned to her. "I can't think of a way to disprove that. If we're drooling on the ground next to a shed, I can't do anything to address that. But if we're not, and this is real, we lose nothing by trying to address it."

Just as he was about to open the door, her paw lifted again. "What if we're hallucinating, but walking around?"

"Then your mom will check us into rehab…" He cast her a sidelong look. "…which may solve the problem."

"Ah, the Hollywood lifestyle." She nodded. "We never had a chance."

Heading inside, they found Laura in the kitchen, phone cradled against her ear. "No, we can't title it Police Lion: Do Not Cross." She grabbed a leftover shrimp cocktail from the fridge, then swatted the door closed with her tail. "Look, we can put it on a character poster." Tiny shrimp in paw, she waved to the pair before tossing the morsel in her muzzle. "Comedic expectations are lower there."

218

Max managed a weak wave, like he'd only ever heard of the gesture. He noticed Kylie staring, then looked down at himself. They might be in different bodies, but they were no less on the same wavelength. He slackened his posture and donned on a smarmy smile. His eyes even darted to her, eyebrows subtly raised, like they were back on set and he was checking if she needed to direct him.

Her mother chattered on, eyes out the kitchen window. "If the part calls for a zebra, hire a zebra. I don't care if you have a horse in the running." She poured herself a glass of water. "I'm sure she's great at painting on stripes. It's the 21st century. Hire a zebra." She waddled back upstairs. "Audiences have never been stupid. They just have social media now, so they can complain to their friends and tank the movie…"

Kylie let out a long breath. Then she patted Max on the back, nearly tipping him over "See?" She smiled down at him. "We're fine."

~ ~ ~

Kylie hustled him to his room, then into the adjoining bathroom. "Still think it's decadent to have a toothbrush in both our bathrooms?"

He snorted, amused. It came out as more of a squeak.

The toothbrush felt tiny and fragile in her huge hand. Being in Max's body unlocked the "destroy object" option in pretty much any context.

A light high noise she soon recognized as an otter throat being cleared. Her throat. She'd only ever heard it from inside her body. Only this time it was her boyfriend trying to get her attention

He offered her his toothbrush. Discomfort contended with resolution on his face as he shrugged.

Trading, she studied the somewhat-larger brush. The bristles sprouted out at slightly different angles, with the idea it had been designed to better clean canine dentition. That's what the TV commercials claimed, anyway. She glopped a bunch of toothpaste on it and got scrubbing. Having someone else's teeth in her mouth was super distracting. Brushing her teeth only brought that fact to the forefront. The husky's mouth had a lot of acreage to cover. In reaching the back teeth, she poked herself really hard in the cheek, then overcorrected and choked on the brush head.

Watching in mild judgement, Max brushed his borrowed teeth with care. His gaze dipped to the sink before it could cross his own reflection.

Her eyes flicked to the mirror. An involuntary twitch of her eyebrows caught her intention. Realizing she had the power, she started contorting his face into every expression she could think of, brushing all the while.

She caught his reflection staring. He raised his ears at her.

"Wha?" She spit an impressive volume of foam. "I get to make all new faces with your face."

A deep sigh stretched his supple body. She marveled at how much it made her body stretch, even with Max's formal posture.

Once they rinsed and spit, they padded back out into his bedroom.

"So we're just going to bed now?" He lifted his palms.

"I think we should." She pulled her shirt off. "It's tiring to stay in character as you."

She watched her boyfriend hop in place, over and over, trying to reach a pair of pajama pants.

"Why do you let me put these PJs on this shelf—" He jumped again, again failing to snag the PJs. "—if you can't reach them?"

"Because I know you'll be there." She reached up and gathered the garment in one giant paw.

He accepted it.

"If we only used shelves I could reach, the top half of each floor would be empty." Lifting his scrawny arm fully, she drew an invisible line to the same height on the wall. Then she stretched to see how far she could reach. "Oh man, I can touch the ceiling!"

"How are you okay with this?" He crossed his arms. "It's scary."

"It's fun!" She poked the ceiling again, tiny crumbs of plaster falling where her claw punctured it. "That's the opposite of scary."

Wilting with irritation, he cast her a weary look. "That is a very lutrine attitude."

She took a deep breath, examining her emotions. "Scary would be if you were missing or something."

A long moment passed. "Let's just go to bed." He sighed. "Maybe this will have worn off by morning."

They climbed into bed.

Max lay on his back. Freed from the swimwear bra, his breasts spread to either side. He kept trying to push them upright, only to have them droop back to the sides. It was pretty amusing to watch.

She snickered, which came out unusually deep, almost a growl.

His webbed hands flew from his breasts. "I'm not just playing with them."

"That's the main thing I do with them." Kylie flung the covers off. "Ugh! I suddenly don't need a blanket. It's like a season change."

"And your shoulders aren't in the same zip code." She tried to wriggle her body into a more comfy position, but without a powerful otter tail she just ended up falling face-first into a pillow.

Her boyfriend squeaked with the bedsprings as he was flung halfway out of the bed.

"Sorry." She pulled him back up by the tail. "How are you supposed to sleep on your side?"

"By stacking pillows." He tried to wrap his arms around her, but found they were far too short. "Or supporting your head with your arm."

She nodded and rolled to her back. Using one of her gigantic arms, she scooped him toward her and held him against her broad chest. They lay in silence. Sleep took forever to arrive. Probably couldn't find her new address.

II

The next few hours passed in a montage of inconvenience.

Max slammed his tail in a door.

Kylie whacked her head on the doorframe.

Max couldn't type with webbed paws.

Kylie dropped her phone for the tenth time.

Max knocked over a cereal box atop the fridge.

Kylie opened the cereal too hard and detonated it across the kitchen.

Max couldn't reach things in his own bedroom closet, which he put there 48 hours before.

Kylie could be tracked through the house, since she barked at every zap of static electricity.

Unsure what to do with himself, Max padded into the kitchen, smacked his tail on a chair, and then glared at his own rudder. "My butt's going all sorts of places I didn't tell it to."

"Yeah, just wait until you walk past a table full of breakable stuff." His girlfriend dumped most of a bowl of cereal into her muzzle. "You doing okay?"

He shrugged, then panicked a little when the motion translated down his entire form. These shoulders felt way too light, flying around even as he tried to emulate her body language. "Can't get comfy."

"What'd ya mean?" She waved a spoon at him as she put the empty bowl in the sink. "That body'll morph onto just about any surface."

His ears flicked down modestly. "I keep laying on my breasts."

Kylie barked a huge laugh. "Be nice to the ladies!" She grabbed a small, frost-tinged box from the freezer. The slogan "Eel Good, Feel Good" adorned the cardboard. She attempted to open the package with her claws, like normal, and destroyed it. The frozen pie clattered to the countertop, rattling like partly-dried clay. She tried to catch it and smacked her watch on the stove.

Max winced at the antique clank.

A whirl of activity, she tossed the pie in the microwave, then set it droning toward warmth. With a quick glance around, she seized a pickle jar from the fridge and popped it open with ease. "I could unscrew every lid in this kitchen."

He propped his hands on wide otter hips.

"I won't!" She rolled her eyes as she tried to puzzle her way through getting her hand into the jar. After many arcane gestures, she secured a

222

pickle. She nudged the fridge door shut, clattering the wristwatch on the steel surface. "I'm just saying: how do you contain this much power?"

"Practice and worry." Max waddled forward and gestured for her hand. Upon getting it in his webbed paws, he took his his watch off her wrist.

She munched through the whole pickle she'd thrown in her muzzle. "Sorry."

He stashed the timepiece in one of the fishing vest's myriad pockets.

"Hey, my life isn't smooth sailing either." She stroked his hair. "I keep finding new ways my nuts can get squeezed between my thighs."

A small chuckle rose from him.

Setting down the pickle jar, she rinsed her damp hands. "I did figure out how to wash my hands."

"I just did too." He jerked a thumb back at the bathroom, only stretching his webbing a little. "Did you just take a shower? The curtain's wet."

"I had to pee. I'm scared to pee standing up, so I'm practicing in the shower." She pranced in place.

Max pressed tiny paws to his face. "It's point-and-shoot."

"Boys aren't user-friendly!" The microwave beeped. She retrieved a steaming pot pie and set it on the counter, only firing a small volley of eel gravy. "Your hands are heat-resistant, though, so that's nice."

The scent of hot eel filled the kitchen. He handed her a fork and took a seat at the counter. "Cereal and pickles and eel pie?"

"Mom used to make this when I was a kid. It's a comfort food!" She scooped up a massive bite, forked it into her smiling muzzle, and became disappointed.

Max sat up and looked at her. "Are you not comforted?"

She slid it toward him. "I'm going to need you to eat this eel pot pie and tell me how nostalgic it tastes."

He broke off a bit of the crimped pie crust and a quick nibble confirmed its tastiness.

"Your body's a bonfire." Her heavy hands flailed in the air, much less responsive than otter ones. "I just keep throwing food on the fire. Dunno how you have time to do anything but eat."

Max speared some chunks of eel meat and ate them while giving her a weary look.

"Are you getting a mystical sense the mojo will wear off?"

His small ears popped up readily. "No?"

She half-frowned. "Neither am I."

He continued eating the pie, which turned out to be warm, savory, and comforting. "What should we do?"

She shrugged. "Wanna watch cartoons?"

"How will that help?"

"I dunno. Can't hurt."

He smashed the top layer of pastry and pushed it into the pie filling. "Fine, let's watch cartoons."

She grabbed his pie for him and they headed to the living room.

He spied the remote control under the sofa, but failed at lifting it to reach the device. "Agh, this is frustrating! Your little noodle arms can't lift anything."

Kylie scampered up next to him, beaming an otter's smile with husky teeth and hefting the sofa with one paw. She cackled maniacally: "Bwahaha! I am the god of upper body strength!"

He snatched the remote off the floor and made a mental note to vacuum up the dust when he got his body back. "Put that down."

She lowered the couch too fast, slamming it on the carpet, then plopped down on it, slamming it against the wall. Her thick paw grabbed him by the tail and hauled him onto her lap.

He briefly traded her the remote for his eel pie.

Together, they navigated through the menus to find a suitably distracting cartoon. A heavy metal intro shot lightning across the title sequence, which was composed mostly of graphs and charts.

"We should get groceries later. I want to try out more foods with your tongue." She stuck it out a short distance.

He shook his head. "If we go out, people are going to notice we're acting weird."

"Everyone in town acts weird."

He crossed his arms at her, swishing his breasts in the process, then uncrossing his arms to glare down at them. For being so sensitive, these things got in the way of a lot of gestures.

Kylie woofed. "We can't just stay in the house forever." She spread a giant paw at the manor. "I'm going stir-crazy."

He nodded. "We can't let this derail our whole lives. Tomorrow morning, I'm going to go for a run."

Creaking down the stairs, Laura breezed into the living room. "I want you both to know that yours truly has written an exemplary script for In Brief."

The younger otter perked up. "That show's still on?"

Max's eyebrows rose. "I guess I haven't seen it."

"That's because we don't watch TV." Kylie pointed at him. "The main character only designs men's underpants, so he has lots of time left over to get into wacky situations with the other characters at the company who all design ladies' undergarments."

"You're just cranking out a generic script, then?"

"No, no, you don't call Laura Bevy just to write any old episode. I'm making it a great callback to all these unresolved plot threads." Pride gleamed in Laura's smile. "But I didn't want to watch 100 hours of middling sitcom just to get the canon right."

"So, what? You used the show's fan wiki?"

The middle-aged otter shook her head, whiskers swaying over a smile. "It doesn't have a wiki, but it has something better: underpants perverts."

"Seriously, M–?" Kylie's muzzle snapped shut halfway into the word "mom." She cleared her throat. "Mz. Bevy."

"Yes, Mr. Saber." She winked at her daughter, who currently inhabited her daughter's boyfriend's body. "Perverts are actually quite knowledgeable. And they've been very helpful to me in writing the script."

"We're living in a golden age for talking to anonymous hornballs online." His girlfriend rolled her eyes.

The plump otter waved her glasses back and forth in one paw. "Most of them want to remain anonymous. A few have asked for their real names to be used."

Max brushed back the long reddish hair that kept falling in his face. "Good for them, owning their perviness."

"You said it, hun." The older otter slid her glasses back on. "Gotta love yourself."

"There's some good advice." Kylie cast a wolfish grin at her boyfriend.

Max's tiny ears gave a bashful dip. "I don't know why we should be surprised by any of this from Mom."

Laura chittered through a laugh. "I write things the fans will love, even if it's the fans of an 11pm sitcom. If I go into a space where people expect mediocrity and raise the bar a little, maybe they'll realize that's what they actually want."

Max rolled his eyes. "Elevating the art form. Mom."

"You know it." The older otter cleaned her glasses on her shirt. "What are you kids up to?"

Kylie shrugged broad shoulders against the back of the sofa. "Idle youth."

Onscreen, flying luxury cars revved and fired lasers from their headlights. A radical dude shouted: "Let's make an early withdrawal, bros!"

Laura tsked. "I leave Hollywood for a year and this is what happens."

Max raised a webbed finger. "It's underwritten by the National Credit Union Administration."

Kylie paused the cartoon and scrolled down to the description. "'Mars has a much more advanced banking system, so the Banker Mice from Mars fight against evil bankers who would introduce sinister alien financial products that Earth is not equipped to regulate.'"

He tried to sound chipper like Kylie, while still sounding cynical like Kylie. "They all have names like 'Escrow.'"

The cartoon mice, accompanied by electric guitar, explained various banking practices that had been outlawed over the past few centuries on Earth, then compared them to more advanced scams imported from the Martian financial sector. Fist-bumps abounded. It took one of them responding "Consider my interest compounded, bro!" before Laura squawked with outrage.

"This is all terrible!" The writer waved a webbed paw at the screen. "I'm going to make some more calls about the rights to Majestica. Maybe we can get the ball rolling on that again."

"Never give up the dream, Laura." Kylie smirked at having used her mother's name without sounding like a complete weirdo.

The lutrine emitted a sound like a rusted door hinge as she waddled back upstairs. "Someone has to save television."

As soon as her mother's office door closed, Kylie wiggled with pride, shaking the sofa. "See? If we can fool Mom, we can fool anybody."

He crossed his arms, more carefully this time. "You seem not very freaked out by all this."

She shrugged. "If freaking out would solve this, we'd have switched back right away."

"I can't tell if I'm freaking out or having heart palpitations or if this just the speed it's supposed to being."

Reaching to his throat, she felt an artery. "Nah, that's normal." She tapped her chest, which made a hollow thump. "I keep thinking yours has stopped."

His little ears flicked up. "So, this doesn't scare you at all?"

Kylie took a deep breath, then let it out, buying herself time to reflect. "I am not scared about this because we're doing it together." She grabbed his paw with her gigantic one, completely covering it. "If we can flip this switch, clearly we can switch it back."

Max nodded. "And if we can't?"

She hugged him to her broad chest. "Then you're going to have to show me the finer points of jerking off, because I have not been good at it so far."

"Work the sheath." He made a lewd, but vague gesture.

"Oooh!" Interested, Kylie sat up straighter on the sofa. Then she dismissed the topic with a wave of her paw. "The thing that matters is that we've still got each other and so we're fine."

"Mmf." Max found himself really enjoying being held. The warmth. The support. The things he'd normally be providing.

"Eventually, hiding in the house is gonna be just as suspicious as going out in public." She patted his back with a powerful thump. "I can only take so many days off from this job before I just don't work there anymore. You might eventually have to sit behind a counter for a few hours."

He nodded as the hug tapered off. An empty fork reached his lips. He finished the eel pie, much to his surprise. He still wasn't sure if he liked eel pie. Squirming, he felt hazy, disconnected. Not a sensation he liked, though enough easy to ignore. For a moment, he considered raising the topic, but Kylie seemed content. Would stressing her out help anything? Maybe she was right. Maybe waiting this out was the answer. They'd dealt with weird stuff before. Getting back into his routine might help too. Resolving to do so, he nuzzled up against her chest and settled in for another round of terrible cartoons.

"How did CyCorg even get an animated series?" He extended a paw at the screen, the light glowing through his finger webbing. "It's an R-rated action film."

"Mm." Kylie nodded against the top of his head.

A moment dragged on. "I get that the extendo-limbs are easy to animate, but this is just going to make a bunch of pups watch a gunfight movie." Another stretch of silence, aside from cartoon sound effects. He wasn't used to being the one to carry a conversation. He looked up at her.

She grinned down at him.

He gave her a weary look. "What?"

Her giant canine head rocked back and forth with mirth. "Soooooooooooo, fooling Mom was super easy. We could do this all the time."

He rolled his eyes, which he apparently did wrong because it hurt a little. "We barely pulled that off with the one person who least wants to believe in the supernatural. We cannot keep this up."

"We'll be fine. We're actors. And I bet this will wear off in the morning or something and we'll miss it when it's gone." She tapped blunt claws on his rainbow bracelet.

Max stuffed the concern down. If Kylie was doing fine, he could tough this out too. No need to disrupt her with his problems. He might be in his girlfriend's body, but he was still himself. He was the stable one in the relationship, the bedrock. His job was to stay strong. They'd figure something out.

~ ~ ~

Max awoke in his bedroom, but in Kylie's body. Laying in a too-large, empty bed, he took stock of his situation. Still an otter. That wasn't a dream, then. Birds chirped outside, drawing his attention to the full-risen sun. His borrowed body had decided to sleep in. He had, however, managed to sleep without twisting into a pretzel, so at least some of his habits had come with him. A deep sigh stretched his chest in uncomfortable new ways. Max wondered if this was normal. He then reminded himself that nothing about trading bodies with his best friend was normal.

After a brief fight with that gigantic tail, he sat up. In an additional unforeseen complication, he had no clothes to wear in his own bedroom. Waddling to his feet, he pulled on pants, even though Kylie rarely dressed so modestly in the morning. His breasts wobbled. He found himself cupping them with both hands, purely to stabilize. He recovered her discarded bra and after several attempts that sent it springing to the floor like a rubber band, he managed to puzzle it on. Thank goodness otter underwear had more in common with swimsuits than lingerie. The occasional drag of his tail along the carpet managed to distract him every time, throwing off his stride even more. Sure, his dog tail had been the demise of many cans of soda, but this new butt was all over the place.

Letting out a breath he'd been inadvertently holding for several minutes, Max opened the bedroom door.

Kylie stood at the counter and munched her way through an entire bag of bagels. "Hey."

"Hey." He turned to sit on one of the kitchen chairs and his tail sent it clattering to the floor. With a groan, he stooped and righted it. With greater care this time, he managed to thread his tail through the slot at the back of the chair. At last, he sat.

"How's life on the otter side?"

Leaning on the table, he gave her a bleary look. "I'm beginning to understand why otters make so many rusty-hinge noises."

Muzzle stuffed with salmon lox, she cast him a wry look. "Rough night?"

"It should have been." He shrugged, a motion which didn't stop and instead translated down his entire spine. "But I was too exhausted to stay up worrying."

She nodded and stuffed another bagel in the toaster. "I slept like a rock. I was brushing my teeth before I was even conscious."

He nodded. Unsettling as the situation was, he had to admit it was interesting on an academic level. Thinking about it from that distance also kept him from freaking out.

"Ouch!" She yapped. "I keep biting my tongue." She stuck it out to check for damage. "How do you keep this thing in your head?"

Max scowled. "I want to be mad at you for adapting to this so fast."

"Oh, c'mon M— Kylie." She winked conspiratorially. "There has to be some part you like."

His tiny ears flicked down. "…I liked the part where you held me."

"Awww, tiny boyfriend." Ducking over to the table, she hugged him until his shoulders popped.

"Ack!" He wiggled free.

"You want some orange juice?" She grabbed a citrus from the fruit bowl and gave it a testing squeeze. "Pretty sure I can crush these with my huge paws."

"No, please." He plucked it from her and placed it back in the bowl. "Those paws stain really easily."

"Okay, fine. Maybe something to eat?"

He grabbed a bran flake that had fallen between the box and its internal bag, then popped it in his mouth. His pointy otter teeth crushed it, then vanished behind a frown. "Even the cereal tastes weird."

"Cereal always tastes weird first thing in the morning. It's how my body works." She propped heavy paws on her hips. "Why do you think I like bagels with smoked salmon instead?"

"Because that's one of the few breakfast fishes." He looked up at her. "And you're an otter."

"Well, I'm the Max now." She snatched a spatula from the drawer. "So I'll cook you whatever you want."

"I think I want to go for a run." He sighed. That usually made him feel better. "Clear my head."

"Okay. I'll be here." Putting the fruit back, she patted his shoulder with an orange-fresh paw. "Not like I can fit behind the wheel of the Amphicar to drive anywhere."

~ ~ ~

After a kilometer of waddles, wobbles, and stumbles, Max returned to Bourn Holt. How Kylie got anywhere on these stumpy legs, he had no idea. He trudged up the driveway. From his lowered vantage point, he noticed the gravel consisted largely of clam shells run over by countless trips to town.

Not only did his legs hurt, but his breasts did too. They bounced around all over the place, even in a bra. Plus, running with an otter tail felt like running with sandbags tied to his butt, so he'd been slowed to a walk for fear of throwing out his back. His feet hurt too, lacking their thicker shock-absorbing pads. The world around him smelled muted with only a lutrine nose.

He slumped in the front door, then shut it. On his tail. He squeaked with pain, jumped forward, and clattered the door back open. With a scowl, he shut it with marked determination.

Standing on the stairs, Kylie looked up from her phone. "Ouch. Careful there, Maxie. Did you have a good run?"

Max sighed deeply. Wobbling on one foot and then the other, he pried off the sneakers with a grunt of relief, feeling the webs between his toes stretch as he flexed them. The webbing had begun to pinch almost immediately into the run, each step squishing the sensitive skin between his toes. He could tell he'd have been in for blisters had he continued, which would have been its own special kind of nightmare.

Kylie grimaced, wincing over the railing as she watched him massage his toes. "Yeah, uni-species shoes are fine for most things, but for running you need special sneakers with padding for the webs." She tilted her head. "I'm sure we could find you a pair easy enough."

He gave her a tired look.

"Okay." Towering inadvertently, she propped her hands on her hips. "What's up?"

"I don't know." A sigh trailed out of him. "Maybe I need more coffee."

"I'm an expert in how much coffee that bod runs on." She looked him up and down. "And I think it's more than that."

His hand tipped toward her, the gesture practiced and nonthreatening, even as the rest of his body bounced and leaned, battered and tense. "And you're doing just fine?"

"I guess? I've mostly been distracted by my new superpowers. Did you know you can move the oven?" She gave a thumbs-up review to his body. "Sure, I hit my head on all the cabinet doors, but we're replacing those anyway, so I'll have my revenge."

He nodded.

She'd thought that was pretty funny. "So, are you going to tell me why you're so bent out of shape?" Conscious effort kept her tone relaxed. She didn't want to railroad him, like his mother had done on the phone to her before. "You seem more stressed out than when you left."

Pulling off his socks, Max said nothing. The counterweight of his tail almost tipped him over. He bounced off the door and kicked his shoe under a kitchen chair. An attempted growl emerged as a squeak extruded through frustration. "Because this body won't cooperate!" He threw his arms out to the sides. "Because I'm anxious all the time, since I'm too small to protect you now. I have no idea if any of this will ever actually get better or if I'm stuck being someone completely different from who I was my entire life. I can't reach stuff or lift stuff or even go for a run without my butt flinging itself all over the place." He stood, panting and stammering and slightly shaking.

Padding up, she hugged him. Those big, strong arms did feel reassuring. Those large paws wrapped around his tapered waist. That felt nice too. Then she picked him up.

He squawked in surprise. "Hey!"

"Settle down." She patted him on the rump. "I've gotta show you something."

Carrying him all the way, she traipsed into the great hall. A path led her through the vast sea of boxes and furniture. Her ancestors had no doubt charted more graceful paths across the dance floor. She knocked over at least one floor lamp with his tail, but instead of falling it slumped lazily against crates of knickknacks and other otter ephemera.

She booted open a side door and toted him through a succession of smaller rooms. A claw-footed cast-iron bathtub appeared in their path, only to be dodged. Beyond lay a room clad in tile with a U-shaped pool set into the floor. Sunlight gleamed through tall windows, shimmering across the surface of the water. She snagged the phone from his pocket and stuck it in hers.

Max realized she planned to stick him in the pool. "Kylie. I'm sorry, okay? I wasn't bad-mouthing your body. Kylie!"

Woofing a chuckle, she again picked him up and gingerly dipped his tail in the pool.

Max squirmed in her iron grip, twisting to see the rippling water beneath him. His body curled up as he tried to stay out of the water. "Kylie, I'm serious. Don't you dare—"

With an impish smirk, she hefted him like a sack of flour and tossed him into the pool.

A heartbeat of weightless anticipation dragged out before Max hit the water. He clenched, bracing for the shock of cold, the rush of water filling his nose and ears, the added weight as it soaked his fur and began to drag.

It never came.

Instead the water enveloped his body in a vast, cool embrace, a gentle pressure from all directions that pressed in without penetrating his layers of dense, oily fur. He opened his eyes and was surprised at the clarity of his vision, suspended upside-down in the chest-high water. He righted himself with shocking ease, his body curling around itself in a flurry of instinct and muscle memory. Every twitch of one of his webbed paws seemed capable of spinning him in any direction he desired.

With a giddy lurch, he shot forward, slicing through the water like an arrow, propelled by the rippling of his curvy body and a flick of the tail that had been such an impediment on the jogging trail. The far wall of the pool came rushing up fast, but he barely had to think about turning before he veered in a graceful arc and corkscrewed back to face the way he came. Excitement thundered in his tiny otter breast. this water, all water, belonged to him. He was made for this. It was incredible, electric; his body moved like it was just another current beneath the waves, the only drag coming from the running clothes he still wore.

The pool was too small to achieve the speeds he knew he was capable of, but he did another half-dozen laps, skimming the floor of the pool and letting the water rush through his whiskers. He surfaced, more because his brain wanted air than because his lungs did, and saw Kylie watching him with a patient smile, sitting on the edge of the pool with her feet dangling in the water. She'd stripped down to her boxers, and when she saw she had his attention she slid into the water and grinned at him. "Pretty cool, huh?"

"Yeah…" He tried to think of a way to talk about it. The first thing he noticed about the water was how dry it was. A husky's fur soaks up water like a sponge, but an otter pelt was a built-in drysuit. He glanced at the myriad tiny bubbles trapped in his fur.

Big, strong husky paws angled him to float on the surface.

His dog body didn't float. But the length of his body buoyed at the surface. "Huh. Cool."

"I know, right?" She leaned over the side of the pool and gave him an upside-down kiss.

Ears dipping, he kissed her in return. In contrast to the chill of the pool, her lips felt warm. Their whiskers touched. Her dry muzzle fur rubbed along his for a sweet moment before she sat up.

"See? Otter bods are great." She laughed. "You've been using it wrong. I'm not trying to use your big, burly husky body like an otter—I'd probably dislocate something if I tried. So maybe you should try chilling out and ottering, okay?"

He nodded. Seconds passed, ripples calming with each bounce across the pool. "Still. I'm not big enough to protect you."

"Aww. You're more than just the muscle." Her voice softened as she smiled down at him. "You're smart. You stop me from being too reckless."

He lifted his wrist, the snap bracelet the only garb he wore. Its abstract 90s pattern darkened a few shades from the soaking.

"Okay, you mostly stop me." She leaned against the tiled wall, watching him float. "And you make me feel sane."

He smiled.

"This is temporary." She played with the bracelet on her own wrist, so light, yet so stubbornly in place. "It'll work out."

"Our magically switching bodies..." He lifted an eyebrow. "...will just work out?"

"If we can survive a TV series, outsmart an alien handyman, and overcome Turkeyzilla..." She jerked a thumb toward the kitchen, where the poultry colossus had lingered in the fridge for weeks, even with a hungry husky doing his best. "...we can do anything together."

Clad only in underpants and bobbing in a weird lutrine pool, Max felt less vulnerable and more relaxed than he'd been since the switch. He did trust Kylie. She was his partner in all this craziness.

"I know this is weird." Kneeling, she leaned in to talk more intimately. "But we'll be okay."

"We waited a whole night and we didn't switch back." He floated in a slow spiral. "We should go back to Joe's shed and look for clues."

"Yeah." She tugged the wristband. "Even your muscles can't get these loose."

He nodded. "We could probably cut them off, but I don't want to damage them."

"Or fry our brains." She wiggled thick fingers at her cranium.

He lifted a hand out of the water to point at her. "Now you're learning."

"I try to listen to you, Maxie." She winked.

A long moment of peace passed through the pool room, accompanied only by the subtle sounds of water and breath.

"I'll let you hang out here." She stood, seeming excessively tall. "You might try stripping down to your skivvies. Clothing is a drag." With that, she ducked out the door and shut it after her.

Left alone in the quiet, Max floated in the pool for a time, then began idly removing an article of clothing at a time. Very little held clothing on an otter, so soon he his entire outfit sat as a wet pile at the edge of the pool. He bobbed on the subtle waves, ghosts of the currents he'd stirred up before, clad only in a sleek two-piece swimsuit. Being in his element felt good, now that he realized what it was. It seemed obvious in retrospect. It was fun. He paddled around. Frictionless ease propelled him along the surface of the water.

After a long while, he climbed from the pool and marveled at the water sloughing off his pelt. Upon toweling off, he began the long trek back to the inhabited portion of the house. He wove around stacks of boxes and draped furniture, then froze when he glimpsed his unfamiliar reflection in the large windows of the smoking room. He smirked. He'd been attracted to this body for years. The smooth curves and shiny pelt stood out all the more in his damp state and minimal clothing. Even the modest swimwear clung in pleasing ways to his body. Realizing he was perving on himself, he blushed and continued padding through the vast entertaining room. He took care not to drip water on anything delicate.

Cutting through the kitchen, he trooped back to the laundry room with the rest of his soaked clothing tucked under one arm. He tossed the wet clothes into an accumulating pile of darks on the far wall, careful not to hit Kylie's sundress, still hanging by the dryer where he'd left it. Only then did he realize the clothes compatible with his body were upstairs. Maybe changing into fresh clothes would help him start the day over.

His still-damp paws padded up the stairs. His hands and feet reported back an unusual amount of detail on the steps and railing, compared to husky paw pads. As he reached the top, he stepped on an especially creaky board.

"That you, cork float?" A voice rang from Laura's study.

Max froze at the top of the stairs. Not being a dog, his smell-radar was next to useless. "Yeah?"

Leaning back in her chair, Laura eyed him, as he stood in nothing but damp fur and Kylie's underwear-slash-swimsuit. The older otter smirked. "You're gonna give Max a heart attack, running around the house looking like that."

Max flushed, then shrugged to Laura. "Clothing is oppression."

She cackled, though a tinge of bitterness clung to her tone. "You never did like staying dressed. Always scandalizing the neighbors."

Keenly aware of his immodest state, he scooted across the hall to Kylie's room and twirled into a fluffy, pink bathrobe. He gathered his wits and poked his head into the office. "Something up? You sound a little down."

"Oh, I don't know." Her paw lifted her lucky coffee cup, but found it empty. "I've just been drained lately."

He nodded, looking for an excuse to bail. But Laura's whiskers seemed in a particular downturn, and he decided Kylie would start chattering on at this point. Surely he could cheer her up without spilling the secret. "You—ya know, you're cooped up working a lot."

She tilted her head back against the chair. "I suppose I could get out a little more."

"You're not going to offend K—Max and me—" He feigned a cough. "—by hanging out with other people once in a while." He swept one of his tiny paws at the sprawling mansion. "You grew up when this house had a bunch of people in it, so it's normal for it to feel a little empty with just the three of us."

"I know." She heaved a sigh. "It's just tough making new friends when you're an adult."

A slow nod bobbed his oddly-lightweight head. "I thought you were going to those wine-and-painting classes."

"I did." She rocked side to side in the office chair. "But when your last name is a local boogeyman, it dampens the mood."

"You grew up here, though." He jerked a webbed thumb at the window. "Aren't there people around the area you want to reconnect with?"

"I guess. Well, one for sure." A faint laugh crept, nervous, from her muzzle. Her gaze flicked toward town, obscured though it was by the trees. "I just don't know if that's a canal we want to dredge back out."

A moment passed in silence. Max found difficulty seeing past his own discomfort to discern an awkward silence versus a thoughtful one. Would Kylie know who she was talking about? It had to be her estranged father, right? He was the only other person in the area she spoke to with any regularity. Maybe it was best to clarify. "Ya mean Greg?"

Her keen eyes scanned his posture. A slight twitch translated down her frazzled whiskers: a slight smile of bemusement. "Yes…"

He squirmed. Then he stopped squirming, worried it would signal something unintentional.

Laura snapped out of it. "Of course, that's not the only thing distracting me."

"Of course." Easy response. He'd had to put it in a writing assignment for her sometime.

"I'm closer than ever to my pipe dream of securing the rights to Majestica and the Defenders of Pegastar."

He nodded, then remembered to add more chatter. "That's cool. That's cool, right?"

"It is." She sighed. "I'm just not used to this level of wheeling and dealing. Up 'til now, everything I've worked on had been someone else's property or something I got to invent. I don't want to screw up and tip my hand."

He straightened unruly whiskers and tried to replicate Kylie's confident tone from yesterday. "We have lawyers in the family."

A tiny cackle burst from Laura's muzzle. "You're actually suggesting Julie?"

Julie: that was Greg's wife's name. He shrugged. "Why not?"

Laura slumped back in her chair to examine him. "I guess you're right. She's handled IP contracts before." She studied his face. "If it doesn't make you uncomfortable."

He felt super uncomfortable. Trying to spread his fingers, the webbing made them feel like stretchy gloves a size too small. "Why would it?"

"You always surprise me, kiddo." She crossed her arms. "I never can predict when you'll have character growth."

Max shrugged.

"I guess I've been too careful about anything more than polite socializing with Julie. She seems like a nice lady, not objecting to me talking to Greg in spite of our history." Leaning out of the chair, she hugged him. She rocked back and kicked her feet up on the battered writing desk. "You're not just saying this so I have to drive to New Hampshire all the time, are you?"

He shrugged. "You could stand to get out more." He followed Laura's gaze downward and saw that his tail had begun to wag, though the stupid thing was so heavy that only the last foot or so was getting any real movement.

Laura clucked her tongue, shaking her head in mock disapproval. "Been spending too much time around canines, kiddo?"

He chuckled, buying himself time to think of a sufficiently Kylie thing to say. "Hey, you're the one who hired him."

"Yes, I should have anticipated all this." She nodded. "Thanks, though. Glad I managed to raise a daughter who can give me some perspective."

A small peep of pride escaped him. He hugged her and started for his girlfriend's bedroom. Once inside, he took a seat on her bed and contemplated the array of fishing vests in the closet with a contented sigh. He guessed he was a passable Kylie after all.

~ ~ ~

Kylie was a better Max than Max. She knew it. Or at least a more confident one. Standing in the living room, she had formulated a great plan. She could totally handle calling his mom and straightening this all out. All it would take was confidence.

The phone rang a few more times, then a soft click announced someone had picked up. "Well, this is a surprise."

She cast her tone in cheerful determination. "Hi, Mom."

A large electric mixer whirred in the background. "And how is my wayward son today?"

"I'm fine." Pleasantries out of the way, she cleared her big, growly throat and barreled on. "Look, I wanted to talk to you about all these texts about me coming back home."

"Oh, so you have been getting those." An innocent yap echoed from the other end. "I wasn't sure."

"Yeah, look." She took a deep breath. "I've got a good thing going here and I'm an adult now. I need you to respect that."

Seconds of silence rolled by. A cool tone breezed from the phone. "Are you feeling alright?"

"Yeah, I'm fine." Kylie found her heavy-duty canine teeth clenched. They fit together in unfamiliar and distracting ways, like she was wearing plastic vampire fangs. Shaking off the distraction, she tried to imagine a really confident Max. "I'm just letting you know I'm going to be sticking around here."

"I got that impression at Yuletide." Something metal clanged in the background of the call. "Do you ever plan on visiting us again?"

Kylie stumbled over the guilt trip. "Of course I do."

"When?" The word came through like a predator's step in deep snow. The soft whine of a computer fan whirred through the speaker.

Glancing from side to side, the husky imposter cast about for ideas. Maybe this hadn't been such a great plan. "I don't know." She shrugged, even though she knew it wouldn't translate over the phone. "Sometime."

"Oh." The syllable carried every volume of the encyclopedia of social obligation. "Soon then?"

A nervous laugh escaped her muzzle, which she clacked shut. Another involuntary shrug failed to assist her. "Whenever it all works out."

"Great! Let's make it work out now." The sound of paws on a keyboard clattered through the phone speaker. "Looks like there's a deal on one-way tickets. I'll get back to you with the details." A smile shaped her words. "We can see what works out for everybody. Two weeks?"

"Umm—"

"Three? Three. I'll have to call you back, Max. Customers. Duty calls, you know." A chair scraped across the floor, counterpointed by distant voices. "But thank you for taking time out of your busy day to chat. Can't wait to have you home."

Straightening to her increased height, she put on her most confident voice. She could still pull this plan together. "Let's—"

"Bye, dear! Love you bunches!" The line clicked to silence.

Kylie blinked stupidly at the little red phone icon. Okay, maybe Max wasn't exaggerating about his mom being a conversation magician. She'd made Kylie's carefully-prepared arguments disappear and transformed them into whatever she wanted. No wonder her boyfriend hardly said anything: he'd been trained his whole life to not give her anything to transmute.

After several minutes holding the tiny phone, she set about cooking him an apology breakfast, then realized she'd eaten that breakfast and started a new one. It wasn't a problem, though. The whole kitchen was within arm's reach, which made it super easy. Once she had coffee, eggs, and toast ready, she grappled with how to pick the plate and cup up. Husky paws had worse grip, but more acreage. And while giant dumb paws could only fit a couple fingers through the mug's handle, it turned out it was possible to use non-webbed fingers a couple at a time. Armed with these new discoveries, Kylie managed to carry the meal to his room and open the door. "Hey Maxie—"

With a surprised squeak, he curled up into an otter ball under the sheets. His gaze flicked to the doorway, in the direction of her mom's office.

With a half-suppressed laugh, she shut the door after herself, set the breakfast tray on the nightstand, and sat on the bed beside him. "I didn't mean to startle you." At first, she thought she'd just startled him, but then a tingle of pheromone buzzed from her nose down to her crotch. "Wait, were you...?"

He buried his nose in the covers. "Sorry. I tried to lay down to chill out, couldn't get comfortable, and then it was too warm for your pajama pants and things kind of...spiraled."

"Sorry?" She barked a laugh. "What'd ya think I've been doing? Twice yesterday and once this morning."

With a groan, he rolled over to face her. Amusement and resignation, not surprise, clung to his features—along with a lingering shyness.

She patted his flank, ignoring the fireworks in her nose. Did she always smell that good to him she was turned on?

He sat up and accepted the steaming cup, then blew over the liquid, vapor curls guttering like candles. Relaxing a little, he leaned against her.

She nuzzled atop his head, seeing now why he found it so convenient to do so. "Before we go, though..." She slipped an arm around his small body. "Don't you have a little unfinished business?"

"Heh, I don't know... Mood's kind of spoiled." He curled up against her, half in her lap. "Plus, I was just sort of messing around."

"Yeah, and now you've got an expert to help you." She slipped a paw down his side, groping the side of his jeans. Her fingertips slowed to an intimate trace, trailing over the fabric of his swimsuit-style panties. "First, ya gotta relax..."

Halfway through a groan, the noise slowed to a chittered growl of pleasure. His paw joined hers, guided to all the best places.

Sturdy paw pads brushed across the material covering his slit. His arousal clung to her paw fur, soaking to the skin with exotic speed. "Already wet, huh?" She explored his body; well, her body on loan. Her fingers slipped inside his panties.

With a distant nod, he let her take the lead. Finger web over his clit, fingers wiggling to either side.

"Ya know how I like it when you play with my nipples?" Using her muzzle, she pushed his shirt up. Her long canine tongue proved really good at licking otter nipples. "That's why."

Max squirmed and gasped for breath. His passage clenched around her thick fingers.

Kylie slowly let her lips lift off the pert otter nipple, giving it one final swipe of her big husky tongue. She licked her lips, watching Max's breasts rise and fall with his labored breathing.

With a squeak, her boyfriend tensed. His limber form contorted with bliss. Then he relaxed against her. Max panted around a tiny pink tongue. This close, she could feel every breath against her throat fluff.

Once he'd caught his breath a little, she leaned down for a deep kiss. Kissing with Max's silly dog lips impeded her efforts only for a couple seconds. She lapped at his lips, a bit less gracefully than she hoped, then nuzzled her nose to his.

Her boyfriend moaned as her fingers slipped from his entrance. Scooting back onto the pillows, his paw settled on her crotch, detecting a major erection. He froze, not moving his fingers away, but not exploring the denim-covered length either. He squirmed. Those little round ears sank. "This is kind of weird."

A sudden giggle overtook her. "This? This is the weird part?"

He straightened, cute but grumpy: hair mussed, breath unsteady, posture fluid. Did she look that cute after she came? She'd have to ask. Perhaps when he wasn't looking offended.

"I'm not making fun of you, I promise." She extended her pinky finger toward him.

"I know." After an instant, he gripped her pinky with his own, giving her a classic Max eye-roll.

"A sticky pinky swear is the most sacred of vows in otter culture." She waggled her eyebrows.

Still slightly dazed, he squinted at her. "You're making that up."

She shrugged. "You can't prove anything."

He wiped his hand on the sheets.

"Sooooooo." Kylie failed to think of a reason she could put off telling him about her phone disaster with his mother. "As of about fifteen minutes ago, you're taking a vacation back home this summer of no less than three weeks."

"Okay…" His head tilted, ears up. "Care to explain why?"

"No."

"Kylie…" Silence settled over him easily, as he waited her out. It took forever, which was about a second.

The confession bubbled out of her. "Because I started at zero weeks, and your mother started at two weeks, and she's really good at negotiating."

"She is that." A deep sigh slumped him against the pillows. "Did she call you?"

Kylie winced. "…Someone called someone."

His gaze kindled into a glare. "Remember the conversation we had about swimming into shark-infested waters?"

"I didn't know she was waiting to chomp! She was prepared!" A soft woof escaped her throat. "I think she had notes!"

"I'm sure she did." His fingers attempted to interlace, then settled for steepling. "She's likely been rehearsing that conversion for months."

She studied the grim expression so rarely seen on otter faces. "…You're angry."

"I'm frustrated." His tone rolled with tension, like a marble on glass. "It's tough enough not being able to do anything. I didn't need you to call my mother and ship me off to the homestead."

"I'm sorry, Maxie. I thought I could handle it for you." She shrugged. "This isn't going the way I planned, but were you ever gonna go back?"

A quiet nod.

Kylie eyed him. "When?"

He crossed his arms over his breasts, which bounced more than dignity preferred. "As little and as late as possible."

"That's harsh." Harsher than she was used to hearing it. "They're your family."

Lutrine jaw muscles flexed around a statement he stifled. "I was about to say something unkind. Am I in caffeine withdrawal?"

Coffee math tallied up in her mind. "Is this the first cup you've had today?"

"Yes."

"Then yes."

He groaned. "Let me drink some coffee while you tell me about how you ruined my life."

Her freakishly-long arms allowed her to grab the cup of coffee from the breakfast tray and hand it to him. "Sometimes, the conversations we avoid are the ones we need to have the most."

"Yes. Thank you. I know." His muzzle tipped down to sip the steaming liquid.

She squirmed, then stopped when the bed frame creaked. "Are you mad at me?"

"A little." Still sipping, he looked up at her. "I'm also mad at myself because I let it get this far." His breath stirred the steam and cast ripples across the dark beverage. "I was doing this balancing act with Mom where I didn't want to upset her, but I also didn't want to cave and go home. Now I'm caving and going home."

She paused him with a raised paw and replied automatically: "Just tell her it was me who said it."

Max's eyebrows rose. He sipped more coffee.

Considering her statement for a moment, she allowed her hand to drop back to her lap. "Yeah, it sounded smarter in my head. That wouldn't work at all."

He handed her the cup. "If we're going back to Joe's shack today, I should get cleaned up." Eeling off the bed, he scampered off to the shower.

"What about your breakfast?" She sat up. Even a quick little bounce in this body squeaked the mattress springs.

He trudged toward the adjoining bathroom. His voice lapsed into his Russian accent from the early seasons of Strangeville. "Is food now. Will still be food after I shower."

A gruff laugh bubbled up from inside her. "You can't be that mad at me if you're quoting the show."

He didn't look back as he waddled into the bathroom and shut the door twice: once on his tail, then again for real. Faint scampering echoed across the tiles. The water sputtered on a second later.

Laying on the bed, she contemplated addressing the bulge in her pants, but guilt nagged at her. Even after an orgasm, he seemed freaked out. Poor Max: everybody forgot how sensitive he could be. Even she did sometimes. Deciding to check on him, she padded up to the bathroom and knocked on the door. "It's me." Her knocks of unexpected strength bounced the door open.

Cute little otter Maxie stood in the shower, hands on the wall, processing. He didn't look up. Water coursed down his dark pelt, streams shifted and merged with even the barest movement. "Hey."

"Hey." She poked her nose through the partly-open door. "Can I come in?"

A weary chuckle echoed off the tile and glass. "Nothing you haven't seen before."

He squirted a dollop of Pelt Plus into his paw.

He rubbed the goop onto himself, only to have it run straight onto the floor. "The shampoo just slides off."

She used her new, rumbling voice to narrate an imaginary TV commercial. "You need otter-strength shampoo and conditioner."

"I'm used to being the reliable one, the muscle." He wrapped his arms around his tiny body. "It's weird to feel...vulnerable."

"Vulnerable? That body has no handles to grab onto. You can wiggle away from pretty much anything. Or escape by sea."

He chuckled. "I've caught you a few times."

"Oh Maxie." She patted his shoulders. "I let you."

The otter rolled his eyes. A calming sigh left his supple frame, leaving his posture a little lighter. Water scattering off his downturned muzzle, he watched the glop of shampoo vanish down the drain.

Taking off her clothes, she managed not to tip over, which was an improvement over this morning. She stepped into the shower behind him, placing a paw on his shoulder that nearly covered it. Her large body took up most of the shower stall. Pattering rivulets soaked her fur. She wrapped muscular arms around him.

He allowed himself to sink into the standing cuddle. Then he wriggled, his tail bumping her crotch. "Is that what I think it is?"

"Yes." She shrugged, rubbing her half-unsheathed dick against his tail. The wet fur brushed, soft and exotic, against her growing erection. She resisted the urge to hump.

He buried his face in webbed paws. "Even as me, you're ridiculous."

"We'll worry about that later." Kylie tried to relax, hoping it would be contagious. "Right now, I think you just need me to hold you."

He leaned back against her, tucking his head under her chin. "I guess it's nice to be held."

Her paws traced down him, as she marveled at how well their bodies still fit together. "Yeah."

"This is super weird, though." He patted down his long otter tummy, which scattered droplets in fine arcs in front of him. "I feel...out-of-place."

"Yeah." Muzzle between his ears, she nodded. "Honestly? I'm starting to get sick of there being so much of me everywhere I look." She stretched out an arm, amazed she could reach across the entire interior of the shower stall. "Your body's weird too. It's really strong, but it's like gravity's taken a special interest. I have to slow down my hands when I let them drop or I'll whack them on something."

"It has a significant learning curve."

"I constantly have to be careful not to break everything. Or hurt you."

Her boyfriend nodded. "The key is to stop before you hear popping."

She chuckled against his ear. Hot water sloshed down her fluffy body. "Sound advice."

Under the hiss of hot water, a slow sigh rasped from Max's muzzle. "What if we're stuck like this?"

Kylie shrugged, arms wrapped around his lithe form. "We won't be."

His hazel eyes glinted up at her. "But if we are?"

"Dunno." She dwelled on the thought. "Guess you'll still be the only person in the world who doesn't think I'm nuts."

"True." He snuggled back against her with a quiet, comforted chitter. The water bounced off his pelt and soaked into hers as he snickered. "I know it for sure."

III

Joe's Quonset hut lay stripped bare. Door open, every scrap of material gone, down to the last roofing nail. Faint drag marks on the floor dust all led to the door, the only sign anything had been there.

"Where'd it all go?" Kylie dropped character, flapping massive arms up and down, cracking a knuckle on the ceiling and then snarling at the injury. As she cradled her paw, she spun around the darkened steel-and-concrete space. "Okay, seriously, what happened to all the boxes? The tools? The alien artifacts?"

Max knelt to examine the dirt tracks. "Somebody brought a truck in." He pointed a webbed finger at the trampled grass leading to the door. "Those shoe prints aren't big or small enough to be ours."

"So literally any adult." Her growl sounded very authentic, like she'd been a frustrated husky for years. "Can't you use your farm dog powers to find who it was?"

"I'm not currently the canine in this relationship." His phone snapped pictures of the tire and shoe treads.

"Right. Right." Angling her nose into the air, Kylie posed dramatically and sniffed. Wind danced across her fluff. Her ears flipped down as she turned to Max. "I don't know how to be a dog."

He rolled his eyes. "First of all, it's easier if you're close to the smell." He swept a paw along the ground and at the door handle. "Whoever did this probably touched the door a number of times."

Her mouth fell open in disgust. "I don't wanna smell some weirdo's hand."

With an extended blink, he unrolled a sigh. "Just smell the door, Kylie."

She crouched by the door, aimed her muzzle at the handle, and breathed in. "Okay, I think I smelled door."

"Quick little breaths, in and out, mouth shut." His index finger lifted her lower jaw into place. "Panting can blow the smell away from your nose."

"I mostly smell grass. And dirt, I guess." She sniffed again. "Grease. Maybe a little rust?"

"Good." He nodded. "Between deodorant, perfume, shampoo, and detergent, most people smell like something artificial. Smell anything like that?"

Kylie took a very deep breath. Then sneezed. Hardly the cute little sneeze of an otter, the explosive woof rattled through the empty shed and into the woods. Birds took flight. Crickets unnoticed fell silent.

With his tiny otter ears blasted flat against his skull, he turned to her. A deep breath steadied him. He steepled his webbed paws and pointed at the door. "Try not to sneeze. It can disperse the scent."

Sharp blue eyes cast him a glance. She returned to sniffing at the door around elbow height. "Okay, I smell a smell."

"Great! What is it?"

"I have no idea." Straightening, she propped large white paws on her hips. "I thought dogs could identify smells!"

"We can. It's something you practice." His webbed hands paddled at the air for a metaphor. "Like telling wines apart by taste."

The towering husky scoffed. "No one can actually do that."

He sighed. "Focus, rudderbutt."

"I've been smelling everything since I got into this body. I've been try-ing to filter it out." She rolled her eyes. "Now I'm supposed to focus."

Crossing his arms over unfamiliar breasts, he tossed her a questioning look.

"Sorry, I'm not trying to be grumpy. I just keep forgetting your body needs to breathe constantly and giving myself a headache." She sighed, heavy shoulders slumping as she rubbed her face. "How will this help us? No way I'm going to be able to follow this smell down the road."

"One step at a time." He raised an index finger, a little surprised when webbing tugged the middle finger halfway up too.

"Okay, I smell it again." She looked around the Quonset hut and dirt tracks. "How do we know this smell wasn't here before?"

Still crouched beside her, her boyfriend closed his eyes and let his mind drift back to when they'd walked into the shed. "When we came here the first time, Joe's shed smelled like steel, motor oil, old cardboard, dust, paint, wood, tar, plastic tarps…"

Kylie blinked. "That's actually really impressive."

Modesty squirmed through him. His thick tail wagged against the grass about a centimeter in either direction.

She waggled a thick finger at him. "I still say Strangeville jumped the shark with that episode where you could smell things before they happened."

He rocked from side to side. "Aw, I liked that one. That's like, the origi-nal canine superpower."

She rolled her eyes, only to be startled by a too-cloudy nictitating membrane. She blinked it away, then turned to him. "What's step two?"

"Wander around town until we find a truck that matches these im-prints." He held the phone up at her. "And/or you smell something."

"Very funny." She rolled her head side to side, blocking the sun out with those erect ears. "You're kidding, right?"

Max just smirked. Then he started back toward the car.

Still standing by the entrance to Joe's storage shed, she threw her hands in the air. "At least tell me I don't look that sinister when I smile with that mouth."

~ ~ ~

Windfall wasn't that big of a town, but it had a large population of smells. Some fantastic, some horrible, all of them presented in high resolution and clamoring for space in her brain. Kylie worried people would think she was nuts, sniffing at the air every few meters, but nobody seemed to pay much attention to that particular activity from her giant canine body. But that didn't help her sift through the smells any faster.

After spending hours wandering around downtown, smelling everything, she halted with a growl. "I'm tired of being a dog. I only wanna breathe to get oxygen."

Her boyfriend crossed his arms over his breasts. "What do you think panting is about?"

"The constant overheating, obviously." She fanned the collar of her t-shirt. "And I can't even swim because I'd probably drown once this fur soaked through. Or dissolve like a packing peanut."

He pulled out his phone, flicking to a weather app. "It is 12 Celsius." He fought to stuff the phone into his tiny, useless girl-pants pocket. "And my body is not a packing peanut."

A pachyderm pedestrian happened to pass by for that part of the conversation and judged them both down the length of her trunk.

Groaning, Kylie stroked paws down her jowls. "Mom's gonna lose her mind when we tell her we found and then lost her cabinet doors."

Max perked his little round otter ears. "Think she'll also lose her mental block against the supernatural? Then we could at least explain the situation."

"She could never be that mad." His girlfriend rolled her eyes. "We could punch a hole in the house and, so long as we did it in a flying saucer, we'd be fine."

"Something's been bothering me." He furrowed his brow. "Whoever beat us back to the shed scooped it all indiscriminately. They had to be after supernatural evidence too. Most of Joe's stuff wasn't worth stealing…"

Hopping over a curb, Kylie spun to face him and waved paws at her crotch while doing hip thrusts. "Ugh! What is up with the constant gymnastic routines in my underpants?"

A mother possum cast a dark glance at her, then dragged her daisy-chain of offspring away from the rude display.

Max rolled his eyes. "We're in public. You can stop talking about your junk."

"Guys never stop talking about their junk. Except you. You're weirdly modest about it." Standing beside him, she gripped his shoulders and leaned in to deliver a lecherous combination of grin and eyebrow waggle. "Not that you have any reason to be."

"I don't know what guys you've been listening to." Her boyfriend sighed, but made no move to shake her off. "Please stop being lewd."

"It's super distracting, though! Everything's flopping around down there." Bowlegged, she pranced down the sidewalk. "My balls keep doing this thing where they raise and lower without orders."

"That's for temperature regulation." Max folded his paws behind his back. "It's a sperm production thing."

Head tilted back, she groaned. "Guys are so weird. You don't see my ovaries doing pull-ups of their own accord."

He snorted. "Yes. Ovaries being known for only doing exactly what you want them to."

"Wait a minute…" Kylie paused, nose in the air. She stood before the front door to the Windfall Chamber of Commerce building. The scent led here. She was certain of it. Far more certain than she'd been when she briefly had a passing vixen's musk fry her neurons. "Hmmm… I think…"

Max watched her, hands on his streamlined hips.

She smiled. "I found it."

"You found it?" He looked around and wiggled his ottery nose in vain. "You're sure?"

"Sure, I'm sure." She nodded at the glass door. Invisible lines of smell-destiny led her there, even now.

"You're sure it's…" He leaned around her to read the sign's sensible font. "…the Chamber of Commerce?"

Her massive paws curled into fists. "Max, we're going in."

"What?" He waddled up beside her. "How?"

She flashed a wolfish grin down at him. "Well, if I've learned anything from this, no one can physically stop your body."

He studied the front door and noted its lack of armor. "…Good point, but—"

She swung the door open and stepped inside. The pleasant cool of air conditioning washed over her, reminding her how overheated she'd become just walking around on a sunny day.

Real paintings and fake plants decorated the interior. The ionized tang of computers hung in the air, accompanied by the scent of paper. The gray, short-pile carpet scuffed under her every step.

Behind the front desk sat a white rabbit. Her ears popped up. The rest of her body remained still as she studied them in silence. The nameplate in front of her read "Justine."

"Hello!" Kylie's voice boomed in the enclosed space. "Looking for a load of weird stuff that got brought in here."

The door clicked shut as Max followed her into the office.

Still seated, the bunny gave her a quizzical look. Were it not for the subtle tuning-in motion of those tall ears, she could have been mistaken for a statue. Her white blouse and black headset shone, spotless. Her dark hair was drawn into a tight coil at the back of her head. Dispassionate brown eyes studied the interlopers.

"I'll just talk to whoever's in charge." Voices perked Kylie's own ears. Though the rest of the office sounded quiet, muffled conversation rumbled from a closed room, marked "Conference." She pointed a thick finger at it. "In here, right?"

Before she could take two strides to the door, the rabbit sprung out of her seat and scampered to stand between her and the door. For being only shoulder height on the husky, she sure put on an unflappable expression. Whenever the intruder reached for the doorknob, she sidled in front of her hand.

"Excuse me." Kylie moved the admin to one side with a slow, but unstoppable hand. Before the bunny could bounce up in front of her, she seized the knob.

Justine, in an admirable effort, grabbed the husky's wrist and kicked off the door frame with both powerful legs. While this maneuver would've thrown most people in town back, it only managed to rotate Kylie. The rabbit herself ended up on the floor with quiet grunt.

Finding the path into the conference room clear, Kylie walked into the room. She tripped only a little as the rabbit clamped onto her ankle with a silent glare.

Max covered his face with a webbed paw. "I'm really sorry about this…"

Kylie marched into the conference room, a rabbit administrative professional wrapped around her leg. The space held a large oak table, around which three surprised middle-aged men sat. A flight of waterfowl paintings hung in formation on one wall, flanked by a globe split in half to reveal a small glass city of scotch bottles. Faded posters from town festivals, including a death worm in bell-bottoms inviting her to "Get your funk on!" gleamed inside expensive wooden frames.

A frazzled squirrel clutched his coffee cup, as if the intruders had come to take it away from him. A ferret spun in his office chair to face them, crumbs on his muzzle. Unmoved, a cougar in a brown tweed suit watched with slitted eyes.

For a moment, everybody in the room watched each other in silence.

Leaning back in his leather chair, the big feline purred. "Your efforts are appreciated Justine, but the town's favorite TV couple is welcome to crash our meeting."

Feeling the grip on her shin loosen, Kylie lifted her leg free of the admin. "Sorry about that."

The secretary picked herself up. After a few steps back, she glowered at them from the hallway, methodically straightening her skirt, ears, whiskers, headset, and bun. Within seconds, she'd reset perfectly to the state they'd first seen her in, foot tapping with impatience.

"Well. Hello." The squirrel spread his paws. "I'm Marv, the owner of UFO Safari. If we'd known you kids were so eager to talk, we'd have put you on the schedule."

"And brought more of my famous mini-cupcakes." The ferret slid the plastic platter of pastries toward the newcomers, then picked the one he'd been chewing at off the table. "I'm Bob. I run Salad Days and Arkham Hors d'Oeuvres."

"So…" Trying to salvage the situation, Max straightened to his unremarkable height and surveyed the room's occupants. "You're the Chamber of Commerce?"

"Some of it!" The ferret set down the mini-cupcake he'd been nibbling at.

Without a wasted movement, the big cat steepled his fingers. "Gary, head of tourism for the city."

Taking his girlfriend's arm, he tried to sound like an otter. "I'm Kylie and this is Max."

The cupcake-munching mustelid wobbled in his seat. "Oh, we know who you are."

"What's that supposed to mean?" Kylie's massive paws tightened into fists. "You've been spying on us?"

"Not exactly spying! Hard to miss when TV stars show up and start stirring up business." Marv twirled and clicked a pen. "What'd ya say, Bob? A ten percent uptick in online merchandise just from them movin' to town?"

"Oh yeah. I'd say." Bob bobbed his triangular head.

The cougar glanced to them with an unreadable growl. "Why did you barge into our meeting?"

Kylie straightened a few inches taller. "Look, we know you took Joe's stuff. You've gotta let us have it back. You don't know what you're messing around with."

A smile shone on the big cat's muzzle, not touching his eyes. "The situation is under control."

A dark woof launched from Kylie's muzzle. "You mean now that you stole all the stuff in Joe's shed."

"We detected some strange activity going on there." Gary swept some crumbs off his portion of the table. "We removed some items in the interest of public safety."

"Public safety?" Kylie barked with derision.

"Strange activity?" Max chittered with interest.

"Once in a rare while, something dangerous will crop up in Windfall. We take steps to make sure it doesn't interfere with business." The middle-aged feline lifted his clawed hands. "Tourists like to feel brave, not actually be brave."

"We also don't want anybody takin' the good stuff!" The ferret gave a self-impressed laugh. "Selling it online—that's our golden goose they're cooking!"

Kylie jabbed a finger at them. "So you admit supernatural stuff happens here?"

"It gets a little crazy, yes." Gary leaned forward, fangs glinting in another practiced smile. "But it's never been something we couldn't handle."

She blinked. Having someone admit they believed in that stuff, in a serious setting with serious plaques on the walls, threw off her expectations. She assumed she'd have to fight to make them admit it. "So you knew Joe was going home?"

"So, what happens now?" Max crossed his arms across his breasts. "You cover this up and ignore it, like you covered up Joe's house collapsing?"

"What are you talking about?" The squirrel looked up from pouring another sugar in his coffee, scattering tiny white grains across the dark wood table. "We didn't cover up anything. We may have…discouraged the papers from talking about it, but that's only because we don't want people getting spooked about the mines collapsing. What do you mean, 'going home'?"

"To his home planet, or dimension, or whatever." She jabbed a thick finger at the ceiling. "He didn't give us a lot of details."

Ferret, squirrel, cougar, and rabbit straightened in silence. Ears perked around the room.

Bob raised a pink paw. "Whoa, whoa, hang on. Joe was an alien?"

Marv twitched to face to his cougar companion. "Did we know about that?"

"No." Gary straightened his suit. "He didn't exactly put it in the meeting minutes."

Justine watched from the hallway, her face unreadable, her opinions unasked for.

Another moment stretched on in silence. Max and Kylie exchanged a glance of intrigue. Maybe these guys didn't know everything after all.

"Oh! I get it!" The ferret tittered a laugh and clapped his little paws together. "You're spinning Joe's disappearance into the town lore." He drummed his hands on the table, his feet on the floor. "Man, Bevys really are an asset."

"No, really. Joe was an alien in a beaver suit. He tried to kill us to get something he needed to go home. Then he imploded his alien lair on the way out." Kylie jabbed a thick finger in the direction of the vanished building. "That's why his house collapsed into the ground."

"Really? Wow." Marv scratched a tufted ear. "Guess that explains a few things."

The ferret bobbed his head rapidly. "Yeah, like why he never went out for drinks with us."

"Or why someone as private as Joe wanted to take our meeting notes. Must have been keeping tabs on us." Gary's sharp claws scratched through his chin fur. "How long had he been in town?"

"Technically..." In the face of a slight squeak, Max cleared his unfamiliar throat. "He'd been around for centuries in one disguise or another. You could even say he founded the town. His first attempt at getting home blew up and exposed all those silver veins the first settlers were after."

The cougar studied Max carefully. "You think he's coming back?"

"Not if he can help it." Kylie laughed. "Once he had what he needed, he couldn't get out of our reality fast enough."

Marv fluffed his bushy tail. "Guess we can stop reserving his parking spot."

Bob nodded his whole body in agreement. "Dibs."

A soft clicking noise announced Justine making a note of it on her phone. Once done, she nodded to her bosses.

"Don't you guys care?" Kylie glared down the table at them. "We were this close to him blowing everybody up. His machine messed with those leyline things under the town. Who knows what else it did?"

The ferret's ears popped up, followed by the rest of his long torso. "That was you?"

"We always suspected you kids did that— What was it?" The red squirrel snapped his fingers. "That thing Martha from the Open Chakra was going on about… About the leylines being all jazzed up…"

The ferret adjusted his long, slender necktie. "Psychic convergence?"

"Yeah!" The squirrel sloshed his coffee. "She calls it psychic convergence." He winked at the younger mammals. "I call it year-round tourist season."

"That thing is real?" The ferret blinked. "I thought she was crazy."

"Doesn't mean she's wrong." Marv leaned on the conference table, which wobbled a little, then gave the intruders a thumbs up. "Anyway, you kids keep doing your thing. Great for business."

Kylie propped her fists on her hips and struck a statuesque pose. "Our thing is exposing the supernatural."

"That's the spirit!" The ferret nodded. "And if you could maybe talk up the Cryptozoology Jamboree?"

Kylie slammed her palms down onto the table so hard that one of the mini-cupcakes tipped over. "We'll take you down if we have to."

"Oooh!" Bob patted his ferret paws together. "A 'fight the power' narrative. We can make it a theme next year."

"Yeah!" Clattering down his coffee onto the table, the squirrel punched a fist into his own palm. "Fighting the sinister authority. We could play the bad guys. You could search lead a search for the truth."

"Stop it!" She woofed with outrage. "That's what we've been doing!"

"And you're being a big help!" Marv patted her on the shoulder. "We haven't seen this kind of push since your uncle burned down that house."

Kylie shoved his hand away and bounced in place. "An alien monster was in that house."

"You heard that part, huh?" Bob nodded. "It did have some staying power."

"You're playing with fire." Kylie barked. "You're going to get us all killed."

"That's a good angle. Good passion too." Bob oozed his long body forward onto the table and grasped another mini-cupcake. "I guess it really shows when you're working with professionals."

"And now you kids did this leyline thing?" The squirrel poked a finger straight down against the table, then gave them a thumbs-up. "Keep it up!"

She glared at him. "We will!"

His bushy tail fluffed. "So how can we help you with this 'fight the power' act?

"It's not an act!" The otter bounced with outrage. "And you can't!"

Max straightened, hands behind his back. "By definition."

"Right! Right. But still? Oh, I know…" Marv rifled through his briefcase. "Here are some of our 'close encounter' upgrade coupons. If you kids could stash them in weird places around town, that would be just super." He slapped a stack of paper tickets into Max's paw.

Max tilted his head at the offering. The coupons had a pith helmet emitting a tractor beam, with UFO Safari in Papyrus font. "Shouldn't you laminate these? If they're going to be outside…"

"See, Bob?" The squirrel chattered a laugh. "This is just the sort of fresh thinking we need around here."

"No kidding, Marv." The slender mustelid nodded his entire body in agreement.

"Max!" With an urgent whisper, Kylie prodded him with an elbow. "Don't help them."

As soon as he regained his balance, Max cast her a quick glare. Having a big otter tail made balancing difficult.

The feline narrowed his eyes at them. With what might have been a purr or a growl, the cougar leaned back to unlock and reach into a drawer of the cabinet behind him, plucking out a tiny filigreed music box. After winding it, his clawed fingers clicked a little lever down. It began tinkling merrily. He set it onto the solid-oak table, letting it resonate through the sudden silence.

The chatter between Marv and Bob ground to a halt. The squirrel blinked at it, then at them, oddly appraising. "So, uh, you kids get hit with some kinda psychic energy lately?"

Kylie straightened. "No!"

The bushy-tailed rodent jerked a thumb at the silver clockwork device plinking soft notes on a shelf. "Because that music box only works when there's spooky brain stuff going on."

"Something you want to tell us?" The cougar steepled his paws. "Maybe we could help."

She crossed her muscular arms. "The only spooky brain stuff here is you trying to give us the run-around."

Max waved a paw between himself and his girlfriend. "We're in each other's bodies."

"Oh!" Bob chattered through a laugh, brandishing half a cupcake at them. "That lines up better with what we'd heard of the two of you."

"Hey!" She barked back at the businessmen. "What's that supposed to mean?"

"You kids know how TV works, right?" The squirrel spread his paws on the table, then raised them with displeasure and scrubbed them clean of crumbs. "People can see what you do on it."

Max patted his girlfriend on the chest. "Please excuse her; she's not herself right now."

A narrow-eyed look of incredulity dropped on him from his much-taller mate.

The three of board members looked at each other. Little shrugs rippled around the table. Quiet agreement bounced between the trio.

With the other two's silent assent, Marv twirled a finger in the air. "Justine, could we get the urn in here? Thanks." Ears flipped back suavely, he again leaned forward on the table, this time with a bucktoothed, snake-oil smile. "This usually works."

The secretary vanished, ducked into an office, and returned a couple seconds later with a polished gold burial urn. She popped the lid off, dumped a collection of loose candy wrappers into the trash, and offered it to the intruders.

Kylie cast a sidelong look at the container. "Does this...belong to somebody?"

"Yeah: me." The ferret jerked a thumb at himself. "Hopefully, I won't need it for a while, but I want it back."

Max narrowed his gaze at the trio of businessmen. "Why would you help us?"

The cougar interlaced his fingers, flexing claws in and out. "We haven't helped you yet."

"But what's the catch?" Kylie eyed the three business mammals.

The ferret wiggled. "We keep Joe's stuff."

"No deal!" She slapped hand down on the heavy wooden table. The whole thing tilted down a few degrees, then rattled back onto the floor. "We need it to prove aliens exist."

The squirrel snapped his fingers at them. "And we want you to do a radio ad."

"No radio ad. And we get the cherry wood cabinet doors." Max crossed his arms over his breasts. "We'll sign ten Strangeville t-shirts."

Rapidly tapping his fingertips together, Marv stared down the apparent otter negotiating with him. "Fifty."

Max nodded with a confidence cool enough for Hollywood producer. "Done."

The ferret sputtered into a whisper. "You shoulda asked for a hundred."

Marv patted his shoulder. "A hundred's not a limited edition in a town this small."

"Seriously?" Kylie dropped a glum look on her boyfriend. "The cabinet doors?"

"What?" Flipping a webbed paw toward the door, he wiggled his whiskers up at her. "They're bought and paid for. And they're still shrink-wrapped. They're perfectly fine."

Rolling her eyes, she examined the urn. She turned it over in her heavy white paws. The still-strange reflection gleamed back at her. She glanced back to the squabbling Chamber members. "Do we have to do, like, an incantation?"

"What? No." The squirrel snapped his head toward them. "It's not magic."

"Blocks the signal." Quick pink tongue flashing over pointy teeth, the ferret licked crumbs off his fingers. "We don't know what the signal is, but gold blocks it."

A growl rose from Kylie, rumbling through the room. "Don't you want to know how any of this stuff works?"

"Hey now!" Marv laughed and jerked a thumb at the tiny device. "We don't know who built this music box or why. All we know is it plays around strong psychic energy. If we took it apart, it might not do that. So we don't take it apart. That's how the town works."

Bob poked a finger in the air. "Except the town makes us money."

The cougar looked up from his claws. "And we take steps to ensure its stability. Especially from disruptive outside influence."

Max watched her glower down at the seated cougar. Before the situation could take a turn for the worse, he deposited the urn in her gigantic hands, then stepped toward the trio. "So you guys aren't going to try to stop us from studying the town?"

"Why would we?" Gary cleaned some invisible speck of dirt off one claw with another. "Supernatural tourism has been paying our bills for half a century."

"Yeah, go nuts." Marv waved a paw. "We've seen you run around town. You obviously know what you're doing. But I guess we shouldn't expect anything different considering your mom made a TV show about us."

Reaching for another mini-cupcake, Bob nodded. "Best thing that ever happened to this place." He grinned as he unwrapped the pastry. "How else do you think I'd be able to afford a gold urn?"

The cougar steepled sharpened claws. He lifted his chin toward the container. "What're you waiting for?"

Max glanced to his girlfriend. Borrowed hazel eyes suggested the door with a fleeting glance.

She waggled the urn, fluorescent light shimmering off its polished surface. As she backed out of the room, she flashed the Chamber of Commerce a toothy canine smile. "We'll take it to go."

Bob popped up. "Remember I need that back!"

"Cripes, Bob." The squirrel rolled his eyes. "They live in the most famous house in town."

"Yes." The cougar purred, his gaze locked on the couple as they exited. "We can always go knock on their door."

Clutching the urn, Kylie cast him a stern look, even as Max pushed her down the hallway, toward the front door and out onto the street.

Once they were a block away, she inspected the gold jar with obvious interest, stumbling over gaps in the sidewalk. "Heh. Being this big, I could have just taken the urn. And whatever else."

He stopped her by the wrist. Checking that nobody was within earshot, he faced her. Exasperation flickered in his eyes. "Okay, here's the deal: you—" He poked her in the chest. "—are not a tiny lady right now."

"Yes." She hefted the metal container with a grin, then hefted the urn in an amiable way. "But if this thing works like they said—"

"No, Kylie." He paused her comment with a raised hand. "You're too large to be talking about your junk in public and slamming your hands on tables. You need to show some restraint."

She propped her hands on her hips. "Restraint?"

"When you're my size, losing your cool freaks people out. Nobody knows what rules you'll break next and it's super clear they couldn't stop you." His brow furrowed. "You can't just walk like you're going to bowl everybody out of the way. You can't suddenly start yelling because you're excited." He took a deep breath, trying to steady his frantic lutrine heart. "There's stuff you can get away with when you're small and cute that you can't when you're big. When you get annoyed and growl at someone, it's endearing. When I do it, it's a threat."

She threw her arms in the air. "It's not like I'm gonna hurt somebody!"

"But nobody else knows that. They just know you could and you're signaling that you want to. I put a lot of effort into making sure people aren't scared of me. I don't want to be known as a bully. And it only takes a few slip-ups to get that reputation."

She straightened, muzzled closed. Hearing Max that insistent, even in her voice, took her aback. And seeing him visibly upset prompted a pang of guilt, enough that she stopped to reassess how she'd look in her borrowed body. Much as she liked how big and gentle he was, she'd never considered that he was gentle because he was big. After a silent second, she slowly nodded. "Okay, I see how that could be a problem. You could have told me sooner it was a big deal."

"I know. I've been meaning to." He glanced down.

A car rumbled past. Birds flitted overhead. In the distance, unseen citizens laughed and shouted in the park. Kylie angled her muzzle down at him. "You can tell me stuff."

He wrapped himself in his arms, glancing around to see if anyone had heard his outburst. "I know..."

"And you will?" She extended a giant white paw. "I don't like making you mad, Maxie."

He brightened a little at the nickname. His webbed fingers curled over hers. Hand in hand, they walked onward to her tiny car.

~ ~ ~

They pulled up at Bourn Manor, finding Laura's car gone. Hurrying inside, Max dragged his girlfriend to the living room sofa, knowing they had the house to themselves. Once seated facing each other, he surveyed the immediate area for dangers. With a thick tail he'd only begun to figure out, he scooted the coffee table out of head-butt range.

His girlfriend sighed. "Is this really necessary?"

"Last time, the switch knocked us both on our tails." He propped her up with pillows, then packed some around himself. "For all I know, we could have a seizure or something."

She drummed thick fingers on the sofa arm. "So, can we try it now?"

"I guess?" He shrugged. "Switching our bodies back seems like the sort of thing you don't just…do."

She rolled his eyes. "Okay, I'll count to three."

"On three?" A small whine escaped his throat. "Or three, then go?"

"Ugh." Kylie shoved her hand in the urn.

A metallic ping rang out inside the container as the bracelet popped loose. Max's own bracelet snapped free and sprung against the wall.

Blink.

Max opened his eyes to find his hand stuffed into the gold cylinder. Across from him, sat Kylie—in her proper body, and wearing it much better than he'd ever felt.

"Woo!" The otter sprung up from the couch, twirling on her toes and frolicking about the carpet. "It worked!"

"Huh." Max nodded, glancing down at familiar white paws, one still covered in the urn. "I guess switching back to our own bodies isn't as big a deal."

"Guess that makes sense." Leaning in, Kylie fished the bracelet from the golden vessel, careful not to let it snap around her wrist. She retrieved its mate from behind the sofa and linked them together with a victorious wiggle. "Maybe it just switched off whatever was on, ya know? Like, the brain link." She pointed slowly at her head.

Max rolled his eyes. It felt nice to have his own eyes again. Reassuring. He glanced to the bracelets. "Maybe we should keep these?"

Kylie savored a supple wiggle. "Yeah, then we can use them whenever I have my period."

The husky crossed his arms. "And this is when we cut to a shot of the wristbands tumbling down into a gorge."

She patted her fishing vest, then, with a chatter, started swapping the contents of various pouches. "You have brought chaos into my pockets."

Very gently, in case he'd forgotten his own strength in the past few days, he took her wrists and drew her close. Softly and deliberately, he kissed her.

She giggled. Dancing in place, she bumped his nose with hers. "What was that for?"

He shrugged, a shy blush warming his dipping ears. "Just happy to have us back."

The otter's entire body waggled, building up energy.

Max eyed his girlfriend. His ears perked at the variety of squeaky giggles rising from her. Taking a seat on the sofa, he found gazing at her only made her wiggle more. He wasn't sure he liked whatever she was planning.

Chitters of anticipation bubbled up from Kylie. Her nimble form bounced from foot to foot. After a wiggle of deliberation, she plopped down on the couch and slapped the bracelet back onto his wrist.

The world tilted wildly under Max. A whirl of vertigo, a blinding blur. His vision blanked out, then reappeared from another position in the room, from another body. "Ugh! Kylie!"

She was towering in his body again. Apparently, swapping bodies wasn't so bad the second time around. Having not even keeled over, she flashed him a winning smile.

Sprawled out on the sofa, he chattered with shock and annoyance. Webbed paws scrambled to prop him back up, then pressed to his eyes. He glared up at her with borrowed eyes. "Really?"

"I wanted to see if it still worked!" She crossed her arms, then almost tipped over from the change in weight distribution. A quick wobble of her giant paws stabilized her.

"It worked…" He groaned and dragged fingers down his face, then shook his head. "I feel like I was turned inside out."

She placed a paw on his arm, the heavy white digits curling most of the way around it. "You okay?"

A moment passed as he wiggled all his borrowed limbs, then he nodded. "Warn me next time."

"Good." She attempted a wiggle, which arrived as more of a top-heavy wobble. "'Cause I have something I wanna do." Her paw closed fully around his. "If you're okay with it? Something naughty."

With a suspicious look, Max considered her for a second, then slowly nodded.

Brimming with excitement, she attempted a scamper and managed a stomp. It carried her up the stairs nonetheless. She leaned down over the top of the railing. "Wait here! I gotta get it all ready!" With a deep giggle, she vanished into the bedroom and closed the door. A great clatter rattled from behind it.

Max sat in his borrowed body. Whatever Kylie had planned, he felt more at ease knowing they could switch back any time. He'd figured she might want to try something like this. He was curious too, he admitted. And he trusted her to take care of him. That felt good, somewhere deep inside.

His small paws flexed before him. This body didn't feel so strange anymore, though he reminded himself it was on loan. He'd been careful with it, especially since it wasn't as durable as his own. Leaning back against the wall, he managed to not step on his own tail: a testament to days of practice. On the other side of the wall, he heard the heavy footsteps of his own body and the jangling of hurried activity. He rolled his eyes. The strain of switching bodies certainly hadn't dampened Kylie's enthusiasm.

On a lark, he slipped off the sofa and padded to his room. The sundress lay draped over a chair. He could put it on, he supposed. It was cute. He could be cute for her. Shutting the door with his tail, he at last realized that maneuver was the trick to not slamming it on the appendage. Unsure how much time he had, he hurried out of his clothes and into the dress. Tying it behind his neck took a little doing, but he managed after a few tries. A soft spin before the mirror showed it off: a thin cotton twirl of greens and yellows. With nowhere to hurry to, he admired himself in the mirror. Being small had its upsides. His normal body wasn't built for this dress, even if it came in his size. Running paws down his curvy hips, he considered taking off his panties, but decided with a little smirk he shouldn't do all the work for her.

From upstairs, his girlfriend woofed with glee. "Okay! You can come up now."

He crested the stairs and rounded the corner to her room.

She grinned, tail swishing. Her big white paw creaked the door open theatrically. Jazz crooned. Rose petals lay scattered on the waterbed.

He nodded, impressed. "You really went all out."

"I have a plan sometimes." Her massive frame scampered around the room, lighting candles. She spun to face him, almost tipped over, then planted fluffy white fists on her hips. "Not bad, huh?"

Red wine chilled in a clam bucket full of ice.

His tiny ears flicked up. "Where's that from?" He picked up the bottle, ice slushing.

She tried to eel around him, but ended up stomping around the room, shaking loose the corner of a Sugar Gliders band poster on her wall. "Stole it from Mom."

"Where is she anyway?" He looked out the window with a shy laugh, but saw only Kylie's car in the driveway. "Won't she hear us?"

"Pretty sure she's at the plant store again." She jerked a thumb toward the door. Her massive paw pressed to the small of his back, drawing him near. Her paws traced the open back of his dress, just below where it was knotted. "We've got some time."

As they swayed into a slow dance, he looked around. "What prompted all this?"

Her ears dipped. "You said our first time wasn't like you pictured it." She swept a paw around the room. "So I painted a picture."

He nodded. "That's actually really sweet."

She propped a paw on her waist. "We gonna let all these candles go to waste?"

A nervous chuckle rattled from his muzzle.

"Seriously…" She winked. "…I can promise you'll like it."

He hesitated, tail curled in front of him.

"C'mon, Maxie. It's the most natural thing in the world to get plowed by a great big slab of dog meat." With several rude hip thrusts, she gave him a scandalous wink.

He snickered. Even in a dog body, she was still very much an otter. He leaned against her hulking form and swayed to the soft music. Allowing himself to be swept up, in the music, in the arms of the woman he loved, he found his supple form dancing with relaxed ease.

Her massive hand cradled his muzzle. A big reassuring smile broadened across that black and white muzzle. "More romantic this time? How's it compare?"

A roll of his eyes came naturally; a little introspection took a few seconds longer. But they weren't in a hurry. "I was in my body and used to holding your body, so, aside from a lack of pants, it was quite familiar." He leaned his head against her chest. "And even then I was a little terrified."

She brushed a lock of hair from his face. "And now?"

"Less so." Max guided her hands to his breasts.

Big, clumsy fingers toyed with those stiff nipples: tugging, squeezing, gently twisting through fabric.

The waterbed sloshed as they sat down. Kisses rained down. Clothes fluttered to the floor. Flower petals danced after them.

Kylie ground her hips forward, glistening cock slipping against Max's swollen, needy sex. She took her time. With absolute familiarity, she caressed his body. Everywhere. Letting him know, with every grip and whisper, he was in good hands.

Max had closed his eyes, panting up at the ceiling. He whimpered and arched his back as Kylie's fingers teased across his nipple, and, as she slipped her cock down to press the tip against his sex, his legs seemed to spread of their own accord, inviting her in. "Mmmf! Kylie…"

His girlfriend grinned down at him with a canine smile, beginning to apply the very barest amount of pressure, beginning to press forward. "But then I was so very gentle with you and you realized the truth." The tip of her cock sinking into him made them both shudder. "Nnngh… See? Just fits." She rocked her hips forward.

Chittering in pleasure, he wiggled atop the sheets. His curvy hips bucked up against her cock.

She bit her lip and sank into him. A slight resistance slowed her penetration, as she outpaced his lubrication. She giggled as she watched her length sink into him, a sound that came out deep and passionate growl.

His paws traced her fluffy pelt. "Mmf! Keep going…"

Growling, Kylie's jaw dropped open as she started thrusting into him. That big, stiff husky cock filled him. The silky slick of his excitement eased her fully in with each stroke.

Webbed paws gripped at her fur, urging her onward. His passage clung to her with hot, slippery tension. Such a strange and wonderful feeling, wanting that cock buried deep inside him. In addition to the textures, the friction, the slickness —all of which kept him buoyed through a sea of endorphins— the novel sense of fullness is what left his eyelids fluttering, his toes curling against the sheets.

She slipped, clumsy, from his slit. He squeaked at the sudden stimulation of his clit. Together, they giggled at their own ungainliness. The waterbed sloshed under them, echoing their haphazard movements.

He urged her faster. That muscular tail swished under her balls. His legs wrapped around her waist. "C'mon, Kylie! Faster! Please!"

A big grin broke out across her muzzle. Sure enough, she couldn't deny a request like that. Her huge body slammed him against the bed again and again. Lucky she had practice with the waterbed, after all those nights alone and, more recently, together in it. Timing each hump of her hips, she bucked hard against him. Before long, her knot bounced against his lips.

Whimpering with pleasure at the new stimulation against his clit, Max moaned. His quick little paws dove to frantically rub at his clit. Novel pleasures swept from his borrowed paws, those paws that had brought him to so many orgasms over the past months. With a tremendous squeak, his streamlined body arched up. His passage clutched around her, squeezing her shaft.

She grit her canid teeth, panting happily as he writhed in orgasm around her dick. Her massive body loomed over his. She gripped his shoulder, holding his little body against her hips. That thickening knot slipped out.

Eyes rolled back, he collapsed back onto the sloshing bed. Measureless time radiated through him, buzzing in the haze of afterglow. Webbed paws, sticky with his juices, trembled to her knot. Rubbing, squeezing, gripping, they rubbed all the right spots. With so many years of practice, he knew how to get his dick hard to the point of dripping.

A wolfish growl rattled the room. Thrusts sped. Climax overcame her. Those powerful hips slammed fully into him. She shuddered atop him, buried in him to the knot. Throbs pulsed up her length and deep inside her boyfriend. Tension rippled through that muscular body, so much larger than his current one. Her expression showed a singular surprise, like she'd been been caught off guard by the instinct to tie and blown away by the sensation. Hazy, she looked him in the eyes as if to ask, wordless, if it always felt this good.

He smiled up at her and gripped her trembling hips. The unfamiliar, but welcome, fullness of being tied pressed the breath from Max. His hips rocked gently, his crotch firmly affixed to hers. His girlfriend's cock spurted heat against his walls. The warmth radiated through his sensitive body.

Spent, she flopped down onto him. At her impact, the bed frame scuffed against the floor. Rose petals rushed up, only to fall in graceful spirals. A confined tidal wave sloshed inside the waterbed. Her massive lungs panted like bellows, greedy for air.

Max rode atop the ripples, his supple body conforming to every crest and trough. In a body made for wiggling, he explored how every little shift of his hips felt with that knot buried in him. Afterglow stretched on, impossibly drawn out. He found himself caressing her naked pelt. He could feel it so well with her paws, webs and all. Maybe he should start using more fur conditioner.

Time lost its meaning. She lay atop him, a weight as comforting as it was warm. He knew she'd take care of him. A very primal part of his brain hummed with safety. His legs rested on her hips. Buffeted by slow waves of pleasure, he squirmed atop the sheets.

"Mmm…" Face still buried in his hair, she chuckled. "Better this time?"

He nodded into her shoulder. "The best."

Her fluffy tail bounced between his feet. "Good."

Another spell of serenity settled over them. Their breathing slowed. Even his frantic otter heart slowed, though it still pattered on with pure joy. He felt so warm and loved, inside and out.

Once she'd regained some degree of coordination, she shifted to her elbows. Still very much tied, this position at least afford them the luxury of looking each other in the face. "I'm sorry I made you mad."

"Mff?" Anger was the furthest emotion from his heart at the moment.

"By being a brute." She shrugged her heavy shoulders. "And accidentally promising you'd go back to the farm."

His eyes closed. Ah yes: real life. "Long term, I guess it's just as well you talked to my mom. Going home was inevitable."

"Yes!" Face fluffing back into the pillow, she pumped a fluffy fist in the air. "Absolution."

A faint groan rumbled in his throat. "Just don't do it again."

"I think I can manage that." She flopped a paw down their bodies to grope his thick tail. "How 'bout this idea?"

"This was a surprisingly good idea." He caressed her shoulder. "Though I still like being myself."

"Yeah!" Her powerful paws gripped his hips. "I never imagined I'd be so good at knotting you."

The husky groaned, burying his face in her throat fluff.

"Aww, shy Maxie." She stroked him from shoulder blades to tail. "Want me to grab the urn?" Under the weight of afterglow, she rolled her head to one side to face him. "So we can switch back?"

Max heaved a sigh, still stuck on her dick. Being under her fluffy bulk like this, having her buried inside him like this, felt safe and pleasant on a very deep level. He doubted her picking him up and staggering downstairs to get the urn would feel as good. Maybe they'd have to keep something on hand for next time. A blush heated under his cheek ruffs at the thought of a next time. They had all the time they wanted, so long as they kept working to understand each other. And, having been Kylie for a little while now, he decided he had a lot left to understand. He rubbed a webbed paw down her flank, a smile blooming in his voice. "Later."

~ ~ ~

In the grocery parking lot, Kylie watched as Max and two of the suits from the Chamber of Commerce loaded cabinet doors into the back of her mother's car. She leaned against the hot steel of a fender, clutching a never-used burial urn.

Carrying one door at a time, the ferret weaved around his companion. "We should hire an intern to do the heavy lifting for us."

Marv chattered. "Pay some some college kid minimum wage and ask tell him not to tell everyone aliens exist? Yeah, that'll go well." His bushy red tail twitched with impatience. "In a small business, you gotta do the legwork yourself."

Max, returned to his husky brawn, grabbed the last five doors and placed them inside the hatchback.

The slender mustelid slithered up to Kylie and extended a paw. "My urn?"

With both hands, she plopped it into his grasp.

"Thank you!" He snatched the vessel away. From his pants pocket, he produced a lens cloth and polished the paw prints from it. When able to admire his reflection on the golden surface, he grinned.

Marv vibrated them both a jittery handshake, in turn. "Pleasure doin' business with you kids! Look forward what you can cook up for the industry."

Her boyfriend's gaze stopped her from snapping at him

They headed back toward the Chamber of Commerce building. "Why's it gotta be my stuff we loan out?"

The red squirrel laughed. "Because you have the most stuff."

"You can't prove that." A pout entered the ferret's tone.

"I've seen your storage unit, Bob..." Their voices faded out of earshot.

The otter watched them go, palms resting on the hood of the car. "Well, we made our deal with the secret cabal." She heaved a sigh. "What'd we do now?"

Sidling up to her, Max slipped an arm around her shoulders. A moment passed in comfortable silence, as he pulled up a document on his phone. Then he smirked down at her. "Your mom did want us to pick up groceries."

They headed into the store. Max texted Laura for the shopping list. Kylie extrapolated a rough approximation of it into their cart before he got a reply. The main difference was a generous stack of frozen eel pies. They rang up at the self checkout, smiled with sympathy to the kid who had to collect the carts in an alien costume, and headed back across the parking lot.

Noon light shining off every car in the lot, Kylie waddled to her mom's hatchback, a giant paper-wrapped salmon fillet in her paws. Heat leached from her paws into the refrigerated fish. She opened the back and placed the meter-long prize inside. One good thing about being an otter again was that she wouldn't demolish the whole thing before she got full.

Max loaded the six bags he'd been carrying into the car. He climbed into the driver's seat. The suspension creaked under him, though it didn't rock nearly as much as the Amphicar. He started the engine.

She popped into the passenger side, shut the door, and buckled up. Upholstery radiated heat through her pelt. Her fingers danced over the AC controls, so nimble compared to borrowed husky paws. It felt good to be herself again.

A heavy claw rapped on her window.

"Ah!" She squawked and turned to face the intruder.

A big cat in a business suit stood just beyond the door—the cougar from the Chamber of Commerce meeting. He made a roll-down-the-window gesture with a few extended claws.

She glanced to her boyfriend.

He shrugged.

Putting on her most serious expression, she rolled down the window. She looked the muscular feline over. When she realized his height advantage, she thumbed the seat's motorized controls, slowly rising without breaking eye contact.

The cougar leaned in, his forearms resting on the window well, his shoulders filling the entire opening. "You know, Joe was a buddy of mine. Came to the meetings for years." A pause, then his tone darkened. "Maybe he was an alien. I don't know."

Max's ears rose. "Should…you be talking about this in public?"

A midnight laugh rumbled past the cougar's teeth. "Do you have any idea how many people shout about aliens in this parking lot?"

The otter's heart pattered. She hadn't fought off an alien weirdo in her own living room to be intimidated by some suit. Now if only she could stop the cold flood of adrenalin in her limbs.

Gary's claws drummed on the steel of the car door. "I just thought I should have a little chat with you." Spring sunlight shone off his pelt.

Wiggling whiskers in annoyance, Kylie crossed her arms, still holding the giant slab of fish. "About what? Revenge?"

"Revenge? You think there's any money in revenge? No, we need to talk about how things work around here. This town, it's a performance. Sure, a few things around the edges are supernatural. But the money comes from how we stage it. We all have our parts to play." His slitted eyes narrowed. "You kids are from Hollywood, right?"

Ears up, the husky tilted his head. "Yes?"

He snapped his fingers into a little pistol gesture at them. "Right. So you understand everything is really about money."

She considered whacking him with the salmon, but she didn't want to bruise it. Maybe she could open the door really fast and whack him in the knees. She filed that away as a backup plan.

The big cat looked between them. "You two keep in mind what part you're supposed to play. Save your dramatic scenes for the public. Otherwise, you could end up with nothing."

Kylie looked at her boyfriend. The dog looked back at her like the cat was out of his mind.

"That got your attention, huh?" He straightened the collar of his brown tweed suit, picking a tiny fleck of lint from the lapel with a single sharp claw. "I hope today demonstrated that everything works better when we all play ball. You help us. We help you."

She crossed her arms over the slab of fish. "And if we don't wanna work with you guys?"

"Hey, you're big names. I get that. But you should be happy with your piece of the action." He grinned. "The Chamber runs this town. Previous Bevys never caught on, but we still made plenty of money off their antics."

The otter jabbed a claw toward the middle-aged cougar. "Now, listen here—"

With rapid-fire clicks, Max sent the window creeping up a centimeter at a time between Kylie and the cougar. "That all sounds good, sir." He nudged the pane of glass up another few clicks as he began idling the car forward. "Thanks for the heads up. Gotta get these frozen eel pies home."

Gary stepped back, ears askew as the car puttered away and out of the grocery parking lot. For a long moment, he stood, watching them go. As they pulled onto the street, he adjusted his power tie and stalked off toward his large luxury vehicle.

"Hey!" Kylie popped up in her seat and chattered at her boyfriend. "Why are we driving away?"

"Because you're from the city, where people talk tough but don't act on it." Both hands on the wheel, he studied her from the corner of his eye "And I'm from the country, where nobody finds the bodies. I don't want to find out where on that spectrum this town falls."

"I was turning the scene around!" She threw her paws toward the up-holstered ceiling. In a refreshing twist, they didn't hit it, since they weren't on gigantic Max arms. "It was a dramatic reversal."

"Rudderbutt, it doesn't work that way." He allowed a microcar with a "Waldorf's Psychic Whisker Tuning" vinyl decal on the back window to merge in front of him. "Don't antagonize these guys for no reason. They're probably some kind of ancient merchandising cult."

With a half-sincere pout, she crossed her arms. "You never let me chew the scenery…"

"Nor do I let you crawl out the window and bite a city official on the ankle." He steered around a pair of grizzled grizzlies sweeping the air above a storm drain with homemade electronic devices. "Which is what I suspect was about to happen."

"At least we still have these." She pulled the bracelets from a vest pock-et. They looked so innocent, something she could have seen clipped on her middle school backpack.

"And that's a victory." He nodded, then furrowed his brow. "I'm trying, but I'm not sure how we can test them."

"Oh, I can think of a way…" Her elbow nudged him in the ribs.

"I mean outside the bedroom, you hornball." His massive paw dialed up the air conditioning. "To in prove the supernatural."

She waved a bracelet in each hand. "We'll just use them."

"Two sci-fi actors acting like they've switched bodies?" His gentle blue eyes flicked to her, then back to the road. "I feel like we'll get dismissed before we can prove anything."

She waved a webbed finger toward him. "See? That's smart." She brushed a lock of hair back from her eyes. "Told ya you weren't just the muscle."

Tail swishing against the back of the seat, Max cast her a demure smile, ears tipped back. Then they popped back up as his muzzle switched to a smirk. "And you're very brave to take on the world, being so small."

"Hey!" She punched him in the arm. "I'm pretty tough per kilogram."

He nodded. "I'll be careful to only put things on high shelves if you don't like them."

Wiggling in her seat, she chattered in triumph. "Finally, the respect I deserve."

He patted her thigh.

Her paw rested atop his. "We'll just have to find some sap to test them on."

"Someone who won't sue us for subjecting them to however those bracelets work."

"Yeah!" Her lithe body bounced in the seat. "Like Mom."

"You think your mom won't sue us?"

She pulled out her phone and skimmed through her favorite sites. "You wanna post a blog entry about this?"

"I took some notes, but it's still too weird." He shrugged. "Soon, though."

"No rush." She waved a paw. "The Internet's distracted by this cake that's also a pinball machine right now."

"Oh?" His ears perked.

"Yeah. You know those little metallic cake decoration balls?" She held her fingers up as if pinching an invisible grape. "Turns out they make big ones."

The canine nodded at the road ahead. "What a time to be alive."

Minutes later, they ground their way up the gravel driveway to Bourn Manor. The faded mansion, with its vines up the side like a kraken from the depths of the lawn, now held a sense of familiarity and safety. When did that happen? As Max pulled parallel with the house, Kylie spied her mother tending the plants in the sunroom. No sooner had the car stopped than Kylie burst from it and scampered across the lawn. Laura looked up from the water lilies in the reflecting pool and managed half a syllable before her daughter grabbed her by the paw. "Check out what we found!"

With only minor objections, the middle-aged otter plodded with her offspring to the car.

"Mother!" Once in full view of Max, Kylie snapped a bracelet on herself, then flourished the other one at Laura. "Allow me to change your life." She slapped the bracelet on the older otter's wrist.

Nothing happened.

"Well, in a small way, yes." Laura examined the bracelet. "Are these cool again? Am I cool now?"

"No, Mom." Kylie shrugged to her boyfriend.

He shrugged back.

Her mom shrugged too, having no idea of the mystical powers at work. She took the bracelet off with ease and dropped it into her daughter's hands.

With a quiet chitter of disappointment, the younger otter wondered why it hadn't swapped them. Not that she especially needed to run around in her mom's body. She'd get to do basically that in twenty years or so. But it would have been nice to get her to admit supernatural stuff was happening around this weird town. Maybe it needed to charge back up? Or it was keyed to her and Max now? Or it only worked across species? Magic artifacts from the 90s really needed better documentation.

"We did have another thing to show you." Max popped the hatch at the back of her car, revealing a full set of cherry wood cabinet doors.

Laura bounced in place. "Hey, wow!" Her paws clapped together, then traced over the intricate patterns. "Where'd you find these?" Fists on her hips, she turned to make sure the younger mammals appreciated the woodworking. "Look how nice that nautilus turned out."

The large canine restrained a smirk at his mentor's sudden enthusiasm.

"They were in Joe's old shed. We had to fight the Chamber of Commerce to get them." Kylie socked a webbed fist into the air.

"Well." Laura nodded. "I won't be commenting so I cannot be implicated."

Max pulled the phone from his pocket, winced at a link to airline tickets, and put it back. "Story idea: intern to the evil conspiracy. Lying to the world at minimum wage."

The plump otter's whiskers rustled. "Why wouldn't he tell the world?"

His index finger rose to the question. "Why indeed?"

His mentor nodded. "It has potential. Give me a draft by Tuesday."

"Ha ha." Kylie stuck her tongue out at him. "You got homework."

"You do too." Her mother turned to face her. "We have to start getting the house ship-shape."

"Umm, why?" She flung a gesture toward the sprawling manor. "I thought were we just letting most of it return to nature."

"As part of my continuing initiative to talk to more people than just you in a day…" She peered down her muzzle, through wire-framed glasses. "You father and his family are stopping by for dinner next week."

Kylie spun to her. "What?"

"Yeah!" Her mom waddled the first stack of doors into the house. "Greg was delighted to hear you thought of him."

"Thought of him?" She scratched her head. "When?"

But her mother had already disappeared into Bourn Manor, chattering happily.

Max cleared his throat. "Umm, that may have been when I was you."

Finding her way back from being lost in thought, she glanced to her boyfriend. "What?"

"Well!" The hulking canine picked up the entire stack of cabinet doors in an effortless load, with an arm still free to shut the car's back hatch. "I'd better get these inside." He trotted swiftly into the house.

"Wait a second!" A chitter of outrage rose in her throat. Arms flailing, she scampered onto the porch after him. "Get back here! You hypocrite! What was that about shark-infested waters?"

About the Author

Tempo is a husky in a cowboy hat. Raised on a horse ranch, he lives in North Dakota with his very understanding wife. He's been writing stories about talking animals since he learned to write and has been guest of honor at furry conventions as far afield as Toronto and São Paulo. He teaches creative writing and game design part time at the local college and has been interviewed about his writing on National Public Radio twice. He is also staff writer for the furry pop culture analysis series Culturally F'd.

FurAffinity: Tempo321
SoFurry: Tempo
Twitter: TempoWrites